PUCK YOU

PUCK YOU

FLYNN NOVAK

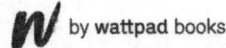

An imprint of Wattpad WEBTOON Book Group

Copyright© 2025 Flynn Novak.

All rights reserved.

No portion of this publication may be reproduced or transmitted, in any form or by any means, without the express written permission of the copyright holders.

Published in Canada by Wattpad WEBTOON Book Group, a division of Wattpad WEBTOON Studios, Inc.

36 Wellington Street E., Suite 200, Toronto, ON M5E 1C7 Canada

www.wattpad.com

First W by Wattpad Books edition: November 2025

ISBN 978-1-99834-134-4 (Trade Paper original)
ISBN 978-1-99834-156-6 (eBook edition)

Names, characters, places, and incidents featured in this publication are either the product of the author's imagination or are used fictitiously. Any resemblance to actual persons (living or dead), events, institutions, or locales, without satiric intent, is coincidental.

Wattpad Books, W by Wattpad Books, Wattpad WEBTOON Book Group, and associated logos are trademarks and/or registered trademarks of Wattpad WEBTOON Studios, Inc. and/or its affiliates. Wattpad and associated logos are trademarks and/or registered trademarks of Wattpad Corp.

Library and Archives Canada Cataloguing in Publication information is available upon request.

Printed and bound in Canada

1 3 5 7 9 10 8 6 4 2

Cover design by Leah Jacobs-Gordon
Typesetting by Delaney Anderson

For all the older sisters, but especially mine.

PROLOGUE
Sebastian

Two minutes and one goal were all that stood between me and the national championship. I'd imagined this moment to the point of obsession, but never once had it played out like this: a tied score with only one hundred and twenty seconds on the clock, triggering a wild scramble to win in the final moments of the game.

The only person I could blame was myself. For the first time in my hockey career, I'd allowed something outside the rink to follow me onto the ice. It was a mistake that had cost us an early lead, a mistake I couldn't afford to make in the NCAA Frozen Four national championship. As the clock continued to wind down, it was all I could do to remind myself that nothing else mattered in this moment, not even the woman I loved.

From the bench, I watched as our third line fumbled the puck straight into the waiting sticks of Minnesota's defense. My gloved fingers tightened around the edge of the metal beneath me. This game was never going to be easy. The Bulldogs were a powerful force on the rink, a seasoned team with years of experience under their belts, but we had an edge—*me*—and I was going to do whatever it took to make sure our team was celebrating when the confetti rained down.

Ninety seconds left.

My pulse skyrocketed as Rowling intercepted a slapshot from the Bulldog's right winger. The junior had barely gained control of the puck when number six from the opposing team landed a nasty cross-check. An uproar swept through the arena as the referee blew his whistle, and number six was sent off to wait out his time in the sin bin.

Go time.

Back in possession following the face-off, and with added advantage of outnumbering the opposing team, we moved the puck around in quick passes, keeping Minnesota at bay as we soared into enemy territory. I concentrated my energy on finding the perfect gap: a brief opening that would cement my name and the Dallard University Ravens in history forever. But Kent jumped the gun: his snap shot went high, bouncing off the plexiglass and tangling in the back of the net. There was a momentary scramble before the referee blew his whistle to signal the play was dead. I glanced at the game clock. Forty seconds was more than enough time.

Focus, Sebastian. All you need to do is focus.

All I could hear was the sound of my own rushing blood as I fell into place at the perimeter of the red circle. I was on the puck less than a second after it dropped, backhanding it to Devon as he shot off from the board side into position behind me. He caught it with the very tip of his stick and pushed out for a quick-release shot, one that I knew would inevitably be blocked. I drove toward the net as the puck flew by and ricocheted off the goalie's kneepads. The rebound met my stick with a satisfying crack, hurtling the puck back toward the goal just as a massive form descended on me. There was no mistaking the sickening pop that tore through my knee as I was struck from the side, or the burning agony that followed. The ice rushed toward me as the horn blared. A furious pain overwhelmed my senses, drowning out the roar of the crowd and the clash of celebrating bodies above me. As the exhilarated faces of my teammates swarmed above, I knew something was terribly wrong. I'd won us the game, but at what cost?

CHAPTER 1

Sebastian

"You won't get any second chances this year, Sebastian. I made allowances for your poor grades while you recovered from your injury, but that won't continue."

I gritted my teeth and forced myself to remain silent in the wake of Dean Adler's scolding. His weathered face was not a kind sight, and there was a tiny piece of unidentifiable food hanging from his overgrown mustache. It moved up and down as he berated me about my academic performance last semester. Apparently, this school had only been willing to make exceptions for me when I was their star athlete. Now that I was damaged goods in their eyes, that special treatment no longer applied.

"I can assure you my grades won't be a problem this semester," I told him. "I'm recovered and well."

Recovered—yes. *Well?* That was an entirely different matter.

"Your academic advisor will be checking in with me on a regular basis. If there are any issues, I will know."

I nodded politely in response, but my eyes conveyed something entirely different. *Fuck you*, they said. *Fuck you for treating me like a washout after everything I did for this school.* If I wasn't so practiced in my control, I might have let the words slip. But mouthing off wouldn't do me any favors. I couldn't afford to piss anyone off, not with my future on the line. Soon enough, the entire school—Dean Adler included—would realize how wrong they'd been to assume I was even close to finished.

"You're free to go, Sebastian."

I retreated from his stuffy office without so much as a goodbye. In the past, Dean Adler had gone out of his way to kiss my ass. After all, as the star of the hockey team, I was Dallard University's golden boy. Even after I tore my ACL, everyone was hopeful I'd make a quick return to the ice. But my surgery had been more complicated than expected, which extended my physical therapy for several months, so I'd rushed back to the rink prematurely. I'd wanted to prove that I was still the same player. More importantly, I'd needed to show the Red Wings that I was ready for the big league. But even after ten months of recovering, I wasn't in the same shape I'd been in the year before, and my attempted return to the ice had been nothing less than mortifying. After that, everyone was quick to forget my part in leading the men's hockey team to their first national championship, as a sophomore no less. All it took was one terrible performance for the dean to lose interest in his favorite toy. It made me all the more determined to spend my final year proving everyone wrong.

Despite the early hour, campus was buzzing with activity as I emerged from the administrative building. Over the last few days, students had trickled back into town as summer break came to an end. With classes set to begin on Monday, the last-minute scramble to get ready for the semester had begun. I set off for the hockey facility under the gaze of intrusive eyes, keeping to one of the tree-lined paths that cut through the school grounds. Everyone at Dallard knew who I was, and that notoriety couldn't be avoided. Even before my injury, I'd never liked being goggled at. I could tune out the attention on the ice, but it wasn't just when I was playing: it was media interviews, student newspaper features, and a heightened profile once NHL scouts were involved. After the initial story broke about my injury, the buzz had eventually quieted down. There were a few articles speculating about my return to hockey, but I wasn't interested in publicly discussing my healing process. That didn't curb the students' interest in me, though. If anything, people stared more than before, but now they looked at me like I was someone to be pitied.

Once I ducked into the safety of DuLane Arena, the tension in my shoulders released. Since freshman year, the state-of-the-art training facility had served as my place of refuge. Within these walls, I felt a deep sense of belonging. On game days, the building was always packed with thousands of fans, but today the place was empty, and I gave myself a moment to bask in the solitude.

I spent most of my time in the lower levels of the DuLane. The locker room was just below the arena, but even further underground was an expansive training facility, recovery center, a second rink, and several offices for the coaching staff and head trainer. I took the set of elevators off the main entrance down to the locker room, holding my badge up to the sensor above the button panel and selecting B1. Even after five years, the place still had that new-construction smell, with the exception of the locker rooms. Fortunately, they were bleached in the offseason, so there were no foul odors to turn my nose as I slipped inside. Every inch of the room was bathed in Dallard blue and green, and a large, jet-black raven—the school mascot—was painted across the center of the floor.

After my miserable meeting with Dean Adler, I wanted nothing more than to lose myself on the ice. In a matter of minutes, I was changed into my gear and walking through the sloped tunnel leading up to the rink entrance. A burst of cool air hit my face as I entered the arena, and I was immediately met with the sound of blades carving through the ice.

An unfamiliar form flew over the recently zambonied rink, maneuvering through a long line of cones with a puck at the tip of his hockey stick. I allowed myself a moment to appreciate the sight of him cutting across the ice in clean, precise sweeps. He moved with a grace most guys spent years trying to perfect, as if the hockey stick was a natural extension of his arm. I inched closer to the rink, eager to get a better look. The player was slim, much smaller than the other guys on the team, and I wondered if he was a freshman. You didn't have to be massive to play hockey—if anything, size could be a hindrance—but this guy was tiny. Despite his small stature, he clearly knew what he was doing. Maybe the coaches thought they could bulk him up in time for next season. They'd have to if they wanted him to survive the league.

He didn't notice me until I slipped inside the players' bench. Ice shavings flew from beneath the blades of his skates as he came to an abrupt stop at the opposite end of the rink. He glanced around, as if to check if anyone else was watching, before pushing off and heading in my direction. When he was close enough that I could begin to make out his face behind the cage, he gripped underneath his helmet and pulled it off in one clean motion. A thick brown braid fell over his shoulder.

No, not his shoulder—*her* shoulder.

She was covered in a thin sheen of sweat, several strands of her dark hair clinging to the skin around her face. A pair of wide brown eyes fringed with thick lashes peered back at me in open curiosity. Slowly, my gaze traced the outline of her arched eyebrows, traveling down the slope of her freckled nose and settling on a pair of slightly parted lips. She had a dangerous mouth, one I was immediately tempted to taste. Lips with the power to make me forget all about my girlfriend.

"What, never seen a girl before?" Her words came out in a teasing rasp that caused the hair on my arms to rise.

In that moment, I felt as if the entire English language had abandoned me. She was a wet dream come to life, my perfect woman. Someone who, based on the way she skated so effortlessly, knew the ice as deeply as I did. But why was she here? Only the men's team practiced at DuLane.

"What are *you* doing here?" It wasn't my intension to sound so accusatory. In truth, her appearance had caught me completely off guard. But before I could apologize, an unexpected thought struck me—*don't explain yourself.* This girl was a stranger, one I didn't owe anything. The mere sight of her had rendered me speechless, and for the first time in three years, I was unsettled—uncertain, even—within the walls of DuLane Arena; it was a feeling I didn't like.

She raised a brow. "Isn't that obvious?"

"You must be new, so I'm happy to clear up any confusion," I said, trying not to sound as rattled as I felt. "DuLane Arena is the men's hockey facility. The women have their own facility—McKinley Rink. You're not supposed to practice here."

The girl stilled at my response. If I hadn't been watching her so closely, I would have missed the subtle movement of her fingers tightening around the hockey stick.

"I know," she said, the playful note in her tone vanishing.

Then why the hell was she here carving up *my* ice?

Before I could voice my question, she continued, "The women's facility is on the other side of campus, and I don't have a car to get my equipment over there. This rink was closer."

"I don't see how that's my problem," I said with a shrug. "You're chewing up my ice."

"*Your* ice?"

"Male hockey player"—I pointed to myself, then to the rink—"men's ice."

"Is it illegal for someone with boobs to skate here? I didn't think guys your age were still afraid of getting cooties. Or maybe you're just scared of being shown up by a girl?"

"Scared of what, exactly? You might be good for a girl, but you have nothing on me. In fact, you couldn't keep up with anyone on the men's team. We're bigger than you, faster than you, and more competitive. The women have their own facility for a reason," I explained, a smug grin on my face. "Use it next time."

Her lip curled up in an expression that could only be described as contempt before she sidestepped me to enter the player's bench. She started removing her gear in haste, eventually stripping down to a dry-fit long sleeve and leggings. With a mind of their own, my eyes tracked her movements, taking in the shape of her toned body beneath the skintight clothing, lingering over her muscular legs and the distracting curve of her ass. When she glanced over at me again, her eyes were narrowed. "Don't ogle me after that response. Assholes don't get the right to look."

I scoffed. "I wasn't *ogling* you. Don't think so highly of yourself."

"Oh, my apologies," she said, pulling her braid out from under the sweatshirt she'd tugged on. "I must have imagined you eye-fucking me."

"Look, there's no need for you to be snippy with me. I'm trying to be helpful by explaining the rules around here."

She gave me a saccharine-looking smile that somehow felt as far away from sweet as possible. "Then understand I'm trying to be helpful when I say this—removing the stick lodged up your ass might make you a more bearable human being."

My jaw clenched, but I chose to ignore her comment. "The women don't play here, that's a fact. You should learn it before your first day of school."

"I'm not setting up camp here," she hissed, cheeks turning a deep shade of red. "I only needed a little ice time."

"Again, not my problem."

Her eyes filled with a glimmer of something I couldn't decipher, and the sight triggered a warning bell inside my head. Her next words made my muscles tense.

"I'm happy to make it your problem."

Was this girl threatening me on my own ice? I searched my brain for an adequate response, but nothing came to mind; I was too caught off guard by her audacity.

"As delightful as this conversation has been," she said, gathering her bag and slinging it over her shoulder, "I'd rather eat shit than spend one more second in your presence."

I moved to stop her before I could even think about the implications, my fingers curling around the sliver of bared skin at her wrist. Unexpected heat surged up my arm and through my body when our skin met, and I dropped her hand as if I'd been scalded. The girl stared down at the spot where I'd touched her as if she'd experienced the same strange sensation.

"What's your name?" I asked after a beat of stunned silence.

Her brows pulled together at my question. Gone was the

animosity behind her stare. In its place, something entirely foreign had taken root. I had no idea what to make of the expression.

"Please, tell me," I commanded in a soft whisper. I couldn't hide the desperation in my voice. Knowing her name was more important than my own pride. For whatever reason, I was convinced that the sound of it would put an end to this fiery feeling inside me. But rather than concede, she shook off her shock and offered up another vexing threat.

"You'll know soon enough, asshole."

>> <<

Grace

The promise left my lips before I even knew what it meant. In my anger, I would have threatened just about anything for the chance to wipe the smug expression from his face. *So long, douchebag.* I refused to waste another second of my life speaking to this guy, even if he was outrageously attractive. *No one with eyes that green and hair so perfectly disheveled should be allowed to exist.* Without another word (and there were *several* choice words I would have loved to use), I stepped around his annoyingly tall frame and made for the exit. Hockey was a relatively small world. I'd met guys like him before, players who thought that good looks and talent on the ice meant they were superior to everyone else. There was no shortage of arrogance within college athletics, but this guy really took the cake. I wouldn't have been shocked to learn he was nothing more than a cherry-picking bender.

With my morning now thoroughly ruined, I made the short trek back to my on-campus housing. The sun was peeking over the buildings as I stepped outside DuLane Arena. Burning light bathed the grounds in yellow-orange hues and cast tree-shaped shadows across the grass. Several students shot me strange looks as I struggled down the path with my equipment bag in tow, muttering vague threats under my breath. When I caught a glimpse of the ivy-veiled stone structure at the end of the road, I let out a sigh of relief. After three flights of killer stairs, I slipped inside the apartment, dumped my bag on the floor, and let out a huff of frustration.

"Did you bring your hockey gear with you for a morning stroll?" My roommate's voice carried from the kitchen.

Caroline Hart stood over the stove, her long hair piled into a messy bun as she stirred the contents of her pan over the burner. In the three days since we'd met, I'd learned a lot about the tall blond, the most important being she was the captain of the women's hockey team and our first-line right defense. Her socials were public, and I'd spent my first night in the apartment lying in bed, digging through her online profile. Alongside her captain duties, she also served as treasurer of the student pre-law organization, volunteered at the local animal shelter, and posted weekly vlogs about fashion. I didn't know how the girl had time to sleep, let alone pursue a degree.

"I really needed to clear my head this morning, so I stopped by DuLane to get a little ice time," I explained, taking a seat at the counter. Her brows rose in surprise. "Yes, I know, that's where the men play. But, in my defense, I didn't think anyone would be there so early this morning."

Caroline chuckled. "I take it someone else had the same idea. Let me guess—tall, extremely handsome, probably a little bit rude? Hard to narrow it down because that's literally the entire team."

"A little bit rude? He was a complete dickhead! I couldn't

believe how offended he was that I deigned to skate on the *men's* ice."

"The players are protective over that rink. Five years ago, it was completely renovated with funds that were donated by a wealthy alumnus. The guys think they're hot shit because they have access to one of the best hockey facilities in the country. Plus, the entire school panders to them. You would think they were famous by the way they're treated around here." She pressed her lips together, as if stopping herself from revealing any more information.

"What aren't you telling me?" I asked.

"She left out the part where we practice in a rink that should have been condemned years ago. Meanwhile, the men live in luxury at DuLane Arena," a voice said behind me.

Our other roommate, Lydia West, was leaning against the arched entrance to the kitchen. She wiped at her sleep-bleary eyes with long, ring-covered fingers, the gold jewelry flashing against a beam of sunlight pouring in through the window. A yellow scarf tied around her head prevented a mass of dark curls from falling into her eyes, and she clutched a sketchbook against her hip, one I'd rarely seen her without since we'd met. The right winger was one of the highest-ranking female hockey players in the NCAA. Since her freshman year, Lydia had been an unstoppable force on the ice. I was in awe at the opportunity to play on the same team as her.

"You can't be serious," I said, glancing between them in disbelief.

"She is," Caroline replied. "Despite the fact that we have a better record than the men—two whole national titles better—they're treated like freakin' celebrities while we're forgotten in the haunted rink on Third Street."

"Haunted? We have to practice in a haunted rink? Please tell me no one died there."

Both girls laughed.

"Not that I know of," said Lydia, "but the building is really old and makes strange noises, so everyone says it's inhabited by spirits."

That was a relief to hear. The last thing I needed was to worry about a potential haunting. As a firm believer in the paranormal, one who spent her teen years chronically on creepypasta, I took that stuff seriously. It was always smart to be cautious of ghosts—some had the potential to be vengeful and nasty—just like it was smart to be cautious of dickhead hockey players.

"Is there nowhere better for us to train?" I asked.

"Yes and no," Caroline said. "We used to practice at a facility in Big Creek, which is only ten minutes north, but they had an electrical fire this summer. There was too much damage to make repairs, so they tore the whole place down. The next closest rink is our home-game arena, but it's forty-five miles south. The distance is doable for weekend games, but driving an hour there and back during the week messes with almost everyone's class schedule. The administration reopened McKinley Rink, which was built in the fifties but closed a few years ago. It's not great, but it's somewhere for us to get ice time."

Knowing this made my encounter at the arena even more frustrating. Having played hockey my whole life, I'd seen firsthand how different the boys' programs were from the girls', how underdeveloped our training was when compared to the male leagues. I'd even played on the boys' team in high school because that was the only way I could reach the level of competitiveness I craved. And here I was, at one of the best hockey schools in the country, and it was more of the same.

"I need to figure out who that guy was so I can mail him a box of dog shit," I muttered.

"What guy?" Lydia asked.

Caroline, who was finally happy with her scrambled eggs, dumped them into a bowl and took a seat beside me at the counter. "She decided to get a little skating in at DuLane Arena this morning. One of the guys ran her off."

"It was probably Sebastian. No one else would be at the rink this early, don't you think?" Lydia looked at Caroline to confirm her suspicion.

"Does he have intense green eyes and think that the world revolves around him?" I asked.

"That's the one," Caroline confirmed. "He's the team captain."

I filed that piece of information away for future reference. Now that I knew his name, it would be easier to track him down and accidentally spill my morning smoothie down the front of his shirt.

"I guess that means he's officially back," Lydia said.

"Back from where?" I asked.

"Sebastian was out last season with an injury. Freshman and sophomore year, he was the team's star player, but he messed up his ACL in the Frozen Four championship game. They won, at least, but he hasn't been the same player since. He came back for a game in the spring, and it was pretty bad," said Caroline.

Lydia nodded in agreement before saying, "He was drafted by the Red Wings at eighteen. Everyone thought he was going pro after the championship, but then he busted his knee in the last few seconds of the game."

Damn, that must have been one hard pill to swallow. I would have felt more sympathy for the guy if he wasn't such an arrogant prick.

"Is your friend still stopping by?" Lydia asked as she poured herself a cup of coffee.

At the mention of Sam, I shot out of my seat. How had I forgotten she was coming by the apartment today?

"I'll take that as a yes," she said as I searched the room for my phone.

It was lying on the floor where I'd dropped my hockey equipment. The screen lit up, displaying a photo of Sam and me from high school. There was a long list of email notifications but no missed texts. I let out a sigh of relief and checked the time. It was still early enough for Sam to be sleeping.

"I should probably finish unpacking," I said to myself, thinking about the mess in my bedroom.

Even though I'd moved in three days ago, I still hadn't put away the majority of my things. Thankfully, Caroline and Lydia had the common spaces covered. It was their second year living in this apartment. I'd taken over the third room, which had previously been occupied by a player who'd graduated last semester.

"She'll be here by eleven. If you guys want to go for coffee then, feel free to join us. In the meantime, I'll be panic cleaning," I said then retreated toward my bedroom to the sound of quiet laughter.

Inside, the floor was barely visible beneath the mess of my belongings. It would be much tidier under normal circumstances, my clothes neatly organized in the closet and the bed made to perfection. I *hated* clutter, but I'd been avoiding the task since my arrival. In my haste to pack for my senior year of college, I'd forgotten my most prized possessions at home: my headphones and portable speaker. Both were an essential part of my ability to function, because I always wound up overthinking when I was left alone with my thoughts. Without the distraction of music or a true crime podcast, I was forced to endure the never-ending monologue inside my head—a voice capable of rendering me completely useless. At this point in my life, I pretty much lived with a pair of wireless headphones in my ears, and that's why Sam was visiting today: she was dropping off the items I'd mistakenly left behind.

The only option I had for background noise was to use my phone, so I switched on an episode of *In the Dark* and turned the volume all the way up. It was better than nothing, but it didn't compare to my sound-isolating headphones. Over the next two hours, I did little more than move things around to new spots on the floor. When Sam finally arrived, I was sitting on the ground surrounded by clothes, playing with an old Game Boy I'd discovered in the bottom of a bag. Her text sent me running down the hall in excitement.

"You are an angel sent from heaven," I said after flinging open the door. It was the first thing that came to mind at the sight of Sam standing outside, a bag of my forgotten essentials slung over her shoulder. Her cheeks were flushed from the lingering summer heat, several pieces of unruly auburn hair sticking to the side of her sweat-slicked face.

She snorted. "I promise you I don't have a halo. That's just my hair." On humid days like today, her mane could double in size, even when pulled into a bun like it currently was.

"Come in, come in," I said, ushering her inside.

As she stepped over the threshold, Sam glanced around the living room curiously, eyes slipping over the faded blue rug, lumpy sofa, and wooden coffee table decorated with dents and water rings.

"It's cute," she commented, her gaze shifting to the large

wooden bookcase being utilized as a TV stand. It was stuffed full of worn novels, a strange mixture of rom-coms and horror movies, and a scattering of peculiar-looking knickknacks. Having spent a few days with my roommates, I could only guess the horror belonged to Lydia, as well as the assortment of trinkets lining the shelves. Sam handed me the bag.

"Right? I love it," I replied. "Seriously, though, thank you so much for bringing my stuff."

"No problem. It's not like you're far from home, anyway. Wasn't that the point of transferring here?"

Dallard University was only a forty-five-minute drive from our hometown in northern Wisconsin, which had been one of the deciding factors in my decision to transfer. The other had to do with their phenomenal women's hockey program. The Dallard Ravens had secured three national titles in the last eight years, and playing with them would offer me the chance to participate in a more competitive conference. ECAC Hockey was no walk in the park, but most national titles were held by teams in the Western Collegiate Hockey Association. Playing amongst the best in the country was a dream come true.

"Let me drop this off in my bedroom." Sam hovered behind me as I threw open the door to reveal the barely improved mess in my bedroom.

"Seems like I arrived just in time. If I'd waited another day, you might have been buried alive," she teased.

"It looks worse than it is."

Sam didn't respond, but the curve at the corner of her mouth told me she was biting back a sassy remark. She rarely pulled her punches, which told me everything I needed to know. Sam was worried about me because I was worried about, well, everything.

"I'm fine, I promise," I told her. "I'm just concerned about how things have been since I left."

"The house is still standing," she assured me. "They'll survive without you."

After spending the summer at home with my father and sister, I wasn't so sure. Sometime in the last year, the little kid who used to follow me around and beg to have sleepovers had transformed from a sweet, impressionable girl into an adolescent nightmare. Gabby's alarming shift in behavior was the main reason I'd left Boston College and transferred to a school closer to home. If I was thousands of miles away, I couldn't keep tabs on her, and ever since I'd learned about her behavioral issues at school, a sense of unease had sprouted inside me. It wasn't like Gabby to skip class or talk back to teachers. She was only thirteen, still a year away from high school. Of course, my dad insisted that it was nothing for me to worry about, but I couldn't shake the feeling that he wasn't telling me the whole story. I was missing a few pieces of the puzzle, and I didn't want to be blindsided when they fell into place.

From my experience, bad news never arrived in one tidy package. Disaster *always* struck more than once. The last time our family had received bad news, it wasn't a single message but rather a series that had left an open wound my family was still struggling to heal from. It wasn't as simple as my mom leaving one day because she was unhappy. First there were the manic episodes, times when she was so happy that it was hard for me to understand how something could be wrong with her, and then came the soul-deep depression. The confirmation of her bipolar disorder diagnosis was only the beginning. Hearing my parents whisper to each other about a family history of mental health disorders did not prepare me for the reality of seeing my mother succumb to one. After months of perfecting her medication and treatment plan, her mental health was derailed yet again by a severe bout of postpartum depression following Gabby's birth. The next three years were like a roller coaster, my mom ebbing and flowing between the highs and lows of her mood disorder. And then, almost a week after she returned from her in-patient treatment program, I had to watch her leave. That was the last bit of bad news—waking up a few days after my twelfth birthday to find that my mother was gone.

Since then, I'd spent my life fearing the possibility of losing another person I loved or, even worse, becoming my mother. But during all those years, I'd never considered that fate befalling my little sister.

"What about Gabby? What if she's—"

Just like our mother?

Sam didn't have to ask what I meant. "Gabby's a teenager. She could very well be going through the angsty stage of adolescence."

More than anything, I wanted to believe her, but Gabby had always been a sweet, bright presence in our family. If this recent change was more than just a teenage phase, I needed to be close enough to step in and help her. I would not lose my sister like I'd lost my mother.

"You're a senior in college, Grace. This is your last year to be a non-adult adult. It's hard not to worry about the people you love, but you also have to think about yourself."

Deep down, I knew that going back to school was the best thing for me to do. I was a senior. Taking a year off before I was supposed to graduate was not an option, at least not in my father's eyes. Even though he didn't have a background in the performing arts, he loved to say that the show must go on. Truthfully, I was terrified to see the second act, but with the way my sister had been behaving, it felt like the curtains were already rising.

"Hey," Sam said, giving my arm a gentle squeeze. "I'll be right across the street, remember?"

I closed my eyes and took a deep, steadying breath. After twenty years of friendship, Sam was an expert at reading my emotions. Growing up with someone bonds you in a unique way; she had far more insight into my life than any other person I knew. With Sam still living at home, she'd promised to keep an eye on my family while I was at school. I had to trust that she would look out for them.

"You should meet my roommates," I said, knowing that a change in topic was needed before I started to spiral. "You and Caroline have a lot to talk about."

CHAPTER 2

Sebastian

I'd been expecting several scoldings upon my return to school, but I hadn't been prepared for the second to follow the first in such quick succession. Perhaps that's why I'd been so prickly with the mysterious hockey player—I'd still been recovering from my first beatdown when I'd discovered her inside DuLane Arena. Now, as I stared into the eyes of another beautiful brunet, one who just so happened to be my girlfriend, I braced myself for a third tongue-lashing.

"Practice doesn't start for another week, Sebastian. You might live and breathe hockey, but food and water are also necessary for survival." Kate's voice reverberated through the empty arena. "Come get lunch with me."

Was it already afternoon? The massive clock at the opposite end of the rink confirmed in large red numbers that it was fifteen minutes past twelve.

"You said this would be a quick session," she added. "That was almost three hours ago."

It was easy for me to lose track of time when I was training, which caused quite a bit of contention in our relationship. To be the best, I had to work the hardest, which meant prioritizing hockey over everything and *anyone* else. Given my current situation, that was more important than ever.

"I didn't notice the time," I admitted.

Kate was always cranky at the start of a new season, when our time together became increasingly sparse. It didn't help that she was used to the injured version of me, which, at this time last year, had been in no shape to practice or train. Now that I was healed and the summer was over, the next few weeks were bound to be a difficult transition for her. Kate didn't like to share me with hockey. But when the injury happened, she stuck by my side throughout my entire recovery. She drove me to rehab, listened to me bitch about my life, and rarely got mad when I snapped at her in moments of pain or frustration. That unwavering loyalty was the only reason I was relatively patient with her outward dislike of my passion.

"Is it too much to ask for a few hockey-free days together before the season completely consumes you?"

Hockey-free days were a rare occurrence in my life, and practically nonexistent in the weeks leading up to a new season. She knew that by now, which made her question even more frustrating to hear.

"How about this—I can give you lunch *and* a pre-lunch snack if you join me in the locker room for a shower. We won't have the place to ourselves once practice starts up."

Rather than give her time to consider my offer, I leaned forward and pressed a deep kiss against her mouth. She tasted like her vanilla and brown sugar lip gloss. It was a new development. Last month had been strawberries.

"I promise to make it worth your while," I whispered. Exhaustion and limited time aside, I would never turn down the opportunity to have sex with my girlfriend. It was the only other release that came close to the high I got while playing hockey.

"You can't distract me with sex," she said.

"We would be saving water. The planet is *very* important to you." Kate was pursuing a degree in environmental science, and I took more showers than the average person, which meant my proposition was bound to be successful at some point.

"Please tell me you two haven't done that before. The locker room is a sacred space."

I glanced up to find Dallard University's best defenseman standing at the entrance to the players' bench, muscled arms closed over a broad expanse of chest. *Colossal* would be the first word I'd use to describe Bryce Hillford; *intimidating* would be the second. At six feet six inches tall, the guy resembled a humanoid bear. And despite being one large motherfucker, his size didn't detract from his speed on the ice. If anything, it made him a lethal weapon, one that I'd had the pleasure of playing alongside for my entire NCAA career.

My best friend stalked forward, his tree-trunk legs eating up the stretch of space between us in three steps. I hadn't seen Bryce in over three months. He usually spent the summers at home in Miami, soaking up the sun at his family's beach house. Despite his love for hockey, Bryce detested the cold.

"I'm glad to see you're alive, Evans," he said. "I could have sworn you were dead, given I haven't heard a peep from you since summer started." For the usually cool-headed hockey player, that was as good as a fist to the face. But beneath the surface-level anger, there was something much worse: disappointment.

"Hey, man," I said, bringing a hand to the back of my neck, fingers massaging the skin at the base of my head. "Sorry I've been a little MIA."

His mouth smoothed into a firm line, and his eyebrows rose in an expression that seemed to say, *That's it?*

"I should've let you know that I was going dark for a little bit, but it was easier to turn everything off and hide from the world. I've been trying my best to get my shit together since . . . " *Since I made an absolute fool of myself returning for a game I wasn't remotely ready to play . . .* "It hasn't been easy."

Was it shitty to pull a disappearing act on my best friend? Absolutely. But the past eighteen months had really messed me up, and I was still working through a lot of stuff. Bryce knew that better than most.

"Are you okay?" he asked.

Truthfully, I was several hundred miles north of okay, but it would take severe inebriation for me to admit that out loud. "Never better."

I knew that both of them could see through my lie, but rather than call me out, Bryce offered a genuine smile and said, "Good. We need you if we're going to win another national title."

Hearing those words from someone I could trust eased a bit of my apprehension, though it was only a drop in a bucket. We both knew I had an uphill battle on my hands. At this point in my hockey career, I was unlikely to be offered a contract. Most players skilled enough for the pros did one or two years in college before moving up to the NHL. If not for my injury, I would have been one of them. But I refused to let one accident take away from the fact that I was a first-round draft pick at eighteen. The Detroit Red Wings had my rights until my NCAA career was over, which meant I had eight months to prove that I was the same player who had led the Dallard University Ravens to a national title at age twenty. Some days, I couldn't help but wonder if scoring that game winning-goal was worth the pain I'd endured over the last year, or the uncertainty it had cast over my future.

"Lunch?" Kate asked.

"I'll join," Bryce said. "I have to ensure our locker room isn't defiled by the likes of you two."

A chuckle escaped my lips as we headed out. I paused at the exit and peered over my shoulder, allowing myself one last appreciative glance of the arena. Despite my less than pleasant talk with Dean Adler and my run-in with little Miss Attitude hockey girl, I was finally starting to think that things were looking up.

>> <<

After seven long days of boring lectures, whispered stares from my fellow students, and building anticipation, stepping onto the rink for the first practice of the season felt like coming up for air after being trapped underwater. Before my injury, I hadn't realized that being on the ice was just as vital to my survival as breathing. Now that I had one final chance to secure my future in this world, I wasn't going to waste it.

"If my mom looked at me the same way Evans looks at a hockey rink, I wouldn't be in therapy twice a month." Kent's drawling comment was met with a chorus of laughter from our teammates. The right winger was only teasing, but I was still tempted to whack him over the head with my stick.

"It's the same way Bryce looks at Boss Subs from the grocery store," said Landon, our first-line goalie.

It came as no surprise that he felt the need to chime in. Landon and Kent's relationship was built on the need to one-up each other. Bickering was their favorite pastime, just like any old married couple.

"And the same way I look at your mother when she crawls into my bed at night," Bryce quipped.

Thankfully, Coach Dawson called for our attention before anyone else could join in on the gag. "All right, boys, enough of that. Time to warm up."

Bryce held out an arm to stop me from entering the rink, and when I met his eyes, I already knew what he was going to say.

"Quiet mind, steady heart."

He spoke those same words before every game. They were a promise to himself as much as they were to his teammates. Today was no game, but hew knew I needed the reminder.

"Quiet mind, steady heart," I repeated, and then I was off, my skates tearing across the ice as I led the pack around the perimeter for a few warm-up laps. Each loop around the rink felt like another gasped breath of air, as if I'd broken through the surface after nearly losing myself to the icy depths of a bottomless ocean. When we split into smaller groups for circle passing, I found myself with the usual suspects, most of whom doubled as my roommates as well as our first line. In addition to Bryce, Landon, and Kent, that included Bishop at left wing and Richie Torres, otherwise known as RT, on defense. Together, the six of us were typically an unstoppable force.

We completed several more warm-ups before breaking out into skill development. Coach pushed us through drill after drill until everyone was sweating beneath their equipment. The entire time, I monitored my knee, waiting for a twinge of pain that never came. By the end of practice, my blood was hot and my heart drummed in my chest. Right before Coach dismissed us, his eyes roamed over me with a gleam of something that looked like hope. That alone sent me strolling toward the locker room with a sweet sense of vindication flowing through my veins, and I wasn't alone. There was a palpable sense of excitement amongst the other players as we showered and dressed for class. Bryce settled beside me on the locker room bench, a knowing expression written across his face.

"It's good to see you smile," he said.

I looked around to make sure no one was listening. "No pain today," I said, glancing down at my knee.

"You looked like you out there." It was a simple statement, one that might not have seemed very meaningful from an outsider's perspective. But something in Bryce's words made me *feel* like myself for the first time since my injury.

"We're doing a team breakfast in the dining hall before classes. Everyone get your asses moving," Kent hollered.

Bryce gave me a gentle elbow to the side as he asked, "You coming?"

I shook my head. "Go on without me. I need a little bit longer."

It was wrong of me to stay back, especially given my title of team captain, but I needed some time to myself. I sat there for a while once the place emptied, replaying the practice over and over again in my head, committing it to memory. For a few moments, it was enough to block out the ceaseless ticking inside my head, a clock that had begun winding down the moment I returned to school.

>> <<

Grace

Where Boston College was gothic grandeur and perfectly manicured lawns, DU was understated charm. The campus was deeply entwined with the surrounding nature. Each and every building had been overtaken by plants; vines extended over the cluster of stone structures in multitudes, expanding across the grounds in a vast network of greenery. As fall approached, there came a shift: in a matter of days, the school transformed into an explosion of warm colors and fallen leaves, students strolling around in cozy sweaters as they made their way to class along pathways lined with red maples and white birch trees. I felt at ease here, being in such a familiar environment. It was a considerable difference from Boston, where people honked first and screamed second. Clearly, I hadn't realized how homesick I was until I was back in the Midwest. Who needed the ocean when you had the Great Lakes?

In the first few weeks of school, I'd settled into a comfortable pattern with classes and my roommates. Despite being complete opposites, Lydia and Caroline complemented each other perfectly. Caroline was intense, organized, and carried a sense of urgency in everything she did, while Lydia exemplified the term *laid-back*, spending her time drawing or scouring the local thrift shops for her next jackpot find. What amazed me most was their dynamic on the ice. It was as if they were capable of reading each other's thoughts from across the rink.

Meanwhile, it was nearly impossible to get a text back from my sister. Given that she'd spent most of the summer with her face glued to her phone screen, I assumed she was going out of her way to ignore me. I was lucky if I got a thumbs-up or a one-word response. No amount of update texts or funny TikToks seemed to pique her interest.

Feeling helpless in my effort to connect with her, I turned my full attention to the one thing with the power to distract me: hockey. I could lose myself in the sport. Being on the ice gave me the ability to tune out my racing thoughts, even without the help of my wireless headphones. But unfortunately, the replacement rink for the women's hockey program was sorely lacking. Nothing could have prepared me for the state of our training facility. At first glance, it only seemed to be outdated. But after several weeks of practice, I'd uncovered a plethora of issues that made spending almost two hours there every day feel like an impossible task. Now, my one source of comfort left me more frustrated than relaxed.

The facility was located on the opposite side of campus, which happened to be a twenty-minute trek from where I lived in the Athletes' Village. While the earlier than expected wake-up call was manageable, at least for me (Lydia had to be dragged from bed every morning *Freaky Friday* style), the mile-long walk in eerie darkness was bound to feel unpleasant once the air turned cold enough to hurt your face. I was also beginning to think that the facility was indeed haunted, despite Lydia and Caroline's reassurances. McKinley Rink creaked and moaned like it was inhabited by noisy spirits, and there was a strange smell of must and something slightly spoiled that no amount of air freshener could fix. Anyone who knew anything about ghosts knew that strange smells signified a malevolent presence.

Worst of all was the refrigeration system for the rink. Our first few days of practice, the ice had been so brittle it was nearly impossible to make a decent hockey stop. But after several days, the building started to grow humid, transforming the rink into a choppy mess of snow. Every morning when I arrived at practice, the fury inside me blazed a little bit hotter. Today was no exception. The ice was in a rough enough state that our scrimmage had devolved into chaos. I was convinced that either the thermostat had a mind of its own or the ghosts wanted us to suffer.

"Last shot!" Coach yelled, voice echoing across the rink.

Thankfully, Lydia took pity on us and slammed a shot that

ricocheted off the side of the goal post. I had no doubt it would have gone in if the ice were in better condition.

"All right, ladies, let's bring it in."

All twenty-three players gathered around Coach Riley. She was a formidable woman built with lean muscle and teeming with endless hockey knowledge. Though I'd only known her for a few weeks, I liked her attitude and coaching style. We meshed well.

"We're lifting heavy tomorrow. I want to see every single one of you with a foam roller before and after practice. Our first matchup is a week away, ladies, and I want us to be ready."

My teammates were quiet as we set off toward the locker room to shower and change. Despite my growing anticipation for our first game, all I could focus on was the fact that we'd had another lackluster scrimmage due to the state of our rink. This team was great, but our training facility was holding us back. We needed the best conditions to prepare for our upcoming matches.

"What's that look on your face, new girl?"

Dena, who mainly went by Big D (I had yet to learn how she'd earned that particular nickname), was watching me from across the locker room, her right eyebrow raised in a questioning arch. At left wing, she made up the final part of the forward line. Caroline and a junior named Pearson served as our blueliners with Liv, another transfer student like me, likely to start at goalie.

"I'm struggling to wrap my head around the fact that we have to practice in this dump. How are we supposed to prepare for a game in these conditions? I've skated on ponds better than this rink."

Mumbles of agreement broke out across the room. Clearly, I wasn't the only one severely disappointed with our circumstances.

"I've already spoken to Coach about the issue. There's nothing she can do," said Caroline.

"I might go crazy if I don't say *something*," I admitted.

The look on Caroline's face was clear; she knew exactly how the conversation would go and had little faith that it would do any good.

Lydia gave me an encouraging smile all the same. "Go easy on Coach, okay? It's not her fault we're stuck with this shitty rink."

I waited for most of the girls to clear out before I knocked on the office door and entered. The windowless room felt more like a closet that an office, the fluorescent light above head flickering as I slipped inside the tiny space. Coach Riley motioned for me to sit down at the armchair in front of her desk.

"I don't understand why we're forced to practice here," I said, the words spilling out of me before I could finish lowering myself into the chair. "This place is a dump, and I'm not just talking about the ice quality; it's the lifting equipment too. Those machines are a day away from crumbling into a pile of rust." The minuscule weight room in the basement of the facility looked like it hadn't been updated in over fifteen years. Most of us girls chose to train in the student gym that was accessible to non-athletes, even if it meant lifting at strange hours to avoid the crowds.

Coach Riley glanced down at her notepad, jotting something down on the paper. I couldn't tell if it was related to my complaints or if she was artfully avoiding my gaze. After a few seconds of awkward silence, she finally met my eyes, her lips pressed together in a thin line. Her expression told me everything I needed to know: this wasn't a conversation she wanted to have.

"I'm sorry, Grace, but this facility is the best we have." She spoke slowly, voice low. It made me think she was trying to keep her composure.

I refused to give up so easily. "It doesn't make sense. The men have access to one of the best hockey facilities in the country, which also happens to have *two* rinks. Why can't they share it with us?"

She let out a dejected sigh. "I understand your frustration, but this matter has already been discussed with the athletic director and Dean Adler. They have inspected this facility and ensured that it provides all the same amenities as DuLane Arena."

"And the extra rink?"

"Is apparently used by more than just the men's team. They host student classes there and open it up to the public some days."

In other words, it was more important to give the public access than the school's *female* team.

I resisted the urge to bang my head against her desk. "That's total bull and you know it!"

When we were on the ice and running drills, Coach Riley was a terrifying force to be reckoned with. But right now, there was not a single hint of that woman in the eyes staring back at me. If this was what giving up looked like, I didn't want it.

"I wish things were different, I really do, but this is the reality of women's athletics," she said. "We're overlooked, and our success is underappreciated."

I'd heard it all by now: the men brought in more money, their games were better attended, people actually wanted to watch them. It didn't matter that the women's team had a better record or that we'd won more national titles. It didn't matter that we had just as much of a chance at going pro now that the new women's professional league was pulling in record attendance numbers.

"What if we put on a gala like the men's hockey team does?" I'd only heard about the party after practice yesterday, when Pearson had mentioned she would be attending with her boyfriend. Apparently, the fundraiser brought in thousands for the men's program every year. As if they even needed the money.

"That event is completely funded by alumni. If you can find a free venue, free catering, and volunteers to run the event, I'm happy to approve it. But we don't have the money to host something like that."

None of this was fair. Outside of throwing my head back and screaming like a toddler, I didn't know how to react. What would it take to prove we deserved as much support as the male athletes at this school? At the very least, we deserved a facility with good temperature control and safe equipment. And one less likely to be haunted.

Lydia's voice rang through my head, reminding me that it wasn't Coach who deserved my anger. Ignoring every muscle in my body screaming to fight, I shoved down my growing frustration and exited her office. A few girls on the team had remained behind, eager to hear the outcome of our discussion. They watched me stomp back into the locker room with wary expressions.

"I take it the talk didn't go well," said Lydia.

"Apparently both the dean and the athletic director think this facility is up to standards." I couldn't help the sarcasm drenching my every word.

"They're men."

"I told you."

Big D and Caroline spoke at the same time, the latter reminding me that she'd been right. But there was nothing smug in her tone. If anything, she sounded bitter.

What an utter load of crap. If the administration at this school didn't want to listen to Coach, to me, and to all the women who came before us, I was going to turn up the volume so loud that it blew out their eardrums.

CHAPTER 3
Sebastian

"This is *our* game. We're skating circles around them out there. Do not let up. Do not get comfortable. I want everyone to know the Ravens mean business this year, all right?"

My voice was a steady boom that echoed across the locker room, one answered by a chorus of roars. Tonight might have only been an exhibition game, but it was also our chance to set the tone for the entire season. So far, we'd done that by shoving the puck right down the throats of our competition, and I'd spent every moment on the rink proving that I belonged there without a shadow of a doubt. I was flying higher than I had in a long time. In fact, I hadn't felt this good since I'd taken the ice the night we won the national championship.

The final period began with Providence trailing by three, scrambling to keep us in the neutral zone. The moment my skates touched the ice, the world righted itself. Bishop gained possession after the face-off, dumping the puck just moments after Kent shouted, "One hard!" in warning. All three of us chased after it, hurtling over the blue line and into the neutral zone. Bishop regained possession after the puck cycled the boards and quickly flung it to Kent, who had nothing but wide-open ice. His shot banked right, just missing the edge of the goalie's stick and whipping into the net. The horn blared for a fifth time, announcing our now four-goal lead over Providence.

I looked out across the ice, blood thrumming in my veins and heart thrashing against my ribs like a mallet to a drum. We flocked to the bench for a line shift, keeping our excitement at bay. It wasn't the norm to overtly celebrate during a game. Youth hockey had trained us to leave our emotions, even the good ones, off the rink. I grabbed my water and settled on the bench between Kent and Bishop, both stoic behind their cages.

"We're a different team with you out there, Sebastian. I don't know how to explain it, but there's a sort of energy you bring to the ice that's unlike anything I've ever experienced," said Kent.

Bishop grunted from beside me in agreement as Bryce and RT plopped onto the bench, the metal groaning beneath their weight. Bryce grabbed a towel and wiped it across the sweat gathered at the back of his neck.

"They're right," he said through panted breaths. "You're the key to his team. It's time everyone remembered that."

Music to my ears.

>> <<

The first game of the season was always celebrated—win or lose—at the shared hockey house at the end of Sampson Street, which was perched on an overgrown corner lot scattered with rusty lawn chairs. The three-story Victorian was probably glorious in its heyday, but after years of wild parties and neglect at the hands of rowdy hockey players, the place had fallen into disrepair. The famous property was owned by an alumnus who had lived in the house during his own hockey days. He'd imparted a list of rules that governed who could live there, ensuring that upperclassmen players got first choice in order of starting line. Currently, the five-bedroom house was inhabited by myself and four other seniors on the team.

Initially, I'd been ecstatic to move in. It was a rite of passage for the best hockey athletes at Dallard. As the youngest captain in history, I was able to move in my sophomore year. At the time, I hadn't considered the woes of living in a house packed with strangers every other weekend—strangers who left a mess of beer and puke behind when they finally departed at two in the morning. During my first two years on the team, I'd let myself fall into the habit of partying more than was good for me. But after the injury, I vowed to stay away from alcohol for the sake of my future endeavors.

Tonight's party was in full swing by ten-thirty, the place packed tight enough that it was nearly impossible to move from room to room without brushing against the sweaty arm of a stranger. Landon had assumed the role of DJ, which meant the music was loud enough to shake the house every time the beat dropped, and the beat dropped *a lot*. He was going through an EDM phase that made me regret our shared bedroom wall. Despite the fact that I was sober, my head was pounding. My only solace was the knowledge that eventually the party would move to the bars just a block away in downtown Trimont. The small town didn't have a plethora of establishments to choose from, but locals treated us hockey players like kings, giving out free drinks like candy at a parade.

Once the place finally cleared out, I'd be in bed watching a movie on my projector, but until then, I was happy to observe the flow of people coming in and out of the house from my balcony. As an introvert, I preferred watching others mingle over partaking in the festivities. People always revealed interesting things about themselves once they'd had a few too many. From the safety of my perch, I could learn a lot about a person by studying their interactions, all while avoiding the uncomfortable sensation of being trapped in a crowd.

The autumn air was crisp tonight, but that hadn't stopped the party from spilling out onto the front yard. A cold breeze rushed over me as three girls approached the house, the sound of their laughter carried up by the wind. The light on the front porch was just bright enough for me to make out the familiar form of Caroline Hart. The captain of the women's hockey team was easy to spot, her bright blond hair a dead giveaway. That meant one of the others had to be Lydia West. The two of them were almost always together.

"Why do I feel like I'm going to regret tonight?"

The question came from the girl in the middle. Though I could only see the top of her head, the rasp of her voice was instantly recognizable. For a moment, I was back in DuLane, staring into a mesmerizing pair of wide brown eyes. Although weeks had passed since our tense meeting, thoughts of her still crossed my mind on occasion. She'd taken root in my head like a stubborn weed, determined to last through the fast-approaching winter.

"You can't attend Dallard as a hockey player and not go to this party. It's a rite of passage. Anyway, it's our last weekend free before our games start. Let loose," Caroline said.

"She's right," said the other girl—it was definitely Lydia. "Just avoid the basement at all costs. That floor has never not been sticky."

I held back a snort of laughter. I wasn't sure how many years of spilled beverages had gone into creating that mess, but there were usually a few unlucky partygoers who lost a shoe to the basement floor. One particular Adidas sneaker had lived here longer than me.

"Hey, Bryce," Caroline said. "Congrats on the win this weekend. You absolutely crushed Providence."

"Thanks. It was amazing," he replied. "How come you guys didn't have an exhibition game?"

"St. Thomas pulled out last-minute." She sounded disappointed. "An exhibition would have been great, but I'm not too worried. Having Grace out there with us has really rounded out the team." Caroline gestured to my mystery girl.

Grace. So that was her name.

"You used to play for Boston College, right?" Bryce asked.

I wasn't surprised that he knew who Grace was. His sister, who was just as skilled on the ice as he was and practically as tall, also played division one hockey. They'd both headed for higher ground after high school, Bryce settling down here while his sister made the East Coast her new stomping grounds.

"Holy shit, are you related to Faith?"

"She's my twin sister," he confirmed. "She was sad to see you transfer. They won't be the same team without you."

I watched from my spot as they continued to chat about hockey, hanging on to every word that left Grace's mouth.

"These are some of my roommates. Landon plays goalie and Kent is at right wing. Our other two roommates are somewhere around," Bryce said, referring to me and Bishop.

Kent was only a few beers away from being drunk, based on the way he swayed clumsily to the beat of the music. If anyone embodied the term *dancing machine*, it was him. All he needed was a little booze to become the world's best and most embarrassing wedding date. Right now, he was ignoring Bryce's introduction in favor of trying to make Caroline laugh. At least, that's what I assumed he was attempting, based on the movement of his arms and the awkward way he was gyrating back and forth.

Meanwhile, Landon shook Grace's hand, overly eager to make her acquaintance. Nobody took advantage of their athlete status around campus to land hookups quite like he did. I was pretty sure he had half the dance team on speed dial at this point.

As more people arrived, it became increasingly difficult to hear more than a few random words of their conversation. I was fighting the temptation to make my presence known, just to see how Grace would react, when Kate slipped out onto the balcony. I'd been avoiding her for the last hour. She still hadn't congratulated me on our big win, and though we usually avoided the topic of hockey to keep the peace, I wanted to hear that she was proud of me.

"You can't hide up here forever. Come on, let's dance a little," she suggested.

Kate's manicured hand wrapped around my bicep, pulling me away from the railing. When she saw how reluctant I was to go, she stood on her tiptoes and kissed the side of my jaw. "When everyone leaves for the bar, we'll have this place to ourselves."

"All right," I said in surrender, "but I need something with caffeine if you want me to stay up. Do you want anything?"

Kate shook her head and motioned to the cup in her hand. "I'll be with Mace. Find me as soon as you grab your drink."

I followed her out of my bedroom and down the hallway. As we reached the bottom of the stairs, Kate peeled off to find

Bishop's girlfriend, Macy, disappearing into the mass of bodies occupying every inch of the first level. It wasn't difficult navigating the crowd; they parted easily at the sight of me. I could sense a shift in energy from the students. By now, they had either witnessed or heard about my return to the ice. Though they were no longer watching me with pity in their eyes, I still disliked the attention.

Tucked into the corner of the living room was our sad excuse for a bar. The makeshift table was comprised of two stools and a large piece of plywood that was beginning to sink in the middle from overuse. The players stuck on bartending duty nodded to me as I ducked under the plywood in search of something with caffeine. I was elbow deep in the cooler when I heard my name.

"Evans is grabbing himself a drink. He can make you something before he leaves."

Bryce was speaking to someone on the other side of the bar. My hand clasped around a can of Diet Coke, and I straightened from my position crouched over the cooler to stand at full height. *Grace.* Her eyes flashed in recognition as they met mine. She was dressed in a denim skirt that showed off the lean muscles of her legs. Her hair was pulled back into a braid, and her cheeks were flushed pink from the heat. I let my gaze linger on her lips. They were shiny with something I was sure tasted just as sweet as she looked.

She's a weed, I reminded myself. *An unwanted growth that is taking over your mind.* I couldn't allow myself to think of her as anything but.

"Hey, man, mind making these ladies a quick drink while you're back there?" Bryce asked.

For a moment, I considered taking the polite route. I'd make her a drink, smile accordingly, and flee into the crowd. But something wicked inside me wanted to make her feel as unsettled as I felt in her presence, and the burning desire to watch her cheeks flush even brighter won out. It was a foolish decision, but I couldn't help myself.

"I'm happy to provide refreshments for Caroline and Lydia, but I don't make drinks for people I don't know," I said, making a point to look directly at Grace.

Her eyes remained glued to me as I popped open the tab on my soda and took a long drink. I could feel the question in Bryce's gaze.

"This is Grace. She's the new starting center for the women's team," he explained.

I didn't bother to respond. Instead, I pulled out two red Solo cups and loaded them with ice from the cooler.

"Don't be an asshole, Evans," Bryce warned.

"That's his only setting, unfortunately." Grace spoke up for the first time, voice barely audible over the pounding music.

"You two know each other?"

She shook her head quickly. "I had the misfortune of running into him at the start of the semester. But don't worry about the drink. I wouldn't trust anything he handed to me anyway."

My jaw ticked in irritation as she pivoted and disappeared into the mass of students. I abandoned the half-made drinks in pursuit of her, ducking under the bar as soda sloshed over the side of the can gripped in my left hand. Bryce called my name, but I was already lost in the crowd, following the path Grace had carved though the living room. She was nearly to the front door when I threw myself forward to block her exit.

"Don't act like you know me," I said, reaching out to stop her as she attempted to dart around me. I wasn't going to let her get away that easily, not after that insulting insinuation about the drink.

"But I do. You told me everything I needed to know the first time we met. And trust me, I don't want anything from someone like you," she hissed.

"Someone like me?"

"Someone who thinks they're better than everyone."

That made me laugh. "I am better than everyone. At least when it comes to hockey. And a few other *strenuous* activities."

"A chauvinistic prick," she continued, pretending she hadn't heard me speak. "A pompous, rude, entitled—"

"I get it, you don't like me. The feeling is mutual," I interjected.

I didn't hate the girl, but I wasn't exactly pleased with my inclination to throw caution to the wind every time I laid eyes on her. Grace was undeniably beautiful, and equally unwilling to put up with my shit. In other words, she was a dangerous distraction waiting to happen, and that was the last thing I needed in my life. Yet here I was, chasing after her like an impulsive fool. Emotions could do a lot of damage if they were given free rein. I needed to find some semblance of control, and fast.

"Then I suggest we get on with not liking each other from a distance," she said.

"This is my house," I pointed out. "Are saying I should leave?"

Grace shook her head in disbelief. "You stopped *me*, remember?"

Over her head, a familiar pair of deep blue eyes caught my attention. My gaze lingered on Kate for a brief moment, hoping that the sight of her would help douse the raging fire lit within me by the presence of Grace.

"Don't worry," I said, lip curling upward. "I'm not stopping you now."

I shifted a fraction of an inch; it was just enough room for her to squeeze through the front door. With one last withering glare, Grace shouldered her way past me. Foolishly, I stole a glance at her retreating form, my traitorous eyes lingering on that perfect ass. Who could blame me really? She had a phenomenal backside.

I had barely a second to collect myself when Kate appeared from the crowd, snaking her arms around my body.

"I was wondering where you went," she shouted over the music, her lips hot across the bottom of my jaw. "Thought you were getting a drink?"

I held up my soda in answer, but Kate wasn't convinced.

"Who was that girl?"

I schooled my face into an expression of disinterest as I said, "No one important, babe. The new center for the women's hockey team."

"Did she make a move?"

A snort of laughter escaped through my lips.

"Don't laugh at me," she said, shoving me away in a playful manner. "The girls at this school are desperate to get with you." Kate wasn't the jealous type, but she was aware that there was a long line of girls willing to take me to bed whether we were together or not.

"That's not why I laughed," I assured her. "She'd rather hit me than hit *on* me."

Somehow, Kate looked even more interested at this bit of information. "What did you do?"

"Why do you assume it's something I did?"

"Because, Sebastian Evans, you're a shit-starter."

I shrugged. "It's nothing, I promise you."

Kate finally relented, pulling me back to the heat of her body.

"Let's get dinner tomorrow night. Something fancy. I'd like to dress up."

"Tomorrow won't work. I have a ton of homework, so I'll probably post up at the library."

Her lips formed an all-too-familiar pout. "Come on, we haven't had a proper date since the hockey season started. It's already October."

"You know my schedule, babe. Sundays are homework days."

"You seriously can't make an exception this one Sunday?"

"I need to pass my classes, Kate. They almost didn't let me back in this semester, and you know that."

Three times. We'd had this talk *three* times, once before the school year started and twice since. I'd been very honest with Kate. This year, more than ever, I was going to be busy. I had to keep up my grades if I wanted to play on the team, and my only chance to sign an NHL contract at the end of the year was to prove myself on the ice. I had to be better in every respect, which left little time to plan extravagant dates.

"Seb, please. I feel like you always choose hockey over me."

And I always would, but she already knew that.

"Is this really how you want to spend the night? Fighting about how I don't make enough time for you?"

She scoffed. "Well, when you say it like that—"

"Pointing out the obvious, babe."

"You're being an asshole!"

"Because all you want to do when we *are* together is complain about how we don't spend enough time together!" Anger and frustration had my voice rising. "If you want to fight, find someone else to do it with."

I shrugged off her touch and made a hasty retreat through

the back door in the kitchen. The stragglers outside grew quiet as I thumped down the stairs and collapsed into a lawn chair. With one stony glance, I sent everyone around me scrambling back into the house. At least some people were back to treating me with the respect I deserved. Letting out a long sigh, I let my head fall against the back of the chair to look at the sky. The scent of woodsmoke and burning leaves permeated the air. It was a major upgrade from the stench of alcohol and sweat from inside the house, one that helped ease some of the tension in my shoulders. Fall was my favorite time of the year. The familiar smells, the shift in weather, the darkening days—they were all changes I looked forward to because they signified the start of the regular hockey season. When the heat of summer began to fade, I could sense the shift within me; it was as if my body knew what was coming.

Tonight, despite every single person who'd doubted me, I'd proved myself an asset. No one had expected me to make such a successful comeback, not after my performance in the spring. The entire hockey world had written me off. But any uncertainty about my return to the team was squashed the second my skates hit the ice tonight. And instead of congratulating me, or even acknowledging my success, Kate complained about how little time we spent together. She knew that my dream was to play professional hockey. She knew how important it was for me to honor my father's memory. But it was never enough for her. I was starting to doubt she'd ever understand.

Later in the evening, after the party had died down to a few drunkards, Kate found me out back. Without a word, she sat down in the chair beside me and settled into the silence.

"Today was an important day for me," I explained, twisting my head to the side. "Everyone expected me to fail, but I didn't.

And rather than congratulate me on the win, on all the hard work we've *both* put into my recovery, you picked a fight. I don't have the energy to fight, Kate. I'm exhausted. I'm exhausted, and I still chose to spend time with you at this party rather than catch up on sleep."

She studied me with careful eyes, her expression unreadable. But after a long moment, Kate nodded her head and reached for my face. Her hands were a shock of warmth against my chilled skin.

"I'm sorry. I should have congratulated you."

I swallowed down a painful lump in the back of my throat. *Are we destined to repeat this same fight time and time again?*

"You were amazing out there. I even watched the whole game, I swear." Her voice grew softer as she dragged her fingers through the ends of my hair.

I was caught off guard by her confession. Kate didn't like to watch me play, not since the injury. I liked to pretend it was because she didn't want to see me get hurt, but it was more complicated than that. At first, I'd blamed her for the accident. She was the reason I'd been so distracted on the ice that night: we'd had a massive fight right before the game. I wouldn't have been scrambling in the final seconds of the game if my head had been in it from the moment the clock started. At the time, I'd wanted to find fault in anyone other than myself. It had only taken a few days for me to come to my senses and apologize, but by then, it was too late. The damage was done. Even though she'd forgiven me, there was an underlying tension that had everything to do with my dedication to the sport and my need to get back on the ice. Maybe a part of her longed for me to quit, like she'd finally realized exactly how much of my life I was willing to sacrifice for hockey.

"Why don't we go back to my place where it's quiet and watch a movie?" she suggested.

I didn't have the energy to walk back to campus, even if it was only a few blocks. My body was sore from the game. I'd taken my fair share of hard hits.

"We can stay here," I suggested. "I'll meet you in my room in a few minutes."

Kate pressed a soft kiss to my cheek before she disappeared into the house. The past few weeks had gone much better than I'd expected. My knee was feeling strong, the team was shaping up to be unstoppable, and I was keeping up with classes. Life hadn't gone this well for me since before the injury. But every time I felt high on hockey, Kate was there to drag me down. It was complicated, feeling both gratitude and overwhelming frustration toward the person I trusted the most. She was the reason I was here now, but I wasn't sure that was enough. Not anymore.

CHAPTER 4

Grace

Someone had taken a sledgehammer to my head. That someone was me, and that sledgehammer was five tequila shots downed in the span of twenty minutes. With deep regret for my late-night decisions, I heaved myself up and into a sitting position and tried to piece together my memories of the evening. After running into Sebastian at the hockey house, my planned two-drink cap had gone out the window. It was all I could do to forget that smug expression he wore like a badge of honor.

Head pounding, I stumbled out of my bedroom and into the kitchen. Pearson and Big D were passed out in the living room, the former on the sofa and the latter splayed out across the floor in front of the TV. I was pleasantly surprised to find Lydia awake, nursing a cup of coffee. She didn't hesitate to grab another mug and fill it for me.

"Thank you," I whispered, grabbing the creamer from the fridge.

"No need to whisper," she said with a chuckle. "Those two can sleep through a tornado warning."

I closed my eyes as the hot liquid warmed my stomach. After taking another long sip, I filled an empty glass with water and drained it in a single go.

"How are you feeling?" she asked, and I let out a low groan in answer. "I figured that might be the case. You probably should have stopped at the fourth shot."

"I shouldn't have had a single shot." Letting loose every now and then was fun, but last night had been a desperate attempt to rid my mind of one frustratingly handsome hockey player.

"Do you remember everything?" she asked.

My cheeks heated under her teasing smile, and I nodded.

"Honestly, everything you said was spot-on. I agree wholeheartedly."

Before I could reply, Caroline appeared at the edge of the kitchen wrapped in her fluffy pink robe. "You agree with what?" she asked.

"Grace's drunken rant about the power of protest."

The discussion had sprung from an unfortunate conversation with a guy named Landon, who ate up at least five minutes of my time bragging about the perks of DuLane Arena. I'd been close to pouring my drink on him when Lydia rescued me. After that, I spent the rest of the night scheming ways to right our ridiculously unfair training conditions.

Caroline poured herself a cup of coffee and hummed in agreement. "You did have some good ideas. Enough to convince those two to come back and make plans," she said, gesturing to our still sleeping teammates.

Though the end of the night was a bit blurry, I distinctly remembered sitting around the coffee table with a whiteboard and several bags of chips. I could have sworn Caroline took notes as we shouted out different ideas.

"Gate-crashing the men's fundraiser would be epic, but it could get you in big trouble," said Caroline.

According to Pearson, the fundraiser took place at the Vincent Hotel every year. She'd be attending with her boyfriend, who worked as the team's student manager. This year, they would be honoring the man who'd funded DuLane Arena. He'd put millions of dollars into rebuilding the facility, one that only the male hockey players got access to. It felt like the perfect opportunity to make a stand.

"If we expose the disparity of the training conditions between the men's and women's programs, it could bring about the change we need. There will be a lot of important people attending that gala," I argued.

"If you sneak into a private event and disrupt it, it could get you into hot water with the university," Caroline warned. "I want you to be sure you're okay with taking this risk."

If I were being honest with myself, I didn't have much experience when it came to taking risks, at least not when it came to my future. Following the rules was second nature to me. But rules were meant to ensure a sense of rightness, and nothing about this situation was right, or fair. What did it matter if I got to play hockey when our practice conditions made training miserable? We deserved better, and so did all the women who would come after us. This was something that I had the power to fix. If there was any chance to make a change or start a conversation, I wanted to be part of it.

"I'm willing to do it," I said confidently. "I just need help getting into the venue and documenting everything."

The three of us turned to the living room, where Pearson was curled up on the sofa. All I had to do was convince her to let me in through the back door and record my announcement. I'd handle the rest. She'd already agreed last night, but I felt it was only fair to ask her when she was sober.

"If you're willing the take that risk, then the rest of the team should be more than willing to help with what comes after. We need to let the students know just how little DU cares about their national championship-winning women's hockey team," Lydia said, and I didn't miss Caroline's firm nod of agreement.

Thus far, she'd been the voice of reason warning me to be careful. But even I could see the fire in her eyes. Just like everyone else on the team, Caroline despised the hand we'd been dealt. It was time we were heard, no matter what it took or how many parties I needed to crash.

"What happens after the gala? I don't think posting to my five hundred followers on Instagram is going to do much, especially since most of them don't go to school here. How are we going to get people to see this?"

I could practically see a light turn on in Lydia's head. "I know the guy who runs the unofficial DUpdates TikTok—Austin. He's a wannabe journalist and big social media guy. Most students here follow him for random updates and school news. Sometimes he even interviews students on campus. Last year, one of his videos went viral. He went around campus with a girl from the basketball team and recorded her challenging guys on campus to a shoot-off. There were a lot of bruised egos that day. I'm sure I can convince him to help spread the news."

"And we'll have everyone from the team share the post. This could work," Caroline said.

"It could help to hang posters around the school. My girlfriend does graphic design, and I'm sure she'd be up to creating some," Lydia added.

I looked back and forth between the two of them as a seed of excitement planted itself within me. Things were actually coming together. "Are we really doing this?"

Caroline crossed her arms over her chest in a stance of defiance. "They can't punish us for sharing the truth. Protesting the patriarchy is well within our rights as students and athletes."

Hockey meant the world to me. It had taught me the power of commitment and the strength of patience, exposed me to new hardships, and helped shape the person I was now. Without hockey, I wouldn't have the confidence to fight for myself and the other girls on this team. So really, there was no question of whether I wanted to go through with this. The only thing I needed to ask myself was: How far was I willing to go?

>> <<

"Did you take away Gabby's phone?"

A loud car horn sounded from the other end of the line; my dad was most likely on his way home from work. I'd told him time and time again not to answer the phone behind the wheel, but the man was stubborn and rarely listened to anyone.

"No, she has her phone. She's been doing okay at school too."

As relieved as I was to hear that she wasn't getting into trouble, his words were confirmation that Gabby had been deliberately ignoring my texts.

"That's good," I said. "Maybe mention that I'd like to hear from her? She's been slow to respond to my messages." That was a nice way of putting it, seeing as she hadn't responded to me in over a week.

"She has a lot on her plate with dance and school, so don't distract her too much," he told me.

Was my sister alive and breathing? That was all I needed to hear; it wasn't like I was asking for a ten-page summary on how her week had gone "I'm not distracting her. I'd like to know she's okay."

"She is, I promise," he assured me.

As usual, Dad kept things short and to the point. He was bad at making small talk in person, and even worse over the phone. To avoid the inevitable awkward pause, I said goodbye and ended the call. My music kicked back on in an instant, blaring through my headphones like a banshee's scream. Pain sliced through my ears, bringing me to a sudden stop as I rushed to turn down the volume. A steely force crashed into me from behind. By some miracle, I managed to avoid kissing the cement as I was sent stumbling forward. There was an apology at the tip of my tongue as I whirled around, but the notion shriveled up and died when I saw the person half responsible for our collision.

Of course, I thought, craning my neck back to take in the full image of him. Sebastian looked as though he just walked off the set of a sports photoshoot. He was dressed from head to toe in brand name activewear that outlined his lean muscles like it was hand tailored to his body. His thick head of hair was perfectly windswept, stray pieces of the chocolate brown locks falling over his forehead. *Too bad the guy underneath all that brooding beauty is a sour little asshole.* My eyes narrowed on the hockey player towering over me and I took a hasty step back.

"Everyone on campus might part like the red sea when you walk by, but you don't own the sidewalk. Other students use it too. It's not polite to run people over," I said.

If only I had a smoothie on hand; that would really give people something to stare at, though it seemed that we'd already gained an audience. Several people had made a point of stopping mid-conversation to catch a glimpse of the famous Sebastian Evans—the quad was crawling with his adoring fans. Good thing I was dressed to impress in my nicest pair of sweatpants.

"And be denied the opportunity to witness your distress at crossing paths with the school's most talented athlete? Not a chance," he said, his words lacking their usual malice and an unexpected tilt at the corner of his mouth.

In fact, if I didn't know better, I'd say Sebastian was teasing me. *Maybe even flirting?* As soon as the thought crossed my mind, I dismissed it with a shake of my head. Sebastian being anything other than rude was deeply unsettling.

"You know what, never mind. Keep walking with your head down. Do it in that direction, say, for about ten minutes." I pointed toward the path to our left where the pavement split, one branch of the sidewalk disappearing into the forest. East Point Lookout was a half mile up the trail, a spot I'd discovered within my first week at school. It was a great location for romantic picnics, owing to the beautiful view of the lake, but it also happened to be perched on a thirty-foot cliff.

"You really dislike me enough to want me dead?" he asked in a falsely wounded tone, clutching at his heart for dramatic effect.

Warning bells blared in my head. Sebastian was *definitely* flirting with me.

"The only thing I wish is for you to leave me alone. And if you happened to fall off a cliff, I wouldn't be heartbroken over it."

"I'm not that bad, I swear. What can I do to make it up to you?" he asked with a glimmer of mischief in his eyes. "Come on, there has to be something."

"If you can help me convince the administration to let us use the extra rink at DuLane, everything will be forgotten." My words caused an immediate shift in the dynamic between us, leaving absolutely no room for Sebastian's earlier playfulness.

"Why? You have your own facility."

How quickly that humorous tone disappeared . . .

"Because ours is falling apart. It should be condemned."

"Compared to DuLane, every facility looks bad. That doesn't give you the right to encroach on our space."

The sun flickered out as a cloud shifted overhead, casting shadows over the path where we stood. Tension hung thick in the air. I drew a deep breath before speaking, willing myself to remain calm.

"You wouldn't say that if you had to practice at McKinley. The smell alone would be enough to turn you off. "Our record is as good as yours." It was better, actually, but I didn't think mentioning that would help the situation. "Imagine what we could do if we had decent training conditions."

Sebastian crossed his arms over his chest and spoke in a low, firm voice. "My training is *extremely* important. I can't give up time on the ice or in the gym to make room for another team. It's the same for everyone else."

A bitter smile formed on my lips. Sebastian didn't want to help. He didn't care about anyone but himself; that much had been apparent from the moment we met. I needed to remember that.

"Then don't expect me to waste another fucking breath talking to you."

I couldn't wait to see his face when I took the stage at the gala. He had no idea what was coming.

CHAPTER 5

Sebastian

There was something devious in Grace's parting expression that set me on edge. I couldn't shake the feeling that she was scheming something in that obnoxiously pretty head of hers. It wouldn't surprise me, especially after her—

"Golden boy," said a familiar voice. "How does it feel to be back on top?"

I tore my eyes away from her retreating form, confusion sweeping over me at the sight of my old teammate. Devon Bowman had graduated two years ago, right after I blew out my knee to win us a national hockey title. Since then, he'd moved to Minneapolis and started working for a sports marketing firm. And, apparently, grown a rather impressive beard.

"Hey, man," I said. "What the hell are you doing back at Dallard?"

"Touring the campus with my little brother. He's looking into colleges this year," he explained.

"Great game last weekend!" someone said and clapped me on the back as they walked by. It happened so fast that I didn't catch a glimpse of their face.

"Seems like nothing has changed since I left. You still have all your adoring fans," Devon teased. If he'd been here last year, or even last week, he wouldn't be saying that. "I look forward to seeing you back on the ice. If you're ever in Minneapolis, drop me a line. Let's catch up."

I stood rooted to the spot as I offered Devon a halfhearted wave goodbye, still stuck on my conversation with Grace.

It was impossible to enjoy my return as king of the campus with her around. Where did Grace get off thinking she had any claim over DuLane Arena? I hadn't been serious when I'd offered to make things up to her; I was just curious to see if there was anything she wanted from me.

For a brief moment, when her eyes had filled with the faintest spark of hope as she'd asked for my help, I'd been close to saying yes without considering the consequences. Clearly, I needed to keep Grace at arm's length for my own sanity, because there was something about her that made me act recklessly. I admired her skill on the ice—maybe that explained some of the fascination I had for her. And even after my less than friendly welcome to school, she'd been willing to put aside her pride in asking for help.

But I couldn't help Grace without compromising my own goals, and when she was in close proximity, I made stupid, impulsive decisions—flirting, for example. The girl was a threat to my hockey season *and* my sanity. It was simple, really: Grace was trouble waiting to happen, which meant I needed to keep my distance.

>> <<

"Are you seriously leaving?"

My eyes flickered between the bulge in my pants and Kate,

who, up until a few seconds ago, had been licking the side of my neck and exploring every inch of me with greedy hands. Now, she was frantically searching the floor for her baby-blue sweater as her phone alarm blasted through my bedroom.

"My blowout is in ten minutes," she exclaimed, a note of panic in her voice. "I need to be in Clearwater like now, and I don't—oh, thank God." She plucked her sweater off the top of my dresser and silenced the alarm. We hadn't had sex in over a week, and I must have flung it over there in my haste to get her undressed.

"You're going to leave me like this?"

Kate's head poked out from the neckline of her top as she righted the material over her chest. "I'm sorry," she said, but she didn't sound like it. In fact, she seemed entirely unbothered that neither of us had come close to finishing. "I need to look my best at the gala. The head of the UVA grad program will be there tonight. His son made the team this year. I think he's a freshman."

Kate had been talking about the University of Virginia's environmental science graduate program since sophomore year. Her mom was an alumnus of the program, and she'd played a huge role in Kate's decision to apply.

"Will you be ready by six?" I asked, glancing down at my watch. "Coach wants us there a little early, so you'll have to wait around a bit before the event starts."

She shook her head as she grabbed her purse. "I'll meet you there. Macy is driving separately, so she'll take me."

Kate rushed over to the bed and planted a kiss on my cheek before hightailing it out of my room. I stared down at my cock for a long time after, wondering if it was worth beating one out before the gala. The answer was a resounding yes, given I was still half hard and desperate for a release. As I worked myself out in the shower, I pictured thick brown hair grasped between my fingers and a wet, hot throat swallowing me down. Just as I fell over the edge, the image shifted; the head bobbing up and down on me tilted up to meet my eyes. But it wasn't the familiar blue I was expecting. Instead, I was greeted by the sight of wide chocolate eyes glossed over with moisture, tears streaming down her face.

After finishing, I left the shower feeling worse off. I was no longer sporting a raging boner, but I felt slimy for picturing Grace when it should have been Kate. What I needed right now was a distraction, and seeing as we didn't have to be at the gala for another two hours, I had time to kill. I set off down the long arched hallway, knocking on doors and calling for my roommates to meet me in the kitchen. Everyone was home, and in about fifteen minutes, we were seated around the kitchen table, Bryce spreading out a deck of cards in one clean line.

"Pick for teams," he instructed.

When we were on the ice, I was in charge. But outside of the rink, Bryce was the glue that held us all together (and made sure we paid the electric bill on time). Landon and Kent sat across the table from us while Bishop perched on the kitchen counter with a beer in hand. He wasn't much of a card player or a talker, but he liked to watch our euchre games. Kent and I selected the lowest cards and were paired together. We picked next for first deal, and as usual, Landon selected the highest card. He was always lucky that way.

"Don't go soft on me," I said to Kent, looking at him from across the table as Landon dealt the first hand.

Kent was a timid player, always afraid to take chances. I wanted to beat them, and for that to happen, he'd have to make big moves. The first hand went to Landon and Bryce, then the second to us. By the sixth round, we were down by three, and my hand was stacked with tens for the second time. I was convinced that Landon had both jacks and an ace up his sleeve. Lucky bastard.

"I'm surprised Kate isn't here," Bryce said, dropping a trump on the table and sweeping the hand.

"She's getting a blowout."

"She's getting blown?" Landon chuckled.

"It's a hair appointment with no cut or color. They just wash and style," Kent said, and I didn't miss the snarky look Landon shot him.

"Anyone else got a hot date, or is it just me and Bishop?" I asked.

"This stag is riding solo, of course. The lonely wives at these events can never get enough of me," said Landon.

"What he means"—Kent slammed down the ace of hearts—"is that he was too chicken to ask out the girl he's been drooling over."

Landon must have kicked Kent under the table because he let out a pained grunt.

Bryce's gaze briefly met mine before darting away. "Maybe let's not talk about—"

"Don't act like you haven't stalked her IG," Kent cut in, reaching across the table to punch Landon in the shoulder.

"You can't blame me. She's hot."

"Who?" I asked.

"The new center on the women's team. Grace," he explained.

Immediately, I was back in the shower with Grace's face looking up at me. *Fuck.* It was starting to feel like an impossible task to keep my thoughts about her at bay. I wasn't surprised to hear that Landon was interested in Grace. No one that hot flew under the radar at a school this small. Maybe I could introduce her to the basketball team. They'd keep her busy. I was willing to try anything if it meant she'd be out of sight and out of mind.

"She's not that special. What about that girl on the dance team you've been talking to?" I asked.

Bryce couldn't hold back a snort of laughter. "Evans here got off on the wrong foot with the new girl, but he won't tell me why."

Landon's eyes widened in realization. "Grace is the girl from the party?"

I didn't like that my teammates were gossiping about me and Grace, but I couldn't blame anyone but myself. I'd made it clear in front of multiple witnesses that we were not on friendly terms.

"I'm done with this game." I tossed my cards down on the table.

"She really has your panties in a twist. Why is that?" Landon was wearing his best shit-eating grin.

Refusing to engage, I crossed my arms over my chest and said absolutely nothing. None of them needed to know the real reason Grace had taken up residence in my head, rent-free. How could I admit to them that my dream girl had skated right out of my imagination and into reality, only to appear at the worst possible time? Right now, I needed to be laser-focused on training. Plus, I already had a girlfriend, one that gave me enough to worry about outside of hockey and school.

"All right, that's enough," Bryce said. "We should get going, anyway. Coach will lose his mind if we're late to the fundraiser."

I shot him a grateful look and pushed up from the table. "I'll meet you guys there. I'm driving separately."

>> <<

The hotel was a fifteen minute drive, which gave me a little time to collect myself. But even with the windows rolled down and the crisp October air rushing over my face, I couldn't banish Grace from my mind. She was like a never-fading echo, a shadow that remained even after the sun went down. Even when I closed my eyes at night, she was there, taunting me with a sweet smile and the promise of a heated exchange. As I pulled into the parking lot, I willed myself to forget about her. It was for my own good.

Coach gathered the team in the parking lot and mentioned the big names who were attending tonight. He warned us to be on our best behavior, emphasizing our role in charming the rich alumni who funded the program, and then cut us free just as people started to arrive. I waited in the lobby for a few minutes before Kate and Macy walked through the front door. Kate was wearing a tight black dress with a slit up the back—a feature I discovered when she did a little spin for me while approaching—and shiny red heels. Long dark waves fell down her back, and a smile painted in bold red pulled my attention to her lips.

"It's so nice to see you out of that sweaty uniform or workout clothes," she said, taking my outstretched hand.

Of course, I thought, my body tensing at the snark behind her words. Kate couldn't help but continually remind me how I chose hockey over her. But now wasn't the time to start a fight. Instead, I grabbed her hand and led her through the lobby and into the ballroom. The place was decked out with fancy chandeliers and cocktail tables piled high with hors d'oeuvres. Waiters wandered in and out of the crowd holding trays topped with champagne flutes. A few people had already moved to the dance floor and were swaying with their partners to the soft notes playing from the piano stationed at the back of the room. The annual fundraiser was always held at the historic Vincent Hotel. Though the ballroom looked identical to last year's event, something felt different. I couldn't put my finger on it.

"Do I look nice?" Kate asked, stepping into my line of vision and giving me another spin.

"You always look nice," I said, glancing around the room as I tried to work out why the atmosphere felt off. Not a single thing looked out of place.

"You're not even looking at me, Sebastian."

I let out a long sigh, still frustrated at her earlier jab, and turned to face Kate. The disappointment etched into her features felt like a punch to the gut. I felt guilty all over again for picturing Grace in the shower.

"I'm sorry," I said, pulling her close. "You are especially ravishing tonight. I'd kiss you if it wouldn't mess up those perfect lips." Even to my own ears, the words sounded rehearsed, like I'd said them a million times before. *I'm sorry I can't spend more time with you. I'm sorry you wasted so much time on someone who can't give you what you want.* It wasn't healthy to spend more time apologizing than enjoying each other's time, and we both knew it. But neither of us had the strength to pull away.

Kate assessed me with an expression that was hard to read. "Macy and I are going to get drinks," she said after a moment, then grabbed Macy's arm and pulled her away from Bishop, who was busy amassing a large pile of appetizers on a tiny silver plate. They disappeared into the crowd, Kate whispering into her friend's ear, no doubt complaining about my lack of enthusiasm. My stomach let out a loud growl. I turned to appraise the food and found that the closest display happened to be a spectacular charcuterie board loaded with every cheese, meat, and nut possible. I was almost within reach of the plates when a hand fell on top of my shoulder.

"Sebastian, great to see you," Elijah Peters said, a smile stretched across his bearded face.

He was still a handsome man, even at sixty-six years old. Despite the wrinkles around his eyes and mouth, there was something genuine in his expression that brought forth a warmth in his features.

"You as well, old man," I said as he pulled me into a brief hug.

Elijah was a close family friend and an alumnus of Dallard University. He was the reason I'd chosen this hockey program in the first place. Not only was he a fellow Raven, he was a regular donor to the program and the university. He and my stepfather had worked at the same company for years before Elijah left to start a private consulting firm.

"You were incredible last weekend. I was glad to see you back on the ice. The team is looking fantastic."

"Thank you, sir."

"I'm confident you'll lead the team to another championship this year."

"That's the plan," I said.

"I'll get in touch with Bill to see what games he'll be attending this year," Elijah said. "Hopefully we can see one together."

Suddenly, someone slammed into me from the side. My reflexes kicked into gear, and I reached out to steady them. The eyes blinking back at me in surprise made my pulse jump.

Not again. What the hell is she doing here?

Grace quickly pulled away and righted herself. Her hands shook as she wiped them along the front of her silky green dress. The material followed the lines of her body, outlining the shape of her curves in all the right places. My mouth watered at the sight of her thigh peeking through a high slit in the material. She was more done up than I'd ever seen her, eyes outlined in dark makeup and cheeks dusted pink. I forced my expression to remain neutral despite the spike in my pulse.

"I'm sorry," she forced out the apology through gritted teeth.

"Do you normally throw yourself at men?" I asked, unable to help myself. There was nothing I could do to avoid the girl when she was so keen on colliding with me. I deserved to have some fun before she undoubtedly stormed off.

"I tripped, you imbecile," Grace said. "I would much rather have fallen into the cheese table than you."

Beside me, Elijah cleared his throat.

"I'm so sorry, sir," Grace said, reaching out to shake Elijah's hand. This time, the apology was genuine. "I'm Grace. As you can tell, I don't wear heels very often. I'm not the steadiest in them."

"Please, no apologies are necessary. I take it you and Sebastian know each other?"

He was looking between us with a bemused expression.

"She plays for the women's team. Transferred this year," I said stiffly.

"Ah, I hear you ladies are some of the best in the NCAA."

"Yes, we're looking to bring Dallard a fourth national title." She turned to me with a sweet smile that promised nothing but trouble. "I guess it'll be five if you count the single championship won by the men's team."

Elijah let out a bark of laughter. "I'm sure you keep this one on his toes."

"If you'll excuse us for a moment," I said, taking Grace's wrist and leading her toward the back corner of the room.

"Are you going to manhandle me every time we meet?" she asked.

"Are you going to run into me every time we're within ten feet of each other? What the hell are you doing here?"

"It's none of your business. I'll be sure to stay far away from you for the rest of the night." Grace pulled out of my hold, and the effort caused her to stumble before she regained her balance.

"If you don't know how to walk in heels, don't wear them. The next person you fall on might not be as nice as me."

"Nice?" She barked out a caustic laugh. "You and 'nice' don't belong in the same sentence. 'Asshole' would be a much better descriptor."

I bit my tongue. It was all I could do to keep myself from conceding to the overwhelming urge to squabble with her. Why did I so thoroughly enjoy bickering with Grace? Something within me burned with desire every time her cheeks turned pink or her eyes narrowed in my direction. She made the blood in my veins run hot.

"You're up to something," I accused, my eyes narrowed in suspicion. "And I'm telling you right now to cut it out. This isn't the time or place."

"Again, it's none of your business why I'm here. Maybe I'm someone's date. Which reminds me, shouldn't you get back to your girlfriend?"

The mention of Kate had me searching the room, eyes roaming across the growing throng of attendees. I spotted her with Macy and Bishop, who were whispering to each other like a love-drunk couple. Kate stood beside them with one hand planted on her hip, eyes trained directly on me.

"Stay out of my way," I said under my breath, not looking away from my girlfriend. I knew if I did, Grace would manage to suck me back into her gravitational pull. "And try not to trip again. Next time, I won't be there to catch you."

CHAPTER 6
Grace

My hands shook as Sebastian disappeared into the crowd, leaving a faint trace of cologne in his wake. The delicious mixture of pine and citrus filled my head with thoughts that were undoubtedly foolish to be having about him. For a few seconds, I seemed to forget where I was and the reason I was here.

Focus on the plan, I reminded myself, eyes surveying the room for my teammate. Pearson's boyfriend had pulled her away to discuss something with his parents nearly twenty minutes ago. Slowly, I headed toward the other end of the ballroom, searching for a hint of dark purple amongst the many gowns. After another few sweeps of the crowd, I landed on her familiar form. Pearson was already watching me, and, when our eyes connected, she gave me a firm nod.

It was now or never.

There was a long booth to the right of the stage covered in computer monitors and cords. As I approached it, someone clinked their glass with a utensil, effectively hushing all conversations. A guy wearing large headphones and thick glasses looked up from behind the screen of a laptop. I gave him a shy smile and nodded toward the stage. "I know they have a little presentation planned, but I have a few extra slides. I'm the honoree's niece, and we wanted to surprise him with some special feedback about how much his generous donation has helped the children of this community."

Glasses guy looked down at his computer, then back up to me. To our right, Coach Dawson was clambering onto the stage with a drink in his hand.

"Do you have the slides with you?" he asked.

I nodded my head and reached into my cleavage to pull out the flash drive, holding eye contact with him the entire time. He gulped slowly as he accepted the small device.

"I'll let you know when to share it, okay?"

After a few slow blinks he nodded and then dragged his attention back to the screen. The Ravens' coach cleared his throat and started speaking.

"Hi, everyone. I need a few moments of your time before we get back to the drinking and dancing. First, thank you for attending another Ravens Gala. We're here to raise money for this incredible team of young men and to honor the man responsible for bringing this program to new heights. As a reminder, please don't forget to check out the silent auction items at the back of the room. And now, I'd like to give a special thanks to the man of the hour himself, Jerome DuLane."

The screen behind Coach Dawson lit up with a beautiful shot of DuLane Arena. As he continued to sing praises for DuLane's donation, the presentation filtered through different photos of the facility.

"Sir, your generous support for this team cannot be understated. DuLane Arena is one of the best hockey facilities in this country, and in the last five years, it's helped bring some of the best hockey players to this school."

Dawson droned on for another five minutes, eventually pulling an elderly Mr. DuLane up on the stage to share his own words. My pulse raced as the presentation continued, flashing through photos of the facility, showing off all the resources the men had access to. Finally, after another reminder for people to participate in the silent auction, Dawson wished the group a good night. The moment he stepped off the stage, I swooped in.

My only shot was the element of surprise.

A bright light beamed down on me as I nodded toward the booth, signaling to the AV guy to load my slides. I made my way slowly to the podium and gripped the microphone tightly between my hands. Not everyone was paying attention, so I cleared my throat into the microphone.

"Excuse me. Sorry to interrupt. This will be quick. My name is Grace, and I play for the women's hockey team at Dallard University."

Thankfully, the stage lights made it impossible for me to see most of the faces in the crowd. Hands shaking, I glanced back at the screen to check that my slides were up. With that final confirmation, I took a deep breath, turned back around, secured the slide advancer in my right hand, and started speaking.

"I'm so impressed with the resources this program has to offer, and I wanted to take this opportunity to praise Mr. DuLane and the other generous supporters who helped make this life-changing facility possible."

I clicked through several slides of the arena that had already been shown in the previous presentation. "Hockey is an incredible sport, and everyone competing at this level deserves access to a safe environment that helps foster great athletes. DuLane Arena offers this and more to the *men* who play for the Dallard Ravens."

I paused for a moment, heart thumping against my chest in anticipation. Somewhere out in the crowd, Pearson was doing her best to inconspicuously record my speech.

"Meanwhile, the female hockey players at DU are forced to play in a run-down, out-of-date facility that is nearly falling apart."

My words rang out, and an even deeper silence fell over the crowd. I advanced the slide again, bringing up photos of our current practice facility.

"The training equipment is old, the facility can barely regulate temperature enough to keep the rink frozen, and it's located inconveniently far from the student athlete housing."

I could see someone making their way to the stage and knew my time was up. With a deep breath, I gripped the microphone tightly and shared my parting statement.

"So again, please take a moment to honor Jerome DuLane for his generous donation to the *men's* hockey team. As we women work under worse conditions to gain our fourth national title, the men have all the resources they need to acquire their second."

A man was at my side, pulling me away from the podium while simultaneously apologizing into the microphone. Adrenaline pumped through my body as I was escorted off the stage. The ballroom and the lobby passed by in a blur, and before I knew it, I was being pushed out the front door and into the hotel parking lot. Triumph pulsed through my veins, even as I stumbled forward and nearly face-planted into the pavement.

"What in the hell were you thinking, Ms. Gillman?" The words were spat with utter fury.

I righted myself and turned to face my aggressive escort.

DU's athletic director loomed over me in a tall wall of muscle and hardened features. Mr. Castillo looked just about ready to flay me alive, though the fact that he knew my last name—knew exactly who I was—was far more concerning.

"Yes, I know who you are. I'm the one who approved your full-ride here," he said, "and I'm the one who has the power to take it away."

A small voice in the back of my head warned me to be cautious, but my heart was leading tonight. There was still too much adrenaline pumping through my veins to act rationally.

"Nothing I said up there was a lie," I told him. "I didn't exaggerate the situation or spread any false information."

I waited for him to set me straight, to tell me right then and there that I was being kicked out, but he didn't. Instead, a loud, shrill sound came from his pocket. Castillo extracted his phone from his dress pants and answered the call with a gruff "What?" before swinging around and stomping toward the entrance. He paused in the threshold to look over his shoulder.

"You will go home and not speak a word about this to anyone. Tomorrow, you'll receive an email with the date and time for a meeting with me where we will discuss your future at this school. Right now, I have to clean up your mess."

All the fight left my body as he disappeared into the hotel. I stood in silence, the truth of what I'd done settling over me slowly, my adrenaline waning. *Move*, I commanded, eventually managing to shake myself out of a stupor. I stumbled through the parking lot with only one goal: get the hell away from here as fast as I could.

A wave of changing emotions washed over me like fleeting dream: there one moment, gone the next. Disbelief shifted to elation, which quickly morphed into an overwhelming sense of dread. I made it nearly four blocks before the pain in my feet could no longer be ignored. All at once the shock wore off, a penetrating cold settling over me. I only managed a few more steps before I had to lean against a lamppost to remove my heels. After another couple of blocks, my feet were numb.

Why didn't I call Lydia to pick me up? It was the first sane thought I'd had in the last half hour, one that brought me to an abrupt stop as I pulled my phone from the small clutch in my left hand. At the same moment, a pair of blinding headlights flooded the street. I squinted against the light as a car came to a screeching stop beside me, stumbling back several steps as the door swung open and a tall figure exited the vehicle.

"What the hell is wrong with you?" demanded a whiskey-smooth voice.

Sebastian Evans ate up the space between us in three long strides, the light from his car casting shadows along the side of his jaw and under his cheekbones. He was beautiful and terrifying, all intensity and sharp lines.

"I can't do this with you right now." I tried to move around Sebastian, but he stepped into my path and placed both of his hands on my shoulders. The shock of his touch was like a volcanic eruption, heat rushing over my skin and spreading down my arms in a blazing trail of fire.

"You're freezing." There was a touch of concern in his voice, which was surprising enough to jolt my brain into gear, and I flinched away from the contact.

That was when I realized how cold I really was. *Have my teeth been chattering this whole time?*

Sebastian let out a huff of irritation, and in the next moment, I was being ushered over to his car. "You're going to freeze to death out here," he grumbled, opening the passenger door and guiding me into the seat.

Warmth enveloped my skin in an instant, and I held my shaking hands close to the hot air pouring from the vents as Sebastian walked back around the hood and slipped into the driver's side.

"What the hell were you thinking trying to walk back to campus, especially without a coat?!" he asked with a stony glare.

I shook my head in disbelief instead of answering—this entire night was taking a wildly unexpected turn. I'd gone from feeling empowered to terrified to unable to form a single word in the span of thirty minutes. A sudden burst of laughter escaped from between my lips. From across the center console, Sebastian was watching me with his head cocked to the side, mouth parted in bewilderment. Maybe I was losing my mind, or maybe this situation was so ridiculous there was nothing else to do but laugh.

"Why am I in your car?" I asked once my laughter died down. My eyes darted around the vehicle, taking in the pristine space with skepticism. Was Sebastian kidnapping me? Did he plan to drive me to an isolated spot along the coast of Lake Michigan and throw me in? More laughter bubbled to the surface.

Sebastian reached over and placed the back of his hand against my forehead. Surprisingly, I didn't shrink away. The strangest expression had overtaken his features. Was that more concern I detected in his eyes, or was I seeing things?

"I'm not dying," I assured him. "Don't get your hopes up."

He looked at me skeptically, brows raised. "Did you hit your head when Castillo tossed you out of the fundraiser?"

"He did not toss me out!" I exclaimed. He had *indeed* tossed me out, or, to be more accurate, shoved me through the door. But I wasn't going to admit that to Sebastian.

"I'm taking you home."

Dumbfounded, I watched as he shifted the gear into drive, the veins in his hands bulging as he gripped the steering wheel tightly. The sight of his clearly defined blood vessels did stupid things to my stomach. *Get a grip on yourself.* I shoved those dangerous feelings to the back of my mind as we drove. There was no music to lessen the uncomfortable tension in the air or keep my thoughts from running rampant. When campus finally came into view, I let out a sigh of relief, unaware that I'd been holding my breath. It was all I could do to keep myself from word-vomiting all over his pristine car.

"Do you know where I live?" I asked, unable to bear another second of awkward silence.

His eyes remained on the road as he said, "You're a transfer student and a hockey player. I'm assuming you're in the Athletes' Village?"

"With Caroline and Lydia," I confirmed. "Why are you helping me?"

No answer. I scoffed and looked out the window, irritated by his refusal to answer me.

"A thank-you would suffice," he said at last.

"I didn't ask for you to drive me home." Thankfully, we were nearly there.

His jaw clenched. "That doesn't negate the fact that I did."

"And that doesn't negate the fact that I hate you, and you're a jerk," I retorted as we pulled up beside my apartment.

Sebastian watched me tug on the locked door handle. After several long moments of struggle, he leaned closer, eyes shining with mischief. "Do you really want to know why I helped you?"

The taunting tone of his question made me freeze.

"The truth is I wanted to say goodbye. It was a pleasure

witnessing your final moments at DU, and it will be an even greater pleasure never seeing you again." Sebastian flashed me a final smug smile then reached across the center console. Heat rolled off of his body, and I tensed as his forearm brushed against my chest. The door clicked as it unlocked, and a moment later, he was leaning away.

When I didn't immediately exit his car, he made a shooing motion with his hand. "You can get out now."

As if my seat had burst into flames, I hopped out and slammed the door shut behind me. Even though I was embarrassed, I couldn't help but glance back over my shoulder; my mind and body were at odds with each other. The first demanded I listen to logic, reminding me of all the cruel things Sebastian had said, while the other remained inside the vehicle, craving the warmth of a body I knew I shouldn't want. Thankfully, the bite of cold cement against my bare feet tore me free from the struggle. I collected myself in time to flash Sebastian the finger as he pulled down the street and out of sight.

>> <<

Caroline bolted off the couch the moment I stepped inside the apartment. A bowl of popcorn went flying from her lap, scattering kernels across the living room floor.

"What happened?" she asked. "How did you get home?"

Her surprise was warranted; I had strayed from tonight's plan. After giving my speech, I was meant to call Lydia so she and Caroline could pick me up a few blocks from the hotel.

"Grace, we need words," Lydia urged, gently guiding me toward the couch. I plopped down onto the middle cushion as they sat on either side of me.

"Sebastian."

"Sebastian what?" Caroline asked.

"Sebastian brought me home."

"You're saying that Sebastian drove you home from the gala," Lydia repeated slowly. "Did he catch you sneaking in?"

I shook my head. It was no use explaining our strange interaction, not when I was still struggling to make sense of his behavior. "I gave the speech."

"And?" Caroline pushed, eager for more details.

As long as Pearson didn't get removed from the gala for helping me and I didn't cost the AV guy his job, tonight had been a success. But when it came to my future at Dallard, I wasn't too confident.

"Maybe she's in shock," Lydia whispered.

"We didn't get a call from the local jail, so I assume you weren't arrested," Caroline said.

I let out a snort of laughter. "I might have preferred that to being hauled out of the event by Castillo."

The words were barely out of my mouth when the couch started to vibrate. All three of our phones were going off, which probably meant—

"It's Pearson," I confirmed, holding up my phone to display the name that flashed across the screen.

Caroline paused the TV just as I hit play on the video. Like any normal person, I cringed at the sound of my own voice. But despite how nervous I'd felt up on that stage, my words were steady and clear. I held my breath for the duration of the video, trying not to pick apart every bumbling movement and awkward pause. At one point, someone in the crowd shifted, their body obstructing the camera view. Pearson stepped to the right just as Castillo strode onto the stage and pulled me off.

"That was amazing, Grace," Caroline said, giving my arm an excited squeeze. "Austin has a ton to work with. He could even post the whole thing, but I'm sure he'll scrape together the best lines."

Lydia's head bobbed up and down in agreement. "I'll send it over now."

I felt an undeniable rush of anticipation at the thought of my speech making its way around campus. This video could very well be the reason I got kicked off the hockey team or expelled from school, but it also had the power to change everything wrong with female athletics at DU.

Lydia must have sensed the unease building inside me because she leaned over to rest her head on my shoulder. "If they even consider kicking you off the hockey team, every single one of us will be there to protest. They won't risk losing us all."

I hoped she was right. Either way, tomorrow would come, and I'd face the consequences, but knowing I'd have them by my side the entire time was a comfort.

"Don't worry about anything else, not tonight. We can get started on phase two tomorrow, okay?" Caroline suggested.

Phase two involved plastering posters all over the campus, but we hadn't gotten much further than jotting down some high-level design ideas. I was much too exhausted to think about it right now. Caroline was right; it could wait for tomorrow. Before I left the room, they surrounded me in a crushing hug that stole the air from my lungs. The show of affection was a comforting surprise, but the warmth of their embrace didn't last. As soon as I was inside the privacy of my bedroom, the full gravity of the situation settled over me like a waterlogged blanket. How could I be proud of myself and feel so terrible at the same time? Pressure built behind my eyes, but I blinked away the moisture, refusing to shed a single tear because of Castillo's threatening words or Sebastian's haughty parting remarks.

I willed both men out of my mind and started preparing for bed. After fifteen minutes of self-care, I was ready to slip under the covers and put an end to the night when my phone buzzed. The name *Matt* rolled across the screen, and just the sight of those four letters was enough to soothe my weary heart.

I answered the phone without a second thought. "Hello."

At first, there was nothing but silence. Then my ex-boyfriend released a long breath.

"I didn't think you'd pick up," he said. It was soothing, hearing his voice. We hadn't spoken over the phone in weeks. No, months.

"I've been avoiding you," I admitted. "I'm sorry."

The sound of his chuckle was like a sip of hot chocolate on the coldest day of the year.

"You're an expert at avoiding. I know better than anyone."

He was right. It had taken him almost a year of chasing after me for our relationship to move beyond friendship, and several more months before things were official. I needed to know I could trust him before opening up about my past. And now things were even more complicated because six months into our breakup, he was still holding on to the hope that we'd get back together. There was never any big fight or hurtful betrayal, but I knew that we weren't right for each other.

"Tell me about your day," I asked, eager for a distraction from my own life.

"Come on, Grace," he said in exasperation. I must have sounded too eager. "You can talk to me. I know things have changed, but that doesn't mean you can't trust me anymore."

How can I lean on him after breaking his heart? That was the question that kept me from texting him when my thoughts turned dark.

"I don't want to talk about me."

"Of course not. You're always so focused on something or someone else so that you don't have to face your own problems. We dated for two years, I know—"

"I didn't answer the phone for a lecture," I said. "Don't make me regret picking up the call." I told myself I was cruel to him because I had to be, but that was a damn lie. I was cruel because he was right, and I hated that.

"When you want to be honest with me, and honest with yourself, give me a call. You know, I really thought I could do the friendship thing, but I don't know. It's a lot harder than I expected." His voice cracked at the admission. Though he said nothing else, I could tell there were unspoken words just fighting to free themselves from within him.

The line went dead a moment later, and I was seized with the need to throw something like a child mid-tantrum. I reached for the closest item—a round decorative pillow near the edge of my bed—and chucked it across the room. It flew into my open closet and collided with the top shelf. Through the darkness, I saw something teeter off the edge and fall to the floor with a thud.

Amazing.

After turning on my lamp, I crawled out of bed to see the damage. A familiar red shoebox had fallen on the floor, the lid several paces away, unopened letters scattered across the ground. *What the hell is that doing here?* It usually resided under my bed at home, and I hadn't packed it when I left for school. How—*Gabby*, I realized. My little sister had probably snuck it into my room when she was here to help move me in at the beginning of the school year. For ages, she'd been pushing me to read the letters from our mother. We both received one on our birthday every year, but I never got around to opening mine. I had no interest in hearing what that woman had to say. When I knelt on the floor to collect the letters, a numbness set in. By the time I placed the shoebox back on the top shelf and slipped into bed, I could barely feel a thing.

CHAPTER 7
Sebastian

The ghost of Grace's presence accompanied me the entire car ride home. More than just the scent of her cherry perfume lingered; it was the sound of her quiet breaths and the warmth of her shy glances across the skin of my knuckles. My eyes darted back and forth between the road and the passenger seat, desperate to find her beside me, that long stretch of exposed thigh peeking out from the slit in her dress. When I finally pulled into the driveway, I turned off the car and sat in silence, trying and failing miserably to ward my mind against her. *What kind of voodoo witchy shit is this?* Grace made me feel unstable, as if I couldn't predict my own next move: like someone else was pulling the strings, and they were acting on instinct alone. I hated that she had so much power over me. The girl was practically a stranger, yet I could feel her presence in a room packed with a hundred other bodies.

The car grew cold and still as I sat there, wallowing in my pathetic feelings. When I could no longer stand the sound of my own thoughts, I abandoned the vehicle and went inside. The house was quiet and bathed in darkness, the only source of light coming from a dim yellow bulb above the kitchen stove. I walked on autopilot to my bedroom and stripped off my clothes, needing to rid myself of Grace's scent if I had any hope of sleeping. I'd just pulled on a fresh pair of boxers when my bedroom door flew open and a furious-looking Kate stalked in.

Oh, shit.

"You *left* me there." Her words were as cold as ice. "What the actual fuck, Sebastian."

"I'm so sorry, Kate." There was nothing else for me to say. It wasn't like I could confess that I'd completely forgotten about everything and everyone else once Grace appeared on that stage. In that moment, the only thing that had mattered was speaking to her, understanding why she was so hell-bent on disrupting my carefully planned life. And when I'd found her walking home without a coat, half frozen, I'd intervened on instinct.

"That's it?" Kate exclaimed. "Are you really going to give me a half-assed apology and zero explanation? Why didn't you say anything? And why haven't you answered your phone?"

"I thought you'd head home with Macy." It was a terrible excuse, and we both knew it.

"That's bullshit! You disappeared from the fundraiser without a damn word. Who does that to their girlfriend?"

"I'm sorry," I said, stepping toward Kate, but she stumbled back in an effort to keep some distance between us. "I was shaken up by Grace's stunt. This season is really important to me, and we can't risk losing ice time to the women's team. I'm worried it could impact our training schedule."

"Of course," she scoffed. "How could this be about anything other than hockey?"

"It was wrong of me to leave without telling you. But you can't blame everything on hockey because you hate that it dictates so much of my life."

I knew immediately from the darkening of her eyes that it was the wrong thing to say.

"You're right," she said. "I've been misplacing my anger this whole time. I can't blame hockey for your lack of consideration. That's all on you."

"It's not a lack of consideration! It's always going to be like this, Kate. You knew that when we started dating. And it worked—we worked. But ever since the injury . . ."

She shook her head in disappointment. "It always comes back to the injury, doesn't it? You can say you don't blame me, but it's clear that you do."

"Kate—"

"Have you ever considered that you're the one who's changed, not me? It's not easy to love someone who—" She cut herself off and shook her head. "I need some space to think."

Kate slipped out of the room before I could respond, closing the door with a gentle tug rather than slamming it closed in rage. I listened to the click of her shoes across the hardwood floor until only silence remained. Somewhere deep in my chest I could feel a pull, one that grew tighter the longer I remained alone in my bedroom. But after minutes of standing still, waiting to see if she would come back, the tension snapped. As the dust settled, I couldn't determine which was worse: the feeling of instant relief or the pang of guilt left in its wake.

>> <<

"I was wondering if you were ever going to call me back."

My mother's voice was soft and teasing; the sound was an instant remedy for my lousy mood, especially after I'd missed her call last week.

"I was swamped with schoolwork," I said, placing my phone on the kitchen counter and switching on the speaker function. None of my roommates were in, and I was desperate for something to eat.

"I'm glad you're staying focused, honey. And I'm sorry I couldn't make it to the fundraiser this year. I always love to hear the coach brag about you on stage. Your dad would be so proud."

Memories of my dad flashed across my mind: our skating lessons on the frozen pond behind the house, me perched on his shoulders at the United Center, the proud look on his face at witnessing my first successful hockey stop. The day he left for an ice fishing trip and never came back. Nine years wasn't enough time with your best friend.

My mom wasn't one of those people who shut away their grief in a box. The only way she knew how to live her life was to honor his memory by keeping it alive. But thinking about him, knowing that he was somewhere watching me from afar, often felt like a weight pressing down on my chest. He was the reason I'd made it this far in my hockey career, he'd taught me everything he knew, and the thought of disappointing him was unimaginable.

"I streamed your exhibition game last night. You had some incredible assists," my stepdad shouted in the background.

I could picture them both at the kitchen table, Bill reading some war hero's biography and my mother journaling her daily affirmations. If she didn't write things down, she was likely to forget them.

"You're both coming for a home game this season, right?"

"Yes, of course," Mom replied. "Bill spoke with Elijah last night to find a date that works. We're going to come in February for the Penn State game."

I propped open the refrigerator door to survey my options, eventually deciding to grab all the essentials for an egg sandwich. "Did Elijah mention anything about the fundraiser?"

She chuckled. "He mentioned something about a player from the women's team stealing the show. From what Elijah said, she made some pretty good points."

I wasn't surprised to hear that he'd had nice things to say about Grace. I could tell he liked her from the moment she insulted me.

"Mom, I need your advice," I said, eager to change the subject. "Kate and I got into a huge fight last night, and I have no idea where we stand."

I walked my mom through the night, starting with the gala and ending with our argument back at the house, keeping Grace out of the conversation. By the time I was done explaining, my sandwich was made, and I'd taken a seat at the table to eat.

"I can't believe you left her there," she said, and I would have bet a million dollars that she was shaking her head.

Ravenous, I took a large bite, nearly halving the sandwich in one go. I spoke as I chewed, managing a somewhat intelligible response. "It was awful, I know. I wasn't thinking straight."

"Do you think anything she said is true?"

I'd stayed up all night thinking about her words, trying to understand her side of things. *Have you ever considered that you're the one who's changed, not me?* I supposed she wasn't entirely off base. Before the injury, I'd had more time to spend with her outside of hockey. But my recovery was a full-time job, and I'd taken some of that with me into the new season. I had to if I wanted to get back to where I was before blowing out my knee.

"Maybe we've both changed." I glanced down at the remainder of my breakfast, no longer feeling hungry.

"How do you feel about that?"

"Confused," I admitted. "It was wrong to blame her, but I apologized, and that was more than a year ago. I thought we'd moved past it."

"Maybe she hasn't."

It definitely seemed that way. "I owe her so much, and I don't want to let go."

"But?" she prompted.

I closed my eyes and leaned back, the old wooden chair groaning under my weight. "But I also felt relieved after she left. We've been fighting so much lately."

"Kate is a wonderful person, Sebastian, and she chose to make sacrifices for your relationship. If you're not willing to do the same, it might be time to let her go. Even if you don't want to."

A part of me didn't want to accept that my mom was right.

"And what if it's a mistake?"

"Sometimes mistakes are good," she said. "They teach you important lessons."

>> <<

Grace

My stomach was a mess of anxious flutters when I woke in the morning to find an email at the top of my inbox from Castillo's assistant. Rather than a meeting time and location, it contained a brief explanation of why he no longer expected us to meet—something to do with an inflexible schedule. There was also an attached letter signed by the athletic director himself.

Ms. Gillman,

I apologize that we will not be able to discuss this matter in person. However, I have a gridlocked schedule for the next few weeks and consider the conversation we had at the fundraiser a sufficient verbal warning. Your actions last night were an embarrassment to this institution. The disruption of a school sanctioned event held to honor one of Dallard's most generous supporters is unacceptable behavior, especially for a student athlete of your caliber. Fortunately, I was able to convince the hotel not to press trespassing charges. Please be advised that any additional disruptions that violate our student athlete policy will be met with appropriate disciplinary actions. If you would like to raise an official complaint regarding the school's facilities, please do so through the proper channels as outlined on the student website.

Best,
Howard Castillo
Director of Athletics
Dallard University

I reread the letter several times, searching for any indication that I was being kicked off the team. After my fourth scan of the email, my heart rate slowed to a normal pace. How the hell had I gotten off with a verbal warning? Last night, Mr. Castillo had been furious.

Mind reeling, I slipped out of my bed and into the kitchen. My roommates were seated at the breakfast bar, sipping their coffee and murmuring to each other quietly. At my appearance, they fell silent. Glancing back down to my phone, I tried to string together an explanation, but words were hard to come by this early in the morning. Instead of reading them the letter, I walked over and placed my phone on the counter in front of them. Both girls hunched over to read the message.

"I can't believe you're getting off with a warning. That's incredible," Lydia said.

When Caroline finished reading, she pushed my phone back to me with an almost clinical calmness, like this was exactly the outcome she'd expected.

"Why do you not seem surprised?" I asked her.

"Well," she replied, tucking a piece of her long blond hair behind an ear, "after you went to bed last night, I did some research. While you technically could be charged for trespassing, which would be a misdemeanor, our student policy only outlines the consequences and processes for felony charges. Honestly, I'm not surprised Castillo got the hotel to back off. They're probably more worried about the truth getting out than they are about you crashing the gala. I read a few articles that exposed several universities for sexism and discrimination, and it seems like this could be a real media mess for the school. And none of the information you shared was untrue, meaning they can't accuse you of slander."

Had Caroline stayed up all night researching for me?

An overwhelming sense of relief and gratitude filled my body. "I—thank you, Caroline. That was really thoughtful of you."

She shrugged. "I'm going to be a lawyer, Grace. This is just a warm-up for what I'll be expected to do in law school."

I nodded in understanding then asked, "Did Austin post last night? Are we on our way to causing a media storm for the school?"

"Not quite a storm," Lydia interjected, looking down at her phone. "At least, not yet. But the post has over ten thousand views, and the comments are picking up. By next week, everyone on campus will have heard your speech. Especially with Sebastian's successful return to the team. The guys are back under a microscope now that their star player is back."

"I wonder if Castillo knows about the video," I mused. He probably wouldn't have let me off so easily if he knew there was a recording of the whole thing.

"Don't worry about him, trust me." Caroline said.

It was silent for a moment, then both girls exchanged a conspiratorial look.

"Grace, I know you're probably exhausted after last night, but we could use your help," Lydia said. "My girlfriend, Nina, agreed to make posters to put up around campus, but we need some eye-catching content. Any ideas?"

My mind flashed to an image of Sebastian's smug grin as he told me to get out of his car, and I got the perfect idea to knock him down a peg. I couldn't wait to see his face when he realized I was still here.

>> <<

St. Cloud didn't stand a chance against us. Back in the offensive zone, our forward line functioned like a well-oiled machine, cycling the puck around the net and making quick passes to create a solid gap. There were only ten seconds left on the clock when one opened. Lydia's wrister flew high, bounced off the goalie's chest, and ricocheted straight for Big D. The left winger slapped the puck my way, and the pass connected at the perfect time. A sliver of space opened as one of the defenders shifted to cover Lydia. It gave me just enough room to sink the biscuit between the goalie's legs.

The horn blared just as the clock hit zero, and I was

immediately surrounded by a swarm of my teammates, their celebratory cries echoing across the ice. A chorus of excited chatter followed the team as we headed down to the locker room. Everyone was high off the win. As Coach Riley congratulated us, my teammates' exhilaration mirrored my own. Tonight's game was further justification of our worth as competitors. I was positive that we would make history, either as the team that made it all the way despite the odds stacked against us or as the team that fought for and ensured a future of equal treatment for female athletes at Dallard University.

The bus ride home was long, but it gave me time to debrief the team on my efforts at the gala and our plan to develop a campaign to help raise awareness around campus. Coach Riley didn't make a peep from her seat at the front of the bus, but she was listening in. At one point, I could have sworn she was smiling.

"With the momentum coming off the gala, we need to act fast. The next phase in our plan is widespread awareness. We want support from our fellow students, which means they need to know all the dirty details. Thanks to Lydia, we've already drafted a flyer to spread around campus, and I'm hoping to get a piece into the school paper. Grace and I are meeting with the editor of the *Dallard Spectator* on Monday to talk details." You could practically feel Caroline's determination through every animated word she spoke.

"These look amazing," Liv voice was full of awe as she inspected the draft poster on her phone. A copy had been sent to the team group chat for everyone to see.

"My girlfriend helped with design," Lydia said with a prideful gleam in her eyes. "She said we could include a QR code at the bottom that will link to the article."

The poster design was simple but effective. Two pictures were cut and pasted together, one side colored blue and the other pink. The blue portion featured a picture of DuLane Arena while the pink half displayed an image of McKinley Rink in all its outdated, run-down glory. The stark difference between the facilities was jarring to the eye. A strip of bold text had been placed over each photo. The blue side read ONE NATIONAL CHAMPIONSHIP while the pink side read THREE NATIONAL CHAMPIONSHIPS. Directly in the middle of the poster, where blue transitioned to pink, was a large equal sign with a slash down the middle.

"If anyone wants to include a quote in the article, let me know," Caroline said. "But not a single word of this can get out before it's published, so keep things quiet for now."

I watched the formidable blond from my seat across the aisle with deep admiration. Since I'd stuck my neck out for the team, Caroline had thrown herself into the plan wholeheartedly. She was a natural leader, and her connections around campus were already paying off. It also didn't hurt that she had more organizational skills than the entire team combined. Without her, none of this would have come together so seamlessly. But it wasn't just Caroline stepping up. Lydia was proving just as resourceful. Bringing Nina into the fold and watching them put their creative brains together had resulted in an amazing centerpiece for our campaign. I'd never experienced this level of camaraderie before. It was foreign to feel so much support, especially from people I'd only known for a month and a half.

By Monday afternoon, I was buzzing with anticipation. As planned, Caroline and I met up after our morning classes and set off for the student union. Maggie O'Neil, the editor-in-chief of the *Dallard Spectator*, got straight down to business the moment we joined her at a corner table in Coaler Café. The place was packed with chattering students meeting for study groups or picking up their afternoon energy boost. Despite the lack of privacy, the sound of the indie folk music in the background accompanied by the hum of machinery ensured that our conversation went unheard. Maggie typed away furiously at her laptop, her brow furrowed in concentration as Caroline and I took turns speaking about the women's hockey program. Every so often, she would interrupt to ask a question or pause to loop a finger through one of her thick black curls.

"This is exactly the kind of story we need," Maggie said, pushing her cat-eye glasses up the bridge of her nose. "I had no idea that there was such blatant sexism within the hockey program."

"Do you have enough information from us?" I asked.

"Yeah, we have enough here." She paused to do a sweep of her screen. "I'd love to get a comment from the men's team, but I reached out and they weren't interested. If there's some way to convince them, or at least record a conversation where you ask for a comment, that would be great."

Caroline and I glanced at each other, and I nodded my head, silently agreeing to do what I could to get a statement from the men's team. Given Sebastian's notoriety, he was the best person to ask. And if he wasn't willing to go on record with an official statement, I'd just have to get a reaction out of him that was worthy of the *Dallard Spectator*.

CHAPTER 8
Sebastian

Something big was about to happen; I could feel it in my bones. If the video of Grace's speech circulating around campus wasn't warning enough, being contacted by the *Dallard Spectator* was all the confirmation I needed—the gala was just the beginning. I had my suspicions that the girls were gunning for a share of our training facility, and I couldn't allow that to happen. Not when my entire future relied on my hockey performance over the next seven months, and not when Grace was already distracting enough from a distance.

"I want to make this clear." My voice echoed over the low hum of chatter in the locker room, silencing my teammates as they prepared for morning classes. "Not a single person on this team is to speak to anyone from the student newspaper. Not a single comment."

The crowd of familiar faces nodded in agreement. No one dared speak against my order. As the room cleared out, Bryce stayed behind to talk with me.

"Do you think Coach should know about the social media stuff?" he asked.

I shook my head. "It's not out of hand yet. I don't want to worry him over nothing."

"Have you heard from Kate?"

Bryce was the only person I had told about our fight. He was the only person to notice that something had been off with me since the gala. Kate and I hadn't spoken in almost four days, and I was feeling more and more confused about the situation the longer we went without talking. Sometimes I reached for my phone out of instinct, ready to text Kate about something that had happened during my day. But it was also impossible to ignore the relief of not having to explain myself after practice ran long or homework got in the way of our plans to hang out.

"She hasn't contacted me." I hesitated, then said, "Do you think I should reach out? She said she needed time, but now I'm wondering if giving her so much space was the wrong move."

"Sometimes girls say the opposite of what they want. Maybe just send her a text to check in," he suggested.

I secured my schoolbag over my shoulders and followed Bryce's hulking form out of the locker room. He was probably right. Maybe Kate had said she needed time to think because she wanted to see me take the initiative with our relationship.

"Do you think—"

We'd just stepped outside the arena when Bryce came to a sudden halt. I managed to stop myself before running directly into his back. One glance around his shoulder confirmed the holdup. Grace was hovering a few feet away, her brows set in a determined line. She was waiting for me, I realized, drowning in a sweatshirt that was three sizes too large for her body, eyes wide as they connected with mine.

"I'll meet you in the dining hall later," I said to Bryce.

He glanced between the two of us with one brow quirked before nodding in agreement and sauntering off to get breakfast. Grace tensed as I approached her, and I couldn't help but notice that her phone was hanging halfway out of the front of her pocket. I resisted the urge to reach over and slide it back in place.

"I suppose this means you weren't expelled," I said.

"Did you get your hopes up?" She was sporting a devious grin, something halfway between playful and calculated, and that made me wonder what she was up to. Grace *never* sought me out.

"What do you want?" I asked calmly, feeling anything but.

"Honesty."

I waited for her to continue, unwilling to play along with her little game.

"Don't you think, as captain of the men's hockey team, you're responsible for commenting on the lack of equality between the men's and women's hockey programs? The *Dallard Spectator* is going to publish an article about the issue either way. I'm giving you the chance to get ahead of things," she said, and I could smell the bullshit from a mile away.

"Leave me out of your little crusade, Grace. I'm not interested."

"You're against gender equality?"

My nostrils flared as I tried to keep my composure. "Of course not."

"Then you just don't care enough to advocate for your female counterparts, is that it? Or maybe you think we don't deserve the same resources as you," she continued, the fire behind her eyes burning a little brighter with every word.

There was a heat burning in my stomach, flames inching up my throat. *Control, Sebastian. Find your control.* "I don't have any say in where you practice. Talk to the administration if you have a problem."

"But you do have influence at this school. You could help our cause." She leaned closer with every word, her brows set in a firm line. I would have felt amused by her determination if it wasn't directed at me.

"I don't have as much influence as you think," I said through gritted teeth. Despite my recent success, I was still on thin ice with the dean. He was much too prideful a man to go back on his threats.

"All you have to do is say you stand with us. Is that so hard?"

"Why the hell do you need to drag me into this? Is it so wrong for me to want to protect *our* training time? You might like the idea of sharing DuLane now, but when both teams lose time on the ice, you'll regret starting this war."

As soon as the words left my mouth, I regretted them. The shift in Grace's expression—from frustration to satisfaction—only confirmed my suspicions. She'd gotten a rise out of me, and that's exactly what she'd wanted.

"This conversation is over," I said, shoving past her. "Tell the student newspaper that we're not interested in commenting."

For once, I was the one fleeing the scene after one of our confrontations, and I felt like a wild animal retreating to lick its wounds. An overwhelming sense of failure compelled me to reach for my phone and type out a message to the one person I knew would always support me—Kate. It was wrong, but I was desperate for comfort.

Kate

Hi. I miss you
I get you need time to think, but I hate this silence
Stop torturing me

                                                        I'm sorry

        Do you think that's enough?

                                                        I hope so

                                                  I'm willing to grovel

        . . . on your hands and knees?

                                                          Always

                                                Tell me a time and place

                                              I'm sorry. Please talk to me.

        I'll think about it

                              >> <<

The next day, I startled awake thirty minutes late, surprised to find that the sun was already starting to rise. My bedroom was cold, and there were golden streaks of light leaking through the gap in my curtains. I was blinking away the last remnants of sleep when my phone vibrated. I reached for it, hoping to see a message from Kate, only to discover a screen full of notifications from my roommate group chat, the Zamboners.

Zamboners

Kent
Anyone been to campus yet?

Landon
Why would anyone be there this early?

Kent
There are posters everywhere.

Landon
So?

Bryce
Is this important enough to blow up the gc before 7 am?

Kent
Seb is gonna lose his shit, look

The next message was an image of the quad. There were pink and blue posters clinging to everything—the sides of the buildings, stapled to trees. They were even scattered across the ground.

> **Landon**
> I guess Grace wasn't messing around.
>
> **Kent**
> Has anyone read the article?
>
> **Bryce**
> We need to notify Dawson
>
> **Landon**
> There's an article???
>
> *Bishop has notifications silenced*
>
> **Landon**
> Oh shit. There is definitely an article

Before I could type out a response, Bryce barged into my bedroom, a pink and blue poster clutched in his hand. He held it out for my inspection, and my eyes grew wide at the familiar image of DuLane Arena set next to McKinley Rink. At the very bottom was a QR code. My heartbeat increased to a rapid thrum as I scanned the code and pulled up the referenced article. Immediately, I was met with the sight of my own face. The photo was over a year old—one of the professional ones taken for the hockey web page. Growing even more concerned, I began to read.

An Icy Injustice
by Margaret O'Neil

In a flurry of pink and blue posters, the Dallard University women's hockey team has made a bold statement about gender inequality within the athletics department. Despite the success of the women's hockey program, which has brought home three national titles in the last ten years, DU continues to overlook female athletes in favor of their male counterparts. While the men train at DuLane Arena, a recently renovated, state-of-the-art hockey facility, the women are forced to practice at a previously abandoned rink. Several concerns about the facility have been communicated to the administration, but no actions have been taken to rectify the issue.

"DuLane Arena has two full-sized rinks, but only the men are allowed to utilize the training facility," says Dena Jacobs, a senior on the women's hockey team. Another female player who requested to remain anonymous claims to have reached out to the men for their support, only to come up empty-handed. Sebastian Evans, captain of the men's hockey team, refused to make a comment, but in a recording provided to the Dallard Spectator, *he can be heard saying, "Is it so wrong for me to want to protect our training time? You might like the idea of sharing DuLane now, but when both teams lose time on the ice, you'll regret starting this war." To listen to the full recording, visit the* Dallard Spectator *website.*

Red swamped my vision, making it nearly impossible for me to read on. I closed out of the article with shaky hands and launched my phone at the bed. I'd been right about Grace being up to no good, and instead of keeping a cool head, I'd played right into her hands. She'd been recording me the whole time, that's why her phone had been hanging out of her pocket so carelessly.

Fuck me.

This was the last thing I needed. Being called out by name in an article about gender inequality was not the kind of press that would help my chances of getting an official contract. I hadn't spoken to a single reporter since my injury. I wasn't interested in the attention. My only goal was to prove how valuable I could be to Detroit out on the ice. I already had to convince them I was worth the risk after suffering a huge injury.

"You certainly pissed someone off," Bryce said with a grim expression.

He didn't mention anyone specific, but we both knew whom he was referring to.

"Grace is going to regret her decision to transfer here. I'll make sure of it."

>> <<

All that could be heard throughout the arena was a frenzy of panicked chatter. Everyone had read the article by now. It had been shared all over campus; the entire situation was inescapable.

"I need everyone to shut the hell up!" Coach's voice cut through the noise like a bullet.

A hush fell over the group in seconds, and the arena grew still. My heart was a thunderous thing inside my chest, gloved hands balled into fists at my sides. I focused my attention on a spot above Coach's head. It was the only thing I could do to stop myself from ditching practice in favor of tearing down each and every poster plastered across the school grounds.

"There's no beating around the bush: this looks bad for us. Right now, the only thing I want you boys to focus on is practice. When you step on this ice, you forget about everything out there." He gestured dramatically toward the exit, spit flying from his mouth as he spoke. "This matter will be handled by the school administration, not us. If they ask anyone for a comment, the answer is no. Do not engage, and don't even think about retaliating."

I wanted to argue with Coach Dawson even as he locked eyes with me, his expression saying, *Especially you, Sebastian*. How did he expect me to remain silent? I was the only one being dragged in the school newspaper. It was my face in that article, and it was Grace who'd put it there.

"Practice starts now. Sebastian, over here."

The team scattered at once, everyone heading for the perimeter of the rink to complete our usual warm-up laps.

"You're upset," he said in a gentle tone, "and I understand that you want to do something about all of this, but you can't. Can you trust that I'll take care of things?"

"It's my reputation on the line," I snapped. "How am I supposed to just sit back and do nothing?"

"What is it you want to do, Sebastian? Was the recording doctored? I'm happy to file a complaint if you didn't say those things, but if you did, I can't have you going after those ladies. That will only make things worse."

Dawson already knew the truth. I could see it in his eyes.

"I didn't know it was going to be used against me. I'm worried about losing time in our training schedule."

Having to share space with another team, with Grace, would only complicate things. Even now, when the thought of her name made my teeth clench in anger, I couldn't ignore the spark of heat that shot down my spine. Why the hell did she have to be so damn appealing?

"You're under a lot of pressure, which is why I need you to focus on hockey and leading this team. Leave the rest to me, okay?"

It was a bitter pill to swallow, but I nodded my head.

"Good, now get your ass moving," he said, clapping me on the back. "We've already wasted enough time today."

Hockey was normally my distraction from the outside noise, but once I was on the ice, I instantly knew I wouldn't be able to forget the article. For whatever reason, I had a feeling there was more to come.

>> <<

Grace

"I wish I could have seen the look on his face when he read the article," I said as we trudged out of the locker room after a grueling practice.

I'd half considered camping out by DuLane Arena so I could follow Sebastian around campus yesterday. The entire women's team had woken up in the early hours of the morning to decorate the grounds. Seeing the school plastered in our posters was such a gratifying moment, especially after I'd spent half the night rereading Maggie's article, memorizing every word. The only thing that could have made today better was seeing Sebastian's reaction when he realized he was the star of our campaign.

"Someone told me that a bunch of the guys were pulling down posters near the arena," Lydia said with a chuckle.

"It's too little too late. Everyone in my literature class was talking about the article. Even the basketball guys were offended, though I'm sure they're more than happy to see the hockey team taken down a peg." Pearson could hardly contain herself as she spoke. The whole team was buzzing. For once, people were starting to pay attention to our plight.

"Who knows, this might have been our last practice in this shithole," added Liv.

"Don't get ahead of yourselves," Caroline warned. "Coach

hasn't heard anything from the administration. What matters right now is that people are talking about us. Eventually, the school will have to address the issue. We need to be patient until they do."

Despite Caroline's reality check, everyone was on cloud nine as we headed off to class. The moment I stepped outside, my eyes were drawn to a tall wall of muscle. Sebastian Evans, the campaign star himself, was leaning against a birch tree looking particularly prickly. Even from several yards away, I could feel tension in the air between us. A gust of chilly wind blew past, loosening a few strands of hair from my braid. I tucked them behind my ears as he pushed off the tree and sauntered over.

"Ladies," he offered in greeting. "I need to speak with Grace."

Neither of my roommates moved an inch from my side.

"It's fine," I said. "I'll see you guys later."

After searching my face for any sign of distress, they agreed. Before leaving, Caroline sent Sebastian a look of warning as if to say, *Don't you dare fuck with her*.

"I can't imagine you have anything worthwhile to say," I said, turning my attention to Sebastian. "Unless you're here to apologize, that is."

He was definitely pissed off. Though his expression didn't change, I could see his entire body stiffen at my words. "I told you not to involve me. I thought I made myself clear."

"That's the thing, Sebastian. You *told* me. You didn't ask me."

His lip twitched. "I told you because it was a command, not a question."

The fucking audacity of this man. My hand twitched, fingers curling into a fist, but I managed to bury the overwhelming impulse to punch him. "Are you really that blinded by your golden boy status that you can't admit to being wrong? We're breathing in mold and destroying our blades over at McKinley Rink."

The green of Sebastian's eyes was infused with a flame of ire, and it was entirely for me—all that breathtaking anger and intensity pouring off his body in waves. He'd been indifferent when addressing Caroline and Lydia just seconds ago, but when it came to me, Sebastian couldn't hide his hatred.

When he didn't respond, I heaved a sigh. "Why do you hate me?"

"You secretly recorded me without my consent," he said, a vein pulsing at his temple. "That's reason enough."

"No, I'm talking about before that." I was over Sebastian pretending like this was an isolated event. He couldn't act like the victim, not after the last few weeks. "You've been an asshole to me from the moment I transferred to this school."

That made him scoff. "Not everyone has to like you, Grace."

"Not liking someone and actively disliking them are completely different." I felt like I was wasting my breath, but I couldn't keep the words from bursting out. Sebastian wasn't dumb; he knew exactly what he was doing.

"I can't believe they didn't expel you after the gala," he said, not bothering to give me a straight answer. "I bet they'll consider it now, given how much trouble you've caused."

What a shocker. Honesty was too big of an ask for Sebastian.

"They can't expel me if what I'm saying is true, and it's not only me. All the women on the team are protesting this gross display of inequality."

"Protest your little heart out, I don't care. Leave. Me. Out of it."

"I don't think I will. Your face has brought a lot of awareness to the campaign." I could barely speak the words without smiling.

Sebastian took another step forward, no doubt aware that I had to tilt my head back to meet his eyes. "What do you expect to get out of this? Like I already told you, I have no say over where the women train."

He was close enough that I could breathe in the scent of him—why did he have to smell so damn nice?—but it would take more than him invading my personal space to intimidate me. "I'm not stupid, Sebastian. This school would bend over backward if you asked them to."

His gaze flickered back and forth between my eyes and my mouth. The entire time, he looked murderous. "You overestimate my power, Grace. I had to plead my case in front of the dean to even come back this year. The moment they decided I was damaged goods, I lost my clout."

His admission took me by surprise, almost as much as the sincerity in his voice. Maybe I was wrong, but it seemed like I was finally getting a kernel of truth out of him. Even so, it didn't make any sense. Though I'd never admit it, I'd streamed their game against Providence and several of the following matches. Sebastian was by far the most skilled player on the ice. He stood out amongst the other athletes. So why would he have to beg for a spot on the team when he was a star on the ice?

"Fine," I said, shrugging indifferently and setting aside my confusion for the time being. "But you can't deny that people listen to you around here. Your support and the support of the entire men's team would help influence the school to make a change."

"No can do," he replied, that obnoxiously smug tone back in action. "Coach has strictly forbidden us to comment on the matter."

Did Sebastian not realize that I had the upper hand here? He was the one who sounded like a sexist asshole in the school paper, not me. And it was his reputation on the line, not mine. "I don't need your support, Sebastian. It would be nice, of course, and it might even help clean up your muddied reputation, but it isn't necessary."

"You don't want me as an enemy, Grace," he warned.

I cocked my head as I peered up at him. "Do you hear yourself when you speak?"

"I—"

"That was a rhetorical question. Clearly, all you do is listen to the sound of your own voice." We were past the point of playing nice. Right now, I needed him to understand that I wouldn't give up or buckle under his threats.

Slowly, Sebastian leaned down until his face was close enough that I could feel the warmth of his breath. "If you don't leave me out of this, I'll make you regret it."

Without another word, he spun on his heels and stormed away. I didn't take my eyes off his retreating form until he disappeared down a bend in the path.

>> <<

Sebastian

The thorn in my side that was Grace Gillman continued to inch deeper. Things only seemed to get worse in the days following the article's publication and the poster campaign. I could feel the student population slowly turning on me. Not a single person had the nerve to say anything to my face, but that didn't stop the glares and whispers. The basketball players were smug, even more so than usual, class was getting harder to keep up with, and Kate was radio silent. We had never gone this long without seeing each other—almost a full week—but I couldn't bring myself to reach out again. A part of me was afraid that if I heard from her, it would only be more bad news.

"Please collect your papers from my desk before leaving today. And remember, we have an exam in two weeks. I'd like to remind you all that you should already be preparing for it."

After gathering my things, I stopped in the small line of students waiting for their papers. Professor Lang handed me a folder when I got to the front.

"Not your best work, Mr. Evans. It seemed a little rushed. Your thoughts were all over the place."

I peeked inside the folder and found a large red *D* staring back at me. Shit. It was a long jump from the B- I'd gotten on my first paper. The entire thing was marked with corrections and comments. Even my professor had joined the "I hate Sebastian" bandwagon.

"If you need help, visit during my office hours."

Fantastic. I'll get right on that. Except it was impossible for me to make his office hours because they overlapped with practice. I barely had enough time in my schedule to complete the basic coursework he assigned. Chest tightening, I tore out of the building and toward my next class, nearly running over several students in the process. They glared after me, and it took all of my restraint not to growl at them like a wild animal. I felt like I was on the edge of going rabid. I needed some kind of release before I snapped.

"Sebastian, wait up!"

The sound of Kate's voice was such a shock that, for a moment, the simmering rage beneath my skin was forgotten. As my eyes settled over her familiar features, I couldn't help but think her appearance was some sort of sign from above. Without thinking, I lurched forward and swept her into my arms. She seemed startled by the sudden movement but melted into my body all the same.

"I can't tell you how good it feels to see you," I murmured into her ear.

Kate pulled away first. "Is now a good time to talk?" she asked, and I couldn't decipher the expression behind her eyes. "About us?"

My instinct was to say yes, but something stopped me. Just over Kate's head, I could see someone pointing in my direction. There was a group of students hovering around a tree, one covered in blue and pink posters hung courtesy of the women's hockey team. Anger flared deep in my stomach.

"Sebastian?"

I focused my attention back on Kate, unable to keep the frustration from my voice. "I want to talk to you more than anything. But right now, I'm five seconds away from blowing a gasket. I need to let off some steam, and I don't think we should talk until that happens. I want to be levelheaded when we have this conversation."

Her brow furrowed. "Let off steam?"

Usually, Kate was my outlet for letting off steam. But I couldn't ask her to help me like that, not before we had a real conversation.

"I'll go to the gym and beat the shit out of a punching bag after my next class. Or maybe run, I don't know."

Kate studied me for a moment longer before she grasped my hand and pulled me in the direction of Nelson Library. I let her lead me into the building and through the winding bookshelves before voicing my concern.

"Where are we going? I have class in ten minutes, and I really think we should talk after—"

"We don't need to do any talking," she insisted.

My brain stalled as she slipped into an empty study room and motioned for me to follow. I was still trying to figure out what the hell she was doing when Kate closed the door and placed a soft kiss along my jaw. She reached for me slowly, dainty fingers catching on the top button of my pants. My body caught on before my brain, cock twitching to life. She undid my pants and pulled down the zipper.

"Kate, you don't have to—"

A hiss of relief slipped from my throat as her hand slid into my boxers and gripped my aching cock. Meanwhile, her lips found a sensitive spot on my neck.

I knew I should stop her, but I couldn't resist the feel of her silky hand. Who was I to get in the way of a sign from above, anyway?

"Don't be gentle, baby. Grip me fucking tight," I instructed, allowing myself to give in to the temptation.

Rather than gripping me harder, she removed her hand from my pants and dragged her tongue across her palm. I focused on the blue in her eyes—*blue, not brown*—and watched in anticipation as her hand disappeared into my pants. This time, when her fingers wrapped around my cock, they slipped easily from tip to base. Kate repeated the motion, grip tightening until the slightest pain accompanied the pleasure.

It was just what I needed.

A half groan, half hiss escaped me as she continued to move her hand up and down, squeezing tighter and loosening her grip again and again. It didn't take long for me to begin thrusting into her touch, gripping her shoulders for support as I rocked into each of her movements with a powerful roll of my hips. My eyes fluttered shut, and I attempted to paint a picture of Kate laid out before me, dressed in one of her sexy lingerie sets. But when the image came into focus, it wasn't Kate on my bed, it was Grace. She was stretched out along the mattress, tan legs on full display, figure hidden underneath one of my jerseys. Seeing her drowning in a uniform that had my name etched across the back was more erotic than any lingerie. Her hands were tied to the bed; she was left completely at my mercy. The thought of her bowing to my will was enough to push me over the edge. Normally, I might have been embarrassed at finding my release so quickly, but nothing could have been worse than the whispered name that fell from my lips as I did.

"Grace."

It took a moment for the room to come back into focus. When it did, I was too slow to dodge Kate's blow. Her hand met the side of my face with a loud clap that echoed through the space. I was at a loss for what to say; I couldn't even look her in the eyes. Instead, I reached down to tuck myself back into my pants. My fingers met hot, sticky fluid, and I cursed at the mess. There was no way I could go to class now.

"It's not what you think." I winced at my own words, knowing how stupid they sounded. There was no possible explanation that could make her understand why another girl's name was on my mind when she was getting me off.

"It's not what I think?" Kate's voice jumped an octave, her face reddening with every word she spoke. "How could it not be that when you're saying another girl's name?"

"I know it looks bad—"

"Isn't she the one behind the posters and the article?" she blustered on, looking angrier by the second. "I saw you two fighting at the gala! What the hell is going on?"

"We did fight at the gala, and yes, she's the one behind the bad press." I tried to choose my next words carefully, knowing that I was one mistake away from making things worse than they already were. "She's why I've been so angry lately. That's the only reason I said her name. I can't think of anything else when the girl is hell-bent on ruining me."

"So you can say her name when my hand is on your cock, but you can't use it in a regular sentence?" Her head shook as she stepped backward, her arms snaking around herself. "I can't do this anymore. It's hard enough competing for your time and attention with hockey. I won't compete with another girl."

Kate unlocked the study room and propped open the door. She glanced back over her shoulder at me, eyes shimmering with tears, and said, "We're done. For good."

She left without another word, the door slamming shut behind her. Silence blanketed the room, and I fell back against the table, pressing a hand to my stinging cheek. I felt defeated. In the absence of Kate, my fucked-up mind turned to the one person I wanted to forget.

Grace had burrowed deep under my skin. If I didn't do something to get her out of my head or off this campus, I was going to lose more than my girlfriend. The realization elicited a spark of anger, and I latched on to the feeling with all of my strength. I wasn't sure how to solve the problem that was Grace Gillman, but in the meantime, I needed her to know that I didn't make empty threats. If she thought McKinley Rink was bad now, I was going to make practicing there ten times more miserable by tomorrow morning.

CHAPTER 9

Sebastian

"Do you two really think that's a good idea?"

Bryce's voice rang out in stark contrast to the silence of the house. Both Landon and I jumped in surprise, whirling around to face him. Bryce was perched at the top of the stairwell, the outline of his large body all that was visible through the darkness. Though I couldn't see his expression, I was confident that it mirrored the clear disapproval of his tone.

Landon sighed in irritation. "Kent's such a little snitch."

"He didn't snitch. You two are not as inconspicuous as you think."

"Always using such big words," Landon muttered, and it was an effort to stop from asking how he'd managed to get into college. Right now was not the time to offend the only roommate who was willing to go along with my plan. I needed at least one person to keep a lookout while I slipped inside McKinley Rink.

"Why are you letting Sebastian pull you into his mess?" Bryce asked.

"His mess? Everyone on the team is feeling the heat! We should all want revenge," Landon argued. "Besides, it's just a harmless prank."

"Are you going to try to stop us?" I asked.

There was a long silence before Bryce let out a huff of laughter. "Of course not. I'm going to bed. You should consider doing the same."

"We promise to be home by midnight, Dad," Landon teased. Then he nodded his head toward the front door and slipped outside.

I hesitated in the foyer for a brief moment, glancing back over my shoulder at the shadowed form of Bryce. Though he said nothing, I knew exactly what he was thinking. Right now, his judgment was a non-issue. The only thing on my mind was delivering a message to Grace that couldn't be ignored. Without a goodbye, I followed Landon outside and shut the door behind me.

There was only a sliver of moon in the sky, which made tonight perfect for sneaking around unnoticed. Still, Landon and I remained silent as we dashed across campus. I lagged several paces behind him, hauling with me a twenty-quart cooler loaded with several pounds of expired ground beef. The meat was courtesy of Bishop's girlfriend, Macy, who worked at the local grocery store. He might have refused to tag along, but Bishop had been instrumental in helping me acquire the goods free of charge.

We were nearly to McKinley Rink; I could see the outline of the structure in the distance. Though I couldn't do much in the way of retaliation, especially given the target Grace had painted on me, petty revenge was better than watching her walk around campus with that smug smile as everyone turned on me—again. Landon and I ducked down as a campus patrol car rolled into view. Once the headlights were nothing more than dots in the distance, we shuffled across the street. I scoped out the surrounding area as we approached the old training center. The place was completely dark except for a flickering light illuminating the front entrance.

"How are we going to get in?"

Was this really the first time he was considering that?

"I'm getting in with this," I said, holding up white key card that opened nearly every building on campus. I had no idea how the previous captain had gotten hold of it, but he'd passed it down to me when he graduated. "You'll stay out here and make sure I'm not interrupted. If you see anything suspicious, text."

Confident we were alone, I darted toward the entrance and pressed the little white card to the sensor. It flashed green and let out a beep, then the lock clicked open. I rushed inside and closed the door behind me, my heart a steady drumbeat against my ribs. McKinley Rink certainly smelled just as Grace had described it—old and moldy. The stench only grew stronger as I crossed the entryway and pushed open the rink access door. Cool air rushed over my face. I flipped on a set of lights and watched as a soft yellow glow lit up the right side of the rink, where there was a narrow strip that held two rows of benches and some standing room. Even in partial darkness, I could tell this place had seen better days. I felt a momentary pang of guilt at the realization that Grace wasn't being overdramatic. McKinley wasn't just outdated, it was a hazard, but that fact wasn't enough to deter me. She'd lost any and all sympathy from me the moment my face had been plastered across the school paper.

I made my way down the steep set of stairs leading to the basement. The lights down here were even worse, so I grabbed my phone and turned on the flashlight. There was a narrow path carved out by walls of outdated equipment and dusty boxes. Walking through the creepy maze of storage, I tried not to think about the campus rumor that McKinley Rink was haunted. Every so often, a loud creek sounded from the floor above, and my heart rate would jump in anticipation. I cast my phone light along the walls and ceilings, keeping my eyes peeled for a grate. Eventually,

I found one along the back wall of the basement. It looked big enough to hold the entirety of my gift. My lips twitched in a smirk as I pulled out the screwdriver tucked into my back pocket and got to work, quickly removing enough screws to swivel the grate out. Now was the unpleasant part. Holding my breath, I dumped the contents of the cooler inside, gagging as several pounds of expired meat slapped against the bottom of the vent. For the finishing touch, I stuck a large toothpick into the middle of the slop and skewered a note addressed to Grace though the top.

I felt a brief rush of gratification as I fastened the grate back into place and surveyed my work, but it was gone in less than a second. In fact, I had to ignore the turning in my stomach as Landon and I trekked back to the house. The only thing that stopped me from returning to the rink and disposing of the "present" was my own misguided sense of pride.

>> <<

Grace

I couldn't believe the smell had gotten worse. With the end of October looming, I had been hopeful the drop in temperature would kill off the lingering scent of mold that clung to every inch of our training facility. But in just twenty-four hours, a newer, fouler odor had taken up residence. If I wasn't mistaken, something was rotting inside McKinley Rink. It had to be. Nothing else could have produced such a grotesque stench.

"Did someone die in here?" Liv said, holding a hand over her nose to block out the rancid smell. The goalie looked like she was about to retch.

Pearson, who was dealing with a nasty cold, looked equally disgusted. "I've been nose blind for days and even I can tell something is off."

"It's definitely worse than usual," I agreed.

Ah, yes. *Worse than usual.* Because we were already accustomed to playing in a rink that *only* stank of fungus on a good day.

"If there's a dead body somewhere in here, I'm out," said Big D.

McKinley Rink would never kick the haunted rumors if a dead body was discovered on the premises. On the other hand, we'd have an excuse to practice somewhere else if they did find human remains. The impending investigation would no doubt require closing the facility to the public.

"Do you think we should look around?" Almost the entire team was gathered at the entrance, so I couldn't tell who'd made the suggestion, but no one seemed eager to move any further into the building.

"I don't want to be the one to find the body," Lydia muttered.

"It's not a dead body," Caroline said matter-of-factly. "It's probably some kind of critter. There are a ton of traps down in the basement."

"Is that you volunteering to check?" asked Pearson.

"What is going on, ladi—" Coach's voice cut off, no doubt as she registered the terrible smell. We all turned to watch as the look of confusion on her face morphed into one of revulsion.

"Please tell us we don't have to skate in this. I think I'll throw up if I'm forced to be in here any longer," said Lydia.

Coach Riley shook her head aggressively. "No. Right now, I want everyone to take a lap and see if they can find whatever is causing this smell. I'm going to call the emergency maintenance number."

Several girls let out groans of protest. "But what if we find a body? What if the killer is in here somewhere?"

"Killer?" Clara exclaimed, eyes widening.

Coach waved them off. "Don't be dramatic. It's probably a dead rat."

"Told you guys," Caroline muttered.

"Just look around, and we'll get someone over from the school maintenance team."

Despite several rumblings, everyone followed Coach Riley's orders, but our search ended in vain. After nearly twenty minutes of choking down the disgusting fumes, I retreated to the fresh air, unable to endure another moment of torture. The scent of what could only be described as death clung to my hair and clothes. Caroline was the last to leave, aside from Coach. I had no doubt she wanted to prove to everyone that it was indeed a dead animal and not a human body.

"They're sending someone over to check on the smell," Coach confirmed a few moments later, walking out with a tissue pressed to her mouth and nose.

A voice rang out from the back of the group. "Does this mean practice is cancelled?"

Coach shook her head and gave everyone a stern look. "We'll wait here until someone comes to fix the smell. We play Minnesota on Friday, which means we need as much ice time as we can get."

I pressed my lips together, holding back a quip about utilizing the extra rink at DuLane. Surely that wouldn't be too much to ask from the men's team. I dropped my bag and settled on the ground, tucking my knees under my chin to conserve heat. It wasn't terribly cold, but if we sat out here much longer, I was going to get chilly. Caroline already had a textbook propped open on her lap, and Lydia had pulled out her sketchpad. Fifteen minutes later, maintenance arrived, and practically everyone let out a sigh of relief. The two men dressed in identical uniforms spoke with Coach before disappearing into the building.

"Okay, but what if they do find a body?" I heard someone whisper. "Are we going to be suspects? Maybe we'll get to be on the news!"

The idle chatter continued, but I was too distracted by a barrage of texts to eavesdrop.

Sambam

Totally walked in on a big fight between your sis and dad.

Talk about awkward.

I blame you for making me do wellness checks.

> Shit. I'm sorry you had to see that
>
> What was the fight about?

Maybe dance?

It was hard to tell through all the shouting.

> Who was shouting?

Mainly Gabs. Idk much else. I got out of there quick.

> Thanks for letting me know.
>
> Can I call you after classes?

I work late tonight. Tomorrow work?

> Call you then.
>
> And in case you needed to hear it, I love you.
>
> And appreciate you.
>
> And will name my first child in your honor if you want.

No need to get soppy, bitch. Love you too.

I glanced up from my phone just as one of the maintenance men came out of the building. He wore a mask and was holding a large white box as far away from his body as possible.

"Found your problem, ladies," he said, dropping it on the ground in front of us, and I was immediately greeted by a surge of the putrid scent from inside the facility.

Coach Riley waved everyone away and spoke with the man softly, motioning at the discovery. With a curt nod, he reached down and opened the box. Coach covered her mouth as she leaned over to glance inside, her lip immediately curling in disgust.

"Grace!"

I jumped about a mile into the air at the sound of my name. At once, everyone turned to look at me. Ignoring their stares, I pushed up from the ground and shuffled closer, holding my breath the entire way. In every horror movie, this was the part where they uncovered a severed head.

"Someone went through the trouble of hiding it inside a vent in the basement. There was a note, but we didn't find anything else," the maintenance man was saying. His name tag read "Lee."

There wasn't a single particle in my body eager to know why a note had been left, but I had little choice given Coach's demanding stare. As an extra measure to ward of the stench, I pulled the collar of my shirt up and over my mouth before leaning over to peek inside the box. It wasn't a head, but that didn't stop me from gagging as I was greeted with the sight of writhing maggots. The little white larvae covered almost every inch of the box, squirming over what looked like a mound of rotted beef. A short stick poked out from the top of the meat with a note attached. SPECIAL DELIVERY FOR GRACE was spelled out across the paper in bold lettering.

"Definitely don't remember ordering that," I said. "Honestly, Coach, I have no idea what this is about—"

"We can probably guess, Grace," Coach said, then turned her attention back to Lee. "How long will the smell linger?"

"Not sure." Lee dragged his fingers through his scruffy gray beard and shrugged. "We'll open all the doors tonight and let the place air out. You might want to give it another day before coming back."

"Is this their retaliation for the posters and the article?" asked Coach Riley.

"Probably," I admitted.

"Have you done anything else?"

"No," said Caroline, coming up from behind me. "We haven't broken any school rules or gone against the athletes' code of conduct."

"Sebastian's behind this. He has to be," I added.

She nodded her head, a thoughtful expression crossing her face. "I'm going to talk to Coach Dawson—we can't have this escalating all season."

"That's it? What about the guys? Are you going to report this to the athletic director?" Caroline's tone was laced with incredulity.

"Unfortunately, there's no proof, and even if there was, I doubt Sebastian would face any consequences. Now that he's returned to being the star of the team, they won't risk losing him."

Ugh. This school was so far up Sebastian's ass I was sure they could see out his throat. It wasn't fair that he didn't have to abide by the rules like the rest of us. "This isn't *Animal House*, Coach Riley!" I exclaimed. "They can't get away with disrupting our practice schedule."

To my surprise, she nodded her head in agreement. "I'll get us some rink time at DuLane. We'll move practice to the evening." She started typing something into her phone with determination. "In the meantime, I need you ladies to get new posters ready for tomorrow. Bigger ones—get creative. Be at DuLane Arena in the morning before the men's practice. If they want to mess with our facility and make it so we can't practice, we'll be there to disrupt their ice time."

Caroline and I exchanged wide-eyed looks of disbelief. I couldn't help but think that with Coach behind us, we'd be unstoppable.

"We'll work within the rules of the university, but that doesn't mean we can't push some buttons. I've had enough, and you girls deserve better."

>> <<

It was cold enough to see your breath when we arrived at DuLane Arena the next morning. Blue and purple streaks cut across the horizon. Dawn was approaching. Despite the semi-darkness and the still of the early hour, no one looked the least bit sleepy. If anything, there was an excited energy buzzing through the group. A sense of pride filled me as we made our way through the arena and filed into a row of seating directly next to the players' bench. Together, we formed a mass of bright colors and bold words, our anger spelled out over twenty-five different poster boards.

Each player's creation was unique. Caroline's highlighted the women's record in comparison to the men's, while Lydia had crafted the outline of a woman's body with the same repeating phrase: RESPECT MY EXISTENCE OR EXPECT MY RESISTANCE. My poster was simple, though I'd made an effort to cover the entire thing in pretty pink sprinkles just for Sebastian. In bold letters, I'd spelled out: Puck You. Head tilted slightly to the side, I took in the long line of posters with a fierce sense of admiration for every one of my teammates. Liv winked at me as I passed, shaking her sign that said, GIRLS JUST WANT TO HAVE FAST ICE.

At the first flicker of movement from the tunnel leading to the players' bench, Caroline turned on her portable speaker and started blasting her girl power playlist. At once, the quiet arena was filled with the sound of Chappell Roan's masterpiece "Femininomenon." As more men surfaced from the tunnel, we were met with an assembly of dumbfounded expressions. They still seemed half-asleep, utterly confused at the sight of us perched in the seats alongside their bench. When Coach Dawson emerged muttering about the music, he froze at the sight of us.

Sebastian wasn't far behind him. He marched right over to the tempered glass separating us, placing himself directly in front of me. Just as he opened his mouth to say something, Caroline cranked the music even louder. I gave him a sweet smile and shoved my Puck You poster against the glass. Undeterred, he stormed over to the arena seating access door and threw it open. Sebastian took the small set of stairs in one step, bypassing each and every girl until he was standing directly in front of me. He didn't speak immediately. Instead, Sebastian looked directly into my eyes with an expression that seemed to promise retribution.

"Leave." The single-word demand was dripping in acid.

"No."

For a split second, I detected a hint of panic in his expression. But in a flash, his handsome mouth curved into a snarl. "You're not welcome here."

Once again, I found myself completely baffled by his show of animosity. Was this really about the women taking up space in *his* arena? Because right now, Sebastian only had eyes for me. He'd barely even glanced at my teammates.

"Is it that we're not welcome here or *I'm* not welcome here?" I said, motioning to the group of women around me.

"I particularly don't like you, but I'd prefer if everyone—"

"You don't care about anyone but yourself, do you?" I interrupted, and his gaze suddenly dropped in a rare show of shame.

"Sebastian, get your ass down here!" Coach Dawson bellowed his name from the players' bench below. Without another word, Sebastian retreated to the ice.

>> <<

Sebastian

No one spoke as we performed our warm-up laps around the rink, though it would have been hard to hear anything over the blast of music coming from the stands. My nerves were starting to take over, flushing out all the anger and replacing it with dread. When I saw Grace sitting in the crowd with her oversized poster, a storm had swept through my body. The very woman responsible for inciting my impulsive behavior was now invading DuLane, my place of refuge. Just one look at her and my skin felt ready to boil off. But when Coach called me down to the ice, the ringing in my ears settled and the truth of the situation became clear. Grace being here was entirely my fault.

I caught Bryce's eye and waited for the impending "I told you so," but he just shook his head and skated past me. I should have just gone to bed that night. Enacting my revenge on Grace was supposed to make me feel better. But the satisfaction was short-lived. It was a lousy prank, a stupid reaction because I couldn't deal with my emotions. I hadn't been in my right mind then, just as I hadn't been a few moments ago when I'd laid eyes on Grace.

Dawson hadn't joined us on the ice; he was speaking with Coach Riley. Her hands were braced on her hips in a way that didn't bode well for him, though things seemed civil enough. After a moment, she looked out at the ice and pointed directly at me.

Shit. That couldn't be good.

"Sebastian, pay attention!"

I slipped into the line for drills at the behest of our assistant coach. It was nearly impossible to concentrate when I knew *she* was watching. For the next twenty minutes, I worked through different skills, my mind shifting between the ice and the stands where Grace remained. Every inch of my body felt impossibly hot, like I'd been doused with a form of liquid embarrassment that left blisters in its wake. It wasn't an emotion I was used to processing, which left me feeling completely out of my depth.

Thankfully, Coach didn't pull me aside or lecture me in front of the team. Instead, he rejoined practice and instructed us to ignore what was happening in the stands, as if that were possible. A tense atmosphere settled over the rink. No one seemed like they wanted to be the first person to speak, so everyone stayed quiet until we started to scrimmage. Still, Coach never said a word to me. Every time I overshot a pass or missed a goal, I glanced over, ready to take an earful, only to be met with silence. He wouldn't even look at me.

I was the first to the locker room after Dawson released us from practice. I refused to look toward the female players. Head down, I retreated to the showers, undressed, and settled beneath a blast of steaming hot water. Despite spending over an hour on the ice, I still felt like I was coming apart at the seams.

Over and over again, all I could hear was the venom in Grace's voice. *You don't care about anyone but yourself, do you?* She'd meant every word; I'd seen the conviction in her eyes, and part of me agreed with her. Deep down, I knew that Grace was right, but it was hard to see past my resentment. The women deserved a better training facility. All their anger was justified. But I needed to be selfish for the sake of my own future. Nothing mattered more than making my father proud. He'd given up his own dream of going pro to help raise me, and I was determined to get there for both of us. My only hope of getting to the NHL was to ensure I had the perfect season, and with Grace around, that seemed impossible.

I stood under the water, hands braced against the tile wall as I tried to find my center. Never in my life had I felt more off-balance, less in control. Even after the injury, I knew what had to happen next. Everything was straightforward.

Until Grace.

Only when my skin began to wrinkle did I turn off the water and exit the showers, a towel wrapped around my waist. Everyone around me was moving and talking, but I felt like I couldn't hear a thing. The next few seconds seemed to proceed in slow motion. I stopped in front of my locker, opened the latch, and watched in stunned horror as a flood of pink glitter rained down over my head, a bucket's worth spilling out across the floor. With my skin still damp from the shower, the particles clung to my body as if I'd bathed in glue. The locker room fell silent.

What. The. Hell.

Poking out beneath a mound of the egregiously bright glitter gathered at my feet was a small white note. Warmth rushed across my skin as I reached down and grasped the paper. There was a single question typed out in a bold font.

IS IT YOUR PROBLEM YET?

There was no more anger left in me. Instead of a burning heat, I felt a dizzying sense of vertigo. The humiliation set in, a tingling that swept up the back of my neck and across my face, made no better by the silence of the locker room. I felt the overwhelming urge to flee when, out of the corner of my eye, I noticed Coach Dawson leaning against the wall. He didn't speak, and his expression was unreadable. Slowly, he stood up straight and looked around the room.

"Nothing to see here, boys," he said. "Just a little mess that Sebastian has to clean up."

Another painful wave of embarrassment rushed over me as everyone packed up and trickled out of the room. Bryce and Kent hovered near the exit, but Coach looked at them and shook his head.

"This for Sebastian to deal with. I don't want any anyone to help."

As soon as they were gone, Coach confronted me with a look that could only be described as disappointment.

"You're the leader of this team, Sebastian. You better start acting like it."

>> <<

Grace

Mr. Castillo would like to speak with you, Grace. I turned the words over in my head, wondering if Coach Riley knew just how terrified I was to see the athletic director. The last time we spoke, he'd threatened to revoke my scholarship. The man had quite literally tossed me out of the men's fundraiser. Even though

Coach assured me it was nothing to worry about, insisting she'd be there for the entire discussion, I was still a nervous wreck when we met outside of his office at ten minutes to nine. It had only been two days since we'd stormed the men's practice in protest, and I had no doubt this meeting was related.

My heart dropped to my stomach when the door opened to reveal the man of the hour. His eyes swept over me in a brief glance before he nodded for us to join him inside. I hung back, letting Coach lead the way. With a deep breath, I trailed after her, pulling my shoulders back to look more confident than I felt. But what little confidence I had immediately evaporated upon entering the room. Sebastian Evans and Coach Dawson were seated at a long conference table along the far wall. There were still six open seats around the table. Coach Dawson nodded in greeting while Sebastian pretended that I didn't exist.

"Please take a seat and we can get started," Mr. Castillo said.

I didn't hesitate to sit down, opting for the chair furthest from Sebastian. When everyone was situated, the athletic director cleared his throat.

"I'm sure you all know why we're here," he said, placing his hands palm down across the top of the table. "This unpleasantness between the two of you—between the men's and women's hockey teams—needs to end."

No one spoke.

"After further evaluation of the women's facility, and taking into consideration the recent issues," said Mr. Castillo, eyes hardening on Sebastian, "we've made the executive decision to move the women into DuLane Arena. They will have access to the second rink except for Wednesdays, when the space is utilized for figure skating classes at the school."

Disbelief crashed over me like a stack of books. *Am I hearing things, or did Castillo just say we're moving to DuLane Arena?* I turned toward Coach for confirmation, and she gave me a proud nod.

"And what about Wednesdays?" Sebastian's words were sharp enough to cut the tension in the room.

"Your coaches aren't keen on losing ice time. They've decided that a shared skills practice is the best solution."

Combined practice with the men's team? Once again, I looked at Coach Riley for confirmation. The situation wasn't ideal; the last thing I wanted was to be forced into spending time with Sebastian. But putting up with him was better than not having access to a rink.

"You seriously expect us to share a rink?" Sebastian said.

"It's decided," Coach Dawson cut in, his tone leaving no room for argument.

Sebastian slumped back into his chair, slowly shaking his head. Several times he opened his mouth as if to say something. No words were spoken.

"Now," Mr. Castillo said, looking back and forth between us, "I don't want to hear about any further pranks. I don't care how essential you are as players on the team. I will not hesitate to suspend you both if these issues persist."

I tensed at his threat, fists clenching in my lap. This moment should have felt better. Our efforts had finally forced the administration to make a change. If anything, we were owed an apology from Sebastian *and* the university, not a scolding. But I was willing to swallow my pride to ensure the the athletic director kept his word.

"Are there going to be any more problems?" he asked.

I shook my head immediately. "No, sir, no problems here."

We turned our attention to Sebastian. He was still slouched in his chair, lips pressed into a thin line of irritation. Coach Dawson gave him a gentle elbow to the side, and he nodded begrudgingly.

"I'm glad this is settled. Moreover, I hope that this will be our last time discussing the issue," Mr. Castillo said. "You may go."

I tried to process the news as I followed Coach Riley out of the room. As soon as the door closed behind us, she and Coach Dawson stopped. I felt Sebastian at my back, heat radiating from his body.

"You two need to, oh, what's the saying? 'Kiss and make up'?" Coach Dawson said this with a serious face, as if the suggestion wasn't completely absurd.

From behind me, Sebastian let out a choking sound.

Coach Riley registered the look of incredulity on my face and smothered her smile. "Maybe a better phrase is to 'bury the hatchet,'" she suggested. "Moving forward, you'll be seeing a lot of each other. We'd like to avoid any further conflict."

I would have liked to bury a hatchet right into Sebastian's smug face, but Riley was right. Endeavoring to be the bigger person between the two of us, I turned around and held out my hand in an offering of peace.

Sebastian looked down at me like I was offering him my dirty socks after a grueling practice on the ice, clear refusal to touch me written across his face. "The hatchet is buried. Scout's honor."

The words had barely left his lips before he pushed past us and retreated down the hallway. We watched him disappear through the exit, the door slamming shut behind him. The hatchet didn't seem all that buried to me . . .

"I'll have a talk with him," Dawson assured Riley. Before he left, he looked at me. "He might be a cocky bastard, and he's done some questionable things, but Sebastian's had a difficult year. Try to give him a little grace. He'll come around, I promise."

CHAPTER 10
Sebastian

The month of October was cursed, and in more than just a spooky, All Hallows' Eve way. In just a few weeks, my blueprint for the hockey season had been shredded to pieces, my two-year relationship was dead and in the ground, and the press was eating me alive. Despite Dallard's statement declaring a mutually agreeable solution had been reached, one that involved the men's and women's hockey teams working together, people around campus were still sending me dirty looks or whispering to one another when I passed by. Worst of all was knowing that most of it was due to my own stupid, reckless actions.

Be that as it may, I was still happy to cast blame on Grace for her part in it all. I might have lit the spark that started the fire, but she was the one who'd poured gasoline atop the entire thing. And the most frustrating part? The undeniable, all-consuming attraction I felt for her that existed in contradiction to my frustration. I'd never actually hated Grace, at least not in the beginning. All that manufactured loathing had been an excuse to keep her far away. I didn't want to be friendly because I'd desired more from her the very moment I'd laid eyes on her. Even after the article was published, I couldn't deny that I wanted her. But now, that need was more complex. I was angry that she'd tricked me and frustrated that it hadn't changed how much I craved her attention.

All things considered, I was more than ready for the month of October to be a thing of the past. And after suffering our first loss, against Ohio State, I wasn't going to risk stepping outside until midnight hit and we were officially into November. Unfortunately, that didn't stop my roommates from hosting the Halloween pregame in our kitchen. Even in the privacy of my bedroom, I could hear the chorus of muffled voices and shitty party music. It was so loud that I barely noticed Bryce as he poked his head into my room. He was dressed in a giant pickle costume that looked a little too tight for his bulging muscles.

"Hey, man," he said, one brow arched as he took in the mess of clothes strewn across my floor. It was unusual for my room to be anything other than spotless, and usually I wouldn't be lying around in my bed unless I was having sex or going to sleep. I'm sure the sight of me reclining in front of my computer screen was slightly concerning. "You going to sulk up here all night?"

My only response was a curt nod.

"Come on, it's Halloween. You can drink yourself into forgetting yesterday's game," he suggested.

When I remained silent, Bryce stepped further into the room and studied me from head to toe as if just realizing something strange. "Where's Kate? You guys always do a couple's costume."

"We broke up. She dumped me, actually. And no, I don't want to talk about it."

His eyes went wide. In all honesty, I still needed to process the breakup myself. So much had happened following the incident in the study room that I'd barely had a moment to think about it. Some days, it didn't feel real.

"Maybe going out would be a good distraction," he suggested.

"I don't want to be around a bunch of drunk idiots."

"You could be one of those drunk idiots." He held his drink up to emphasize his point, taking a long sip of whatever concoction he'd mixed up in his Solo cup. If I had to guess, it was whiskey and Coke.

"You know I don't drink anymore."

"Okay, sorry for suggesting it. I thought it might help . . ."

I wasn't in the mood for one of Bryce's motivational talks, especially since he was more than a few drinks deep. I'd regret being so short with him in the morning, but right now I couldn't help myself.

"You going to be okay for practice next week?" he asked in a complete one-eighty.

I didn't intend to sound so defensive as I shot back, "What do you mean?"

"You've been weird since they told us we're sharing DuLane with the women's team."

Yeah, and everyone else should be just as concerned . . .

"I'm worried about how this will impact our training. The entire dynamic we've built these past couple months is about to shift."

He examined me with careful eyes before he asked, "Are you worried about our training schedule or are you worried about Grace?"

I shot him a warning look. Bryce was my best friend, but I wasn't willing to talk about *her*. Not now, when everything was so fresh from my breakup with Kate that I still felt guilty wanting someone else. Especially someone who'd had a part in derailing my life.

"Don't play psychologist with me. I'm not in the mood," I said dismissively.

After a long moment of silence, he nodded his head. "Have it your way."

Thirty minutes later, when I was confident the pre-game had ended, I went downstairs to remedy my rumbling stomach. The house was quiet as I stepped into the kitchen and surveyed the mess of empty beer cans and plastic cups scattered across the different surfaces of the room. I didn't have to touch anything to know that every inch of the counter was sticky. With a shiver, I searched the pantry from top to bottom. There wasn't much. Usually, Bryce was the one who stocked the kitchen. He must have abandoned his weekly-scheduled Sunday shopping trip to join the festivities around campus. My stomach let out a low rumble of protest. Given the late hour, I had limited options for food. There was a pizza place downtown that might be open, but my best bet was the gas station on the edge of campus.

I slipped on my jacket and set off down the block, securing the hood over my head. Not only was it cold, but I wanted to avoid being recognized. Booze had the power to make anyone fearless, and people might do more than point and whisper with the fuel of alcohol. Unsurprisingly, the streets were filled with costumed students stumbling on drunk feet. Most ignored me, but a few hollered drunk questions my way. By the time I reached the gas station, I'd already encountered three people bold enough to shout, "Who are you supposed to be?" Head low, I grabbed some snacks and a frozen pizza from the back. It wasn't a typical meal for me—I liked to avoid preservatives and eat a clean, high-protein diet. But nothing else was open, and my stomach was aching from hunger.

I only managed to cross the street before I heard *her* voice. It was impossible to mistake that raspy tone for anyone other than Grace. She was sitting on the stoop of an unfamiliar house with a phone pressed to her ear. After several long moments, I realized she was dressed as Bob Ross, her dark brown locks hidden beneath a rather large wig of curly hair. She'd even gone to the trouble of putting on a fake beard to match the wig. Despite all my conflicting feelings about Grace, I couldn't help the snort of laughter that escaped me. When I pictured Grace dressed up for Halloween (and I pictured it *a lot*), her costume involved zero facial hair and far less clothing.

"Answer your phone! It's really not that hard. You just"—she hiccupped—"press the stupid button and say, 'Hi, so good to hear from you I miss you so much and love you.'"

There was little question in my mind that Grace was drunk. If the hiccups didn't give her away, the slurring did.

"Ugh, you suck!" She slammed her phone down onto her lap and let out a scream of frustration. After a moment's consideration, she picked up the device, typed something in, and held it up to her ear once again.

"Stop ignoring me, you gremlin. I'm your—"

Grace's eyes met mine from across the yard, and she went silent. Slowly, she pulled the phone away from her ear and ended the call.

"Are you, like, stalking me?"

Grace sprang to her feet and swayed as I approached. She was absolutely wasted.

"You're drunk," I muttered, holding out a hand to help her safely down the short set of concrete stairs. Even I didn't want to see her with a bloody nose or missing teeth. But hey, maybe that would kill the appeal.

"And you're a stalker," Grace muttered, slapping her hand into my palm like it was second nature. Her fingers tightened around mine, and she leaned her weight against my arm until her feet were firmly on the ground. Then Grace came to the sudden realization that we were touching and shoved herself away from me. In the process, she stumbled back and ended up with her ass on the lawn of whoever's house this happened to be. At least it was a soft landing.

"I'm not a stalker. I was getting food." I held up my plastic bag from the gas station. I didn't know why I felt the need to explain myself when she was too drunk to even stand on her own. Where the hell were her friends, anyway? I didn't like the idea of her being out alone, even in her ridiculous costume.

"Whatever you say, *Se-bas-tian*," she slurred. Grace was a mess right now, and I kind of loved it. Drunk people were way too honest for their own good.

"Late-night booty call?" I teased, unable to help myself. It was easy to fall into our usual pattern. "Seems like they're not really interested."

Her brow furrowed in confusion, but then she glanced down at her phone, putting two and two together. "You think I was making a booty call?"

"Were you not?"

She scoffed at me like she was offended by the assumption. "I was calling my sister. Anyway, I don't need a stupid phone to have sex with someone. There are plenty of people out and about that would looooove to fuck me."

Me being one of them. But that wasn't a possibility, and it never would be, considering her feelings for me. Plus, I was pretty sure sleeping with Grace would only make things worse.

"You sound very confident for someone wearing a fake 'fro and beard."

Grace looked at me as if to say *challenge accepted*. Before I could intervene, she was shouting at a group of partygoers passing on the sidewalk behind me.

"Do any of you want to sleep with me?"

Their chatter died down, and one of the guys, in a pirate costume, squinted in Grace's direction. He took a step into the yard, and I had to stop myself from blocking his path like an overprotective boyfriend.

"Hey, you're Bob Ross," he said with a laugh.

"I am. Would you fuck me? Even with the wig and the beard?"

The guy looked her up and down from head to toe and nodded his head. "Definitely."

"Okay, that's enough," I said, placing myself between the stranger and Grace.

She was still on the ground where she'd fallen, legs extended and arms on either side of her body. I didn't miss the triumphant gleam in her eyes. Shaking my head in half amusement, half disappointment, I reached down and picked up her phone just as the screen lit up. Grace made a noise of disapproval as I read the name flashing across the front and answered the call.

"Hello, Caroline," I answered.

"Grace, is that you?"

"Do I sound like Grace?"

A sigh of relief met my ears. "Thank God you found her, Sebastian. We've been looking for over thirty minutes."

"Yes, thank God I found her and not some perv with bad intentions. Why the hell is she out here alone?"

"We were heading to the bar and then suddenly she was gone. No one saw her leave."

"She's on her ass in someone's yard," I said as I searched for the nearest street sigh. "We're on the corner of Brentwood and Lloyd."

"I'll be there in, like, five minutes. Don't leave her."

I hung up the phone and turned back to Grace. She was fully lying down now, her back pressed into a pile of fallen leaves as her eyes searched the sky. Without overthinking the absurdity of the situation, I lay down beside her and looked up. Trimont didn't have much light pollution, so there were hundreds of stars visible overhead.

"Why'd you run off?" I asked.

She turned to look at me, and I slowly mirrored her movement. If October was cursed, then November had to be an alternate reality. There was no other explanation for how I'd found myself here, on the ground, mere inches away from Grace. It would have been so easy to lean over and kiss her. We were already more than halfway there, our eyes level, lips closer to touching than ever before.

"I didn't run off," she said. "I stopped walking."

Maybe it was because she was drunk and probably wouldn't remember tonight, or maybe it was because I was tired of fighting, but I let go of my feelings for a moment. At least for tonight, Grace and I could be more than sparring partners. I could be concerned, not angry.

"You're smart enough to know that you shouldn't wander off by yourself in the dark."

"I can take care of myself."

"You can't even walk."

"I can walk!"

Perhaps we were destined to bicker—no matter how we felt about each other or what state of mind we were in.

"Then stand up and show me."

"I like it down here, though."

"You're ridiculous."

"I'm ridiculous? You're the one who's out on Halloween without a costume."

I bit back a smile. "How do you know I'm not dressed up as someone specific?"

Grace considered my words, her eyes roaming back and forth along my body.

"Oh, I see now," she said. "Can't believe it took me so long. I've seen plenty of arrogant athletes around here, but there's no mistaking the captain of the men's hockey team. He's handsome, but he doesn't like to share."

It didn't matter that she was insulting me, not when she called me handsome in the process. This time, I didn't hold back my smile.

"Well, this is strange."

Caroline Hart, or should I say Hannah Montana, appeared above us in a flurry of sequins. Her hands were placed firmly on her hips, and she was gazing down at us like we each had two heads. With a sigh, I pushed myself off the ground, and together we helped Grace to her unsteady feet.

"Get her home safe this time," I instructed. "When she wakes up in the morning and asks what happened, feel free to tell her she said I was handsome and that she wants me."

Caroline's eyebrow rose in speculation. "That last part can't be true."

She was right, but I couldn't deny that a part of me wished it was. It would be comforting to know that Grace wanted me like I wanted her, even if we still loathed each other. I'd feel less crazy knowing I wasn't alone in my madness.

"Maybe not. But it'd be funny if she believed it."

>> <<

Grace

"Your hangover remedy awaits."

Caroline placed a glass of unreasonably green liquid on the counter in front of me, followed by a second glass full of water and a steaming cup of coffee. "Drink them in order of light to dark, and you'll feel better in an hour."

"Never let me drink again," I groaned, sinking onto a barstool.

The water went down first, followed by some much-needed Tylenol. Though I expected it to taste horrible, the green mixture was surprisingly refreshing. Once I got to the coffee, I no longer felt like I was going to throw up. A few minutes later, Lydia slunk into the room looking hungover but in much better shape than me. When Caroline placed the same green drink in front of her, she gulped it down immediately.

"So," Caroline said, pushing a plate of pancakes my way. "Strange night, huh?"

Strange wasn't the word I'd use to describe last night. Unfortunate? Yes. Humiliating? Also yes. *If only my Bob Ross costume had been more believable* . . .

"What even happened?" Caroline asked. "You went missing out of nowhere."

I shrugged, still unclear about certain parts of the evening. One moment I was trailing behind the group, and the next I was sitting on the stoop of some random person's house. "I don't really know for sure, but I drunk dialed my sister at one point."

Lydia snickered into her coffee cup. "Isn't she, like, thirteen?"

"She's been ignoring me for weeks. I wanted to check in on

her." There had to be something more behind Gabby's silence, and I was desperate to hear her voice.

"I don't like runners, Grace. I get stressed out when we're drinking and someone disappears," Caroline muttered.

"I'm sorry," I said. "But you should know there was very little running involved. The opposite, actually."

"I know. I'm the one who picked your drunk ass off the grass and walked you home, remember? If it weren't for Sebastian, I might not have found you."

The irony of Sebastian coming to my rescue was not lost on me. "I didn't take him for the knight in shining armor type."

"He's an arrogant prick at times, but he's not a bad person. I'm glad it was him you ran into and not some creep from the basketball team. *Never* go to one of their parties."

"You're saying I was safe with Sebastian?"

She gave me an odd look. "Did he make you feel unsafe?"

I shook my head. It was quite the opposite, actually. I'd been so worked up after calling Gabby that I was relieved to see someone familiar, even if it was him.

"Did he say something that bothered you?"

I assured Caroline that Sebastian hadn't said anything untoward, and I found myself unintentionally smiling as I recalled the night. If anything, I'd sensed his concern—concern for *me*. The more I thought about it, the less it made sense.

"Do you remember calling him handsome?" Caroline asked, and Lydia practically spit up her hangover cure.

My head fell into my hands as I let out a groan of shame. The last thing Sebastian needed was an ego boost. He was already much too full of himself. "Vividly, yes, and I'm sure he'll be eager to remind me the next time we meet."

>> <<

We spent the rest of the weekend lazing around, watching TV, and eating copious amounts of junk food. It was the only way to survive a hangover. When Monday rolled around, the whole team spent hours after practice exploring DuLane Arena and all it had to offer. The training center was perfectly crafted for anything a hockey player needed, with all the newest weight and cardio machines, a wide-open space for dry skills training, and a recovery room equipped with large tubs for ice baths. It was superior to McKinley Rink in every way.

By the time our first shared practice with the men's team came around, I was anxious to get it over with. Would Sebastian treat me with cold indifference, or would he tease me relentlessly for how foolishly I'd acted over the weekend? I wasn't sure which would be worse.

"All right, folks, I want to make one thing clear. When we're all on this ice together, we're one team. I don't care what you got between your legs. What matters is that everyone is a Raven, and Ravens are family. Got that?"

Coach Dawson's formidable voice echoed throughout the arena. The rink felt impossibly cramped with two full teams forming a circle together surrounding the coaching staff. Even after two days of exploring the facility, I was *still* amazed by DuLane.

"Boys, you call her Coach or Coach Riley. She's owed your respect," he said, gesturing to a stern-faced Riley.

Coach Riley studied the men's team, her shoulders back and chin held high. She exuded the same strength and confidence as Coach Dawson. I had no doubt the men would come to respect her.

"Show them how it's done, ladies," she said.

I found myself looking for Sebastian amongst the group. I hadn't stopped thinking about him since Halloween night, and the more I turned over the memory in my head, the more bewildered I felt about his behavior. Maybe Sebastian was actually trying to be civil. Or maybe (most likely) he was going to hold the whole thing over my head. Only time would tell. Now that we were on the ice together, I was sure to find out.

After our warm-up laps, where I spent my time at the back of the pack, eyes glued to the back of Sebastian's jersey, the coaches announced we'd be focusing on individual skills to ease into the new combined practice format. There were three stations set up across the ice, the cones spaced out evenly to ensure that each group had enough room to run their drills. When the coaches split us into groups, I found myself lumped in with Sebastian. I was sure they wanted to test our ability to remain peaceful around one another.

The skills sequence would have been familiar to any hockey player. It was a basic yet crucial aspect of training, one that focused on fundamental skating technique, puck control, and stickhandling. Within the first few minutes, everyone had fallen into a steady rhythm. It didn't take long for me to realize that Sebastian and I were both hyperaware of one another. His eyes burned a hole into my back as I worked through the drills, and I passed my downtime studying his movement across the ice, waiting with bated breath for the moment things took a turn. I was slightly exhilarated by the thought of quarreling with Sebastian. It was practically second nature by now, and I couldn't deny that I liked watching the self-satisfied smirk melt off his face the moment I landed a worthy jab.

"You might have a bucket on, but everyone can tell you're staring." I'd just returned to the line after completing a sequence when I overheard Liv from a few paces away.

She was talking to Sebastian, I realized, when he shrugged his shoulders and said, "Her form is practically perfect; it's impressive."

"Did you hear that, Grace?" Liv shifted to face me, grinning like a maniac. "Sebastian thinks you're perfect!"

He didn't look the least bit embarrassed as he glanced over his shoulder at me. "I thought you deserved a compliment after this weekend. It took a lot of courage to admit you think I'm handsome."

The group of players around us seemed to freeze, a few chuckles sifting over the noisy sounds of practice. I knew he wouldn't be able to help himself, though I had to admit, it was light work for Sebastian. I was sure he had something more offensive up his sleeve.

"But don't let it go to your head," he said with a playful smirk. "I'm still the best hockey player on this ice."

>> <<

Sebastian

My insides seemed to vibrate at the sight of Grace blushing from behind the bars of her cage. I hadn't known what to expect for the first shared practice, especially after our bizarre interaction on Halloween, but it definitely wasn't this, whatever *this* was. It felt like there was a rope connecting us, one that grew tauter with every shared glance. I was simultaneously scared and excited to know what would happen if—no, when—it snapped.

For the remainder of practice, I kept her within my sights at all times. Everyone here had a certain level of expertise that set them apart from the average hockey player, but Grace stood out amongst them all. Being on the ice was second nature to her, and I wondered if her introduction to hockey had been anything like mine—at the hands of someone she loved during the earliest years of her life. Each time I felt the heat of her stare, I pushed myself to work a little harder, knowing that after today, Grace wouldn't be able to deny that I had every right to be cocky.

At some point, our watchful fascination with each other shifted into something more like a game. It was clear we were trying to show the other up by way of fancy footwork and deceptive puck handling. Everyone around us had caught on to our little contest—even the coaches, who seemed just fine with a healthy dose of competition. Our final battle took form as a series of sprinting drills. The entire time we remained neck and neck, one of us pushing to the lead just to be overtaken by the other. When the coaches finally dismissed the teams, we both ended up on our backs, splayed out across the ice, chests heaving as we tried to catch our breath. We weren't the only ones unable to move. There were several other forms sprawled out like dead bodies.

"So," Grace said as she pulled herself up to a sitting position and removed her helmet. "Do you still think the men are more deserving of this facility? Have we sullied this good ice with our terrible female ways?"

Beside her, Caroline let out a snort of laughter. Both were pink-cheeked and covered in a thin layer of sweat. Lydia was there too, but she was still lying on her back sucking large gulps of air into her lungs. Grace had wedged her way into their best friend dynamic. I'd rarely seen the pair around campus without her.

"I never said the men are more deserving. But I do think we'd wipe the floor with you ladies. No offense."

"Being bigger or stronger doesn't mean better," she quipped.

"What about faster or—"

"Oh, don't even go there," Caroline interrupted. "You and Grace were neck and neck during sprints."

I was playing devil's advocate for the sake of pushing Grace's buttons. The women *were* excellent hockey players. Their record was proof, and their performance today a reminder. None of this ridiculous back-and-forth had ever been about skill level or who deserved what. It had always been about ensuring my success on the ice and increasing my chances of going pro.

"We can all agree strength and size doesn't automatically equate to skill level," Lydia said.

"That applies off the ice as well," snickered Landon.

A chorus of laughter rose from the group. The sound was a shock to my system. I looked around the rink, surprised at the sense of ease I felt being surrounded by players from the women's team. Even with Grace just a few feet away, I was more relaxed than I had been in weeks. Had I been sabotaging myself this whole time, or was this just the calm before the storm? I looked to my left and caught Grace watching me.

"Do I have something on my face?" I asked.

"The look of a smug asshole who thinks he's better than everyone."

At her words, a tingle of excitement shot down my spine. I *knew* she wouldn't be able to make it through today without insulting me, especially after I'd teased her about the handsome comment.

"So much for being civil."

"The truth can be a hard reality," she said.

"Is that why it took you so long to admit that I'm handsome?"

Grace scoffed. "Are you ever going to let that go? Everyone thinks you're hot. It's not your looks that are the problem."

"Oh, yeah? Then what is?"

"The stick that's clearly still lodged up your—"

"Why don't we channel all of this energy into something more productive than bickering?" suggested Lydia. The right winger had finally managed to pull herself into a sitting position, her discarded helmet lying a few inches away on the ice beside Grace's.

"What do you mean?"

"Showing off and trying to best each other in practice today was a productive way to channel your negative feelings for one another," she explained, eyes darting back and forth between me and Grace.

Who did she think she was, our therapist?

"A competition could be a good idea," Caroline said. "Clearly, you both feel the need to prove the other wrong. Sebastian thinks he's the best, and Grace thinks he's a sexist prick."

"No one said sexist," I pointed out.

Grace chuckled. "Oh, I've definitely called you sexist. Just not today. Or to your face."

I rolled my eyes and turned to Caroline. She had a point. There was tension between Grace and me, a tension that had the power to cause more trouble than we'd already gotten ourselves into. Maybe if I was focused on beating Grace, I'd be less focused on how angry I was about the article. Or how badly I wanted to sleep with her. Or that stupid PUCK YOU sign.

"What about a bet?" I proposed, Caroline's voice playing in mind. *Sebastian thinks he's the best, and Grace thinks he's a sexist prick.* "Grace, do you remember that man from the gala? The one I was speaking to before you ran into me?"

She sighed. "What does this have to do with anything?"

"That was Elijah Peters. He's a close family friend and a very wealthy alumnus of Dallard. He's going to make a large donation to the men's hockey program at the end of the season." I paused for dramatic effect. "If you can match or better my stats for the season, I'll convince him to split the donation between the men's and the women's teams."

The annoyance on her face melted away. She glanced between Caroline and Lydia. There seemed to be some sort of silent communication taking place. Behind them, Kent watched in clear fascination. He pushed himself up from the ice and onto his skates.

"How do you know he'll agree to that?" Lydia asked.

"He's very close with my family. If I ask him to split his donation, he will. Plus, he met Grace at the gala. I could tell he liked her."

"What kind of stats are we talking here?" Bryce asked, chiming in to the conversation. I hadn't even noticed him at the edge of the rink, leaning against the barrier. Given that we'd barely exchanged more than a few words since our conversation on Halloween, I assumed this was his way of letting me know that everything was good between us.

"Let's keep it simple," Caroline said. "We can look at overall numbers for assists, goals, and face-offs won at the end of the season."

That would be a piece of cake. "I accept."

"And if I lose?" Grace asked.

"*When* you lose," I said, "you'll publicly apologize for the comments you made about me in the school newspaper and admit that I'm the better hockey player."

CHAPTER 11

Grace

News of the bet travelled fast. By the end of the school day, I was besieged by messages from my teammates who'd missed the action, all of them asking if the rumors about Sebastian and me were true. Admittedly, I was slightly embarrassed by the whole thing, but it would have been stupid to say no. If there was any chance that I could secure more funding for the women's program, I'd take it. Our move from McKinley Rink to DuLane Arena had only solved the issue of our lackluster training facility. There were other problems to address. The team could use new uniforms, for one, and the away-game travel bus had seen (and smelled) better days. But all thoughts of hockey vanished as my phone lit up with a text from Gabby. My pulse leapt. Despite my drunken messages over the weekend, she'd been radio silent. Fallen leaves crunched underfoot as I stopped along the tree-lined path in front of Nelson Library, heart hammering with nervous anticipation.

Gabs

I can't believe you drunk called me 4 times

So cringe

And don't call me gremlin. I'm not a kid anymore

And then something even crazier happened. Gabby's name flashed across the screen as my phone received an incoming call. I'd never answered so quickly.

"Hello?" I held my breath, half-convinced that this was some sort of prank call.

"Don't you have any friends at your new school, or boys to keep you busy?"

Despite the snark in her tone, I let out a breath of relief. It really was Gabs.

"Hello?"

"You've been ignoring me for weeks. I don't even get the courtesy of a thumbs-up anymore, what did you expect?" I tried my best impression of her snarky attitude.

"I've been busy," she said.

That was her excuse? If it were possible, I would have reached through the phone and shaken her by the shoulders. "Sam mentioned that you had a fight with Dad."

"That's why I called," she admitted. "I can't deal with him lately. He's so up in my business all the time, and I thought you could talk to him for me. He listens to you better."

My mouth fell open at her words. Gabby was asking for help? After avoiding me all summer, acting as if she wanted nothing to do with me, she was actually asking for my help? Maybe this was a step in the right direction.

"What's going on?" I asked. There was a long pause on her end, and for a brief moment, I thought she'd hung up.

"I quit dance without talking to Dad, and he's making a huge deal about it. Apparently, I *need* to pick up another hobby outside of school now that I'm not dancing, but there's nothing else I'm interested in."

"Why did you quit?" Something wasn't adding up. Gabby loved to dance, and she was damn good at it. Just last year she was placing at regional competitions.

"Does it matter?"

I bit down my frustration and took a long breath, willing myself to remain calm. "Please just tell me. I'm willing to talk to him if you have a good reason."

"I just don't want to do it anymore," Gabby said.

"That's not a good reason," I argued. "Did something happen? Are your instructors pushing you too hard?"

The front doors to Nelson Library flew open, and a group of laughing students spilled outside. I covered one ear and took a few steps away from the building, worried that I'd miss Gabby's reply.

"You sound just like Dad. I should have known better than to think you'd be on my side."

"Wait," I said quickly. "I'm on your side, Gabs, I promise. Explain why you don't want to dance anymore. Is it taking up too much of your time? Are the other girls being mean?"

"Sure. So, can you talk to him?"

She wasn't even trying to convince me. That was what worried me most. The whole "I don't give a fuck" attitude was so far from her normal demeanor.

"I'll talk to Dad about it," I agreed. "But he's right about finding another hobby. You'll be bored without dance. Trust me, I know you."

"You've been gone for three years, Grace. You don't know anything," she bit out.

It had been hard on Gabby when I'd left for Boston College, but it had been just as hard on me. We were always close, and spending most of the year without her was a huge adjustment. But I always made staying in touch with her a priority, despite my busy schedule.

"That's not fair." After all, she'd iced me out this summer. She was the one ignoring my texts or sending one-word replies every few weeks.

"But it's true," she snapped.

"If I really don't understand anything, then I'm not the right person to speak with Dad. Given that he *has* been around for the last three years, I'm sure he's made right decision."

Gabby remained silent for a moment. I had no idea what to expect from her at this point. She sounded like a completely different person right now.

"So much for the help, big sis. I won't bother you again."

The line went dead.

The chill of November whipped at my hair, blowing pieces into my line of vision as a shiver crept across my skin. There was an all too familiar prick of unease at the base of my neck. It was the same feeling I'd had leaving for Dallard University at the end of summer. Now more than ever, I was doubting that Gabby's attitude shift had anything to do with regular teenage angst. How had I let myself get so wrapped up in hockey and my rivalry with Sebastian that I completely forgot the reason I'd moved home in the first place? Gabby needed help—my help. I just had to figure out how the hell I was supposed to be there for her when she wanted nothing to do with me.

>> <<

Caroline's lips were moving, but I couldn't hear a word she spoke. Remi Wolf was blasting through my wireless headphones, her voice supported by a chaotic combination of instruments and engineered sound production. After a moment of staring at my roommate, I paused the song and pulled off my headphones. I had an inkling that the thirty-four open tabs on my computer were a contributing factor to my slower than normal reaction time. Could your eyes melt off from looking at a screen too long?

"I didn't take you for the suffer in silence type."

I cocked my head to the side, wondering what exactly she meant.

"You've been hiding out in the science building for the last week. What's going on?"

"I—nothing. I've had so much homework. It feels like I have a paper due every other day," I explained.

Caroline didn't look convinced. Nothing was wrong, per se, but I wasn't feeling like my normal self. Gabby was constantly in the back of my mind, and I had no idea how to make things better. Between my stress about her, my ever-increasing workload from school, and a new training regimen to ensure I stood at chance at winning the bet, I was exhausted. There was no taking my foot off the pedal at this point—not for any of it.

"You haven't come to lunch in forever. I'm insisting you take a break from whatever it is you're doing"—her eyes swept across the three open textbooks on the table—"and come eat."

Was *the* Caroline Hart—overachiever extraordinaire—implying that I was overworking myself? I glanced back at the endless tabs open on my laptop and realized how right she was.

"Come on, you need a break," she insisted.

I packed up my things and trailed after her. She kept glancing back as if to check that I was still there. Was she worried about losing me, or did she think I was going to run?

"There's been a new development," she said.

"A new development? In what?"

"You'll see."

I didn't have it in me to question her as we exited Barton Hall, crossed the quad, and entered the dining hall. We slipped into the line and grabbed our food before heading toward our normal spot. When I saw that there were men—hockey men, to be exact—sitting beside Lydia, the dots finally connected. Bryce, Landon, and Kent were perched around the circular table, eating lunch and chatting like it was a normal occurrence. Lydia didn't seem fazed in the slightest.

"I was wondering if I'd ever see you here," said Landon, snatching a carrot off my tray and biting into it with a loud chomp.

Rude.

"She's too busy for us," Caroline snarked in a playful tone.

I gave her an exasperated look. "Professor Lang assigned us an entire book to read before class on Friday." *And my sister is giving me heartburn with all the worrying I've been doing.*

"Meals should serve as an obligatory break," said Kent before he bit into a large sandwich. There was a twinkle in his bright blue eyes, and I was positive it had everything to do with his proximity to my blond roommate. She might not have realized it yet, but Kent had it *bad* for her.

"That's just your excuse to eat, like, ten meals a day," Caroline said.

He flashed her a smile and flexed his biceps. "I'm a growing boy, what can I say?"

"Is this a thing now?" I asked, motioning around the table with my fork. "Two weeks ago, we were deciding whether or not to toilet paper your house and hang tampons from the sad-looking bush in the front yard."

Lydia choked on her drink at my confession.

"It's a historical house, you know. Any damage would have certainly assured your expulsion."

My heart rate spiked at the sound of Sebastian's voice. He appeared over Kent's shoulder, one hand gripping the strap of his backpack and the other palming an apple. Holding my gaze from across the table, he lifted the fruit to his mouth and bit into it. My breath hitched at the resounding crunch.

"Are we all friends now?" he asked, taking the seat beside Kent, placing himself directly in front of me.

"If 'we' excludes you, then yes," I said with a sweet smile.

Sebastian grinned. "Does that mean you won't be attending my birthday celebration this weekend?"

"Finally turning five years old!" I exclaimed. "You must be proud."

"It's a big milestone. I can even count to ten."

"I can bring a cake. Would you prefer dinosaurs or race cars?"

He scoffed. "Cars on a cake are tacky. Anyway, Landon is already handling the cake."

The thought of Landon being in charge of anything that required planning made me laugh. "If you put him in charge of the cake, I'm confident strippers will burst out of it the moment you light the candles."

"Well, too bad you won't be there to see it. I don't allow non-friends access to my family lake house."

"I'm completely devastated," I deadpanned.

"Are they fighting or flirting?" Kent asked.

I promptly kicked him under the table, a silent warning to shut his mouth.

"So," Bryce said after a long moment of silence. "Got any big birthday wishes?"

I didn't miss the way that Sebastian's gaze jumped to me, those green eyes of his blazing with an intensity that, for a moment, looked a lot like wanting. But it was gone in a flash, so quickly that I convinced myself I was imagining things.

>> <<

Gabs

Hey...

Are you ever going to talk to me again?

I just need to know you're alive

Are you done being mad at me?

It's been like two weeks, come on...

I'm sorry. Just talk to me.

Gabs was determined to punish me after our argument. The only reply I'd gotten in the past two weeks was a middle finger emoji.

"Doesn't look like you're getting much studying done."

My head whipped up and I connected with a pair of gray-blue eyes. "Hey, Landon."

I locked my phone and placed it face down on the table. Around us, the student union buzzed with activity. I preferred to study someplace quiet, where I was less likely to run into people I knew, but I didn't have enough time between my morning classes to stop at the library.

"Mind if I join you?" Landon didn't wait for me to answer before he sat down in the empty chair across from me. If he had, I would have told him that I was just about to leave.

My phone buzzed, and I felt a tiny surge of hope that Gabby had finally come to her senses and texted me back. But when I flipped it over, the last name I expected flashed across the screen. *Matt.* We hadn't spoken since the night of the gala. It should have been me reaching out to apologize, but I'd gotten so swept up in the campaign and my sister that I hadn't thought about our conversation in weeks.

Matt

Just saw this: *DUupdates (@DUupdates)* on TikTok

Sucks to see those training conditions. Congrats on taking a stance.

>Does this mean I'm forgiven for being a total bitch?

>I'm sorry by the way

I think I can let it slide this once...

As long as I can see you when we come play Dallard this winter

>I think that can be arranged

"Boyfriend?" Landon was leaning across the table and looking down at the screen of my phone. I'd completely forgotten he was there.

"Ex," I said, snatching up the device and shoving it into my pocket.

He smirked at my admission. "You're a heartbreaker, aren't you?"

I could have sworn my eye twitched. This—Landon flirting, laying it on thick like he did with almost every other girl I'd seen him interact with—did absolutely nothing for me. He was nice enough, but I wasn't interested in him, or at the idea of jumping into another relationship. And even if I wanted a distraction, I wouldn't turn to Landon for it. Hell, I'd rather—

As if my twisted thoughts had conjured him from thin air, Sebastian was suddenly hovering over the table, surveying the two of us with a strange-looking smile. "This is cute. Am I witnessing a first date?"

"No," I said quickly.

"Grace, can I talk to you?"

Sebastian turned to Landon, who was watching the scene unfold with a pinched expression. The goalie let out an exaggerated sigh and pushed back his chair to stand.

"See you later?" he asked hopefully.

"Sure, see you next practice."

Landon's shoulder made brief contact with Sebastian's as he walked by, but the team captain barely flinched. He plopped down into the now abandoned chair. I waited for Sebastian to explain himself, but he simply made himself comfortable and took a long sip of water from the bottle in the side pocket of his backpack.

"Get on with it, then," I prompted.

"Get on with what?"

My eyes narrowed in suspicion. "Whatever it is you need to say."

"Oh, that? I don't actually need to speak with you. It just looked like you needed rescuing. Landon doesn't really know how to read the room."

My mouth fell open in a brief moment of surprise. Now that Sebastian and I weren't directly opposing one another, I didn't know how to interpret his moves. Had he really come here to rescue me, or was this part of some plan to scramble my head? We were no longer at war, but there was still the bet to think about.

"Don't overthink it," he said, as if reading my mind. "This just so happens to be my favorite table at the union, and I need to finish some work on a project before I get to class."

I let my gaze sweep over the straight line of his jaw and those striking eyes. All of this would be much easier if he weren't so nice to look at. Usually, when I disliked someone, it made them uglier in my mind. But for some reason, that didn't apply to Sebastian.

"What, never seen a guy before?"

"Not one with such an abnormally large head."

Sebastian smiled, a real, genuine smile that brought a subtle softness entirely at odds with the sharp lines of his face. "You can thank me later for rescuing you. But if you don't leave soon, you'll probably be late for class."

I glanced at the time on my phone and noticed that he was right. My next class was in less than fifteen minutes.

"I don't need rescuing," I said as I stood up from the table and slung my backpack over my shoulder. "You should know that by now."

"Sure, but I do enjoy the idea of you being indebted to me."

I rolled my eyes. "Don't get used to it."

CHAPTER 12
Sebastian

Grace was at my birthday. Grace Gillman—hockey star extraordinaire, women's activist, and hater of all things me—was currently standing in the front hallway of my favorite place in the world. She was the last person I'd expected to be here. When I'd told Caroline that she had a fat chance of convincing Grace to come, she'd only chuckled and said they were on the way.

"Who is that?" I asked Caroline as she leaned back against the kitchen counter beside me.

"Her best friend, Sam. I'm sorry I didn't tell you, but it was the only way I could convince her to come."

Usually I'd be annoyed that someone had been invited without my permission, especially because I was particular about who was welcome at the lake. But tonight, I wasn't bothered. The only thing I could think about was the long-legged girl who'd taken up permanent residence inside my head.

"As long as she doesn't steal anything or throw up on my mother's favorite rug."

Caroline smirked at me like she knew something I didn't. But before I could pry, Bryce walked into the kitchen with Kent,

Grace, and Grace's friend Sam trailing behind him. Sam was eyeing the back of Bryce as if she'd like to climb him. Next to each other, the difference in their size was almost laughable. She barely came past his elbow. The group stopped in a half circle before us, and Grace stepped forward, her cheeks flushed. She was wearing a crop top that displayed several inches of midriff, a pair of jeans hanging dangerously low on her hips.

"Happy birthday," she said softly.

"You came after all. Does this mean we're *finally* friends now?"

Grace was struggling to hold back a smile. "I'll agree to acquaintances. Anything else might be moving a little too fast?"

I shrugged. "You're the one at my birthday party."

"Okay, then we're one step *past* acquaintances but not fully in the realm of friendship. Fracquaintances." As soon as at the words left Grace's mouth, Sam let out a snort of laughter. Grace elbowed her in the side, face flushing even brighter.

"I think frenemies might fit you two better," suggested Bryce. The sound of his voice pierced the tension between Grace and me, and she seemed to sag in relief.

"This is my best friend, Sam," Grace said, pushing the tiny redhead to the front of the group. "She's met everyone else by now."

"Saved the best for last?"

"I'll let you believe that, at least for tonight," Grace said.

My lips twitched with the threat of a smile, but I forced it down. I couldn't let myself be pulled any further into her gravitational force. I needed to get through tonight without doing anything impulsive. There could be no flirting disguised as fighting, no intentional ruffling of feathers. If I could stay in control for the next twelve hours, seeing Grace at practice once a week would be a breeze.

>> <<

"This is a truth circle," Caroline said, smacking her hands against the hardwood, "where we ask scandalous questions or make people reveal their darkest secrets. If you really want to see how many hot dogs Landon can fit in his mouth, form your own dare circle. But please do it somewhere I don't have to watch."

"No one wants to see that," muttered Lydia.

I surveyed the room, cataloging everyone pulled into the "truth circle." Bryce was sitting on my right with Sam on the other side of him. Landon had squeezed in beside Grace, who scooted closer to her best friend the moment he sat down, leaving Kent, Caroline, Lydia, and Nina to complete the circle. I could have sworn Bishop and RT had fled the room with several other partygoers the moment Caroline had announced her idea.

"There's only one rule in the truth circle—you must tell the truth. You don't get to know the question beforehand, but the questioner must have your approval before they ask."

"You have to ask someone if they're willing to answer your question before they know what it is?" Sam questioned.

I snuck a glance at Grace. I'd spent the first few hours of the evening watching her from afar, imagining what it would be like to drag my hand along her lower back so I could feel the heat of her skin against my palm.

While everyone else was clearly intoxicated, some to the point of slurring their words, Grace's eyes were alert. She was still clutching the same can of beer that Bryce had handed her at the beginning of the night. I knew it was the same because I'd barely let her out of my sight since she got here. So far I'd managed to keep my distance, but as the evening progressed, I grew more restless in my desire to talk to her.

"Yes," Caroline said in answer to Sam's question. "The game is more about if you trust the person asking the question than the question itself. I can go first, if that makes things easier."

She took her time assessing the circle, looking each person in the eyes as she tried to determine who she wanted to pick. Eventually, her attention shifted to Grace.

"Grace, will you answer my question?"

Grace looked like a deer caught in headlights as everyone turned toward her. She pulled her bottom lip between her teeth as she considered. Grace was nervous. Her fingers tightened around the can as she glanced at Sam for either comfort or reassurance. If I had to guess, they'd known each other for most of their lives. I could tell by the way they interacted with each other. And right now, Grace was leaning on her comfort-person for support. I'd never witnessed such apprehension in her before this moment. She always seemed so sure of herself.

"If I say yes, I'll have to answer you? No matter how personal the question?"

Oh, she was definitely nervous. Seemed like Grace wasn't much for sharing, at least not when it came to personal matters.

"Yes, but I promise to go easy on you this first time," Caroline assured.

"Then yes, I accept." Sam's eyes widened in response to Grace's words.

"Tell me the truth—are you having fun tonight, celebrating Sebastian's birthday?"

Grace visibly relaxed as several people in the group booed.

"That's too easy," Landon shouted. "Make it harder than that!"

"I'm having fun," Grace admitted, her eyes meeting mine

from across the circle. "Thank you for having me, Sebastian. And for letting Sam tag along."

There was no suggestion of sarcasm in her response, as I would have expected, and I tried not to let it go to my head. I was sure it was only a matter of time before she went back to loathing my existence. Though, if I were being honest with myself, I didn't mind our bickering. Fighting with Grace was like the thrill of a breakaway. Riling her up, seeing that spark of fire in her eyes, felt like flying across the rink at full speed, nothing but ice and open space before me.

As the game went on, the questions grew dirtier. Sam was eager to answer just about any question thrown her way, while Grace nearly always declined. The only person who was visibly annoyed by her lack of participation was Landon. Each time she turned him down, I could see his frustration rise. After the third time, he shifted his attention to me.

"Birrrday boy Seb," he slurred, taking a long sip of his beer. "Will you answer my question?"

If it got him to stop pestering Grace, I was happy to oblige. "Yes."

Landon threw his fists up in celebration. In the process, drops of beer rained down over Grace. I opened my mouth to scold him, but he barreled forward with his question before I could speak.

"Did you and Kate break up over another girl?"

The circle went silent. I could see the triumphant gleam in his blurry, unfocused eyes. What the hell was he playing at? I'd never even mentioned the breakup to Landon, which should have been warning enough that it wasn't on the table for discussion.

"All right, all right," Bryce said. "Maybe it's time we move on to another drinking game."

"Good idea," Caroline said as she pushed to her feet. "Should we go to the basement? I think they have beer pong set up down there."

"No, come on. It's the rules, Sebby. Yagotta answer the—"

"No more truth circle," I snapped as I got up and stepped away. "And I'd advise you to stop while you're ahead. You're clearly wasted."

The group immediately dispersed, Kent leading the charge to the basement with Lydia and Nina following in his wake. Meanwhile, Landon held out a hand to help Grace up from the floor. Though she looked as if she'd rather touch dog shit, Grace politely accepted his help. He tugged at her arm with far too much force, the momentum launching her straight into his chest. Warning bells blared in the back of my head as his slimy hands dropped to her waist, his fingers pressed to the exposed skin along her lower back. Grace froze on the spot. Her entire body seemed to tense with Landon's newfound proximity. And just like that, my control flew right out the door. In less than a second, I was across the room, and in another I was yanking Landon away from her.

"Don't fucking touch her," I said, and everything grew still.

Bryce was between the two of us before I had the chance to wring Landon's neck. "You should drink some water and go to bed," he said.

Landon glared at me over Bryce's shoulder, looking for a moment as though he might protest before he stumbled off to one of the guest bedrooms, muttering something unintelligible under his breath. His exit did nothing to ease the tension in the room. If anything, the pressure only intensified as I locked eyes with Grace. She was standing stock-still, mouth open in an expression of alarm. No one else spoke. Somehow, the silence was loud enough to make my ears ring.

I did the only thing that came to mind and bolted out the back door. My feet carried me down the slopped hill leading to the waterfront in an all-out sprint. I barely registered the biting cold. Only when my toes were hanging off the edge of the dock, body positioned precariously between solid ground and open air, did I come to a stop.

Happy birthday, Sebastian, I thought. One year older but never wiser. Once again, I'd failed to overcome my own impulses. That's what Grace did to me: she robbed me of my restraint.

"Are you going to jump?"

I startled, head whipping around. The outline of Grace's body was backlit by the moonlight. Why had she followed me out here? I needed space away from her frustratingly distracting presence to set my mind right.

"I wasn't planning to," I said, shifting back to face the lake and looking down at the water below me. "It's a bit cold for a dip."

Grace moved forward until she was shoulder to shoulder with me, her toes curled over the edge of the sun-bleached wood. We both spoke at the same time.

"I'm sorry."

"Thank you."

Silence.

"Why?" she asked, brow furrowed in a look of confusion.

"Why what?"

"Why go through all that trouble for someone you don't like?" she asked.

If only she knew what I really thought about her. All the dirty, depraved things we did in my head. "It doesn't have to make sense," I told her.

Would she even believe me? If I admitted the truth—that I

couldn't stand the sight of Landon touching her—she might laugh in my face, or accuse me of being a liar in addition to an arrogant asshole.

"Make it make sense," she demanded, shifting to face me instead of the water. "Do you and Landon have a history? Why would you—"

Grace stopped herself short, but I knew exactly what she meant to say. She couldn't fathom why I'd help her, not after everything I'd said and done.

"Why does there have to be an explanation?"

"Because there just does!" she shouted. "Will you please fucking look at me?!"

Slowly, I pivoted to face her. Grace's frustration painted a stunning picture. She looked fierce with the moon reflected in her eyes, chest heaving up and down as she tried to contain the rage building within. My body seemed to move without consulting my mind. Several inches of space between us vanished. We were practically touching.

"Do you really want to know why I was seconds away from pummeling my teammate in the face?" I would have happily ruined my hand bashing in his nose if it pleased her.

"Yes. I need to understand."

I shook my head. I didn't even fully understand. With Grace, sense was always an afterthought.

"I do!" She slapped her palms against my chest and pushed out in anger, but I was impossible to move. "Please, tell me."

"Would it change anything?" I could feel the heat of her skin through the material of my shirt. It drove away the little reason left within me. "Would you think of me differently if you knew that watching him touch you felt ten times worse than seeing my face on the cover of that article or knowing that you set me up?"

At last, Grace was speechless. She didn't step away or call me a liar. She just stared at me as if my confession had been given in tongues. There was another way to get the message across, one that was sure to land. Slowly, I placed one hand along the curve of her waist, testing the waters. Grace's breath hitched, but she didn't push me away as I caressed the side of her cheek with my other hand, my fingers slowly pushing into the hair at the back of her head. A little noise of surprise left her lips. I leaned forward until our faces were nearly touching, lips a hair's breadth apart. I paused, willing myself to hold steady and giving her time to come to the realization that she didn't want me. But Grace didn't push me away or ask me to stop. If anything, her body leaned into the heat of my own, eyes dropping to my lips.

Fuck it.

I surged forward, my mouth falling over hers like it was the key to my salvation. As soon as our lips touched, I was met with a terrifying realization: this woman had the power to devastate me. Heartbeat in my ears, I breathed her in. Grace didn't push me away like I was expecting her to. Instead, her hands fisted the material of my shirt, and she pulled me closer, our bodies melting into one another. Everywhere we touched came ablaze with heat. I sucked her bottom lip into my mouth, and she gasped in response. Her tongue swept across the seam of our lips, and I opened up to give her access, white-hot need rushing through my body.

Every single particle of my being could feel the kiss, each nerve connected to the next, sending signal after signal of euphoria. The lines of our bodies pressed together, the feel of her hair clenched between my fingers, the taste of her lips; it was all too much. No amount of lust or wanting could have prepared me for the truth of what kissing Grace felt like. Her body surrendered itself to me as I traced one hand along the dip of her waist and over the top of her shoulder until my palm cupped the skin of her cheek. I wanted all of her, every single morsel she was willing to give over. Her breath, her scent—I wanted it all. I was so swept up in the bliss that I missed the moment things shifted.

Grace came to her senses in a split second, the moan on her lips transforming into a startled gasp. Her grip on my shirt loosened, fingers spreading until her palm was flat against my chest. Suddenly, the world was tilting, the lake rushing forward in an almighty lurch. My body hit the water with a loud splash. Cold shocked my senses, rendering me motionless as I sank below the surface. Everything fell still as the darkness consumed me, but the moment my feet touched the muck at the bottom, I pushed, surging upwards. I emerged in front of the dock with a gasp. Moonlight danced across the rippling surface of the black water.

Grace was fleeing up the hill, her hair streaming behind her as she ran for the safety of the house. I pulled myself from the water and collapsed onto the dock. A sudden, almost hysterical-sounding laugh burst from me as realization dawned. Grace could feel it too, this strong current pulling us together. There was want and need in the way she'd returned my kiss. She could deny it all she wanted, or push me into another freezing lake, but that wouldn't change anything. And now that I knew how she felt, I'd take pleasure in reminding her every single moment of the day.

Happy birthday indeed.

CHAPTER 13
Sebastian

The lake house brought me a special kind of peace that was impossible to replicate. Not even standing inside DuLane Arena had the same effect. Bill had bought the property a year after he'd married my mom. I could still remember the first time we'd pulled down the long wooded drive, patches of sun poking down from the sky after two weeks of nonstop rain. Even though my dad had never been here, I could feel him with us when we were out on the lake after a long day of fishing, or standing around the bonfire cooking pudgy pies at the end of the night. I never felt more like myself than I did sitting on the dock at the break of dawn, watching the sun's reflection slowly creep across the glass-like water.

"Are you ready to go?"

I blinked and glanced away from the lake, eyes shifting to the person standing beside me on the back deck—square jaw, brown eyes, black hair: Bryce.

"Ready."

It was a complete lie.

I did one more pass through the house to ensure the lights were turned off and the security system was set. Bryce followed me out the front door toward the only remaining vehicle parked along the twisting driveway. Everyone had left hours ago, but I wasn't ready to leave. I never was when it came to this place.

"Should I be worried about the team dynamic?" Bryce squeezed his large frame into the driver's seat and started the car.

"No," I said, contemplating the events of last night. "I just got carried away."

After taking a shower to wash off the lake (and avoid hypothermia), I'd stumbled into bed and spent the early hours of the morning staring at the ceiling fan. Learning that Grace and I shared a mutual attraction, that she too was struggling to resist this strange connection between us, came as a relief, but the more I thought about it, the more that relief shifted into concern. I'd never wanted her close to begin with because I knew she had the power to pull my focus from hockey. Now, there was no avoiding the girl. And to make matters worse, I knew that she felt something for me, even after everything that had transpired between us.

"You want to tell me what happened last night?"

"Not re—"

"No more bullshit, Evans. No more snapping at me when I ask how things are going. Be honest with me for one fucking second."

I dropped my head into my hands, letting out a long sigh. It was so much easier to keep to myself. Speaking the words out loud made it real.

"I kissed Grace."

Bryce didn't say anything. He was waiting for me to say more.

"It feels wrong to be fixated on another girl—one who's proven she can't be trusted—when I just got out of a two-year relationship with Kate."

"Feeling guilty is normal," said Bryce, "but it doesn't necessarily mean you've done something wrong. Don't let that stop you from pursuing whatever or whoever you want."

"That's the thing, Bryce. The only thing I *should* want to focus on is hockey. Grace is one massive fucking disturbance to my equilibrium. I'm out of control when she's around."

I was scared that she had the power to make me forget about hockey altogether.

"I don't know what to do," I admitted. "I want her, and I fucking hate that I want her at the same time."

"Have you ever considered that your feelings for her could be a good thing?" Bryce asked.

The last time I'd let someone into my heart, they'd crept onto the ice during the most important moment of my career. And then I spent the next year resenting her, even though it wasn't really her fault. To this day, I still thought about a reality where Kate and I had never gotten together. Would things be different? Would I already be playing for Detroit?

No, letting Grace in would be a mistake. Right?

"It doesn't even matter," I said, shaking my head. "Grace might be attracted to me, but she hates me all the same. She pushed me into the fucking lake last night."

Bryce's booming laugh filled the car. "You and Grace are like different sides of the same coin. She might get under your skin, but that's what you like about her. And I'm pretty sure that's what she likes about you . . . among other things."

"She didn't have to push me into the lake," I muttered. "All she had to do was pull away."

"And what does that tell you?"

"Oh, I don't know. That she hates my guts and wanted to see me drown?"

"It could be that," he said, his fingers tapping against the steering wheel, "or maybe she's just as scared as you are about how she feels."

That was not a possibility I was ready to consider. Thankfully, the exit for Clearwater appeared in the distance, a reminder that we were meeting my mom and stepdad for a late lunch. Seeing my family would be a welcome distraction. They were visiting for my birthday, even though the drive from Illinois was well over four hours. When I'd told my mom that Bryce and I would be heading back from the lake house together, she'd insisted he join.

Bryce took the Clearwater exit and turned left toward the Belle Bistro. We pulled into an almost empty parking lot a few minutes later. Bill's Cadillac was parked in a spot at the front.

"Happy birthday, my love!"

My mother was upon me the moment we entered the establishment. The bell on the door was still ringing as she pulled me into her arms and crushed me against her with the strength of a person three times her size.

"How was the drive?" I asked, pulling away to inspect her. She was wearing a blue and green Dallard hockey sweatshirt that brought out the color in her eyes.

"Long as always, but we stopped at this really good cheese place on the way. And Bryce, it's so good to see you!" As she descended on him, I turned my attention to Bill.

My stepfather was wearing a sweatshirt to match my mom's, though he'd paired it with a long-sleeved turtleneck and a nice pair of slacks. Bill wasn't the best at doing casual, but I appreciated the effort.

"Good to see you, Sebastian," he said, clapping a hand over my shoulder in greeting.

"You too, Bill."

The hostess ushered us to a table in front of a large window that overlooked the parking lot. She went to get a round of water before taking our orders.

"Are you guys staying at the lake house?" I asked.

Mom nodded. "We'll get to see just how well you cleaned up."

"Hopefully nothing is damaged beyond recognition," Bill teased.

We fell into an easy chatter, jumping from one topic to the next until my mom mentioned the upcoming holiday. "Bryce, will you be joining us for Thanksgiving this year?"

It was hard for Bryce to get home on short breaks given the distance to Miami. For the last few years, he'd spent Thanksgiving with our family in Illinois.

"We can't come this year, Mom. Our scheduled is packed, so the coaches are hosting a team Thanksgiving."

"That's too bad," she said with a frown. "Maybe I can send you a pie in the mail."

Bryce and I met each other's eyes from across the table with a smirk. That would be a new one. My mom had a history of sending us care packages throughout the year. Sometimes, we'd come home to find a massive box packed full of non-perishables, toilet paper, and other essential items. I couldn't remember the last time any of us had bought toothpaste.

"Anyway, this is for you." Mom placed a birthday bag on the table in front of me.

She nodded at me as if to say, *Go ahead and open it*, and I pulled the tissue paper. There was a flash of faded blue material, and I sucked in a sharp breath. Slowly, I reached inside and dragged my fingers across the familiar pilled fabric. My dad had worn his Toronto Maple Leafs crew neck religiously. Sometimes, he'd go five days in a row without taking the damn thing off. Slowly, I lifted the relic to my nose, desperate to find if it still smelled of him. An infinitesimal trace of his scent clung to the material. I clutched the crew neck to my chest and breathed in a hint of cedar. For just a moment, he was here in the restaurant, wishing me a happy birthday in person.

"He would have wanted you to have it," Mom said, her eyes shining with tears. "You always begged him to let you wear that ratty old thing."

"Thanks, Mom," I said, voice strained, blinking back tears I refused to shed.

The sweatshirt was stained, a relic from the past, one that had seen better days. But it was a reminder of why I was here and what I was doing all of this for. Hockey was how I honored his memory. It was all I had left of him.

>> <<

Grace

I woke with a gasp on my lips, my body trembling. As the world came into focus, I realized there was a body shifting beside me, unintelligible words drifting from beneath the blanket. Sam's messy curls appeared a moment later. The sight of her face was all it took to trigger a sudden onslaught of word vomit.

"I kissed Sebastian last night."

She blinked away the sleep in her eyes as a yawn escaped her mouth. I gave her some time to digest my words, but there was no immediate response of shock that I'd been expecting. "This is the part where you're supposed to say, 'What the hell is wrong with you?'"

"The only thing wrong with you is that you haven't been laid in months." She looked me up and down with a shake of her head. "If someone that hot nearly ripped off his friend's head for touching me, I would fall straight onto his dick."

"Are you forgetting how awful he was to me when the school year started?" I reminded her. "Sebastian hid rotting meat inside our training facility."

"You won in the end, right? And you got your revenge. Don't you think it's time to turn over a new leaf or whatever?"

Maybe Sam had a point, but turning over a new leaf was one thing. Last night, I'd skipped that step and jumped ahead by like eighty paces. "You promised you would keep me from doing anything stupid! That's the only reason I agreed to go."

"You asked me to stop you from picking a fight with the birthday boy, not to stop you from making out with him," she argued.

To be fair, I'd never considered kissing Sebastian as a possible outcome. I'd been too worried about offending him on his birthday. I barely drank a sip of alcohol out of fear that he'd do something to trigger my sass, especially because I'd promised Caroline I'd be nice. Suddenly the room felt impossible hot. I tossed the blanket off my legs and leapt from the bed. Sam was like a radiator in the morning.

"Was it good?"

I shrugged and leaned against my desk. "He definitely knows what he's doing."

"That's all you have to say?"

"It doesn't matter how good the kiss was, it's never going to happen again."

"Not even after he defended your honor?" she asked with a smirk, pushing herself up onto her elbows in bed.

"Him defending my honor *is* the problem. It makes no sense. What if—" *What if Sebastian is just messing with my head?* I wouldn't put it past him given our tumultuous past, and I couldn't forget about the bet. I knew he wanted to win just as much as I did. Who was to say this wasn't part of his strategy?

"It's pretty simple, Grace. All that tension between the two of you has to go somewhere. Better it be hot sex than murdering each other."

"Maybe you're right," I said, "or maybe this is part of a bigger plan to punish me for everything I've done."

"Punishing you by giving you pleasure?"

No, I thought. The punishment would be making me feel something for him and then pulling the rug out from under me. After all, the reason I'd pushed him in the lake was because I didn't have the strength to pull myself away.

"Just forget about it," I said, stretching my arms over my head. "Why can't we talk about your love life for once? What about that date you went on with the radiologist from work?"

"Apparently he has four kids, and that's four kids more than I want," she said dismissively. "All I'm saying is you and Sebastian are bound to collide again. It's only a matter of time."

I shook my head dismissively. "I can't talk about this anymore." I didn't even want to think about it. Not when I was drowning in schoolwork and still trying to figure out a way to reconnect with Gabby.

"Are you coming home for Thanksgiving this week?" Sam asked, and I nearly sagged in relief at the change of subject.

"We have an away game the night after, so our coaches decided to host a Ravens Thanksgiving extravaganza. They want us all to bond."

She snickered at that. "I'm sure Sebastian would love to bo—"

"Absolutely not," I warned.

"Have you and Gabby talked since your fight?"

Regret tightened my throat at the thought of our argument. I never should have snapped at Gabby, even if she was being a major bitch. It had only served to increase the distance between us, making me feel more helpless in my attempt to fix things.

"No, and I'm really worried," I admitted. "She won't talk to me or listen to what I have to say. I know that seeing a therapist would help her, but I'm nervous about how my dad will react to the suggestion."

He wasn't a fan of medical professionals, especially those working in the mental health sector. It was just another piece of fallout from my mother. Because even after doing everything right—getting her professional help, trying different medications, and admitting her to an in-patient program—she'd still left. These days, he wouldn't even like going to the doctor for his annual checkup.

"If you want, I'm happy to talk to your dad. It might be helpful to hear things from a nurse's perspective."

"No, thanks," I said, knowing how fragile the situation was. "I'll talk to him when I'm home for Christmas break in a few weeks. If he won't listen to me, then I'll call you in for backup."

This is going to work, I told myself. *It has to*.

>> <<

Wednesday was so eager to see the fallout from the weekend that it pressed fast-forward on Monday and Tuesday. Dread filled my stomach at the thought of our shared practice with the men's team, and for good reason. The last time I'd seen Sebastian, he had been plunging into the icy lake. In other words, today's training session had a great likelihood of ending disastrously. Facing him meant facing the fact that we'd kissed, and worse, that I'd liked it. No amount of self-reflection could help me make sense of that night. It wasn't every day you found yourself lusting after someone you loathed.

"Grace, are you listening to me?"

Caroline was waving her hand in front of my face.

"Sorry. I'm a little out of it."

"Lydia and I are worried about you." When I shot her a look of confusion, she added, "You've been MIA since Sunday. I literally haven't seen you in two days. You're almost never home, and if you are, you're sleeping."

I wasn't sure what or exactly how much to say. Since this weekend, I'd felt entirely off-kilter. Sam was the only one who knew about my kiss with Sebastian, and I wanted it to stay that way. What would Caroline think of me if she knew I was locking lips with the devil himself? Would she judge me? I didn't want to find out.

"School's been a lot," I said, glancing down at my feet so I didn't have to look her in the eyes. I didn't feel great about withholding the full truth of why I'd been so distant, especially given everything she'd done to support my crusade against Sebastian. "It's been impossible to keep up with everything."

"I totally understand," she said, tightening the laces on her skates. "I feel like my professors are trying to punish me for being a well-rounded student." She continued to chat as we walked through the tunnel and entered the arena. It took all my strength not to look across the rink in search of Sebastian. "How are you doing after the party this weekend? The whole Sebastian and Landon thing was so intense."

"I'm fine." I recalled a sudden flash of green—Sebastian's eyes blazing in fury as he clutched the front of Landon's shirt.

"You disappeared for a while after. I'm sorry I didn't check on you. I was so drunk, and I could have sworn I saw you and Sebastian down by the lake." She laughed a little awkwardly at the admission, almost as if she wanted me to confirm the information.

"Yeah, no biggie," I said, forcing a smile onto my face. "We've all been there."

Caroline seemed to be dissecting my every movement. It felt like I was getting a glimpse into her future as a criminal defense attorney, and I was terrified.

"So," I said, dragging out the vowel longer than necessary as Lydia sided up beside us. "Are you and Kent a thing?"

Lydia's lips twitched into a smile as Caroline shot me a baffled look. "I don't know what gave you that impression," she said.

For someone so smart, Caroline was clueless when it came to guys. Kent had been flirting with her all night at Sebastian's party. "Oh, come on, Caroline. You guys bicker like an old married couple. But it's in an endearing way. Gives off couple vibes, you know?"

"Totally," Lydia confirmed.

"It's not like that," said Caroline. "He just thinks I'm a know-it-all and likes to remind me."

That was denial if I'd ever heard it.

"He likes to remind you because he likes to talk to you."

"Seriously, Grace, it's not like that," she insisted.

It totally was, but Caroline was being willfully blind because she thought her personality was too much for most men. I, however, loved that she was unapologetically herself. Yes, at times she could be a know-it-all, but there were guys out there who liked dominant women. Kent had this glimmer in his eyes when he spoke to Caroline. There was definitely interest on his end.

"I'm not taking boy advice from the girl who still talks to her ex," she snarked, and I instantly regretted our talk about Matt on the drive to the lake house. Caroline had seen us texting and went straight Nancy Drew on my ass. "That's like the biggest dating no-no."

She was annoyingly good at changing the subject or turning things around on other people. It made her difficult to argue with in addition to the fact that she was usually right.

"Okay," I said, holding my hands up. "I'm dropping it."

Without the immediate distraction of a conversation, I found myself instinctively searching the rink for Sebastian. I caught sight of his practice jersey just as the whistle blew for warm-ups. At first, I kept as far away from him as possible, moving to the back of the group as we looped the perimeter. But once practice was in full swing, I realized there was no point in trying to avoid him because he was already avoiding me. He barely paid me any notice, even as we were forced to team up for a six-passer shooting drill. It was a stark contrast to our first shared practice.

This was the best possible outcome I could have expected after the events of his birthday party. There was no scene in front of the coaches or attempts to expose our moonlit kiss. But even as I told myself this, I couldn't ignore the tightening in my chest or the rush of disappointment that followed. For whatever twisted reason,

I much preferred his relentless teasing to this cold indifference. It didn't make sense; nothing ever did when it came to Sebastian. I'd lost the plot and was descending straight into madness. There was no other explanation, no way to make sense of my feelings. How could I both want Sebastian's attention and detest his very existence?

"Hey, Grace, can I talk to you?"

I was already frowning when I turned to face Landon. At the sight of my scowl, his eyes fell to the ice. *Good*, I thought. At least he had the decency to look ashamed.

"I want to apologize about this weekend."

"Are you always so handsy?" I asked.

Landon's throat bobbed. "No, I promise. That wasn't me. And if my sister were here, she would smack me upside the head for acting like such a loser. I'm truly sorry I made you uncomfortable."

"Apology accepted," I said, sensing that he was entirely sincere—or absolutely terrified of me. I liked to think it was a little of both. "But don't think I can't stick up for myself. Sebastian might have beaten me to the punch, but I'm just as capable of saying no."

Landon smiled. "I'll never make that mistake, not after watching you take down the golden boy in a matter of weeks."

It was as if Sebastian could sense we were talking about him. Over Landon's shoulder, our eyes connected for the first time all morning. It looked as though Sebastian had smelled something truly foul from the way his upper lip was curled in disgust. I had no idea what to make of him or of the way he'd been acting all practice. Clearly, he was mad. That much made sense. But there was something else in his expression that set me on edge. All I knew was that it couldn't bode well for me.

>> <<

Sebastian

"I hate dressing up for Thanksgiving." I pulled at the collar of my shirt. It felt like a trap. What was the point of wearing a button-up and nice pants when the entire goal of the controversial holiday was to eat yourself into a coma?

"But everyone looks so nice."

Kent sounded far off, like he was on another planet. Caroline was standing in his line of vision, dressed in her usual shade of pink and sipping a glass of cider next to the refreshment table. *Shocker.* If he ever worked up the courage to ask her out in a way that she couldn't interpret as joking, I'd buy him a round of shots and a lottery ticket.

Today felt weird. Spending Thanksgiving in a barn on the edge of Coach Riley's property was not how I'd expected to celebrate. At least she'd had the foresight to station heaters throughout the drafty building. In the last few days, the temperature had dropped significantly. Winter was just around the corner.

"Why does it feel like this is a wedding?" Kent mused, looking up at the lights dangling from the ceiling. "Do you think Dawson and Riley hit it off?"

"Coach Riley is married. To a woman," came a familiar voice from beside me. Coach Dawson had appeared out of nowhere, wearing the same exact button-down and dress pants from the gala. "And I'm also married. Thought you'd know that after four years on my team."

I held back a snort of laughter as Kent's ears reddened.

"I need to speak with Sebastian. Give us a moment, will you?" Kent was gone in the blink of an eye, leaving us in an isolated spot near the back of the barn.

"Everything okay, Coach?"

"Yeah, everything's fine. I just wanted to check in with you. Has Duncan sent in his usual progress report?"

Shock stole my breath in an instant. How could I have forgotten? Since being drafted, my scout from the Red Wings always sent a mid-season summary. The report provided an overview of my strengths and instructions on how to improve or further develop certain skills. Given my injury last season, the only time we'd communicated in the past year had been to discuss my recovery process.

"Sebastian?"

I grabbed my phone and started frantically scrolling though my email, desperate to find something from Duncan. But there was nothing in the last few weeks. I went back to the top of my inbox and searched for his email address. Nothing at all.

"Son, it's nothing to worry about," Coach Dawson said, setting a gentle hand on my shoulder. "I'm sure it'll come in the next few weeks."

I could barely hear his voice over the ringing in my ears. What if it wasn't coming? I tried to recall when exactly the report had come in my freshman and sophomore years. It was always *before* Thanksgiving. I was sure of that.

"I'm going to get some air."

Dawson nodded and said, "Take some deep breaths. You have nothing to worry about. I'm your coach, so I can say that with one hundred percent certainty."

I wanted him to be right, but as I tore out of the barn and into the brisk evening air, there was no mistaking the panic crawling up my throat. I veered to the left and rounded the side of the barn, my foot catching on a discarded box of supplies. As I stumbled around the corner, I nearly fell head-first into the side of the barn. Instead, I caught myself against the wooden structure, and cold seeped through the skin of my palms. *Calm down*, I thought, desperate to ease the sudden nausea building in my stomach. Coach was right. There was nothing to worry about, right?

"Are you okay?"

I spun around, breathing shallow, heart seizing within the confines of my chest. Grace was bathed in orange hues from the setting sun, arms wrapped around herself protectively despite the long sleeves of her purple dress. A strange sensation moved through me as she took a hesitant step forward. I no longer felt in danger of asphyxiation; my panic was subsiding. Even my hands felt more steady as I wiped them across the front of my pants and straightened up.

It was pretty fucking obvious by now that I couldn't escape this absurd force pulling me toward Grace, not even if it jeopardized the future I'd been planning since I was twelve years old. From the moment I'd seen her and Landon together at practice, I was done for. I'd tried to drive her away—done everything in my power to make her hate me. And maybe Grace did hate me, but that hadn't stopped her from kissing me back on the night of my birthday, and it didn't change how frustratingly right she felt in my arms. I could pretend all I wanted, but there was no driving her out of my mind. Grace was too far under my skin; the infection had already taken root. I needed her like I needed hockey, and that was a terrifying realization.

"Sebastian, what's wrong?"

Grace took another slow step forward, until she was nearly close enough for me to reach out and touch her. In less than a second, I had her pressed against the barn, my arms on either side of her head, face buried in the corner of her neck. I took a long drag of her cherry perfume, my eyes fluttering closed at the intoxicating smell. Grace held herself deathly still, as if she were fighting the very same instinct that drove me to pin her against the barn. I lifted my head slowly and placed my lips along the shell of her ear. She shivered, but I knew it had nothing to do with the cold.

"Is this wrong?" I asked in a low whisper. "Am I scaring you?"

She didn't respond immediately. Only after a painfully long moment, one that I spent convincing myself that I had completely terrified her, did Grace shake her head. Her admission came as a relief, but it was short-lived. As I leaned forward to press my lips to her jaw, someone called out her name.

"Grace, where'd you go?"

A growl rumbled in the back of my throat, and I tore myself away just as Lydia turned the corner. She stopped dead in her tracks at the sight of us standing close, Grace's back pressed to the exterior of the building. There was no mistaking the hint of concern in her eyes as she surveyed the scene.

"Is everything okay?" Lydia asked.

I didn't miss the accusation in her tone.

"Yeah, everything is okay," Grace said with a shaky breath.

I gave myself one brief moment to take her in, wanting one last look at golden hour reflected in her stare. I'd worship at her feet if she let me, no matter our past. All she had to do was ask. But then she turned and headed back into the barn with her teammate.

"Happy Thanksgiving, Grace."

CHAPTER 14

Sebastian

Despite our unforgettable kiss on my birthday, or the heated moment we'd shared at Thanksgiving, Grace was still in the denial stage of her feelings. There was no other explanation for the lengths to which she went to avoid me. It wasn't entirely unexpected, not considering our past, but that didn't assuage my frustration. And after a week of catching glimpses of her retreating form around DuLane, and seeing her flee from the lunch table the moment I sat down, I was ready to make her pay. If I had to suffer in my wanting for Grace, she'd have to suffer in her wanting for me.

My plan to ambush Grace on common ground was simple, though it required me to roll out of bed even earlier than I preferred, which was saying a lot. The girl was relentless when it came to training, which, rather annoyingly, was only more of a turn-on. Until meeting her, I'd never known anyone who dedicated as much time to hockey as I did. Feeling more determined than ever, I arrived at the empty training facility with a skip in my step. When I reached the weight room, I settled onto a machine along the back wall and waited. It gave me a perfect view of the entrance, and I didn't have to wait long. Grace arrived ten minutes later, her steps featherlight as she slipped through the door. I could hear the faint sound of music pouring from the wireless headphones perched over her ears. Silently, I watched her approach the row of stationary bikes and settle onto one. This *is* going to be fun. If there was anything I'd learned from the past few months, it was that Grace looked incredibly sexy when I got her all worked up. Her head whipped around as I slid onto the bike beside her.

"What do you want?" she asked, pulling her headphones down to sit around her neck.

"It's bold of you to assume I want anything other than a warm-up."

She glanced at the empty row of bikes before returning her gaze to me, eyes narrowed in a look of suspicion. "Do you need to use the bike directly next to me?"

"This is my favorite one. I never have to adjust the seat height."

"Move."

I smirked. "What are you going to do if I don't? Push me off?"

The horrified look on her face was more gratifying than I could have imagined. She could pretend that our kiss meant nothing, but I wasn't going to let her forget about it. Grace looked away ashamedly and, without another word, slipped on her headphones and resumed her warm-up. The entire time, I remained on the bike beside her, allowing my gaze to stray over the length of her body. I knew she could feel my eyes on her, and I took pleasure in the way her cheeks grew warm under my attention.

She finally slowed to a stop fifteen minutes later, abandoning the bike station after a long chug of water. I considered the possibility that Grace was about to flee the scene, but I had a feeling her pride would win out. As expected, I was right. There was a stubborn set to her shoulders as she laid out a mat in the stretching zone.

"What do you want, Sebastian? Why are you following me around?" she asked when I approached.

"I figured I ought to check out your training regimen, given our little competition."

Grace shot me a look of exasperation as I plopped down beside her.

"And," I said, shifting to face her head-on, "I wanted to figure out why you were avoiding me. We are, after all . . . what did you call it again? Oh yes—*fracquaintances*."

"Not my best moment," she huffed. "And I'm not avoiding you. Some people just aren't meant to be friends."

Grace was right about one thing. We were *never* going to be friends. It would have to be more than that, for me. And based on her disappearing act, I was confident she felt the same. What other reason would she have to avoid me?

"Then join me for my lifting session. If you're not avoiding me, that is."

Grace bit her bottom lip in consideration. The sight made me want to lean over and claim her mouth for a second time.

"I'm working on mobility today," she said.

"Perfect, I really need to loosen up." When I saw how unimpressed she was with my words, I added, "Give me a chance to show you that I'm not the same asshole you met in September."

Damn, I sounded desperate, but I was past the point of caring.

"Fine," she relented, though she didn't sound happy about it. "Just this once."

I flashed her a broad smile. "Tell me where you want me."

She only arched an eyebrow in response, but I could see the telltale signs of a blush in the heat that crept up her neck. *Good*, I thought. I wanted her mind deep in the gutter beside mine. If we were both there, I'd feel less alone.

Grace grabbed another mat from the back wall and passed it over. I laid it alongside hers, leaving just a sliver of space between them.

"Let's start with ankle gliders," she instructed, settling onto her right knee.

I mirrored her position, one knee down and one leg bent at a ninety-degree angle. Slowly, we shifted forward, extending our knees over our toes before returning to the starting position. After eight reps on one ankle, we switched to the other. The entire time, I followed Grace's slow breathing cadence, in through my nose and out through my mouth. My eyes lingered along the muscles in her calves and quads, entranced by the way they pulled tight and flexed with each of her movements.

"Do you always come in before practice to work out?"

She shook her head. "I prefer to split things up by morning and evening, but I've been swamped with schoolwork lately. I need as much time as I can get after classes to catch up."

"So very studious," I teased.

"The same could be said for you, Evans," she said, glancing at me from the corner of her eye. "I've seen you in the library more than most athletes."

"I can assure you I'm not the studious type. I didn't even plan to finish school originally. But I need to keep my grades up to stay on the team," I admitted.

"You were drafted by Detroit, right?"

I nodded my head. "They wanted me to get some experience in the NCAA before signing a pro contract. I figured it would happen after sophomore year, but . . ." I trailed off, my throat tightening.

"But you tore your ACL," she finished.

"And a few other things in the knee region, but my ACL was a mess." I looked down at the long scar that stretched across my knee as if to remind myself that it was all in the past.

"What about you?"

"What about me?" She sounded exasperated, as if she'd been expecting the question all along and was unwilling to answer.

Okay. Maybe I needed to be more specific. "Have you ever considered going pro?"

Grace had more than enough talent to pursue a proffesional career in hockey. Not only were her skating and stickhandling skills remarkable, but she made quick, intelligent decisions on the ice. That's what made a great player—the choices they made in high-impact moments. Grace paused at the bottom of her Cossack squat as she considered my question. I was impressed by the depth of her stretch. Most hockey players had chronically tight hip flexors, but she was only a few inches from the floor. The sight brought forth a myriad of dirty thoughts.

"I love hockey," she stated, pushing up and then settling down to stretch out her opposite hip, "and at one point, I considered playing professionally. But I want to go to grad school. I just finished submitting my applications for my master's degree."

I'd never admit it, but a small part of me itched for the chance to do the same—to leave hockey behind and never look back. I often wondered what my life would be like without it, but my love for the sport always won out. It was entrenched into everything that made me who I was. I couldn't let go. I couldn't let him down.

"What kind of programs did you apply for?"

"Social work. There's an amazing program at the University of Chicago, but it's nearly impossible to get into. I want to stay as close to home as possible."

It came as no surprise to learn that Grace was interested in a career that involved helping other people. The girl was annoyingly selfless. After all, the terms of our bet provided no direct benefit to her. Any money donated to the women's program would only impact future hockey players.

"But I could see myself coaching in the future. I like kids," she added.

Nothing could stop the flood of naughty images—ones featuring Grace on the ice dressed in a sexy teacher outfit, with knee-high socks and a long pointer stick. It was impossible not to think of all the ways I wanted to fuck her. Maybe if we slept together, I wouldn't feel so strung out over the girl. Who was I kidding? Grace wasn't the type of girl you fucked out of your system. She was the girl who became even harder to forget once you finally got a taste. This past week had been proof enough of that.

"What's that look for?" she asked. "Your eyes glazed over for a second. Am I boring you?"

"You're not boring me." *Trust me*, I wanted to say, but I was confident that she'd laugh at the suggestion.

Grace switched to a new stretch, lying down on the mat with her back to the ground. She lifted her knee at a ninety-degree angle and folded it over the opposite side of her body. As she settled into the stretch, she focused on keeping her shoulders flush to the mat.

"You're avoiding the question, Sebastian. Tell me what you were thinking."

Unbelievable. After a week of avoiding my entire existence, Grace was calling me out for dodging a simple question. If anyone was being evasive, it was her, and I was more than happy to prove it.

Without breaking eye contact, I lowered myself down to her mat, setting my knee in the space between her legs. Grace sucked in a gasp as I pressed my hand to the side of her leg and pushed, deepening the stretch. Then, with the most wicked smile I could muster, I leaned down until our faces were inches apart.

"Do you remember last time you asked for a peek inside my head?" The memory of her raspy cry was one I revisited quite frequently. *I need to understand. Please, tell me.* I'd never forget the sound of her pleading or the shape of her mouth as she'd uttered that five letter word. "Do you recall what came next?"

Grace didn't speak. I didn't think she was even breathing as I waited for a response I knew would never come. Only after the tension had thickened to a point of discomfort did I whisper, "If that's what you really want, you'll have to ask *very* nicely."

Her pupils expanded, black swallowing the surrounding brown. I knew that if I kissed her right now, she'd let me. I could feel the tautness in her body; she was poised to snap at any moment. Now that she knew exactly what it felt like to have my fingers wrapped in her hair and our bodies pressed together, it was only a matter of time before she gave in. But first, I wanted her to suffer. I let my eyes focus on her lips for one incredibly long second, and then I was pushing away, flopping back onto my own mat feeling entirely too satisfied with myself.

"I want to know why you were so upset Thanksgiving night. And don't say it was nothing. You were on the verge of having a panic attack."

I shot her a look of utter disbelief at the lack of reaction. That was what she was thinking about right now? After all that?

"Share something real with me, something honest, even if it's just this once." Grace spoke in a gentle tone that drove away any doubt of her sincerity. And those eyes. How could I deny her when she was looking at me with such genuine curiosity?

"I got a bit of bad news," I winced at my own words, recalling the panic that had overtaken me at the mention of my mid-year report. "Well, it was actually no news, but that's what made it bad."

It had been over a week with no word from Duncan. Coach Dawson told me to be patient, but every day that went by without news chipped away at my confidence. It was part of the reason I was so desperate to see Grace. When I was around her, I wasn't thinking about anything other than how much I wanted her.

"Hockey-related news?"

"I haven't heard from my scout in a while. I usually get a progress report around Thanksgiving, but there's been nothing."

"Why do you assume that's bad?" she asked, letting her eyes roam over me in a curious perusal. "What if they haven't sent the report because they know you'll be ready by the end of the season?"

"Or what if they haven't sent the report because they've already decided to release me at the end of the season?" I shot back.

"They're not going to let a player like you get away, trust me."

"A player like me, huh? Would you mind telling me what that means?" I couldn't help myself, not when Grace so rarely sang my praises.

She rolled her eyes as if she could read my mind. "I'm not going to sit here and inflate your ego; it's already taking up half the room. You talk a big game, Seb, and you play one too. Why are you doubting that now?"

I felt a little jolt of excitement at the sound of my nickname.

"I know I'm great," I said without a single doubt in my mind. "But it's not always about that. I took a bad hit and was out for a year. Scouts get concerned about injuries like that." The average hockey career lasted five years for a reason: the sport was rough, and after a few big injuries, it was hard to compete at such a high level.

"You're too good a player for them to overlook, even with a past injury." She shook her head in disbelief. "I can't believe I have to tell you that."

Grace's confidence was comforting, but I was beginning to realize that it didn't matter how well I performed on the ice or who assured me everything would be fine. Until I knew with certainty what my future held, nothing would ease my anxiety.

"Why do you train like you're preparing for the big leagues when you're not planning on playing after college?"

"It soothes me," she said. "I'm a bit of an overthinker. When I have something to channel my energy into, I feel less stressed about the things I can't control."

We both liked control, it seemed. No wonder we were constantly at each other's throats.

Grace walked us through the remaining movements in a comfortable silence. At times, she'd reach over to correct my form with a gentle touch or remind me to breathe by catching my eye and exhaling through her nose. At the end of the final stretch, we collapsed onto the mats. My muscles were quivering from the effort of our mobility workout. Grace had sufficiently kicked my ass.

"Was it as terrible as you imagined?"

Her head fall to the side as she glanced at me. "Was what terrible?"

"Working out with me?"

Grace looked absolutely stunning like this: no makeup, rosy cheeks, hair piled atop her head, several loose strands falling along the side of her face. She was practically glowing.

"It wasn't terrible. But you don't seem like yourself today."

"You don't really know me, though," I said with a low rumble of laughter. "Maybe I'm more myself today than I ever have been with you."

A touch of her snarky attitude came through in her response. "Too bad I won't find out since we agreed on *just this once*."

"I thought you weren't avoiding me." My lips curled knowingly. Grace hated that she wanted me—refused to accept whatever this was. I knew what denial looked like after watching it in the mirror for weeks.

"Not everyone has to like you, Sebastian." I recognized her words as a parrot of my own, from the day Grace had goaded me into a heated comment for the *Dallard Spectator*. My lips twitched in anticipation as I stood up and began to gather my things.

"Is that why you pushed me into the lake, because you don't like me?" I asked, and she stilled at the question. "Or maybe you pushed me into the lake because you like me a little too much."

With a parting wink, I turned on my heel and headed toward the exit. I was halfway out the door when another thought crossed my mind.

"Oh, and a word of advice," I said, glancing over my shoulder. "You're better suited to anger than you are denial. Wouldn't you rather play with fire than pretend it doesn't exist?"

>> <<

Grace

Sebastian was giving me emotional whiplash. He was all I could focus on in the week following our training session. One moment, I'd be lost in a daydream about his lips, and the next, I was resisting the urge to smash my own head against the wall for having such ridiculous fantasies. I could still hear his voice like a haunted whisper. *Or maybe you pushed me into the lake because you like me a little too much.* He got off on teasing me and seemed intent on pushing my buttons until I was forced to shove back. But something about his parting words felt like a warning. *Wouldn't you rather play with fire than pretend it doesn't exist?*

I needed to remind myself that Sebastian would do anything to win this bet. After all, he didn't have to like me to fuck me. And yet, even when taking into consideration his past grievances, it was a tempting offer. I couldn't deny our sexual chemistry. For whatever twisted reason, my body came to life in his presence. Would it be so bad to give in? The thought alone sent a jolt of excitement through my body. One more taste couldn't hurt, not if I didn't let it. But that was the problem, I realized. How could I be sure it would only happen once?

"I am not watching that." Caroline's voice dragged me out of my introspection—I kept losing myself in thoughts of Sebastian. It was exhausting work, all this overanalyzing. That was why I'd suggested a movie night. I needed the solid distraction that only horror, true crime, or sleep could provide.

"I promise to let you snuggle tonight if you're too scared to fall asleep."

Lydia was only half teasing. The last time we'd convinced Caroline to watch a scary movie, she'd made us sleep together in the living room under a massive pile of blankets. The girl could do anything she set her mind to with only three hours of sleep, but she couldn't make it through a horror film.

"Why can't we just put on *New Girl* and gossip about boys," Caroline suggested. "We can bore Lydia with our problems as penance for being in a loving, healthy relationship."

Being stabbed in the eye sounded like a better way to spend the night. "I'm in desperate need of a distraction," I admitted. "And *Hereditary* is one of my favorite movies. It's not that bad, I promise."

Lydia caught my eye from across the couch with a barely concealed smirk. We both knew that wasn't entirely true, but if Caroline was ever going to get over her fear of horror, she had to face it head-on.

"What's on your mind?" Lydia asked dramatically, flipping through her sketchbook as she tried to settle on a project to finish.

"Family stuff," I said. "My sister is still pretending I don't exist."

"If it makes you feel better, my brother called me twice yesterday, and one of the times it was to ask me how to boil spaghetti noodles," Lydia said.

Her siblings' helplessness was astounding to me, even after months of overhearing their ridiculous phone calls. Lydia was the eldest of four, though she acted more like a mother to her brother and sisters in the absence of their parents, who spent much of their time working. At least twice a week, one of them would call asking for advice, usually pertaining to something ridiculous like where the fabric softener went or how to boil spaghetti. Her capacity for remaining patient with them was remarkable.

"Isn't he, like, nineteen?" Caroline asked.

"Twenty."

"Sometimes, being an only child has its perks," Caroline muttered as she sifted through a pile of her philosophy notes.

"What does your dad think about it?" Lydia asked me, jumping back to our conversation.

"He's pretending that things are fine, as usual," I admitted. "I never made a fuss growing up. He's entirely out of his depths when it comes to dealing with a rebellious teenager."

"You saved that energy for adulthood, and thank the Lord for that because I was sick of practicing in McKinley," Caroline said. "I guess, for that, I'd be willing to give your spooky movie a try."

>> <<

Resisting Sebastian quickly became a full-time job, one that he clearly relished. To make matters worse, it seemed as though the universe itself was in cahoots with the gorgeous hockey player. Our coaches were now requiring us to integrate our lifting schedules. It was another push for the teams to bond, despite the fact that everyone was getting along just fine. If Sebastian wasn't following me around the weight room, begging to be my lifting partner or asking to stretch me out, he was popping up at my favorite study spots and joining me for meals in the dining hall. The man was relentless, and each day, my resistance grew weaker. Even though I knew getting involved with Sebastian was a bad idea, I wanted him—*badly*. At some point, I was bound to slip up and let a moment between us turn into something physical, so to save myself from the humiliation of giving in to him, I hid.

Everyone had their favorite study spot on campus. For some, it was a particular bench in the quad, if the weather allowed, or a private nook in the campus coffee shop. Mine was a small wooden table between the *U*s and the *V*s of the fiction section at Nelson Library. It was rarely visited by other students, which meant I didn't have to worry about crossing paths with Sebastian, and the height of the table was perfect—not too low and not too tall. Normally, the tranquil atmosphere and musty smell of books eased me into a study trance, but today it was impossible to focus.

After fifteen minutes of struggling to find the right playlist,

I finally started making headway on my advanced psychology statistics project. But halfway through developing my directed acyclic graph, a pair of feet appeared in the corner of my eye. I let out a long sigh of irritation, pulled off my headphones, and glanced up at the figure hovering over me. No hideout was safe, it seemed. And then, as if the situation couldn't get worse, my stomach let out a horrifying growl loud enough to shake the building.

"Good thing I found you in time," Sebastian said, taking a seat across from me and placing a large paper bag on the table. "Your stomach sounds like it's about to start eating itself." He reached into the bag and pulled out a salad container, an apple, and a protein bar.

My stomach let out another clamorous groan.

"You should eat," he said, shoving the food closer to me. "We'll get a noise complaint if your stomach keeps making those awful noises."

"We'll get a complaint if someone sees this food. There's no eating in the library," I hissed.

"Then you should eat fast. It's not a good idea to study on an empty stomach. Trust me."

Sebastian wasted no time in making himself comfortable, reaching into his bag and pulling out his study materials. I was still gaping at him, my mouth parted in disbelief, when he glanced up from his computer screen.

"Good, you're halfway there. Now you just need to put the food in your mouth."

My mouth snapped shut. "What are you doing here? Why are you bringing me lunch?"

"You weren't in the dining hall. Caroline said you might be here, and I figured you'd be hungry since you skipped lunch."

Of course, I thought. This was Caroline's doing, no doubt her way of punishing me after Lydia and I had forced her to watch *Hereditary*. I was impressed that she'd made it through the full movie, even with her childhood blanket covering her face for the entire thing.

"Is it poisoned?" I glanced down at the salad skeptically.

"Would a fracquaintance do something like that?"

I let out a long sigh of irritation. "You can stop referencing that made-up word now. It was embarrassing enough that I said it in the first place."

"I like it better than 'frenemies.' Plus, there's nothing wrong with inventing new words. Shakespeare did it all the time."

Before I knew it, my lips twitched into a half smile. Sebastian looked far too pleased with himself.

"Please just eat. I'll take a few bites if it will make you feel better."

Slowly, I opened the plastic container of salad, fished out the packet of dressing, and poured it over the top. I could feel Sebastian watching me as I mixed it all together and took my first bite. His gaze lowered, dropping to my mouth as I slowly chewed and swallowed. A wicked thought crossed my mind. Without considering the consequences, I brought the fork to my lips and licked off the remaining salad dressing. Sebastian's jaw ticked. After a moment of tense silence, he spoke.

"See, I told you it's more fun to play than pretend," he said in a low, gravelly voice, one that sent a shiver of warmth through me.

I ignored the signals my body was sending and gave him my best look of innocence. "I have no idea what you're talking about."

Sebastian studied me as I tucked in to the rest of the salad. I wouldn't admit it, but I was grateful for the food. He eventually made himself busy, shifting back and forth between his notebook and computer. Scribble. Type. Scribble. Type. It was impossible to focus on anything other than him when he was in such close proximity.

"Why are you *really* here?" I asked, unable to stop from voicing my thoughts. "I'm not buying the nice act."

"Nice act?"

He even played at looking offended.

"Bringing me lunch. Being sweet."

I didn't miss the gleam in his eye as he leaned across the table, lips curled in bemusement. "Do you really want to know?"

Déjà vu. This wasn't the first time Sebastian had asked me a similar question, and I had a feeling it wouldn't be the last. I nodded my head and held my breath.

"You're right. The sweetness, it's all an act. This was more of a wine and dine situation so that I could—oh wait, that reminds me." Sebastian reached into his backpack, pulled out a small bottle of grape juice, and set it in front of me. "As I was saying, I was hoping to wine and dine you for the sole purpose of seducing you right here in this library."

I glanced at my empty salad bowl and considered stabbing him with the discarded fork. "Come on, be for real."

"What can I say, it's always been a fantasy of mine to do the deed surrounded by musty books. There's something about the thrill of being caught that—"

"I want honesty, Sebastian," I cut in before I could lose myself in those dirty thoughts of his. "You can't expect me to believe your sudden interest in me has nothing to do with the bet."

His brow quirked in a curious expression. "Messing with me is clearly your favorite game, but I'm a person, not a toy. I don't appreciate being played."

My words caused a shift in his demeanor that I hadn't expected. The smirk he wore like a badge of honor vanished, replaced by a steely look behind his eyes.

"The last thing you want is honesty, Grace. No, you'd prefer to pretend that all of this is some elaborate attempt at revenge. That way, it's easier to deny the needy ache you feel between your legs when you think about me late at night, or the flush in your face when I catch you looking at me from across the weight room."

Sebastian's declaration left me utterly speechless. My first instinct was to deny—to push back and tell him that he was totally off base—but my tongue was glued to the roof of my mouth. I could hardly breathe, let alone speak.

With a knowing expression, Sebastian packed up his things, slipped his backpack over his shoulder, and came around the side of the table to stand directly beside me. I tilted my head back to meet his eyes.

"Oh, and about the other day," he said, leaning down so that our faces were merely inches apart, "I'm happy to help you stretch out anytime. Just let me know."

Sebastian had already disappeared into the maze of bookshelves before I could think of a parting remark. It took me nearly fifteen minutes to snap out of my stunned stupor, and for the rest of the afternoon, I sat with my legs squeezed together, failing miserably to ignore the burning heat in my core.

I was so totally screwed.

>> <<

Sambam

How's celibacy treating you?

I lost the charger for my BOB, so not well.

You can't refer to your vibrator as
a battery-operated boyfriend if it's
electric.

>Is EOB any better?

Why are we even talking about vibrators
when you have access to the real deal?
And it's gorgeous.

Just fuck him already!!!

>It's not that simple.

It really is. I can explain the mechanics
if you're that rusty.

I sent her a row of middle finger emojis.

Sambam

What's the worst that can happen?

Not considering pregnancy . . .

>It will all blow up in my face, I just know it.

Don't even think about making that joke, Sam. I
swear, sometimes you think like a teenage boy.

You thought about it too.

Give me three good reasons why you
shouldn't have sex with him.

>I have class! Talk later.

Sam just sent me an eye-rolling emoji in response.

CHAPTER 15

Grace

As the days grew colder, my resolve began to melt. I felt as if there there was an inferno trapped within me, and it was all thanks to Sebastian Evans. Each day, he added a little more fuel to the fire in the form of salacious smiles and shameless flirting. And the worst part? I enjoyed it. Despite every instinct, every red flag or warning sign, my will to resist grew weaker. The walls I'd constructed around myself were beginning to crack. Out of pure desperation for relief from the heat, I resorted to my least favorite form of recovery: an ice bath.

By the time I lowered myself into the tub of freezing water, the recovery room was practically empty. The pain hit me immediately, stealing the air from my lungs and forcing a slow hiss from between my lips. The first minute was always the worst. You had to ignore every nerve that screamed in agony and every instinct that demanded you retreat from the freezing water. But the payoff was well worth the bitter burn. Cold water immersion had the power to minimize muscle soreness, improve performance, and reduce the risk of injury. It was an important part of the recovery process that I forced myself to undergo, despite how much I loathed it.

I was nearly numb when the sound of sloshing ice water caught my attention. A pair of familiar veiny hands gripped the edge of the other immersion tub. Sebastian pushed himself up a moment later, water pouring over his naked chest and down the hard lines of his stomach in thin rivulets. His body was a lethal weapon, honed to perfection through pure dedication. I couldn't tear my gaze away as he stepped out of the bath. Now that he was playing nice, or rather fighting by way of flirting, it had become harder and harder to ignore our chemistry. I had to remind myself of our past, but even that wasn't enough to stop me from grinning like an idiot during our playful chats in the library or feeling a tingle of warmth when he caught my eyes from across the lunch table. There was so much pent-up tension between us. I wanted to give in to the temptation, but I was sure that if I did, he'd reveal this was all just a game.

The right side of his lip was curved into a smug expression, one that told me he knew exactly how close I was to succumbing. It wasn't ideal, this power he held over me. Right now, I needed to level the playing field. It was the only way to gain some control over the situation. Without hesitating, I hauled myself out of the bath and into the blessedly warm air. *Two could play this game.* Sebastian's jaw tightened at the sight of my body, his hands curling into fists. His gaze seared into my skin like the needle of a tattoo gun, little bolts of electricity dancing across my flesh. He studied me languidly, starting at the line of my neck and moving across the expanse of my exposed collarbone. It wasn't until Sebastian glimpsed my hardened nipples that his pupils blew wide.

His Adam's apple bobbed up and down as I stepped out of the freezing water. Feeling emboldened by his reaction, I turned my back on Sebastian and slowly bent over to grab my towel. A wicked smirk danced across my lips as I stood, spun around, and dragged the fluffy material over my body, wicking up the moisture dripping down my skin. Without breaking eye contact, I slowly pulled on my discarded sweatpants and T-shirt, enjoying the way his jaw ticked. Satisfaction coursed through me as I sauntered as toward Sebastian's rigid form. When I was near enough to see the gooseflesh that pebbled his skin, I slowed, looked him up and down, and inched closer—close enough that we were practically touching, his warm breath fanning over my face as I tipped my head back to meet his eyes.

"You might need another ice bath," I whispered, eyes trailing down to take in the bulge at the front of his shorts.

He was speechless as I shoved past his trembling form toward the women's locker room. I'd barely made it through the door when a burning hand latched on to my wrist and tugged, pulling me around. In three swift steps, Sebastian herded me inside. My back hit the tiled wall as the door clicked shut. He was so close that I could feel the heat pouring off him in waves, his arms braced against the wall on either side of my head. My brain glitched as Sebastian leaned forward to brush his lips along the side of my neck.

"You're playing a dangerous game, Grace," he said, voice low and full of something that promised sweet torture.

Part of me wanted to reach out and beg for what he was offering. I held still, the vein in my neck pulsing in rhythm with the beat of my heart. I forced my lips apart, breath whooshing out in a rasp.

"You started it."

Despite the warning signal blaring inside my head, I willed myself to meet his emerald eyes. There was little green in them now, his pupils blown wide, the black expanding even further as we locked gazes. I felt something low in my stomach clench at the thought of our lips touching, at the very possible reality of our bodies colliding.

His voice was a dangerous growl as he said, "No, *you* started it the moment you stepped on *my* ice."

"It's not just your ice anymore." I spoke the words in a whisper, as if I was scared to hear them myself.

"You're right," he said, hand reaching up to grip my neck in a gentle, commanding hold. His thumb cupped the side of my jaw as his fingers splayed across my throat. "I've finally warmed up to the idea of sharing."

I had no time to process his words. Sebastian's lips collided with mine in a searing explosion. The kiss instantly transported me back to his lake house, to the long dock that stretched out across the water, surrounded by a darkness that only intensified the sensation of our mouths devouring each other. I chased after that feeling desperately, jumping up and wrapping my legs around his waist as his hands dropped, fingers digging into the flesh of my ass. Everywhere we touched, there was a blazing fire that had the power to consume us both and leave nothing in its wake but ashes.

Sebastian's tongue entered my mouth slowly, easing inside as my fingers found the damp strands of his hair. We moaned into each other as the frenzy enveloping us heightened. I wanted to be even closer to him, to feel every inch of his bare skin against mine. He pulled away for the sole purpose of removing my clothes, reaching for the bottom of my shirt only to hesitate. I made the decision for him in one swift motion, pulling the damp material over my head and tossing it on the floor. And then, as if feeling the need to even the playing field, I gripped the material of my sports bra and tossed that away as well.

Air kissed my bare breasts. Sebastian froze. His hungry eyes devoured every inch of my exposed skin, the ravenous expression he wore shooting molten pleasure straight to my veins. His large hand snaked up my torso and traced along the bottom of my breast. His fingers danced across my skin, inching further and further up until they found the peak of my nipple. I hissed as he pinched the sensitive flesh between his fingers. The sensation shot straight to my core. I threw my head back and ground my hips into Sebastian.

"Sensitive, are we?" he rasped into my ear before lowering his head to take my nipple in his mouth.

The sound I made was truly undignified, somewhere between a whine and a moan. He teased me slowly, trailing his tongue across my burning skin before his teeth gently scraped across my nipple.

"Sebastian," I gasped, threading my fingers through his hair and tugging his head away from my chest.

He looked at me in a way no one had ever looked at me before, like he was entirely consumed with the mere sight of my face.

His next words were nothing short of a demand. "Say that again."

A playful smile broke through my lustful haze. Something in me couldn't help but tease him. "Say what again?"

"Say my name like a good girl, and I promise you'll be screaming it very soon."

As if his words weren't promise enough, Sebastian rolled his hips against mine, pressing the hardness of his erection directly over my center. Again and again, he ground himself against me until I was writhing in his arms and calling out his name in a chant. The entire time, I replayed the sound of his voice in my head. *Good girl.* How could two measly words have such an effect on me? I needed the rest of my clothes off. I had to feel his skin pressed against mine.

"I need these gone," I whined, reaching down to tug at my pants.

"Next time I'm going to make you beg," he rasped.

Astonishment clouded my brain as he set me down and lowered himself to his knees, his hands trailing from the sides of my breasts, along my waist, and down to my hips. He pressed a light kiss to my bare stomach, the heat of his lips sending a zing of pleasure straight to my core. In a sudden movement, he gripped the sides of my sweats and tugged. The motion dragged me forward, my back leaving the wall as my pants and spandex shorts were shoved down to my knees. Cool air whispered across my heated flesh. It was sensory overload, every nerve in my lower body going berserk. Gently, Sebastian pushed me back against the wall and lifted my legs one at a time to remove the last of my clothing.

His mouth went slack at the sight of me bared for him. Exposed as I was, there was no embarrassment or shame. The wanton expression behind his eyes made me feel nothing less than perfect. I wanted to ask what he was thinking. I wanted to know how the hell we'd gone from exchanging lustful gazes from across the room to being naked, but I was too afraid to ruin the moment. Sebastian gripped one of my thighs, tugging my leg to the side. It was a demand for me to open, and I was more than willing to oblige.

"Look at how wet you are for me." His voice was hoarse, eyes wide as he leaned in close to my core. Sebastian blew a wave of hot air over the wetness between my legs. Goosebumps exploded across my skin. A shiver raked my body.

"Tell me what you want, Grace."

I closed my eyes and leaned my head back against the wall. Now was not the time for talking.

"Use your words," he commanded. "I need to hear them."

I let out a little whine of frustration as he blew another wave of hot air over my core.

"You told me," I panted, breathing heavily as his fingers dug into the skin of my thighs, "I'd be screaming your name. I want that. I want you."

Sebastian let out a breathy groan at my admission, one of his fingers finally moving close enough to graze the heat at my center. The slight contact had me bucking off the wall, pressing closer to this touch. He blew out another breath and dragged a finger over my slit, his other hand snaking up my torso and latching on to my breast. Slowly, Sebastian began moving his long finger in light circles over my clit. He increased the pressure before easing off. Again and again, he repeated the same ministrations, switching between levels of pressure in a way that drove me crazy and stole the breath from my lungs. When I started to push myself against his touch, eager for more, he let go of my breast and pushed me back against the wall.

"Learn some patience. I've had to wait a long time for this moment, so you can wait a little longer. I want you dripping down my hand before I give you my cock."

His words were a promise, one that made it even harder to stop squirming. Only once I was completely still did he resume his torturous teasing. His fingers were magic against my skin, so perfectly knowledgeable that I had to resist pleading for more. I was seconds away from losing my head completely when another wave of hot breath was followed by his finger plunging inside me. Pleasure coursed through my body. I cried out and reached forward to grasp his shoulders.

Before I could even fathom that he was inside me, another finger was pushing in and stretching me open. And then his mouth was over my clit, hot lips pressed to the sensitive nerves. His tongue snaked out as undignified sounds poured out of my mouth. All at once, it was too much. My entire body was pulsing with pleasure as Sebastian devoured me, fingers rocking in and out as his lips pressed down on my core. The pressure inside was building rapidly, my body tensing with each wicked flick of his tongue. Just as I reached the top, my body poised to fall over the edge, he pulled his mouth away from me and removed his fingers.

An embarrassing whine slipped past my lips at the loss of his touch. I felt so empty. Breath was escaping from me in staggered pants. I wanted to scream at him to continue. I wanted to ask him why he'd stopped. But something told me that's exactly what he expected me to do. Rather than fall into his trap, I sank my teeth into my bottom lip and bit back a whine.

"Such a good girl," he praised, the corner of his lip twisting into a half smile.

Slowly, he rose from the ground and stood at full height. I dropped my head against the tile wall to meet his gaze. Without looking away from me, he reached down and pushed at the top of his shorts, exposing the stretch of skin under his hip bones. My eyes dropped to his waistband. Slowly, he hooked his finger under the black material and slid the shorts all the way down.

Holy hell, he was beautiful. It wasn't every day that the sight of someone's manhood incited thoughts of beauty, but everything about Sebastian seemed to be a contradiction. If anyone were to have a gorgeous, glorious cock, it would be him. I took in the vast expanse of flesh, eyes traveling over the slight curve at the top of his member, feeling slightly intimidated by the size. My instincts urged me to reach out and touch him, but I hesitated, pressing my hands against the cool tile of the wall. Something told me that Sebastian wanted complete control at this moment, and I was happy to give it over just as long as he kept his promise of making me scream.

"Shit," he breathed out, glancing around the room. "Don't move."

I was too overwhelmed with anticipation to disobey, even as Sebastian cracked open the door and glanced around the recovery room. He leaned outside without fully leaving, stretching his body as far as possible to reach something. When Sebastian found what he was looking for, he shut the door and locked the deadbolt. He was clutching his backpack, one hand digging around until I heard the crinkle of plastic. The bag thumped to the floor.

"Why don't you help me with this?"

Sebastian held out his hand to reveal a condom. I nodded my head obediently and peeled the wrapper open. Gently, I secured the rubber over his tip and rolled it down the length of his cock. He twitched at the contact, a throaty groan escaping his lips. A sudden clarity fell over me—the realization that I was about to let Sebastian inside of me, literally—and I held back a snort of disbelief. We might have been walking a fine line these past few weeks, teasing and bickering and riling each other up at every turn, but I'd never expected this—the two of us stripped bare in the women's locker room, utterly desperate for one another.

Sebastian, too, looked like he was entirely taken aback. But there was something else behind his expression, a mixture of wonder and determination. He eased his fingers under the back of my right knee and lifted, hooking my leg securely over his hip. It brought us impossibly close. I could feel his hardness against my slick center, and my core clenched in anticipation. Slowly, he began to rock forward, dragging his cock along my opening. The leg bearing my weight shook as he thrust up and down, the underside of his shaft dragging over my sensitive skin until my whole body was quivering. Just when I thought he would stop torturing me, Sebastian fisted his cock, lifted it away from my center, then let it fall back against me. I jolted at the shock of him smacking against my swollen flesh. Smirking, Sebastian repeated the movement, his eyes burning with intensity as he continued to string my body along until the slick between my legs coated him entirely.

"Enough teasing, Evans," I growled out, urgency woven into every word.

He nodded in understanding, but there was something I couldn't discern within the depths of his eyes. "I wanted to give you the opportunity to back out." He was breathing heavily, muscled chest rising and falling in the same rhythm as mine. "I need you to tell me this is what you want. Can you do that for me?"

I nodded my head through the heavy haze of lust. Hadn't I already said I wanted him? Why was he—

A realization dawned on me. Sebastian was giving me an out, even now. This entire time, he'd been waiting for me to stop him. Waiting for the moment I realized this was one big mistake. But that wasn't going to happen. We were too far gone. In this moment, there was nothing more that I wanted than Sebastian. Despite everything he'd done and said, I needed this.

"I want you inside of me, Sebastian. Please, I want—"

My words shattered the last of his restraint. Sebastian growled as he lifted me to hover just above his tip. Without another moment of hesitation, he brought me down on his cock.

>> <<

Sebastian

A feeling of pure bliss enveloped me as I sank into Grace's heat. I watched myself stretch her open inch by inch, shuddering at the sensation of her walls sucking me in. She was so close to falling over the edge. I could tell by the way her entire body quivered in my arms and her head fell back, mouth parted in an expression of ecstasy. It was too soon for Grace's finale. If I saw her come undone now, I wouldn't last more than three seconds. With a steadying breath, I willed myself to remain still. Grace needed time to adjust, and I needed time to think about anything other than the warmth of her cunt wrapped around me. After a long moment of nothing but ragged breaths, Grace shifted, hooking her other leg around my waist so she was completely wrapped around me. I sank deeper, and a breathy whimper slipped past her lips. Her hands found my hair a moment later, and she gripped the strands tightly between her fingers.

I closed my eyes, fingers pressing into the flesh of her ass as I willed myself to hold off. "Give me a moment," I groaned, sensing her impatience. She wanted to move just as badly as I did.

Ever so slowly, I pulled out, our eyes never straying from each other. When just my tip remained inside of her, I plunged back in, deep and hard. Grace's head fell back against the tile as she let out a long, throaty moan. I'd never felt so consumed with pleasure—she was gripping my cock perfectly. If this was the end, and the last thing I got to do was be inside of Grace, I'd die a happy man.

Thankfully for me, this wasn't the end.

It was just beginning.

"You feel so fucking good," I said, eyes raking over her naked body as I snapped my hips back and forth in a slow, steady rhythm. I didn't know where to look. Every inch of her was perfection. Her tits bounced with each of my thrusts, the toned muscles along her lower stomach contracting as she urged her hips forward. Was this real? It had to be. I'd imagined this very moment more than I cared to admit, and never once had it felt so fucking good.

Grace's hold on my hair tightened. She yanked my head back and crashed her lips against mine. We both moaned in unison. I continued at a steady pace, bucking my hips into her, using the wall to help support us both. Never in my life had I been so determined to make someone scream my name. I needed to hear her say it again, this time with my cock buried inside of her. Grace pulled away from my mouth and dragged her lips along the side of my neck. She left a trail of hot kisses and love bites over my skin. My pace stuttered as she whispered into my ear, hot breath tickling the skin along my neck.

"I need more."

If I'd had more restraint, I would have made her beg. Nothing would have pleased me more than seeing her on hands and knees. But I'd spent far too long imagining this very moment to risk coming in her mouth. There would be time for that in the future.

The next time I pulled out, I hesitated for a moment, tip perched along the seam of her opening, throbbing with need. Just as Grace's eyes snapped open, another demand poised on her lips, I slammed into her hard, driving the entirety of my length inside her. Something warm rushed down my leg. It was all the confirmation I needed to continue at a punishing pace, moving like a piston in and out of her as the last shred of my control evaporated. Grace let out a string of half curses, half moans. The sound only drove to me to move faster, one hand moving to squeeze her nipple between my fingers.

Her walls fluttered around me. I could sense she was as close to the edge as I was. I tried to hold myself back, tried to prolong the inevitable, but neither of us seemed capable. We moved in tandem, each of us bucking against the other, chasing that impending explosion. I was losing myself to her, to the knowledge that no other woman would ever compare to Grace.

As she began to tense, just moments away from falling over the edge, I reached down and pressed my thumb against her clit. That was all it took for Grace to let out a strangled cry in climax, screaming out my name like a promise. Her back arched as her walls clamped down, squeezing even tighter as she pulsed around me. The sensation was too overwhelming. My own body stiffened, balls tightening as a hot rush of bliss shot down my spine. Pleasure like nothing I'd ever experienced rushed over me as I found my release. I pressed my face into the crook of her neck, riding out the aftershocks of my orgasm with my lips against her delicate skin.

Heavy breathing permeated the air. I didn't want this moment to be over. In fact, I would have happily stayed inside of Grace forever. But eventually she unhooked one of her legs from around my waist and reached for the floor. I pulled out and gently set her on the ground. We met each other's eyes as the silence expanded.

I couldn't have predicted any of this. There had always been a sliver of doubt, despite the weeks of teasing banter and heated stares. I knew she wanted me just as much as I wanted her, but Grace was stubborn and willful. I'd always thought she was too proud to give in to her desires when it came to me.

Slowly, I leaned forward and pressed my lips to hers. I needed her to know that this wasn't some one-time—

Grace gently pushed me back, her bare hand like an iron across the skin of my chest.

"Are you oaky? Was that too much?"

She shook her head, but I could see the looming panic in her eyes.

"Grace—"

"That can't happen again," she said in a rush, frantically collecting her scattered clothes. "We had to get it out of our systems. Right?"

Her words were a sucker punch to my gut, and being braced for the impact only made the pain worse. I was well and truly fucked, that much was obvious. Grace could ruin me with little more than a few words. This wasn't just an attraction I felt for her. It was much deeper.

"You're right," I agreed, watching stupidly as she dressed herself in haste.

"Would you mind keeping this between us?"

Grace wouldn't look me in the eyes; she regretted everything. The shame was so clearly written in the trembling of her hands.

"Wouldn't dream of it."

Somehow, watching her leave felt even worse than hearing her say we had to get this out of our systems.

After a long few minutes of waiting for my heartbeat to steady, I stumbled out of the locker room, startled to discover someone just beyond the door. Lydia sat on the edge of a padded recovery table, arms crossed over her chest and a knowing expression painted across her face. She was dressed in sweats, her long black hair pulled back into a braid. She was a quiet observer, much in the way that Bryce was.

"Interesting choice," she said, nodding to the locker room door behind me.

There was nothing I could do but stand there like a complete idiot. My brain lacked the necessary oxygen to form an adequate response.

"Do you like her?" she asked.

The blunt nature of her question caught me off guard. For a moment, I considered lying. I didn't owe her anything. But something in my gut told me I could trust Lydia.

"So much." It felt both good and terrifying to admit it out loud.

She tilted her head to the side as she continued her silent assessment. Eventually, she slipped off the table, strode across the room, and stopped directly in front of me.

"This better not be about winning a bet or getting revenge," she warned.

"Seems like a lot of effort on my end just to fuck her over."

"I wouldn't put it past you," she told me. "Not after everything you've done."

"She's the one who said it could never happen again." My voice fell flat at the admission. How could I fuck Grace over when she wasn't even willing to admit that she liked me?

"Grace doesn't open up easily. I don't know much about her life outside of hockey, but she was willing to risk getting kicked off the team and expelled from this school if it meant standing up for our rights as female athletes. She did that for me, for all of the other girls on the team, when she barely knew us. Just be careful with her. She doesn't deserve to get her heart broken."

When I'd met Grace, I was convinced that she was out to get me, her only goal to put me in my place. I'd had it all wrong. Coming after me was always about her teammates and making sure that they were treated with the same decency as the male athletes. At the time, I was nothing more than an obstacle in her path. She'd had every right to push me away, but I wouldn't allow it any longer. Not after today. What I felt for Grace was more than just an infatuation. It had been silly of me to ever assume I'd be able to fuck her out of my system. She was exceptional; why else would I have gone through all the trouble of making her hate me? Now, she needed to face the truth of *her* feelings. Because under all of that regret and loathing, there was just as much desire.

Lydia studied me for another long moment before she turned around and headed for the exit. She paused in the doorway, glancing back over her shoulder. "And no more sex in the locker room. Seriously, it's unhygienic."

CHAPTER 16
Grace

I didn't remember walking home. The apartment was empty when I arrived. With shaking hands, I dropped my things at the door and retreated to my bedroom. In the aftermath of Sebastian, I was lost, floating somewhere between elation and denial. I could still feel his lips dusting kisses along the slope of my neck, his hands braced on either side of my hips. My body felt at ease in a way I'd never known before, not even with Matt. What had happened between Sebastian and me was *more* in every sense of the word. It was a terrifying realization, one that made me reach for my phone and FaceTime Sam.

"'Sup, bitch," she answered on the third ring.

The video feed was dark; I could barely see more than the outline of her face and the whites of her eyes.

"I did something I probably shouldn't have."

A bright light flashed across the screen, and she came into view. She was dressed in scrubs and sitting in her car. I looked at the time and realized she must have been on her way home from a shift at the hospital.

"Okay, don't panic yet. Just take a few deep breaths and tell me what happened," Sam commanded.

"You were right," I said, recalling the conversation we'd had after Sebastian's birthday party. "It was only a matter of time."

"You're not making any sense, though I do like to hear that I'm right."

"I had sex with Sebastian."

The was a long pause and then Sam was shouting, her face so close to the phone camera that I could only see her nose and mouth. "That's it? That's your big mess-up? I thought you were about to tell me you'd murdered someone! I was already thinking about ways to hide the body."

A strange sound somewhere between a laugh and a choke escaped me. Sam was still talking, rambling on about how much I'd freaked her out. Apparently, she believed me capable of murder. At least I knew I could trust her to help me get rid of a body if I ever did find myself in that situation.

Totally not the point, Grace.

"But I hate Sebastian." It was the only thing I could think to say.

"Do you?"

"I wish I did," I admitted. "It would be easier to resist him if I really did. I can't believe I let him fuck me in the women's locker room."

"I will refrain from saying something dirty and instead take this moment to remind you that you're a twenty-two-year-old single woman. Being horny is normal."

I let out a huff of exasperation. "But it was Sebastian."

"Yes, and as we've already established, he's a fine piece of ass. You should be clapping yourself on the back for bagging such a hottie."

I rolled my eyes. I needed someone to shake some sense into me, not congratulate me.

"Seriously, Grace. Don't feel bad about embracing your desires. There's nothing wrong with that."

She was right, but there was more to the story than embracing my desires. I was scared of this thing between Sebastian and me because it had the power to shift into something that went beyond physical attraction.

"I'm not ashamed of myself for sleeping with him. I'm scared that this could turn into something more than just sex. I've never felt that good before. It was incredible."

"Better than Matt?" she asked.

"It's hard to compare. With Matt, we knew each other for over a year, and I trusted him with my heart. He did everything right."

"And Sebastian?"

"Everything is more intense with him. When we're together, I feel like I have no control over myself," I admitted.

"Having no control and letting go of your control are two different things. It can be scary to let go, but I think that's what you need."

I shook my head. "I'm not scared to let go. I'm scared that when I do, I'll find out this was all just a game to him."

"Maybe it's worth taking that chance. Think about how things were with Matt. It took you months to let him even take you out on a date. This kind of raw attraction means something—don't you want to find out?"

"It's too late."

She tilted her head to the side and frowned. "Let me guess, you self-sabotaged?"

"I told him that it couldn't happen again."

"You care about him."

I nodded my head reluctantly. "I don't want to."

"You don't always get to choose who you care about. Sometimes it just happens."

I wished she was wrong. If I could choose to, I'd erase every memory of Sebastian from my mind. How could I trust him after our past? I was terrified that everything between us was a lie, a way to punish me for invading his precious arena. As much as I wanted to give in to this overwhelming desire, I couldn't risk letting myself go there with Sebastian.

>> <<

Sleep evaded me. I spent the night staring at my ceiling, failing to silence the voice in my head. Despite my best attempt at counting sheep and progressive muscle relaxation, I was woefully unsuccessful. I felt half dead as I pulled myself from bed an hour before my alarm was set to go off. The only thing with the potential to quiet my mind was losing myself on the ice, so I began the process of dressing and preparing my schoolbag for the day.

The moon was low in the sky when I left the apartment, bundled in my thickest coat and winter boots. DU had been visited by its first snowfall of December overnight, and it was unusually bright despite the lack of sunlight. A thin blanket of white encased the campus, crunching underfoot as I walked to the arena feeling like I was in an episode of *The Twilight Zone*. Operating on autopilot, I scanned my badge and pushed through the front doors. My half-functioning brain barely detected the unmistakable sounds of hockey: the hiss of blades across ice and the crack of a stick meeting puck rubber.

Who the hell would be here at four-thirty in the morning?

I dropped my things off in the locker room and headed out

to the rink, curious to see who was willing to punish themselves at such an early hour. Two forms appeared on the ice as I entered the players' bench, one significantly larger than the other. Quietly, I sat down to observe the training session in secret. It looked like they were working on edge control, based on the series of cones set out across the ice.

"Lead with your head, Tanner. And you're digging in too much; you need to glide." Sebastian's voice was unmistakable. The command in his tone pulled me right back to the memory of us in the locker room. I forced away the image it conjured and pressed my legs together to contain the heat spreading through me.

"Trust your edges," Sebastian said, weaving through the cones in a display of the proper form.

After watching Sebastian's example, Tanner nodded his head and pushed off. This time, he weaved through the cones with a little less dig and a little more glide. Still, he wasn't low enough to the ice, and he wasn't leading with his head.

"That's better, for sure," Sebastian said when he came to a stop. "But there's a few other things you should focus on."

Sebastian went through a few minor tweaks to his form, suggesting that he bend his knees more and skate with confidence. He too had noticed that Tanner wasn't low enough to the ice and that he wasn't leading with his head. Afterward, he showed Tanner a few drills to help improve his edge work. I'd never seen this side of Sebastian. He was patient with the younger hockey player and explained things in a way that was understandable. He was confident, not cocky. It was refreshing to see this side of him.

"All right, let's get some rest in before practice. Coach will wring my neck if I work you too hard."

I realized too late that they were headed in my direction. For a moment, I considered fleeing, but Sebastian had already seen me. Tanner reached the bench first, pulling off his helmet as he stepped off the ice. I recognized him from our shared practices. He was a freshman.

"Hey, Grace," he said in greeting.

I was immediately grateful to have heard Sebastian call him by his name. "Hey, Tanner. Nice edge work out there."

He flushed under my praise. "Not as good as you or Sebastian."

"There's no need for flattery," I teased, glancing up to where Sebastian stood behind him. "Sebastian already has way too many adoring fans singing his praises"

I'd slipped so easily into our normal banter, almost as if nothing had transpired between us yesterday. Playful seemed safer than serious. As long as it didn't turn into anything more than that. Sebastian's expression was hard to read. For a moment I braced myself, half expecting him to spew something cruel at me, to see that familiar anger in his eyes once again, but it never came.

Instead, he clapped a hand over Tanner's shoulder and said, "Mind giving me a moment with Grace?"

Tanner gave us a goodbye salute before stalking to the opposite bench. Once he'd disappeared into the locker room, Sebastian returned his gaze to me.

"You don't usually come in early on Thursdays," he said, remaining at a distance from me on the other side of the bench. There was no hint of the usual playfulness in his voice. I felt a lurch deep in my stomach.

"I barely slept last night. Wanted to clear my head," I said, motioning to the rink.

I could tell he was surprised at my honesty. "Was there any reason in particular you couldn't sleep?"

I swallowed a lump in my throat as his neutral expression started to shift into something much more familiar.

"I would've thought that after last night"—he paused for a brief moment, eyes gleaming with delight—"you'd be exhausted."

My breath caught. I watched him pull his lower lip into his mouth and release it. Images of him, of us, flashed across my mind. My grip on the edge of the bench tightened, fingers squeezing against cold metal.

Get yourself together, I thought. Sebastian knew exactly what he was doing. Despite agreeing that we couldn't repeat last night's activity, he seemed happy to resume his usual lusty gazes and suggestive comments. This man was a true terror. He knew exactly how to torture me, and he loved doing it.

"I would've thought that after last night, all of this would be done," I said.

"All of what?" He smirked. "I'm not sure I know what you're referring to."

"You know exactly what I'm referring to." I jabbed my pointer finger into his chest. "It's the sex eyes and the flirting and the suggestive remarks." His only reaction was a quirk of the brow. "Don't play dumb, Sebastian."

Slowly, he leaned forward until our faces were mere inches from one another. "You're the one who swore off sex with me after I gave you the best orgasm of your life. If anyone's playing dumb, it's you."

My breath hitched, pulse jumping. "Sure of yourself, aren't you?"

"You're desperate for me, Grace. Just as desperate as I am for you. Once you realize that, I'm happy to fuck you somewhere other than a locker room. Though I'm not picky about the location."

Sebastian turned to leave, but I reached out to stop him. It was impossible to ignore the shock of energy that traveled through my palm the moment we touched.

"That's *never* going to happen again."

He looked me dead in the eye and said, "If that's what you really want."

Without another word, Sebastian set off across the rink. My heart raced as I watched his form grow smaller and smaller until he disappeared into the locker room. Despite the sleepless night, I felt wide awake. The fog around my brain had started to clear, and a new realization took form. Sebastian was the kind of all-consuming that could make you forget about everything else. My only hope was a winter break detox. The distance would help clear my head; it would allow me time to focus on fixing things with my sister. I couldn't let myself become distracted by a boy, not when I was trying to repair one of the most important relationships in my life, and not when he held the power to break me.

>> <<

Sebastian

From: sebastian.evans@du.edu
Sent: December 20, 2025 11:46
To: d.howard@redwingsrecruitment.com
Subject: Mid-Year Check-in

Hi, Duncan,

Happy holidays! I'm back home for the winter holiday and would love to stop by Little Caesars Arena. I haven't been out to BELFOR Training Center in a while. I'm happy to make the trip out to Detroit before I head back to school. Any news on my mid-year report?

I hope to hear from you soon!
Sebastian

From: sebastian.evans@du.edu
Sent: 24 December 2025 1:36
To: d.howard@redwingsrecruitment.com
Subject: Mid-Year Check-in

Hi, Duncan,

Merry Christmas Eve! Tell the wife and kids I say hello.
I'll be leaving to go back to school in a few days—we have some big games coming up. Let me know if I should stop by the center for a quick skate. I'm feeling great.
I also wanted to check in about my mid-year report. Is there any chance that it's been delayed? I haven't seen anything come into my inbox, and I just wanted to make sure I wasn't missing anything.

Talk soon!
Sebastian

From: sebastian.evans@du.edu
Sent: 28 December 2025 5:55
To: d.howard@redwingsrecruitment.com
Subject: Mid-Year Check-in

Hi, Duncan,

Did you get a new number? I tried your cell, and my call didn't go through. Should I be worried that I haven't heard from you? Please send an update as soon as possible.

Sebastian

Grace

"Those look amazing, Dad." The kitchen smelled divine thanks to a laborious afternoon preparing my grandmother's famous pierogi recipe. She was usually the one to make them, but this year my grandparents had decided to ditch cold Wisconsin in favor of sunny Florida. The kitchen was a complete disaster, and the dumplings looked slightly deformed, but I'd had fun struggling through the process with my father.

"Thanks, love. Would you mind setting the table? And let Gabby know we're almost ready for dinner."

In a not-so-surprising turn of events, Gabby had spent the day locked away in her bedroom. Since I'd arrived home, I'd only seen her come out for meals and, as I liked to call it, forced family time. Otherwise, she remained behind closed doors, seemingly uninterested in spending time with anyone but herself. But I was determined to have a real conversation with her before I went back to school. After laying out the plates and silverware, I retreated upstairs, pausing in front of her door. Hesitantly, I knocked.

"What?"

It was her usual response. The past few days, I'd just barked out that dinner was ready or that Dad wanted to watch a movie. Today, however, I was determined to try something new.

"What?"

Again, I waited, no longer willing to speak through a door. After a long moment of silence, I convinced myself she was planning to ignore me altogether, but then I heard a loud sigh of irritation followed by heavy footsteps. The door flew open.

"What?"

Gabby was buried beneath a large sweatshirt and oversized sweatpants, hood pulled over her head. She looked tired. I tried not to think about how much she resembled our mother, especially with those dark circles under her eyes.

"It's time for dinner."

"And you couldn't have just said that?"

"Sure, I could have. But Dad asked me to check for signs of life," I said with a smirk.

"I doubt he said that," she scoffed.

I was so tired of her attitude and general lack of consideration. "I didn't want to wait the thirty minutes it would have taken you to get out of bed. We've been in the kitchen all afternoon cooking, and I'm hungry."

I braced myself for a snarky remark that never came. Instead, Gabby slipped by me through the gap in the doorway and stomped away. Downstairs, the table was covered in food. Beside the steaming plate of pierogies was an impressive display of topping selections and three smoked sausages. My stomach groaned in anticipation.

"You want any wine?" Dad asked me, holding up a bottle of red.

I nodded and accepted the glass with a thankful smile.

"Can I have a glass?" Gabby asked.

"You can have a sip," my dad conceded, holding out his glass for her to try.

An air of annoyance surrounded her like a force field. "What's the point of having one sip?"

"And that is exactly why you're too young to have a glass," he said.

We all loaded up, though that was a generous term for the meager amount of food on Gabby's plate. I resisted the urge to comment. The last two times I'd told her she should eat more, she'd given me a scathing look and assured me that she wasn't as hungry since quitting dance.

As usual, my dad and I spent dinner chatting about school, work, and hockey while Gabby sat in silence and pushed her food around the plate. I tried several times to pull her into the conversation, but each attempt was met with a lackluster response or an eye roll. When dinner ended, Gabby practically ran from the table and back to the safety of her room as my father and I cleaned up. Though I had half a mind to chase after her, I'd put off speaking with my dad all week. Tonight was my last chance to have the conversation I'd been dreading. *It has to be done*, I assured myself. The moment Gabby's bedroom door slammed shut, I ripped off the bandage.

"She needs to see a therapist. Someone who isn't us that she can talk to."

There was a long silence. It had taken me over five days to work up the courage to have this talk for a reason. I was bringing up old wounds that were painful to revisit, but this could no longer go ignored.

"I don't know, Grace." There was an unspoken fear in his words as he turned on the sink and began rinsing off the dirty plates.

"Depression doesn't just go away. You know that better than anyone."

His grip tightened around the sponge, and a rush of watery bubbles burst out and over his fingers. "And you think putting her on a bunch of medications until she's numb is the answer?"

"No one said anything about medication." I spoke in a low tone, trying to keep my voice down. "But she needs to talk to a professional. Do you even recognize her right now? She barely leaves her room let alone says more than two words. I really think she hates me, Dad."

"She doesn't hate—"

A knock echoed through the house. I let out a shaky breath and poked my head into the hall. Sam peered through the front window. When she caught my eyes, she held up a bottle of wine and grinned.

"I'll be right back."

Sam started talking a mile a minute when I opened the door. "My mom got me this really good—"

"Mind waiting up in my room for a few minutes?"

Her brow furrowed in a look of concern. *I'll tell you later*, I mouthed as she slipped off her shoes and hung her coat on the banister. With a nod, Sam headed upstairs. My dad was right where I'd left him when I returned to the kitchen, hovering over the sink with a dirty plate in hand.

"Something serious is going on with Gabs, Dad. She's starting to—"

I stopped myself before I went too far, the words dying on my lips. *She's starting to look and act like Mom did.* Gabby took after our mother physically, but that wasn't what I was referring to. There was an emptiness behind her eyes that was all too familiar.

"I know that you tried to do everything right with Mom and she still left. But we can't sit back and watch Gabs get worse."

"I'll talk to her, kiddo." Dad relented, dropping the sponge into the sink and pulling me into his chest for a hug. "If she won't talk to me, I'll speak with a counselor at school about getting her an appointment."

I willed myself not to cry. "I don't want to lose her the same way we lost Mom."

"I won't let that happen," he assured me. "I promise."

We finished cleaning the dishes in a strange silence. The whole time, my dad kept pausing to glance over at me, only to look away when I tried to face him. I couldn't help but feel like he was trying to work up the courage to tell me something, but when everything was put away, he slunk off into the living room to watch the Discovery Channel. *This should feel better*, I thought. With a tightness in my chest I was desperate to alleviate, I grabbed two empty wineglasses and headed upstairs. Sam was lying across my bed on her stomach, paging through one of our old high school yearbooks.

"This was not a good year for my hair," she said, pointing to her sophomore year school picture.

I settled down beside her on the bed. "That was right about the time I went through my weird eyebrow phase."

"That was such an iconic choice," she said with a laugh and closed the yearbook. "So, how did *that* go?"

I shrugged. "Kind of as expected. He didn't say much. You know my dad, he's not a man of many words. He said he would talk to her about going to the school counselor."

"That's a step in the right direction," Sam assured me. "I'll check in on her, okay? I won't let anything happen while you're at school. But you need to focus on finishing your senior year of college. Have fun, let yourself kiss that hot-ass hockey player."

I let out a groan of frustration at the mention of Sebastian. When I'd left for break, I'd done so with the highest confidence that being away from Dallard would help smother the burning need inside of me. But the distance wasn't helping to curb my appetite.

"I want to do more than kiss him," I admitted.

"Why don't you?"

"I've only known him four months, and half that time it was an effort to keep from strangling one another."

"You were hurt by someone you loved, but that doesn't mean every person will let you down," she said. "Sleeping with Sebastian doesn't have to be anything more than sex. Keep things casual. Focus on your physical connection and have fun."

Keep things casual. Was I capable of doing that?

"Don't compare Sebastian to what you had with Matt," she added. "They don't have to be the same."

"Stop reading my mind, you witch!" I threw one of my decorative pillows at Sam, and she batted it down to the ground. I hated when she was right.

"Promise me something, will you?" she asked, her voice quiet. "Put Grace first, just this once. You can't keep showing up for everyone but yourself."

"I'll try, I promise."

>> <<

Later that night, after finishing off a bottle of wine and watching *Elf*, I found myself lying awake next to Sam, listening to the soft sounds of her snoring. Even the alcohol hadn't helped me fall asleep. I pushed off the blankets and slid out of the bed. Before I even knew where I was going, my feet stopped in front of Gabby's room. I pressed my ear against her door and held my breath, listening for a sign that she was awake. After several long seconds of silence, I pushed open the door and stepped inside.

The room was dark save for a thin strip of moonlight that spilled from a part in her curtains. Gabby was asleep with her headphones in. I could her the faint hum of her music in the silence. She was just like me when it came to being trapped inside her head. Slowly, I lowered myself into her bed and scooted up beside her. She shifted as I wrapped my arms around her and pulled her into my chest.

"What the hell," she mumbled, blinking open her sleep-heavy eyes.

I didn't say anything. Instead, I tightened my hold around her and pulled her even closer to my chest. She used to sneak into my bed all the time growing up, usually after a bad dream or during a thunderstorm.

"Grace, get off of me," she huffed, though she made little effort to push me away.

"I miss you," I said, closing my eyes and willing myself to remember the days when she would beg to have a sleepover in my room.

Gabby didn't say anything for a while. I was afraid to move, scared that any sudden shift would have her huffing at me to get out, but it never came. I nearly cried the next time she spoke.

"If you steal the blankets, I'm kicking you out."

That night, just for the briefest of moments, I felt like I had my little sister back.

CHAPTER 17

Sebastian

Campus was buried under a foot and a half of snow. I'd just made it back to the hockey house when the blizzard hit, and it wasn't until I woke early the next morning that the storm began to slowly taper off. I watched out the frost-covered window as snowflakes drifted down from the sky unhurriedly. The plows had yet to make their way through the quiet neighborhood, which meant it was nearly impossible to get anywhere on campus without the use of a shovel or snowshoes. I was going out of my mind trapped inside, alone, with no way to entertain myself. Normally, I relished any opportunity to have the place to myself. It was hard to find a quiet moment living with four roommates. But right now, I needed something or someone to distract me from myself.

If I wasn't in a state of half-panic over Duncan's disappearing act, I was overanalyzing everything that had happened between Grace and me before winter break. I was worried for my future and my sanity—both seemed to be slipping further away from me with each passing day. More than anything, I wanted to know if Grace felt as strung out as I did, like an addict going through withdrawal.

Half of me wished I could turn back time to stop myself from following her into the locker room, and the other half wanted to turn back time so I could experience it all over again.

I shuffled aimlessly from room to room, as if expecting to find something new each time I retraced my path through the house. The storm had delayed my roommates from returning to campus, so for the next twenty-four hours, I had to find some way to keep myself from doom spiraling. Eventually, I queued up an old Toronto Maple Leafs game in the living room. It was only five minutes into the first period when I heard the unmistakable sound of a knock at the front door. Who the hell was out during a blizzard? When another knock rattled the old Victorian, I paused the game and approached the front of the house.

A light flurry blew inward as I pulled open the door. Standing on the front porch, buried under several layers of winter clothing dusted in a fine layer of snow, stood the last person I'd expected to see. Grace looked like a giant marshmallow. Her face was mostly hidden beneath a large blue scarf, a pink nose poking out from beneath the thick wool. We stared at each other for several long seconds before she launched herself forward into my arms, the force of her body colliding with mine hard enough to make me stumble backward into the doorframe as she wrapped her legs around my waist. An icy nose against the skin of my neck tore a startled gasp from my mouth. Before I knew what was happening, Grace was kissing me. Her lips moved over my own in desperate, hurried movements as I stood frozen, so utterly surprised by the sudden turn of events that my brain and body felt disconnected. It took Grace's tongue tracing the seam of my lips to elicit a response. When I finally kissed her back, I did so with haste, as if to assure her I felt just as starved of her touch as she did of mine. There was yearning behind each stroke of her tongue and roll of her body, a deep demand for more. But all too soon, Grace pulled away, peppering a line of hot kisses along my jawline as she did. Her mitten-covered hands came up to grip my face, and the heat of our ragged breaths swirled in the air between us. I smiled at the sight of her lips, which were now as red and raw as the tip of her nose.

"This better not be about the bet," she warned, and as she spoke, I could hear the fear in her voice.

"I can't even think about the bet when you're kissing me," I promised, lifting one hand to brush a piece of hair out of her face. "I want you so badly."

Her eyes glazed over in a haze of lust. "I missed you," she said, leaning her head against mine. And then, as if realizing what she'd just admitted to, Grace quickly added, "I missed your body."

"Only my body? Is that all I'm good for?"

"If you must know, you're also a good training partner."

I tilted back my head and let out a low chuckle. "What else did you miss? There has to be something else."

She shook her head in a refusal to answer my question.

"Did you miss my relentless teasing?"

Grace's lips scrunched up as if she was trying to hold back a smile.

"And the feeling of my eyes watching you from across the ice?"

A flush crept down her neck, but she remained silent.

"What about the suggestive remarks I like to whisper into your ear?"

This time, she bit her lip. I nearly groaned at the sight.

"Tell me, Grace, what do you want?"

She hesitated. I had an inkling she was calculating precisely how much information to share. I hadn't forgotten the way she'd clammed up at my birthday party during our little truth circle. It was easy to see how uncomfortable she felt about the prospect of sharing. Even her best friend had looked surprised when she'd agreed to play that stupid game.

"I want to stop wondering what it would feel like if I allowed myself to be with you," she confessed. "But I'm not ready for anything serious. All I know is that you make me feel good."

She didn't trust me, and I couldn't blame her. Right now, I was willing to accept "nothing serious" if it meant I could have her.

"Anything else?"

"Can we keep this between us, at least for now?"

"You ashamed of me?" I kept my tone teasing, worried I might scare her away if I revealed how frustrating those words were to hear.

"I'm not," she said, reaching up to trail her fingers along the stubble on my chin. "We don't have to hide, maybe just keep things private."

"I can do that."

Her thighs clenched around my waist. "Are your roommates here?"

I shook my head, and seconds later we were stumbling further into the house. The moment her feet touched the floor, Grace started to rip off the winter gear. There were so many layers that by the time she got to the second coat, I was hunched over in laughter, both hands on my knees as she struggled to break free of the clothes.

"You could help me, you know," she said, huffing out a breath as she struggled with the zipper.

"All you needed to do was ask." I threw Grace over my

shoulder without a second thought, taking the stairs two at a time as I ran to my bedroom. She squealed out a high-pitched laugh as I kicked open my door and tossed her onto the bed.

"Stay still," I commanded.

Right now, Grace was going to learn a thing or two about patience. Slowly, I pulled down the zipper of her second coat, tossing it over the side of the bed once her arms were free. Grace watched me intently, eyes glazed over with anticipation as I took my time undressing her, dragging each layer of clothing down her body in a slow promise. I could feel her patience waning, but I didn't rush things. Instead, I took my sweet time removing the layers, letting my hands slide over the curve of her hips and the sides of her legs. Each article joined the growing pile of clothes along the side of the bed until she was down to her lacy blue underwear.

Grace was perfectly spread out for me, her legs parted and her hair splayed out in a halo around her head. I committed the image to memory. My eyes swept across the smooth expanse of skin that was freckled in a strange constellation of beauty marks. A small scar marked the flesh across her upper thigh. I trailed my fingers over every curve of her body, taking care to note the moments she tensed, like when my fingers dragged along the spot below her ear where her neck met her jaw.

"Are you just going to touch me?" she asked, clearly fed up with my slow perusal of her body. In response, I stood up from the bed. The movement elicited a low whine of impatience. But once I began to remove my own clothes, Grace went silent. Her eyes burned into me as I slipped out of my shirt and sweatpants. The tent in my briefs was proof enough of how much I wanted her, and Grace's eyes widened at the sight. With a knowing smirk, I left them on and slowly crawled onto the bed. I wanted this moment to be about Grace, not me.

Our first time together had been a magnificent collision. After weeks of quiet study sessions and flirtatious teasing, we'd come together in an explosion of passion. It had happened so quickly that I'd barely had time to appreciate her. I wasn't going to make that mistake again. My fingers returned to her skin, circling a dusty pink nipple as it hardened under my touch. Grace was watching me with awe in her eyes, as if she couldn't believe this was happening. I continued to explore her, tracing the underside of her breast and dragging my fingers further down her body. Her stomach tensed, and she sucked in a sharp breath when I reached the very top of her underwear.

"If you don't want this—"

"Don't even finish that sentence," she interrupted, hands coming up to cup my face. "I want this as badly as you do."

A wave of relief crashed over me, but I didn't let it show. Reaching down, I tugged at her underwear. Grace lifted her hips compliantly as I slid the material down her legs and tossed it over the side of the bed. As I moved back over her, I spread her legs and settled myself between them, eyes glued to the bare skin of her core. She was a pretty pink, her folds glistening. The memory of my cock sinking inside of her sent a shiver down my spine. Watching myself disappear into her tight pussy had been a euphoric experience, one I was eager to relive. But tonight, I wanted to remind Grace of my promise to make her beg, and to teach her that good girls got rewarded for having patience.

I leaned down over her chest, taking her nipple into my mouth and sucking the sensitive skin. She mewled against me as my tongue flicked across the rosy bud. With my other hand, I trailed a path down her stomach until my fingers met the bare skin above her opening. Her whole body shook as I inched my hand forward and felt the wetness gathered there. Grace buried her hands in my hair just as I latched my teeth around her nipple and bit. Though I was gentle, she arched against me and let out a beautiful whimper of pleasure.

I dragged my pointer finger across her opening and settled at the very top, pressing down against the most sensitive part of her. Her hips surged forward to meet my movements, greedy for more. Slowly, I worked my finger over her in small circles. She let out a throaty groan as I increased the pressure, pushing more deeply against her clit. Soon enough, Grace was moving against me in rhythmic thrusts as my mouth devoured the soft skin of her breast. She reached up and drove her hands through my hair. I felt a slight burn on my scalp as her grip tightened, her entire body writhing against me. I continued to tease her relentlessly until her movements became frantic and her body tensed, all telltale signs of an impending orgasm.

Right before she reached her crest, I released her nipple, and my fingers stilled. A wicked smirk touched my lips as she let out a long whine. Grace's eyes flew open, her pupils blown wide as a desperate look spread across her face.

"Don't stop," she pleaded, chest heaving up and down. "I was so close."

"Don't you remember what I said last time?" I asked, delight sweeping through me at the pleading expression in her eyes.

Grace let out another impatient whine. "Now is not the time for talking."

I let out a tsk. "Only good girls get to orgasm. Think really hard. What did I say the last time you were so desperate for me?"

She looked at me in shock, as if she couldn't believe I was being serious. After a long moment, she tugged at her bottom lip with her teeth in a sign of careful consideration. My eyes zeroed in on her mouth. The next moment, realization dawned across her face.

"You told me that next time I'd have to beg."

I nodded my head, pleased to know that she remembered. Grace looked at me expectantly, as if answering the question was all I needed to continue dealing out her pleasure. When I did nothing, she let out an irritated huff.

"Please don't stop," she said, barely above a whisper.

My eyebrows shot up.

"That's all you got? I'm going to need much, much more if you want to come."

She narrowed her eyes at me, but her cheeks flushed as if the thought excited her. Grace might not have realized it yet, but her body was delighted at the opportunity to surrender to me. I leaned down so that my lips were hovering over her mouth and brushed a soft kiss against it.

"Do you want my mouth on that pretty pussy? Do you want to explode with your thighs wrapped around my shoulders?"

A moan escaped her lips, breath fanning over my face. *I'll take that as a yes.*

"I need a verbal response, Grace," I commanded.

She didn't hesitate this time. "Yes."

"Then you'd better beg me."

Grace looked into my eyes, the fire within hers burning even brighter. She wanted to fight back. It was only natural, given our past. But beneath her struggle, I saw just how much the idea of surrender excited her. Grace was always in control. Handing it over to me wasn't in her nature, but bending to my will had its perks. I was willing to show her just how pleasurable it could be.

"Please," she said finally, eyes fluttering shut.

This time, I could hear just how much she meant it. Exhilaration coursed through me. My cock was impossibly hard, straining to fill her up. Despite how much I wanted to bury myself inside her, I wouldn't. Tonight was about her pleasure.

"Please what?" I asked. My fingers flicked across her clit, and she squirmed beneath me.

"Please don't stop," she begged in a rasp that shot straight to my throbbing member.

I scooted down the bed, trailing a line of kisses down her stomach. My fingers remained perched at her entrance, a reminder of my promise. I pulled her thighs over my shoulders and settled before her pussy. It was a beautiful sight, pink and swollen from my earlier teasing. I ran my tongue across the slick on her thigh, pleased by the moan it pulled from her lips.

"I need you to be more specific, Grace. Tell me exactly what you want. Beg for it."

She looked down at me in rapture, mouth parted slightly, chest rising and falling at a frantic pace. I didn't look away as I puckered my lips and blew across her center.

"Please get me off with your mouth," she pleaded, voice laced with desire. "Please, Sebastian, I need your mouth on me now. Please let me—"

I dove forward, my finger sinking into her as my mouth closed over the sensitive nerves at the top of her opening. Graced cried out, her back arching against the bed. My tongue flicked out, and I was met with a burst of her tangy flavor. She was fucking perfect, and all mine. I wanted her to see stars by the time I was done with her, so I set to work, easing my finger in and out of her as my lips moved over her clit. Grace's response was nothing less than enthusiastic. She moaned loudly, her hands clutching at the sheets as she tried to find purchase.

Grace wasn't quiet as I feasted upon her. Every movement of my tongue drew out sighs and whimpers, all of them tumbling out of her perfect mouth with a breathy gasp. Her entire body shook as I eased another digit into her and curled the tips of my fingers. Grace was frantic, thrashing against me as I pumped in and out of her, my tongue drawing circles along her clit. I could sense she was nearing her climax when her body began to tense and her moans grew louder. Grace's head was tipped back onto the pillow, eyes closed and mouth parted in ecstasy. I watched in fascination as she lost herself to pleasure, body rolling against me.

Grace's thighs tensed around my head; I knew she was about to tip over the edge and into oblivion. I sucked her clit into my mouth while my free hand reached up and tweaked her nipple. She detonated that very moment, and the cry that left her mouth was music to my ears. Grace's inner walls clenched around my fingers, sucking them deeper into her as she thrust herself against my face, riding out the aftershocks of her orgasm. Her pussy was still gripping my fingers as I pulled away from her center.

Grace's eyes fluttered open and immediately found mine. I smiled wickedly at her, content at the sight of her flushed cheeks and general look of awe. She was still struggling to catch her breath, her naked body moving up and down as she tried to swallow large gulps of air.

"What did we learn today, Grace?" I asked arrogantly, unable to hide the smugness in my tone.

Grace could barely form words, but she managed to croak, "You're good at eating pussy."

I shook my head; the smile never left my lips. "Good girls get rewarded. As long as they ask nicely."

She pushed onto her elbows, head tilting to the side as she studied me with open curiosity. I shifted, sucking in a breath as my cock dragged along the side of her leg.

"And what do you get?" she asked with a devious grin.

"The pleasure of watching you come undone is gift enough."

"I don't think so."

Grace tugged me forward with shocking strength, twisting out of the way as I collided with the bed. I rolled over, and she moved to straddle me, assuming my previous position. Seeing her naked and hovering above me was tempting, to say the least.

"I don't need anything," I assured her, though a cold shower would be necessary.

Grace just shook her head. I could see stubbornness behind her eyes as she grasped the waistband of my briefs and tugged them downward.

"Don't worry," she murmured, scooting down until her hands were braced on the bed alongside my hips. "This won't take long."

I opened my mouth to object, but my good intentions were ruined the moment her tongue flicked across my tip. A few seconds later, her lips closed around me. A strangled groan from deep in my throat broke free. She smiled, eyes glimmering in triumph.

"Fuck," I hissed as she took me even deeper into her mouth, her tongue swirling against my shaft.

She repeated the motion, pulling all the way up so that her lips were at the head and then sinking down, taking me as deep as she could into her throat. Her hand wrapped around the base, squeezing lightly as she moved her head up and down. Euphoria coursed through me at the sensation of her mouth against my skin and the sight of her perfect lips swallowing my length. Desperate for something to hold on to, I laced my fingers through her hair and guided her as her hand and mouth worked in perfect unison.

Again and again she took me into her tight mouth, my tip nudging the back of her throat with each thrust. I closed my eyes and tried to picture something mundane to keep this going, but the heat of her lips and the pressure of her fist around my cock was too much. A zing of pleasure shot down my spine, and I tried to pull Grace off, but she resisted, taking me deeper into her throat. I came with a loud groan, hips snapping off the bed as I thrust into her mouth.

"This was supposed to be about you," I finally said once I was able to catch my breath.

"It's about us," she responded, leaning down to brush a soft kiss against my lips, "and I had to remind you that I'm good with my mouth as well."

"Feel free to remind me whenever you want."

Grace chuckled as she reached for her discarded clothes and began to dress. I knew what was coming next. She was going to leave, and as much as I wanted to ask her to stay, I refused. Not after her insistence that we keep things casual. Grace wasn't ready to trust me. She needed more time.

"Are you okay?" I asked, unable to help myself. I had to know if she was already regretting her decision. The last time we'd slept together, Grace had fled the scene before I was fully dressed.

"I'm better than okay," she insisted, squeezing my hand in assurance.

I forced myself to remain cool, calm, and collected despite

the growing turmoil inside me. Grace could make the decision to end this at any time, but I was already well into the deep end. Now that I'd had another taste of Grace, there was no going back.

>> <<

Grace

Sebastian insisted on walking me home. Though the sidewalks were hard to traverse, the roads had been plowed serval times over. We didn't speak the whole way. A calm had settled over campus in the wake of the storm, and neither of us seemed eager to break through the peaceful quiet. After a lingering kiss along the side of my neck, Sebastian said goodbye. A giddy smile curved my lips as I stumbled up the stairs, blissfully ignorant of the interrogation awaiting me. With a nudge of my hip, I pushed open the door and stepped into the apartment. A deafening silence greeted my ears. Caroline and Lydia were perched on the couch, the former watching me with a wary expression as I slipped off my winter gear and eased myself into the living room. The examination began almost at once.

"Liar, liar, pants on fire," Caroline sang in greeting.

And just like that, my post-sex euphoria evaporated.

"I wonder," she continued, "have you and Sebastian been canoodling since the night of his birthday, or has this been going on for longer?"

Lydia shook her head, evidently embarrassed by her best friend's dramatics.

"Did you just use the word *canoodle*?" I couldn't help myself, and I was desperate to ease some of the tension ladening the room.

"You do not get to avoid my question! And yes, I used the word *canoodle*. I could have asked how long you've been having dirty sex—"

"Okay," Lydia said, interrupting Caroline's clear attempt at role-playing her future career as a litigator. "Let's have a grown-up conversation about this. Grace, that begins with you telling us about Sebastian."

This was *so* not how I'd wanted to end my night. Not only had I endured an hour-long motivational talk from Sam on the drive back to school, but I was emotionally exhausted from being vulnerable with Sebastian and physically exhausted from everything that came after. The only thing that sounded better than sleep was a long, hot bath paired with a podcast.

"You can start by telling me what happened at Sebastian's birthday party," Caroline prompted, as if she could sense an excuse was about to fly out of my mouth.

"We kissed. And then I pushed him into the lake."

"So that's why he was wet," Lydia mused at the same time as Caroline asked, "That's all? I need more details. How was the kiss? Why did you push him in the lake?"

I had a feeling it was going to be a while until I got to bed.

"You can trust us. You know that, right?" Lydia's voice was soft, as if she were trying to convey the sincerity behind her words.

I did trust them—as least, I wanted to—but I wasn't used to talking about this stuff with anyone other than Sam. I'd never been close with my roommate in Boston. She was my biggest competition on the team, which meant we were always pitted against one another, and when our coach moved me to the first line, things only got worse. Matt had a reputation as a player back then, and my roommate made it known that I was just another puck bunny on his roster. I was accustomed to people judging me for who I associated with. Growing up, everyone had treated me differently when they found out my mom was in a mental facility. No one had wanted to be friends with the girl whose mother was "insane." Sam was the only friend who'd stuck by my side after the news spread.

"I was worried you might judge me for wanting him after everything that happened at the start of the season," I admitted, forcing words out despite my every instinct. "And then I convinced myself that sleeping with him was a mistake, one that would never happen again, so it didn't make sense to tell anyone. I'm sorry. I know I should have said something, but I was so confused about my own feelings."

"I'm not mad, I just wish you would have been honest with me," Caroline said.

"And it's not like we couldn't tell there was tension. You guys have been eye-fucking each other at lunch for weeks," Lydia added.

I shook my head in embarrassment. "I'm an idiot, and I'm not good at opening up. It takes me a while to feel comfortable enough to share the more private parts of my life, and everyone usually gives up before I get there." Another thought struck me less than a second later. "Wait, how did you guys find out?"

Lydia visibly shuddered as she said, "I heard you two at it in the women's locker room."

Oh. My. God. Nothing could stop the rush of humiliation that doused my entire body in heat. I was seconds away from bursting into flames.

"I don't even know what to say." I stared down at my hands as if they were the most interesting thing in the world. "I'm mortified that you overheard us."

"Oh, me too. I can't un-hear Sebastian calling you 'good girl.'"

Caroline let out a shriek of laughter. They were *never* going to let me live this down.

"I never would have guessed you'd be shy talking about sex," Caroline said. "How was it? If you had to compare to past guys, what would you rate it out of ten?"

I was *so* not cut out for this conversation, and I'd already pushed myself past my normal limits of sharing by tenfold. Nonetheless, I knew how relentless Caroline could be. "There's only one past guy," I admitted, and her mouth fell open as she glanced at Lydia like I'd just shared the juiciest piece of gossip.

"Just Matt?" she asked with an incredulous stare.

I nodded.

"Is he also a hockey-playing enemies-to-lovers type?"

Exasperated, I looked to Lydia for help. At times, she was the only one with the power to talk sense into Caroline, and right now, I was desperate for a reprieve. Her brow quirked in amusement, as if to say, *This is your own fault.*

I glanced back at Caroline and let out a long sigh. "He's a hockey player, yes. But we were friends before we started seeing each other." If I were honest, the only thing that Sebastian and Matt had in common was their love for hockey. Outside of that, they were pretty much opposite.

"Are you and Sebastian dating?"

Ugh. Was this ever going to end?

"We're just sleeping together, it's nothing serious," I said, then quickly added, "I can't handle more than that at the moment."

"Okay, so how was the sex? Did he make you—"

"Please stop, this is going to make my brain explode," I pleaded.

Lydia finally came to my rescue, shooting Caroline a warning look. The blond simply shrugged and asked, "Why are you so scared to talk about him? Or anything related to your feelings, for that matter?"

"Are you my therapist now?" I bit back, my temper rising.

"She would be a terrible therapist, she has no boundaries," Lydia quipped.

"You're a psychology major, Grace." Caroline laughed. "You literally study the mind. Keeping things in is—"

"Bad, I know," I cut in. "My mom, who is severely bipolar, went into a manic episode and ended up accosting someone at the grocery store when I was a kid. None of the girls at school wanted to hang out with me after that. Their moms didn't want them around someone with an unstable parent. And then, two weeks after being released from her in-patient hospital treatment, she decided that being a mother wasn't her thing. So yes, I have a hard time trusting people. That's a potential side effect of being abandoned."

The resulting silence spoke volumes. Caroline's bright eyes were wide as saucers. After several long moments of solid discomfort, Lydia leapt to her feet and pulled me into a crushing hug. "Did that feel good to get off your chest?" she asked as she pulled away, looking over me like a proud parent picking up her kid after their first day of kindergarten.

"I think so," I said, feeling like a tiny weight had been lifted off my shoulders. "If nothing else, it was worth it to see Caroline's face."

"Maybe this is a good moment to admit that I can be a little overbearing at times," Caroline confessed, stepping in front of Lydia and wrapping her arms around me. "I'm sorry for pushing."

"It's okay. I needed the shove."

"You can always be honest with us, Grace," Lydia said. She wrapped her fingers around my hand and gave it a little squeeze.

"You risked your future at school to fight for our team, and for that, we'd never betray you. Know that we're here to talk if you ever need to. And we won't tell anyone about you and Sebastian. You don't always have to keep everything to yourself."

I was finally starting to believe it.

>> <<

January was a frenzied blur of sleepless nights, endless study sessions, and overwhelming success on the ice. With Sebastian taking up so much of my evenings, I had little time to stress about how things were going at home. Even so, some days I found myself idly scrolling through my messages with Gabby, trying to work up the courage to reach out. Her silence was louder than any screaming match or disagreement we'd had in the past. But each time I felt tempted to reach out, I remembered what Sam had said about putting myself first. Right now, I needed to trust my dad to take care of Gabs.

In the moments that Sebastian and I spent together, everything else in the world was ambient noise. I didn't need my wireless headphones to keep from overthinking. Sebastian was the ultimate distraction. In the haze of our lust, we took ample time discovering every last inch of one another. It was proving difficult to remain productive when we were alone. He couldn't keep his hands to himself, and I was only so strong. It felt impossible to resist him when his every touch sent sparks along my skin.

"I need to finish this," I said to Sebastian, glaring down at the hand that was stroking my thigh. It had become routine to spend our Sunday evenings tucked away in his tidy room, catching up on school work while *Parks and Recreation* played on a loop as background noise. His bed was more than twice the size of mine, which meant we could both fit comfortably with our books spread out across the mattress. But studying in bed wasn't always the most productive activity for us, not when there were other things we'd both rather be doing. Tonight, Sebastian seemed determined to halt all progress on my essay. Every few minutes, his fingers would inch further up my leg, and I'd have to spend the next few minutes re-reading what I wrote in an effort to refocus. At this point, I was completely worked up, my underwear drenched from his teasing. My body was hyperaware of Sebastian's warmth as he shifted beside me, his leg pressing against my own.

"Then finish," he said in a smug tone. "No one is stopping you."

The bastard had the audacity to spread his fingers across my entire thigh and squeeze.

"You are diabolical," I muttered, slamming my computer screen shut and turning to face him. "This better be quick. I still have two thousand words to write."

I lay back on his pillows as he set his laptop on the ground. There was a wicked gleam dancing behind his green eyes as I spread my legs in invitation.

"I don't think you'll need much of a warm-up," he murmured. "I bet you're already soaked."

Sebastian grabbed the waistband of my sweatpants and tugged. I let out a surprised squeal as my entire body was dragged further down the mattress. He didn't look away from me as he peeled off my pants. Once they were gone, his eyes dropped to my underwear.

"As I expected."

"You're such a tease; can you blame me?"

I pulled off my sweatshirt and sports bra in haste, eager to feel his skin against mine. All thoughts of my homework assignment evaporated the moment Sebastian started removing his clothes. My throat bobbed. I watched eagerly as he peeled of his shirt and stepped out of his briefs.

"Are you sure you want this to be quick, beautiful? I could get you off three times before even filling that perfect hole of yours."

Sebastian meant every word. At this point, he was an expert at giving me orgasms, with or without the assistance of his—

"Just fuck me," I demanded.

Sebastian settled over me, pressing my legs to the bed on either side of him. His eyes were ravenous as he grabbed his cock and brought it to my entrance. Only once I began to wiggle with impatience did he shift forward, the tip of his engorged member rubbing against my slit. I felt my pussy clench in anticipation and urged my hips forward.

"You're gonna give me one perfect orgasm *before* I fuck you, got it?"

I bit down the urge to scream out in frustration. My body was more than ready to take him, and he knew it. Yet another part of me preened under his command, excited at the opportunity to follow orders. My heart was pounding in anticipation, chest rising and falling more rapidly with every moment that passed.

"Say it."

"I'm going to orgasm before you fuck me." I repeated the words back breathlessly. Sebastian reached for his bedside table and pulled out a condom. He tore it open with his teeth and secured the rubber, sliding it on with ease. In slow, even motions he began to rub the bottom of his shaft up and down my opening. I shifted underneath him, my body surging forward to increase the pressure along my clit.

The dull throb of pleasure low in my stomach started to build with each thrust of his hips. It never took much with Sebastian. The fire between us burned bright and hard when we came together in moments like this. He leaned down to capture my mouth with his own, and I gasped into his lips. The shift in his position sent jolts of pleasure zapping across my skin. He was moving even faster now, his cock pressing further into my folds as he dragged it over my opening, up and down, again and again.

Sebastian's jaw was tight, his muscles tensed as he continued to torture me. I could tell it was getting to be too much for him as well. He wanted to find his release just as badly as I did. The hand pressing my leg into the bed moved between us. At the first touch of his fingers against my heated core, I jolted forward. He grinned at me and rubbed small circles into the concentrated bundle of nerves. In a matter of seconds, the tension deep within me snapped. I slapped a hand over my mouth to muffle the loud moan that poured from my lips. My body spasmed, pussy fluttering as the orgasm whipped through me. The entire time, Sebastian continued to move above me, his shaft slipping over my opening but never inside me.

The pleasure continued to ripple through me, and stars exploded before my eyes. I was still deep in the bliss of my release when he grabbed my hips and flipped me over. With my face pressed against the sheets, Sebastian shoved a pillow under my lower stomach and angled my hips so that my ass was sticking up. He didn't hesitate another moment, pressing into me from behind in a measured thrust. The sensation of his cock sliding into me tore an embarrassing sound from my mouth—something between a moan and a scream. Still reeling from the aftershocks of my orgasm, my pussy pulsed around him as he bottomed out.

"Fuck," Sebastian hissed as my body slowly adjusted to the stretch.

He grabbed my hips roughly, his fingers sinking into the flesh of my thighs with a delicious twinge of pain. Sebastian was steadying himself. Still half delirious from my first orgasm, I pushed my ass back against him in an order for him to start moving. He let out another hiss of breath, pulled out, and drove back into me. The force of his thrust pushed me further into the mattress. I braced my arms above my head and pressed the side of my face into the sheets as Sebastian repeated the motion, his pace remaining steady and hard as he slammed into me from behind.

"Is this what you want?" He groaned and snapped into me even more forcefully.

The moan on my lips was my only response. I could barely think, let alone speak. I couldn't fathom Sebastian's ability to form full sentences as he pounded into me. Each time he bottomed out, a garbled cry burst from my mouth, the sound half swallowed by the sheets. A low, steady pressure deep within me started to grow, heat building in my core as our skin slapped together with every buck of his hips.

The pleasure felt different this time, less urgent but just as all-consuming. His fingers delved into my hair, tightening at the base of my scalp before he gently tugged in a silent command. I pushed off the bed until my back was pressed to his chest, our bodies jolting as he continued at a ruthless pace. The hand in my hair dropped to my throat, his finger curling around my neck in a gentle yet firm grip. My entire body was on fire, burning brighter as we continued to climb even higher together.

"You're"—*thrust*—"fucking"—*thrust*—"perfect."

I was overwhelmed with sensations—the blazing heat of our

flesh pressed together, the drop of sweat sliding down my back, Sebastian's hot breath in my ear as he whispered my name over and over again like I was his favorite prayer.

"Are you up for one more?" Sebastian all but growled the words, and my pussy clenched in anticipation.

"Yes."

Sebastian's pace stuttered for a moment and then picked up.

"Then I need you to say the magic words, Grace."

He was thrusting into me so fast that I could barely keep myself upright, my body wholly reliant on the firm hand gripping my waist to keep from crashing down into the mattress. Through the overwhelming pleasure, I spoke, desperate for release.

"Please make me—*ahhh*."

I couldn't get out the words before Sebastian pressed his finger against my clit, dragging a scream from my throat. My entire body shook as I arched against him and exploded. The orgasm crashed over me in a tremendous wave, sweet bliss rushing through my body as I spasmed around his cock. The force of me clamping around him was all it took for Sebastian to reach his own release. With a groan, his hips stuttered against me three times, and he stilled. We collapsed on the bed, bodies spent, panting to catch our breath. I could feel my pulse between my legs.

For a moment, we lay together in silence, neither of us able to speak. Slowly, Sebastian shifted so that he was facing me.

"Better than studying, right?"

Much better, but now I was completely spent. My body ached deliciously, and the thought of getting up seemed like too much effort. I knew I'd regret not going to the bathroom, though, so I hauled myself into a sitting position and started to gather my clothes.

"I should go home so I can actually get some studying done, and I need a shower," I murmured.

"Shower here."

"I need an everything shower, and you definitely don't have my exfoliating body scrub or deep-conditioning hair mask."

Sebastian didn't argue as I pulled on my clothes and disappeared into the bathroom. Just out of curiosity, I pulled back his shower curtain and looked inside the tub. It was just as clean as the rest of his space, with several female-looking products tucked into the back corner. Were those for me, or were they from his previous relationship? Things between us were so casual at this point that I didn't think it was right to ask about Kate, but that didn't stop me from wondering about her.

Sebastian was half dressed when I finally emerged from the bathroom, a pair of gray sweatpants hanging low on his hips.

"You got a call from Matt when you were in the bathroom," he said, handing me my phone.

I froze at the sound of my ex-boyfriend's name. "You spoke to him?"

"No. But he called twice."

Sebastian said nothing more, but I could read the discomfort in his body language. He stood with both hands shoved into the pockets of his pants to keep from fidgeting, his brow furrowed and lips pressed into a thin line. After a long moment of tense silence, he asked, "Are you seeing other people?"

I would have thought he was joking if it weren't for the low growl in his voice. "When would I have time to see anyone else?"

"You want to keep this casual, and that's fine with me, but we clearly need to define some boundaries. I don't sleep with more than one person at a time, and I don't like to share."

"I only want to sleep with you."

A hint of familiar smugness flickered across his face. "This Matt guy, I don't have to worry about him?"

"No," I said carefully, hesitant to approach my next admission "But I should probably mention that he's my ex-boyfriend." Tension crept back into the bedroom at once, filling the space between us with a sense of tangible uncertainty.

"You keep in touch?" He asked cooly.

"On and off," I admitted. "We were friends before anything else, but the romantic part of our relationship is over."

His shoulders visibly relaxed, one hand retreating from his pocket to rub the back of his neck. "Is there anything you want to know about Kate?"

Sebastian's words left me momentarily speechless, and though I should have said no, I couldn't deny that I was curious about his previous relationship. It only took a few long seconds for my resolve to break. "Do you miss her? You two were together for a while . . ."

"I miss her sometimes," he said truthfully, never looking away from me, "but not in the way you're thinking. Kate showed up for me at my lowest moment. I don't love her anymore, but I love what she did for me."

I couldn't lie to myself, hearing those words stung a little. *This is supposed to be casual,* I reminded myself. Why should his past matter when this was just a bit of fun?

"We weren't right for each other. It took meeting you for me to realize that," Sebastian added, as if sensing my disappointment, the very disappointment I was trying to convince myself I shouldn't feel. He strode forward and placed his hands on my hips, dragging me into the warmth of his chest. "There's something else I need to say," he whispered into my hair. "I'm sorry—for everything. I was selfish. I didn't want you anywhere near DuLane because from the moment I saw you, I wanted you. I don't like feeling out of control."

Was Sebastian trying to make things more difficult for me?

"So you're saying that you were mean to me because you liked me? That is such playground behavior," I joked, desperate to get back to our normal, teasing dynamic.

He chuckled. "It was stupid. *You* make me stupid."

Knowing that Sebastian had liked me from the beginning only made things more complicated. How long could we keep things casual? *Don't overthink it, Grace. Let things happen.* It was Sam's voice, urging me to let go of my worries.

"Thank you for telling me that. I forgive you."

Sebastian placed a tender kiss on my forehead. I melted into his touch, allowing the stress to leave my body, but his next words sent a jolt of panic rushing through me.

"Do you want to stay the night?"

Don't you dare freak out, I told myself. "It's big step, right? I thought we were keeping things casual."

"I'm not asking you to marry me, Grace. You're always going back and forth between our places. Wouldn't it be easier to stay here every now and then? Don't you want to?"

Of course I did—that was the problem. If I started treating this thing with Sebastian like a real relationship, I was bound to develop real feelings. The lovesick, heartbreak-inducing type.

"Maybe next time. Is that okay?"

"Let me walk you home at least."

"Absolutely not."

We both knew that if he walked me home, he'd end up in my bed.

"At least text me when you get there." Sebastian pulled me back into his arms for another goodbye kiss. This one was much longer and much deeper than our last. I had no doubt he was attempting to distract me from leaving. When Sebastian's tongue met mine, I pulled away breathlessly, scared that I'd fall victim to his antics.

"You'll survive without me, I promise."

"Let yourself out," he told me, nodding toward the bedroom door. "If I follow you downstairs, I'll likely follow you home."

Sebastian held up my coat, and I slipped into the heavy material. My backpack quickly followed as he secured the straps over my shoulders. I resisted the urge to glance over my shoulder as I was leaving. Sometimes, all it took was one smoldering look from that boy and I was in deep trouble.

CHAPTER 18
Sebastian

"Watch those edges, Sebastian. You're not deep enough. I need to see more power as you push off!"

I was sick and tired of hearing my name being shouted across the ice. Coach Dawson had been hounding me all practice, scrutinizing my every move. It did nothing to ease the dull twinge in my knee that had set in on Sunday morning in the wake of our back-to-back matches against Omaha. A full day of rest was not enough to ease the inflammation, and after two days of practice, the pain had gotten worse. But I was determined to push through. The last thing I needed was time off the ice to rest, especially given the uncertainty surrounding my future with Detroit. I felt a little more hopeless each day that passed without word from Duncan.

Despite my best efforts to fly under the radar all practice, I could feel eyes on me. Grace had been watching me closely from the moment we hit the ice, as if she could sense something was wrong. For the third time today, she cut in front of me and spoke in a quiet tone so the coaches didn't hear us talking.

"What's wrong? And don't tell me it's nothing. You're favoring your right side."

Damn her for being so perceptive.

"Can't take you eyes off me, can you?" I quipped, flashing a broad smile in an attempt to dissuade her concern. Unfortunately, my words seemed to have the opposite effect. Grace crossed her arms over her chest like she was gearing up to give me a scolding.

"It's just a little dull pain," I admitted, looking around to make sure no one else was close enough to hear. "Nothing to worry about. I don't want to make things worse."

"Then you should rest."

I scoffed at the suggestion. "That's not going to happen. We play Denver this weekend. They're easily our biggest competition this year."

"If you want to be in your best shape for that game, practicing on a sore knee won't help," she insisted, and a few our teammates shot glances our way.

"Don't mom me," I warned in a low tone. "I'm capable of knowing my limits."

I didn't wait around for Grace to tell me off, not when other people had begun to notice our whispered conversation. Instead, I fell back into line behind Kent and prepared for another round of drills. For the remainder of practice, Grace kept her distance, though I could feel her worried glances from across the ice. Knowing both she and Coach Dawson were scrutinizing my every move, I pushed through the pain and finally managed a perfect run through our transitioning and attacking drill. By the time we exited the rink at the end of the hour, the dull throb in my knee had progressed to a steady thrum. I held back a wince as I collapsed onto the bench. I barely had a moment to breathe when Grace was upon me, her helmet nestled between her side and her arm, one gloved hand clasped over the edge of the barrier of the rink.

"Taylor's coming to take a look at that knee," she said matter-of-factly.

I held back a snarl of frustration at the clear concern etched into Grace's eyes. She was doing was she thought was right, but bringing in the head trainer was unnecessary. Pain after an injury like mine was normal occurrence. I couldn't expect to feel in perfect form all the time.

"Don't meddle. I'm fine," I insisted.

"Do you trust me?"

An answer came to me without an ounce of hesitation.

"Yes."

"Then let her look at your knee," she pleaded, and I was prepared to put up a fight until I heard the fear in her tone. "Please, do it for me."

"Fine."

Begrudgingly, I stripped off my gear and folded my socks down to reveal the swollen skin around my knee. Grace let out a dramatic gasp, leaning forward to get a better look. I was seconds away from receiving a lecture when a formidable woman stepped into the players bench. My body was seized by a brief sense of panic at the sight of the middle-aged head trainer. I'd endured countless hours working through torturous exercises with Taylor throughout my recovery period. We'd spent the second half of the previous season working together on a daily basis. While I was thankful for everything she'd done to help me recover, I wasn't thrilled to see her. She placed her kit on the bench beside me and gave me a cautious smile.

"I hear you've been favoring one knee this week," she said in way of greeting.

Taylor had a built-in bullshit detector, so there was no use in lying. I immediately dove into an explanation of my pain, giving an overview of when it had started and how it had progressed. She assessed the knee with careful eyes. After having me extend it, she felt around the swollen area and asked if I had any pain to the touch. Grace remained by my side, watching carefully as Taylor ran her tests.

"I don't think it's anything to be worried about: some inflammation is expected after the severity of your injury. I want you to go back to some of the basic exercises you did when you first started recovery—bridging, calf raises, hip abductions. In the meantime, I'm going to give you a cortisone shot to help with the pain, but I want you to sit out of practice tomorrow."

That was not going to happen.

"I'll do the exercises and the shot, but we have an important game coming up. I can't miss practice."

"You can and you will," said Grace, moving to stand beside Taylor. "Missing one practice won't affect your game. It *will* give you time to get that swelling down."

The head trainer gave Grace an appreciative nod.

"You should listen to her, Sebastian. She also happens to be one of the best players this institution has ever seen."

When I met Grace's eyes, all the fight left in me vanished. She had no idea how much power she had over me.

"Fine."

I sounded like a broken record at this point.

Taylor led us down to the recovery room, where she began to prepare a shot for my knee. To kill time, Grace poured herself an ice bath and stripped down to her sports bra and compression shorts. Before getting in, she slowly bent over to place her phone on the ground, sending me a wicked smirk over her shoulder.

"Ice that knee, but you shouldn't do full submersion for a few days," Taylor instructed.

After administering the shot, she packed up her things and gave me a stern talking-to about listening to my body. The entire time, Grace had a death grip on the edge of the tub, her eyes squeezed closed as she breathed through the overwhelming cold.

"Please distract me," she gasped as soon as Taylor left room, and I could hear the pain in her voice.

"I'm not sure I should get naked here. Anyone could walk in."

She scoffed. "That didn't stop you in the locker room."

"You were naked as well, so I couldn't think straight."

"Distract me," she pleaded. "I need to stop thinking about how cold this damn water is. Tell me about one of your favorite hockey moments. Tell me about your favorite goal, I don't care. Just distract me."

The memory came to my mind without a second thought, an image of a crowded arena and the sound of a raging crowd flooding my senses. I was immediately transported back in time to my youth hockey days.

"After my dad died, when it was just me and my mom, there was no money for me to join a traveling team. But when she married my stepdad, everything changed. I went from playing in house leagues to making the Chicago Fury U12 team."

From that moment on, training became intense. Hockey went from my hobby to my entire world. Even as a kid, I needed to be better than everyone. I worked my ass off and promised myself that I would be the best.

"When I was thirteen, we won the CCM Denver Dash. I remember taking off my bucket and gazing around the arena after the final buzzer rang. I'd never felt larger than life until that win. And then suddenly, I was looking at my dad in the crowd. The pride on his face, the pure amazement, it was like nothing I'd ever experienced."

I could feel my heartbeat in my ears just thinking about that day.

"It was the first time I'd seen him since he died. My mom always said that he came to her at random times, like in the grocery store or outside in our old backyard. If I'm honest, I thought she was delusional. But it finally happened to me, and it didn't take much to realize the significance of him appearing at that very moment."

My chest deflated as I let out a long breath.

"The first year or so after his death, I felt a bit of resentment toward hockey. He was the one who'd taught me to love the sport, and then he was gone. But seeing his face in the crowd and knowing that he was there for my first big win helped reignite my passion. Being on the ice and playing hockey is how I honor his memory."

I'd never told anyone that before, not even my own mother. The memory was sacred, like it was only for me to have. But with Grace, there was no hesitation. I wanted her to know why I was so dedicated to hockey. Maybe it could help her understand why I'd been such an asshole when we'd met.

My mind drifted back to the training room at the sound of sloshing water, as if waking up from a dream. Grace was watching me from the tub with wide eyes and blue-tinged lips. She'd been in the water too long.

"You should get out," I said gently, reaching for a towel from the shelf above her and holding it out. Slowly, she pulled herself from the freezing water and stepped onto the mat. I placed the towel around her shoulders and pulled her against me.

"I didn't know," she said, turning around to face me. Her eyes were filled with unshed tears. "I didn't know that your father died. I don't really know anything about your family, if I'm being honest."

"This is new, Grace. You're not supposed to know everything about me."

"Thank you for sharing that with me." Grace shivered, her teeth rattling as she spoke. Once again, I pulled her into my chest and wrapped my arms around her to share some warmth.

"How old were you when he died?" she asked.

"I was nine. He died in an ice fishing accident."

"I get it now," she said, her breath warm against my neck as she spoke. "I can see how much you love hockey, how hard you work for it, but it's more than that, isn't it?"

It was a rhetorical question. We both already knew the truth. I loved hockey more than anything, but it was more than just a passion for the sport that drove me to be the best. Every time I was out on that ice, it brought me closer to my father and the dream that he gave up to raise me. All of this was for him—maybe even more than it was for me.

>> <<

Grace

"Don't beat yourself up. We all have bad days."

Coach Riley hovered behind me as I pulled my equipment off of the travel bus. I knew she was trying to be nice, but that didn't make me feel better about my performance against Ohio State. I'd been all over the place tonight. The only reason we'd scraped by with a win was because Lydia had picked up my slack.

"Thanks, Coach."

I followed after the stream of my teammates funneling inside DuLane. Everyone chatted about their plans for the night as we dropped our things off in the locker room.

"I'm going to stay here for a bit," I said, glancing over at Lydia as she tossed her warm-up jersey into her locker.

"Is something wrong?" she asked, but I wasn't buying the clueless act, not after she'd spent all game making up for my mistakes.

"Other than the fact that I tripped over my own skates tonight?"

"Come on, it happens to the best of us. You can't be perfect all the time."

"Don't let Caroline hear you say that," I muttered.

After assuring her that I just needed a night to myself, I packed up my locker and headed into the empty arena. The chilled air was an instant relief against the heat of my skin. I settled onto the bench, took out my wireless headphones, and selected one of my playlists at random. But after several songs, I realized the music wouldn't be enough to drown out the world.

Learning about Sebastian's dad had sent me into a bit of a spiral. After he'd opened up to me, all I could think about was the possibility of losing Gabby. Sebastian's dad had been gone in the blink of an eye. I might have lived a version of that, but knowing someone left versus knowing they were taken from you were two completely different things.

When it became apparent that my headphones were useless,

I pulled them off and took in the eerie silence of the empty arena. It felt strange to witness the vast space so empty and quiet. Even during my occasional morning training sessions, there were always staff milling about, preparing for new day. DuLane had been well and truly abandoned for the night, the rink only illuminated by a flickering light from the tunnel behind the bench.

"I thought I'd find you here."

Sebastian's voice was a welcome comfort. The sound glided over my skin and left raised goose bumps in its wake. He slid onto the bench beside me, close enough that our legs were touching, and I found myself shifting even closer to absorb the heat of his body. Sebastian lowered a hand to his thigh palm up, an open invitation for me to touch him. I reached down and traced the tip of my finger over the creases etched into his palm. They were like the lines carved across the rink after practice, right before the Zamboni came through to smooth out the ice.

"You're supposed to hold my hand, not read my palm," Sebastian teased.

I slowly intertwined our fingers, marveling at the sheer expanse of his hand in comparison to mine. "Do you believe in that stuff?" I asked. "Palm reading and fortune telling?"

"Not really. I like to think we pave our own path, not that it's already written."

Sebastian glanced over at me in amusement, as if he'd just discovered something strangely fascinating about me. Was there something on my face, or had my question taken him by surprise? I resisted the urge to brush away a nonexistent crumb from the corner of my mouth.

"If our lives were fated by some predetermined factor, at least we'd have the chance to know how things would play out."

He chuckled. "That would make life very boring."

"I hate not knowing. It drives me crazy."

"I can understand that more than anybody," Sebastian said in a low, pained voice. "But what if you knew how things were going to end and couldn't do anything about it?"

That, I thought, was a very good point. "Why couldn't we have the best of both worlds? A little peek into the future to see what's coming, but the power to change things you don't like."

"You're quite introspective tonight. Any particular reason?"

I was preparing to shrug my shoulders and change the subject when he squeezed my hand, as if to convey something that couldn't be said. I could see it in his eyes. *You can trust me, just like I trust you.*

"I played like shit tonight." Sure, it wasn't a heartfelt confession, but it was a start. Sebastian didn't say anything; I could tell he was waiting for the real answer. "There's nothing you can do to help. I don't even know how to help."

"Help what?"

I could hear Caroline's voice in the back of my mind. *Why are you so scared to talk about him? Or anything related to your feelings for that matter . . .*

"My sister. She hasn't been herself lately," I admitted, biting my bottom lip out of nervous habit. "At first, I thought she was just being a teenager—moody, and stubborn, and a little bit sassy. But it's more serious than that."

"How so?"

"I—well—it's not easy for me to talk about. The only person who knows about my family is Sam," I confessed. Sebastian waited patiently for me to work up the nerve to finish my thoughts. "Gabby is clinically depressed, most likely, or she's in a depressive episode, one that might eventually shift into a manic episode. That's how bipolar disorder works. Both illnesses run in the family—my mother's side—so we've seen this before."

"What can be done?" he asked in a soft, calming voice.

"There's therapy, and medication, of course. But my dad has a hard time trusting mental health professionals. We talked about her seeing a therapist over winter break, but he hasn't followed through. Not yet, at least. I'm just worried he's going to keep putting it off."

"And your mom?"

This time, opening up about my past felt a little easier, as if speaking with my roommates had prepared me to be more vulnerable with Sebastian. Rather than blurting things out in a moment of panic, I spoke softly; each word felt like an unburdening. I recounted my mother's struggles, skimming over the grim details and focusing on the main event: her departure.

"That couldn't have been easy," Sebastian said. "Having someone there one day and not the next is, well . . ."

"It's not the same as your dad. I can't imagine the pain of losing someone that you know loved you with every fiber of their being. My mom wanted nothing to do with me. She wouldn't even let me visit during her hospitalization. I was only twelve, and my parents probably wanted to shield me, but it was too late for that. I was with her during the manic episodes. I heard her and my father fight every night for weeks. I saw her sit in the same chair for over three months and rot. It's hard to hide something like that."

Every time they'd turned me away, I'd felt the knife lodged in my chest slide a little bit deeper. I couldn't fathom why my own mother didn't want to see me. Even to this day, I felt partly to blame. Was it something I'd done? Or was I just not worth fighting for?

"Do you keep in touch with her?"

"She sends me letters sometimes, but I don't read them. She really fucked us up, you know? My dad still hasn't moved on. He'll likely blame himself for her leaving for the rest of his life."

"Why haven't you read the letters?" he asked.

"I'm not interested in hearing excuses for why she left, and I don't want to dredge up those memories. It's painful."

"How often does she write you?"

I frowned, feeling slightly overwhelmed by his barrage of questions. "Every year on my birthday since I turned thirteen. Why?"

Sebastian rubbed the back of his neck in a rare show of nervousness. "I wish I had letters from my dad. I know it's not the same, but I'd do just about anything to hear from him."

Great, now I feel like an asshole.

"I'm sorry, I wasn't think—"

Sebastian seized me by the waist and pulled me into his lap, my legs settling on either side of him. Our faces were mere inches away from each other, the tips of our noses almost touching.

"You don't need to apologize. Thank you for sharing that with me," he said, his eyes roaming over my face in a look of awe. "It can't be easy feeling responsible for your little sister and feeling abandoned by your mother." He paused, a small smile flickering across his face. "You take it with grace."

A laugh deep from my belly burst forth at the same time Sebastian caught my lips in a kiss. I leaned eagerly into his touch, keen to lose myself in the taste of his mouth and the fresh pine scent that clung to his skin. The sensation of our lips moving in tandem brought me to a place of simplicity, one where nothing else mattered but the hunger of our kiss and the urgent touch of his tongue against mine. His warmth fell over me in an embrace. It melted away the frigid grip of fear that had taken hold of my body.

Sebastian pulled away from me with a gasp, as if it had taken everything in him to stop kissing me. "Will you do me a favor?" he asked.

I was already nodding my head before he finished the sentence.

"Put on your skates, will you?" A shred of unease penetrated the blissful haze I'd found myself submerged within.

"Trust me, okay? You can't leave the ice tonight on a bad note."

Trust me. For the first time, hearing those words didn't cause me to tense up. With a leap of faith, I nodded my head in agreement.

"Any other requests?"

He shook his head and said, "Come on, get your skates on and meet me back here."

We departed for our designated locker rooms and emerged a few minutes later, laced up and ready to skate. Sebastian and I met in the middle of the rink, stopping within the line marking the blue circle.

"Here," Sebastian said, shrugging out of his jacket and handing it over to me.

"So chivalrous."

Despite my teasing, I pulled on the coat and took a deep breath of his familiar scent.

"What now?"

He shrugged. "We skate, of course."

Sebastian pushed off and glided in a leisurely circle around me. "Every time we're out here, we're skating with an objective: get the puck, stop the pass, make the hit. Sometimes, it's nice to skate without one."

With gentle nod of agreement, I dug in my edge and pushed off. Sebastian followed close behind me as I swept over the rink without purpose, hands at my side, head tilted back ever so slightly. The only sound to be heard was the whoosh of our blades cutting through the ice. It was familiar and comforting and helped me feel centered after a long day of drifting off course. I closed my eyes and focused on the noise. I let it rush over me until all I could sense was the air against my face and the ice underfoot.

The connection that I had with the ice—that we both had—was more than just a skill or a hobby. Skating kept me grounded. Breathed life back into me. Reminded me that no matter how poorly I played, or how fucked up things got, I still belonged here. If all else failed and nothing made sense, I could always return to the rink and find a little bit of myself on the ice. At that realization, I slowed to a stop and opened my eyes. Sebastian stood just a few feet away from me, the same truth written across his face. I didn't need to thank him for reminding me why this mattered. He knew.

Later that night, after what felt like hours of skating around DuLane Arena with only a dull, flickering light to illuminate the rink, Sebastian and I walked back to my apartment and slipped into my bedroom unnoticed by my roommates. I didn't consider the potential consequences or overanalyze how fast things were moving between us. After he stripped down to his boxers and I changed into an oversized shirt, he pulled me into the tiny bed. We barely fit, but that didn't matter. I lay with my back against his chest, our bodies molded together in a perfect fit. Exhaustion swept over me almost instantly. The last thing I remembered was Sebastian's smooth voice wishing me sweet dreams.

CHAPTER 19
Sebastian

My mind and body were halfway between waking and sleep. A beam of morning sunshine stretched across the bedroom wall. There was a delicious warmth pressed to my chest, and pinpricks dancing across my arm where Grace's head lay, the tantalizing scent of cherries thick in the air. She was still fast asleep, her chest rising and falling in a steady rhythm, hair sprawled over the pillow and along the side of my face. I blinked away the morning cobwebs and glanced around her room.

Grace and I were alike in our preference for order and neatness. Through the gap in her closet doors, I could tell that everything inside was where it should be, either hanging from the clothing rod or tucked away into the built-in shelves. Even her desk was organized; the large pile of books that sat atop it was stacked neatly together under a tiny figurine of a hockey player. Beside the books, there was a dusty purple lamp, a framed picture of her and Sam, and a mason jar filled with different writing utensils. I had a feeling Grace's notes were crafted to perfection. She probably color-coded each subject and had a personalized table for abbreviations.

For some ridiculous reason, I grew hard at the thought of her curled over a book, lip pulled between her teeth as she carefully highlighted the text. All those times we'd spent in silence studying together, pretending as if there weren't some magnetic force pulling us together, played across my mind. Somehow, simply being in her presence was enough to excite me these days. Slowly, the blazing heat of her body pressed against me, and a zing of pleasure shot straight to my cock.

She wiggled again, and without thinking I ground my hips into her ass. The catch of her breath was all I needed to confirm that she was awake and aware. Still, I paused for a moment, my mind finally catching up with my body. Something told me to proceed with caution. Grace had been incredibly vulnerable last night. I could tell how truly exhausted she was after opening up about her family. We'd barely made it back to her place before she'd passed out. The last thing I wanted to do was push her for sex after such an emotionally draining night.

"Don't tell me you fell back asleep," she rasped, grinding against me with another slow roll of her hips.

There was no chance of me falling back asleep now. No chance in hell.

"You can feel how very awake I am," I said, just barely shifting in the cramped space of the bed.

I wanted Grace more than anything. She had to know that.

"Then why did you stop? This is the best wake-up call I've had in months."

At those words, my hesitation vanished. Who was I to deny her what she wanted? If anyone deserved a distraction, it was Grace. I tightened my grip around her and pulled her even tighter against me, burying my face in her neck. She let out a low groan at my touch, back arching as my mouth latched on to her neck. My fingers slipped underneath the hem of her shirt and trailed across the bare skin of her stomach. When I reached the bottom of her breasts, she let out a satisfying hiss of air.

Part of me was still in denial about the fact that I could touch her like this, that she *wanted* me to. I cupped her breast in my hand and squeezed gently. She was the perfect fit, her flesh soft and supple beneath my calloused fingers. My cock twitched as her nipple hardened underneath my touch.

"You're perfect, you know that?" I whispered.

Grace's cheeks flushed even brighter as she glanced over her shoulder.

"Even with morning breath?"

I brushed a kiss to her mouth, taking her bottom lip between my own and sucking. She gasped against me, her body arching into me yet again.

"Even with morning breath," I confirmed.

Grace looked at me bashfully as I shifted back in the bed, creating enough space so that I could pull off her oversized sleep shirt. She lifted herself off the bed to help, holding her arms over her head. Once she was bare, save for the lacy pair of underwear, I allowed myself a moment to admire the view.

"Lie back down on your side like you were when we woke up."

Grace followed my command immediately, making room for me to reach into her bedside table and grab a condom. She was smiling at me with sleepy, lust-filled eyes.

"Good girl."

I pushed down my boxers, slipped on the condom, and pulled Grace against me so her back was pressed along the front of my body. My lips grazed the skin of her neck. At the same time, I reached over her hip and slid my hand below the band of her underwear. She was already wet, my fingers slipping easily through her folds. Grace arched her back the moment I dipped my finger inside her. I worked the palm of my hand against her clit with each teasing thrust of my digit.

Her head fell back, and she released a sigh of contentment. I added another finger, and her hips rolled, meeting every thrust of my hand, her ass rubbing along the length of my already aching cock. She began to shake as I pushed her closer and closer to the edge. Grace was biting down on her lip hard, forcing herself to remain quiet.

"Breathe," I reminded her, and she took in a long drag of air through her nose. At the same time, I withdrew my fingers and pushed her underwear over the curve of her ass. Her back arched, her legs spreading in preparation for me. I rubbed the slick coating on my fingers along my shaft. Then I angled my hips and guided my cock to her dripping seam. Grace's entire body was tense, pulled tight in anticipation of the moment I would enter her. I pushed forward in a slow, deep thrust.

My eyes rolled, satisfaction rushing over me as I sank deeper inside her blissful heat. I gripped her hip and snaked my other arm under her neck and over her shoulder, my hand tracing over her peaked nipple. Grace's walls clenched around me in an enthusiastic response to my touch. I pinched the sensitive skin with gentle fingers and started to move, pushing into her from behind in slow, languid movements. Grace arched into me even further, the angle allowing me to slip deeper inside.

"You're beautiful," I whispered into her neck. Her only response was a low moan of pleasure, one that she muffled by turning her head and burying her face in the pillow. My slow pace started to pick up. I pushed faster, thrusting in and out of her with a bit more force, pulling her back against me each time. I watched greedily as her she arched her back, her ass pushing into me with eagerness. Grace was pulling me deeper, her walls tightening around me each time I bottomed out. The only sound was our ragged breaths, the wet slap of our skin as I rolled my hips into her over and over again. The pleasure was getting to be too much. I could feel my balls starting to tighten, sense that I was just about to fall over the edge.

"Say my name," I urged, reaching down to press a finger against her clit.

Grace hissed out my name in a low moan as her walls clamped down around me, her body shuddering as the orgasm hit. I followed immediately after her. My body jerked as I spilled inside the condom, Grace twitching against me with every last stuttered thrust. She finally stilled in my arms, her body relaxing into mine.

"I can see now that sleepovers have their benefits," she murmured. "Maybe next time, we can do it at your place. I'm not sure this twin will hold up for much longer."

"You can stay with me whenever you want."

I pulled out of Grace and tugged at her hips, guiding her to roll over and face me. Her cheeks were a beautiful shade of pink.

"I know you only like me for my body, but there are other perks to sleeping with me," I said teasingly. "You can tell me anything. You know that, right?"

Grace remained quiet. Her eyes shifted over my face in a slow perusal, like she was trying to commit this moment to memory. I wanted some acknowledgment of my offer, needed to know that she understood what I meant, that I was here for her. But just as I opened my mouth, she nodded her head and buried her face in my chest.

>> <<

Grace

I was starting to wonder how the darkest, most miserable month of the year could bring me so much happiness when reality came flashing across my phone screen in a line of ten digits. The number wasn't saved in my contacts, but I knew who it belonged to. The last time my mother had called me was on the day of my high school graduation. I could picture her perfectly in my mind, standing at the edge of the football field and clutching the strap of her purse like it was a lifeline. She'd shown up looking for forgiveness and the promise of a future with me, and I'd denied her both.

When the call finally ended, I let myself breathe again. The longer I stared down at my phone, the more agitated I grew. She hadn't left a message, so I could only guess why she'd reached out. I considered calling her back just to tell her to fuck off, but the fear of hearing her voice stopped me. There was a strong likelihood I'd fall apart the moment she spoke.

I slipped on my noise-canceling headphones and forced myself to get ready for the day. No matter how loud I blasted my music, it wasn't enough to drown out the sound of my phone ringing or the unease turning my stomach. The morning seemed intent on torturing me with how slowly it dragged on. I went through all the normal motions—practice, breakfast, class—feeling like I was trapped behind a warped pane of glass, the world nothing more than a blur of muffled sounds. It wasn't until Sebastian found me at my study spot in Nelson Library that my senses started to return. Little by little, the filter lifted. Sound flickered on as he spoke, and the scent of musty books filled my nose.

"You seem quiet today," he said, poking my foot under the table with his own. "Is everything okay?"

I'd been rereading the same sentence for ten minutes. "A little tired, maybe."

Tell him, I thought. *Tell him about the missed call.* After all, Sebastian had said that we could talk about anything. I barely had time to consider the notion before my phone started to vibrate against the table. I hesitated for a long second, terrified to flip over the device and watch that familiar unsaved number move across the screen. But it was only my dad, and relief washed over me in an instant as I shot up from the chair, answered the phone, and stepped away from the table.

"Hey, Dad," I said, coming to a stop on the other side of the bookshelves. "Any updates on Gabby?"

There was a long sigh from the other end of the phone, and I held my breath in anticipation of his response. "Well, she's not too keen about seeing the school counselor."

Yeah, I'm sure she's not.

"Did you tell her that it's important?" It was an effort to keep the frustration from my voice.

"I explained that she needed to work on her attitude and reminded her that she'll have to pick up another activity without dance."

I wanted to scream, and probably would have if I hadn't been in the library. He *needed* to put his foot down about this. How could he not see that Gabby required more than an attitude check? She needed professional help.

"You promised."

"It's not that simple, Grace. There are things that you don't understand."

"What if this has something to do with Mom? She called me this morning." A crushing silence followed in the wake of my confession, and I felt my grip tighten over the phone clutched in my hand.

"It does have something to do with your mom."

My heart dropped into my stomach.

"What do you mean?"

It took far too long for him to respond, but even in those tense moments of holding my breath, nothing could have prepared me for his next words.

"Gabby has been in touch with your mother for over a year now. The reason she called you is because Gabby asked her to."

I didn't know what to say. It was hard to think over the ringing in my ears and the panic burrowing a hole in my chest. "How could you let her—"

"Gabby wants to know her mom. I might not like it, but I can't keep them apart. She's old enough to make her own decision about that."

No. No. No. This couldn't be real.

"Grace?"

I felt cold all over. The warmth had been sucked from the room and replaced with a bitter numbness. It seeped into my skin and traveled all the way down to the bone.

"You've been lying to me. Both of you have."

Nothing. He had nothing to stay. He'd let that woman back into Gabby's life and kept it from me. Like I hadn't been the one to pick up the pieces of him when she left.

"I can't believe this has been going on for so long." My voice grew thick, weighed down with the awful truth of what he'd done. "When she breaks Gabby's heart, if she hasn't already, it'll be your fault."

I ended the call. There was absolutely nothing he could say to fix this. Not when my trust was completely shattered. I closed my eyes and took in a long breath through my nose, only stopping when my chest was so tight it felt ready to burst. I needed to hold myself together. At least until I was in the safety of my own bedroom.

I returned to the table without looking at Sebastian. As soon as my eyes fell across the screen of my laptop, I knew there was no point trying to finish my paper.

"Is everything okay?"

I didn't want to lie to Sebastian, but I couldn't talk about this right now. I was moments away from completely falling apart. I'd felt this type of pain before. It was the reason I kept most people at arm's length—so they couldn't hurt me.

"I may have overheard some of your conversation," he added.

His admission didn't come as a surprise given how quiet it was in the library.

"Do you want to talk about it?"

"No."

"Is everything okay with Gabby?"

"I really can't talk about it right now," I confessed.

Sebastian didn't push any further. Instead, he reached out his hand for me to take. Slowly, I wove my fingers through his. But even his touch wasn't enough to block out the sound of my father's voice. *Gabby has been in touch with your mother for over a year now. The reason she called you is because Gabby asked her to.* Was our mother deliberately turning her against me? And all this time my father had known, even encouraged it. He'd let that woman back in, and now Gabby was someone I didn't recognize.

It was incomprehensible.

>> <<

Sebastian

"You have no reason to bench me, Coach!"

There was no hiding the plea in my voice; I was desperate to get back in the rink. This was our first matchup with Boston College all season. The East Coast team was only trailing by one, which meant the game was far from over. Sure, my knee was a little sore, but I could push through the pain. I had to.

"You were favoring your knee, Sebastian. There's no need to push yourself tonight. We have more important games coming up."

I fought back the urge to protest as Bishop took a slash along his shin from Boston's right winger. A whistle blew. I surged forward out of instinct, ready to hit the ice, but Dawson clapped a hand over my shoulder.

"You're done for the night. There's only seven minutes on the clock. We can hold them off without you."

A snarl of frustration tore from my lips as I collapsed onto the bench, watching as number twenty-four on the opposing team intercepted Dean's slapshot. He was a great defenseman, probably the best player on their team, and the reason why my knee was currently aching in protest. The guy played clean, but he hit hard.

"We're not helpless without you." Bryce took the seat beside me breathing hard, having just come off a line shift.

I knew they weren't helpless without me—that wasn't the issue. Bryce didn't know about the unanswered emails or the missing mid-year report. He didn't understand how important it was for me to be out there, proving myself at every moment. On the slim chance the Red Wings were still considering me for a contract, I had to prove my strength. The hockey world needed to know I wasn't a risk because of my previous injury.

I seethed in silence as the clock ran down, itching to throw myself back into the game. I'd spent almost all of my junior year glued the bench, rotting on the sidelines as the team moved forward without me. Sitting here now, even as I heard the final buzzer announce our victory, overwhelmed me with a sense of sickening déjà vu.

I didn't have any words to share with the team after the game. When Dawson tried to pull me aside for a chat, I brushed by him and retreated to the showers. It was childish behavior, but taking a few moments to cool myself down was better than losing my shit in front of him and the entire team. Tonight was supposed to help alleviate my stress, not make things worse. I'd been looking forward to sixty minutes of pure distraction, especially since my study session with Grace on Thursday evening. She hadn't been herself since the phone call with her father. The total shift in her demeanor had thrown me for a loop and I was desperate to know what the hell was going on inside her head.

I turned on the faucet and stepped under the blast of water before it could warm. The cold was a shock to my system, one that I desperately needed. Eventually, the water heated and my muscles relaxed. I stayed there for a long time, allowing the locker room to slowly empty around me as I focused on the sensation of warm liquid running down my back. There were only a few players loitering about when I finally switched off the shower and returned to my locker to change.

"Don't even bother with Evans, you already know he's staying in with Grace."

My head shot up at the sound of her name, and I scanned the surrounding area. Kent and Bishop were hovering near the exit, doing their own sweep of the room.

"They're getting a head count for tonight. They'll be at the bars until the early morning, no doubt," Bryce explained.

Saturday night home games always ended with a contingency of players posted up at one of the bars downtown.

"Are you going?" I asked.

"For a little bit, but I can't be hungover all day tomorrow. I have a test on Monday that I need to study for."

"Such an overachiever," I said dryly.

"Yeah, well, it beats being a killjoy, which was your excuse before Grace came along." Bryce smirked at me as he stood up and pulled on his winter coat. "Tell her I say hi, will you?"

His parting words were a reminder that I was planning to meet Grace tonight, and that she was bound to be back on campus by now. The women's home-game arena was about forty miles south, which meant their matches started earlier in the evening to make up for travel time. Maybe if the game had gone well and Grace was in a good mood, she'd be willing to talk about whatever was going on with her sister. I wanted her to feel like she could open up to me, and focusing on Grace helped me forget about how abysmal my future was looking. With that thought in mind, I packed up the rest of my things and set off to find her. Most likely, she'd be waiting for me near the main entrance of the arena.

As I stepped outside, I was assaulted by a brutal blast of

freezing air. *Just another lovely day in the Midwest.* Over the howl of the wind, someone shouted Grace's name. My eyes landed on her as a genuine smile broke out across her face—the first one I'd seen in days. The sight lifted my spirits, but the feeling of warmth in my chest didn't last, not as she was enveloped by a much larger male form. My heart stalled at the blatant show of affection, only thumping back to life once he slowly set her back on the ground.

I recognized him immediately as number twenty-four from Boston College, the star of their team. He reached up to cup her face, but Grace stepped away from his touch, putting a bit of distance between them. It was a reassuring sight, but that didn't stop the blood from rushing to my head as I stalked toward them, my feet moving faster than my brain.

"It's so good to see you," I heard him say, but before she could respond, I was wrapping my arms around her from behind. I planted a kiss on her cheek, making sure to stare directly into the hockey player's eyes as I did. Grace glanced over her shoulder at me, cheeks flushed and mouth slightly parted.

"You smell good," I said, pressing my face into her neck and taking a deep breath.

There was a long, awkward silence. Grace's mouth opened and closed several times, but no words came out. The player from Boston College stared at me with a furrowed brow and stony eyes.

"Sebastian, this is Matt," she said, finally managing to speak.

My body went rigid at the sound of her ex's name, and then a moment later, the dots connected. *Boston College.* It hadn't even occurred to me that we were playing against Grace's old school. The school her hockey-playing ex-boyfriend still attended.

Apparently Grace had a type, though I was objectively more handsome than the meathead standing in front of me.

"Hi, Matt, nice to meet you," I said, knowing damn well we both knew that was far from the truth. "Tough loss, but you guys put up a good fight."

Matt didn't say anything. Instead, he glanced at Grace with a pained expression.

"I take it you two are together," he said.

Grace's smile turned into a grimace. I wanted nothing more than to enlighten him about our situation. I almost did, but she beat me to it.

"It's complicated."

Oh, I absolutely *hated* that answer. But I wasn't going to say that in front of her ex-boyfriend.

"I meant to tell you," she said, cringing at her own words. "I just . . ."

"Forgot?" he finished for her.

Matt was shifting back and forth on his feet. He looked miserable, one hand clasped across the back of his neck, the other hanging at his side, his fingers curled into a fist.

"I'm sorry. I've been caught up in family stuff and—"

"Don't sweat it," he interrupted, and the half-assed smile he offered did little to mask the pain etched into his face. "I should probably go."

I realized with a sudden rush of dread that he was still in love with her. When Grace and I had talked about our exes, she'd assured me that they were just friends. Either he was in denial or she hadn't been honest with me.

"Matt, can we talk in private?"

The plea in her tone made my stomach lurch, but it wasn't enough to convince Matt. He shook his head, pivoted, and set off in the other direction.

"What the hell is going on?" I questioned, my earlier frustration at being benched swiftly rising back to the surface. Grace stared at the spot where Matt had stood moments before, tears in her eyes. It made me feel sick.

"I'm sorry," she said, turning to face me. "I know that looked bad, but you have nothing to be worried about." She was breathing heavily, her face twisted with guilt. I wanted to believe her, but something wasn't right.

"I thought you two were *just* friends."

"There is nothing going on between us. I broke up with him in May, and I haven't seen him since I moved home."

"He clearly still has feelings for you."

Her silence told me everything I needed to know. Grace was well aware that Matt still loved her.

"You left that part out when we discussed our exes. And the fact that we would be playing each other this weekend. What if the roles were reversed, Grace? What if I spent my time texting Kate and meeting her for—"

"I haven't seen him since we broke up."

"It doesn't matter!" I shouted, unable to hide the anger in my voice. The outburst was a culmination of frustration from the game mixed with the feeling of being blindsided. Had Grace been distant from me because she was stressed about her sister or because she was nervous for her reunion with Matt? I shoved my hands into my pockets and let my head fall back to look up at the sky. *Don't lose your shit, Sebastian. Don't let her see how much this is fucking hurts.*

"I'm sorry. Please believe me when I say there's nothing more than friendship between us." Grace paused, her wide eyes glistening with unshed tears. "The truth is I miss Matt. He was the only person I trusted in Boston, the only one who was patient enough to break down my walls. When you don't have a lot of friends, it's hard to let one go. Especially when they haven't done anything wrong. I was the one who fell out of love with him."

I let the truth of her words seep into my skin, the reassurance in her tone slowly smothering the anger inside me. Grace was a lot of things—stubborn, fierce, and even scared—but she was not a liar. I could trust her. I just needed her to trust me.

"Why didn't you tell me that he still had feelings for you?"

"He's in Boston, and I'm here with you," she said, as if it were that simple. "You are the only person I have feelings for."

Grace rarely mentioned her time on the East Coast, and when she did, it was always hockey-related. She'd spent three years in Boston, and I knew nothing about that time in her life.

"Can you tell me more?" I asked, glancing back down at Grace. Her mouth fell open then closed a moment later like she didn't know what to say.

"More about Matt, or more about how lousy I am at making friends?"

The corner of my mouth curved upward. "Both. Help me understand."

Grace reached for my hand and led me in the direction of her apartment, talking in a low voice as we walked, the sound barely audible over the howling wind. She explained how they'd met during welcome week and laughed through stories of Matt's terrible attempts at impressing her. He'd chased after her for over a year—a whole damn year—before she even considered going out with him. And here I was, thinking she'd been stubborn for resisting my charm for a few weeks. Though it was unsettling to know that Matt was her first big love, I was glad she could look back on it with happiness.

Grace didn't stop talking when we arrived at her apartment. She led me into her room, sat down on her bed, and continued to share stories about the two of them and their time at Boston College. When she mentioned struggling to make friends, a sound of disbelief left my mouth.

"I don't get it. You're not shy."

Not in the least.

"It's not about being shy. It's about being private and protecting myself." Grace paused and looked down at her hands. "It takes me a while before I open up to people."

"Well, you just opened up to me," I said, trying to instill some confidence back into her.

Grace was always so sure of herself when it came to hockey, and school, and what she believed in. She knew what she wanted, and she went after it. She was a force to be reckoned with, but when it came to opening her heart, there was so much hesitation and fear inside of her.

"That's why you have to believe me when I say there's nothing to worry about when it comes to Matt. He stuck around long enough to wear me down, but you?" She shook her head like she was unable to find the right words. "You made me hate you and then want you in what felt like seconds. I couldn't stop myself from coming to you after winter break because you make me feel more than anyone ever has."

I'd needed to hear those words, but a small voice in the back of my mind warned me to proceed with caution. Grace was still keeping things from me. Though she had every right to her privacy, especially with matters regarding her family, I wasn't sure how long I could wander along in the dark. Something was eating away at her. Over the last few days, I had seen the weariness in her eyes.

"Remember what I said?" I asked, cupping her face in my hands. "You can always be honest with me. Please, just be honest with me. That's all I'm asking."

CHAPTER 20

Grace

"You're going to miss out on an amazing night."

Lydia was already tipsy. She had downed one hard seltzer and two shots of tequila to pass the time as Caroline finished getting ready for team karaoke night.

"I really think I'm coming down with a cold."

It wasn't even a decent lie, but I didn't have the capacity to care. The past week had been a lot for me to handle, and with Sebastian out of town at an away game, I couldn't rely on him to distract me with mind-blowing sex. Even though a girls' night out sounded like heaven, getting drunk while I was on the verge of a mental breakdown was a recipe for disaster. My only plan was to binge-watch *Gilmore Girls* until I melted into the couch.

Caroline strolled out of her room dressed to the nines, wearing a pair of loose-fitting denim pants, each leg a different shade of pink, and a white bodysuit that dipped low on her chest. She looked ever the Barbie, her blond hair slicked back into a ponytail and lips glossed to perfection. Lydia squealed at the sight of her best friend, rushing from the kitchen to crush her in a hug. She was wearing a pair of army pants and a cropped Led Zeppelin shirt, black curls hanging loose around her face.

"You guys better bring coats," I warned. It was much too cold for only booze blankets.

"Yes, Mom," said Caroline, reaching for her white puffer jacket.

"If you sing something together, please have someone take a video." I'd heard about their legendary "Take Me or Leave Me" performance from the other hockey players. Apparently, they both had incredible voices and were not afraid to belt the famous *Rent* duet once they had enough tequila in their systems. After another round of shots and a long search for Lydia's keys, they waved goodbye and set off for the bar. Quiet fell over the apartment once they departed, and with it, a rush of worried thoughts arrived.

Sebastian. Matt. My dad. Gabby. Each name I ticked off was another person I'd let down or someone I could no longer trust. Though Matt and I had briefly spoken over the phone about our awkward reunion, and he insisted he wasn't angry, I could tell he was hurting. I didn't like being the cause of his pain. Right now, the best thing I could do for both of us was give him time to decide if he wanted to remain friends.

And then there was Sebastian. After opening up to him about my time living in Boston, I thought things would go back to normal. They had, in some ways. We still spent every night tangled up in one another, but ever since our run-in with Matt, I couldn't help but notice he was acting strange. I'd catch him watching me with this worried look in his eyes, or staring off into space for minutes at a time. And when he wasn't acting weird, he was asking me about Gabby. I knew I couldn't deal with everything on my own, and even though I trusted Sebastian, it was way too soon into whatever *this* was to burden him with my family's betrayal.

It was time to call in reinforcements, so I picked up the phone and called Sam.

"Hey," she answered on the third ring.

The sound of her voice forced a strange sound from my mouth, somewhere between a sob and a laugh.

"Is everything okay?"

Everything was definitely *not* okay.

"Gabby's been in touch with our mom," I told her, and in the silence of the apartment, my words were like a deafening crack of thunder. "For over a year. And my dad knew about it the whole time."

"Holy shit," Sam muttered.

"This has to be connected to her depression. Nothing else makes sense, right?"

There was a long pause. Even without being able to see her, I could tell that Sam was carefully considering her response. She always blundered ahead and shared her opinions freely, so her sudden hesitancy gave me pause.

"It's not cool that they kept this a secret from you. But maybe you should hear them out," she said placatingly. "Maybe there's more to the story."

My mouth went slack. I shook my head in stunned disbelief.

"More to the story? She abandoned us, Sam. She destroyed our family, and now she's back to do it again."

"You haven't spoken to her in years. Maybe things are different now." I couldn't understand why she was trying to reason with me, not after everything she'd witnessed when we were kids. "I'm sure Gabby just wants to know her mother. Your dad wouldn't let them have a relationship if he didn't trust her."

Why was I the only one seeing logic?

"I thought you would be on my side," I said quietly, my words barely above a whisper. It felt like my entire chest had been hollowed out.

"Being on your side doesn't mean blindly agreeing with you. I get you're worried, but maybe it isn't the worst thing that your sister knows both of her parents. Your mom isn't evil. She suffers from mental illness."

Sam didn't know what the hell she was talking about. She couldn't possibly understand the pain of waking up in the morning to learn that your mother had left, and without a goodbye. Not everyone deserved a second chance.

"Grace, just think about it for a sec—"

Without letting her finish, and before I could say anything I'd regret, I ended the call. For a while, I sat curled on the sofa, watching as *Gilmore Girls* played across the screen without really watching. Even when my stomach started to growl in protest I stayed rooted to the spot, half listening to a fight between Paris and Rory as I tried to make sense of how Sam could defend my mother. There was no sense to find in her argument, and only once my eyes started to burn did I finally peel myself off the couch and head for the kitchen in search of something sweet to drown my sorrows in. Thankfully, Lydia's chocolate addiction meant there was bound to be something with sugar in it lying around. I was rifling through her candy selection when a small pile of unopened mail slopped across the counter caught my eye. There was a single letter addressed to me sitting at the top of the stack, the loopy handwriting unmistakably my mother's. *That's strange,* I thought. She was more than several months early this year. My birthday wasn't until June.

For a moment, I considered throwing the letter out. But before I could make that decision, I heard the unmistakable sound of my phone buzzing. I retrieved the device from where it'd slipped between the couch cushions and did a double take at the name flashing across the screen. It was Gabby. The message was short, only three words for me to ruminate over.

Gabs

You're a coward

I stared down at the screen for a while, wondering if she and my mother had somehow coordinated their attacks. With a numbness spreading through my chest, I dragged myself to bed and collapsed onto the mattress. My exhaustion weighed heavily, and I fell asleep with Gabby's three word message repeating in my head, over and over again. When Sunday morning came, I spent most of it lying in bed, staring at the ceiling and drowning myself in music. My phone was bombarded with texts from Sam and Sebastian that I pointedly chose to ignore, dead set on wallowing alone in my misery. By the afternoon, I was restless, my roommates still sleeping off their hangovers, so I pulled on some workout clothes and headed for the training center. It might have been a recovery day, but I was desperate to lose myself in a run. Campus was dead, and the training center was blissfully empty when I arrived. I put on my headphones, cranked the music, and lost myself in a sprint, one I could only hope was long enough to help me forget.

>> <<

"Grace, can you hear me? Grace!"

The sound of my name was a distant echo. I was surrounded by darkness, floating in nothing.

"She's completely out!"

The voice grew louder, and suddenly a light broke through

the empty space. My eyes fluttered open, flashes of a familiar face filling my vision. Sebastian was hovering over me, green eyes wide in a look of pure terror. The shock of seeing him brought all sensation back to my body. I let out a loud groan.

"Can you hear me?"

Placing my palms flat on the floor, I started to push myself up, but Sebastian reached out to stop me.

"Don't move too fast. You might have hit your head."

My gaze swept across the room and stopped on the hulking form of Bryce. He had worry lines etched into his forehead. The last thing I remembered was setting out a mat to stretch after my run. I tried to move my shaky legs, but it was more difficult than expected.

"You passed out," Bryce said.

I'd run pretty hard for about an hour before switching off the treadmill. Though I'd felt a bit lightheaded at the end, I hadn't thought I was close to passing out.

"Did you eat anything today? Drink any water?"

The questions came from Sebastian, who was looking at me with so much concern you would have thought I'd broken my leg or severed an appendage.

"No," I admitted, hanging my head in shame. "I forgot to eat breakfast."

It was a rookie mistake. I knew better than to train with nothing in my stomach, but I felt so unwell when I woke up this morning that I couldn't find it in me to eat breakfast. Just for a few hours, I wanted to forget about everything.

"Why are you here? Sundays are strictly rest days."

"Why are you here?" I shot back. I knew Sebastian was only worried about me, but I was still feeling defensive after my argument with Sam.

He finally helped me into a sitting position, having decided I was aware enough to move. Once I was upright, Bryce handed me a cup of water, a protein bar, and a Gatorade.

"Caroline tracked your location. After I get you home, you're sharing it with me," he said with narrowed eyes. "What are you doing here on a Sunday?"

How could I admit to him that I was here to forget about my rapidly devolving family relations? My own father and sister had betrayed me. Just like my mother had.

"Bryce, can you give us a minute?"

I chugged the water as Bryce disappeared, my body sagging in relief as the cool liquid eased the back of my raw throat. Almost immediately, Sebastian tossed aside the cup and replaced it with the bright blue sports drink.

"What's going on, Grace?"

I didn't answer because it was easier than lying to him.

"You stopped answering my texts last night and didn't pick up when I called you five times this morning. I was really worried."

I dropped my head between my knees and said, "It's just stress. I thought a run could help clear my mind, but I pushed myself too far. It won't happen again." After Sam's reaction, I was terrified to confide in Sebastian. What if he agreed with her? What if he thought I was a coward just like my sister did?

"Look at me," he commanded.

I did as I was told, even at the risk of losing myself in his eyes.

"I don't think you have a concussion, though I'm sure you'll feel sore tomorrow. You know better than to push yourself like that."

I nodded my head in agreement and took a long swig of Gatorade.

"Please tell me what's going on. Let me help you."

He was the only person left on my side, even if he didn't know it. "What if you leave? I can't lose anyone else."

"I'm not going to leave you, Grace. I would never do that."

His words should have soothed me, but they had the opposite effect. Something was truly broken inside me. It was the only explanation.

>> <<

Sebastian

Grace Gillman was going to give me an aneurysm. It had been less than twenty-four hours since I'd watched her faint, and despite my urgings to take more than a day to recuperate, she was waiting outside my Econ class where we usually met up on Monday afternoons. Her stubbornness was unmatched. She needed more rest, but asking her to take a break was like asking the Hulk to calm down: extremely ill-advised.

"You didn't sleep much last night," I said, taking in the dark circles under her eyes.

"Are you telling me I look horrible?"

I bit back the urge to remind her that she'd quite literally collapsed before my eyes. Seeing her crumple like that had been one of the scariest moments in my life. She might be willing to act like nothing had happened, but I wasn't going to let it slide that easily.

"You scared me yesterday, and it's not just that," I said, stopping myself short as I tried to think of the best way to approach my concerns.

"Are you still upset about Matt?" she asked.

I shook my head. "No, this isn't about him. It's about how weird you've been acting since that phone call with your dad. I know something's up, and I just want to help."

"I appreciate that," she said, reaching out to take my hand. "The call took me by surprise. It's more of the same. Gabby hates me, and my dad won't do anything even though she's clearly in distress and acting out."

"Is there anyone else who might be able to persuade her to go to therapy?"

Something incomprehensible flickered behind Grace's eyes. "I don't think so. I was going to see if Sam could—" Grace sucked in a breath, as if just remembering something painful. "I appreciate that you're worried about me, I really do, but there isn't anything you can do to help. At least not directly."

I knew that she was holding back. There was more to the conversation with her father—I'd listened to bits and pieces of their discussion, heard the pain in her voice through the wall of books between us. Why couldn't she be honest with me?

"Come on, we'll be late for lunch," she said, grabbing my hand and setting off down the hall.

Be patient, I reminded myself. It was hard to accept that she wasn't ready to tell me everything, but instead of pushing, I let her lead the way to lunch in stilted silence. The usual suspects were spread around our regular table, and everyone seemed to be talking at once. It wasn't until we sat down that I noticed Lydia and Caroline hunched over a laptop.

"Did we miss anything?" Grace asked.

Caroline spoke before anyone else could, eyes darting up from her computer screen. "I've been calculating the numbers. Are you two interested to see where you stand in the bet?"

For a moment, I had no idea what she was talking about. But

before I could voice my confusion, Grace let out a surprising shriek of excitement, exclaiming, "Yes! Please tell me I'm winning."

"Not exactly," Caroline said with a tilt of her head. "It's more of a tie at this point. You're up in assists, but Sebastian is up in goals, and you're pretty much tied in face-offs."

"Pretty much tied. How is that possible?" I asked.

"Well, technically Grace has one over you, Seb, but you're up higher in goals than she is in assists. It evens things out."

It had been weeks since a thought about the bet had even crossed my mind. To be honest, it didn't matter to me at this point. I was tempted to suggest calling it off and tell Grace I'd make the donation happen no matter what, but I didn't. Something told me that Grace would be disappointed if she didn't have the chance to beat me herself. And from the eager gleam in her eyes, letting her stay focused on the bet could be a much-needed distraction from the stuff going on at home.

"As I was going through the stats, I did happen upon a potential logistical issue. If both teams make it all the way to the Frozen Four, the men will have played more games than us, which gives Seb the advantage."

"Wow, confident, are we?" Kent teased.

"Oh, come on, there's no need to be humble. We're leading our conference, and you guys are neck and neck with Denver. The only other team in the NCAA that's close to your stats is Western Michigan. Even if you lose to Denver in the conference championship, you'll still progress to regionals," Caroline said.

"Okay, if that happens, then we can count the games with his best stats and put that against the number of games Grace plays," Bryce suggested.

It wasn't the best solution, given I'd have more chances to rack up better stats than she would, but Grace didn't complain.

"That's not really fair, though," I pointed out.

Grace nudged me in the side with her elbow. "I'm not worried about it."

"But—"

"Who knows, you might need the advantage," she said in a mocking tone.

It was a relief to see that the promise of a competition put some fire back into her eyes, though it wasn't enough to ease my concern. Things between Grace and me had moved far past the point of casual, but she still wasn't ready to let me in all the way. It made me feel dejected, like I was powerless to help the woman I was undeniably falling in love with.

>> <<

As we moved further into the month of February, the same pattern repeated. Grace and I spent countless nights wrapped in each other's arms, fucking on every possible surface of my room. We couldn't get enough of each other. But with each passing day, Grace drifted further from me. There was no mistaking the distance in her eyes. Every time I asked her what was wrong, she resorted to kissing me or making up an excuse about schoolwork. She was half present, always using sex as a distraction. Maybe Grace still had doubts about my intentions, or maybe she was scared to admit that our relationship was no longer casual. And she sure as hell didn't want to face her family problems. If we did speak, it was only in those teasing moments right before sex. I didn't know how to handle this far-away version of her. She was disappearing before my eyes.

With our game against Penn State a day away, I could think

of only one thing that might help Grace understand just how deeply I felt for her.

"Which one of you wants to paint my number on their stomach?" Kent asked. He was lying on his back and staring up at the ceiling, not even attempting to look productive in his efforts to stretch. The rest of the group—Bryce, Caroline, Lydia, and I—were suffering through a foam roller session, and just a few yards away, Grace pounded away on the treadmill, ever-present headphones secured over her ears.

"We're not puck bunnies." Caroline scoffed at his suggestion. "But I suppose I could wear your number. I mean, if you have an extra jersey."

It was impossible to miss the way her cheeks flamed as she spoke. Kent's head snapped in her direction in a display of utter disbelief. For a moment, an awkward silence fell over the group.

"I was only joking—"

"I have an extra jersey," Kent rushed to say. "I'll bring it over to your place tonight."

He was beaming at her with shining blue eyes and a smile so wide that a dimple cut into his cheek. For the first time this season, the women's team would be able to watch us play in person at our home arena. They had a bye week that just so happened to line up with our matches against Penn State. My mom and Bill were visiting for the weekend, and all I could think about was introducing them to Grace. If she knew that I wanted her to meet my family, she might realize how serious I was about us. I didn't know how else to get through to her.

"I take it that Grace will be wearing your number?" Lydia asked.

"She better," I said, unable to keep from smiling at the thought of her wearing my jersey, watching me from the crowd.

"Hey, I was meaning to ask you something. Has Grace seemed, I don't know, like she's distracted lately?"

Lydia glanced over her shoulder and gave Grace a long, assessing once-over.

"She has some family stuff going on. Has she said anything to you?"

"Not a lot," I confessed. "I'm worried, but I don't want to push her too hard."

"She hasn't been herself in a few weeks. I thought it was because she was so caught up in you," Lydia admitted. "I try not to pry about her personal life, but it might be time for you to stop playing it safe. She likes you more than she lets on; I know that much. I don't think she'll run if you push for her to open up a bit. Not anymore."

Lydia's assurance was all I needed to hear. After the group was done stretching, I rolled up my mat and sidled over to the long line of treadmills. Grace was laser-focused on the screen displaying her run time and miles. When she noticed me hovering next to her she jumped off the belt, planting her feet on either side of the machine.

"Hey," she said breathlessly as she pulled her headphones down to rest around her neck. "What's up?"

I looked at the time on the display screen. Forty-five minutes. Grace had been running an eight-minute pace for nearly an hour, and that was on top of the women's regular morning practice. If she kept pushing herself like this, she was going to faint again.

One problem at a time, Sebastian.

"Can you come over tonight?" Her phone buzzed, and she looked away, her brow furrowing at whatever notification she'd received. "Grace, I have something I want to talk to you about. It's important."

She remained focused on her phone, as if I wasn't there and hadn't spoken. I let out a long sigh of irritation and said, "I have to meet with my study group later, and I have a test tomorrow. I won't be able to see you before the game against Penn State. Please tell me you'll stop by tonight, after? I could come to your place if that's easier."

Grace blinked up at me. "Yeah, of course."

Even as she agreed, I wondered if she had heard a word I'd spoken.

>> <<

Grace

Twenty-three missed calls. Fifteen from my father. Eight from Sam. And even with them blowing up my phone, I'd never felt so alone. It was part of the reason I was desperate to keep Sebastian away from it all. He was my only escape, a reprieve from the darkness closing in around me on all sides.

"Why aren't you ready to go?"

Lydia poked her head into the living room. She was halfway through the process of braiding her hair, arms raised above her head as careful fingers wove the thick sections of waves together. In the last few days, both of my roommates had started to hover. I wasn't blind to their concern, but I didn't want to talk about my family. Not to them, and not to Sebastian.

"Sebastian wants to hang out tonight."

"Doesn't he have his study sessions on Thursday nights?" she asked.

"Yeah, he's going to come over in a few hours," I explained.

"Then come out with us for a bit. It's just a few drinks. We never get to go out on Thirsty Thursday. It will be fun!" Caroline said as she strode into the kitchen, opened the fridge, and cracked open a White Claw.

My gut instinct was to decline, but the alternative was moping around the apartment all evening until Sebastian arrived. Sometimes, his study group ran late. A few hours of drinking might be good for me.

"Fine," I agreed, peeling myself off the couch. "But I need twenty minutes to look less . . ."

"Unhoused?" Caroline finished for me.

I stuck out my tongue at her before retreating to my bedroom to get ready. Preparing didn't take long. In under three minutes, I managed to brush my teeth, pull my hair into a ponytail, apply a clear layer of lip gloss, and throw together an outfit that consisted of jeans and a top that I'd stolen from Sam three months ago. Five minutes and two tequila shots later, we hurried out of the apartment bundled in our winter coats.

"Where are we going?" I asked, shivering as we were blasted with a particularly frigid gust of wind.

"Remmy's," Lydia said. "They have half-off drinks for ladies every Thursday."

The bar was packed when we arrived, but Lydia managed to claim a tiny table in the back. I was starting to feel fuzzy around the edges as we pushed our way through the crowd, my pre-game shots finally catching up to me. Red and green ornaments dangled from the ceiling, and there were multicolored lights strung up along the walls. As usual, going out with Caroline came with perks. Just a few minutes after we sat down, the bartender came over with a tray of shots and three cocktails, kissing Caroline on the cheek in greeting. "Have fun, ladies," she said in a thick British accent before weaving her way back to the bar.

"Cheers!" Lydia shouted as we clanked our glasses together and downed another round of tequila.

My eyes fluttered closed as the heat of the alcohol burned a path down the back of my throat. For the first time in weeks, I wasn't preoccupied with thoughts about Gabby. The alcohol had put a stop to my incessant inner ramblings and all at once, I felt light as a feather.

The time passed by in a blur of lively chats and endless fits of laughter. I was thankful that neither roommate made mention of my recent moodiness. Lydia eventually gravitated over to the pool table that was crowded with student athletes. She spent the next half hour hustling a group of lacrosse players while Caroline and I tried desperately to run off a group of middle-aged locals who insisted on buying us another round of shots. *Just a few drinks*, Caroline had said . . . yeah, right.

"So, what are you and Sebastian supposed to be talking about tonight?" Caroline shouted, leaning closer so I could hear her over the rowdy group of men at the table next to us.

I shrugged. "I don't know, but he seemed a little agitated when we spoke. What time is it, anyway? I should probably—"

"Oh, shit," Caroline said, her eyes widening at something over my shoulder.

I turned around, slipping off my barstool in the process and nearly crashing to the ground. The guy next to me held out a steadying hand as my eyes met a pair of burning green embers from across the bar. *Oh, shit* was right. Sebastian was here, and he looked furious.

"Wait!" I called after him as he turned on the spot and left.

I shoved my way through the throng of people rather ungracefully, stepping on a few too many toes in my desperation to catch up with Sebastian. A wall of freezing air slammed into me as I stumbled out the front door and onto the sidewalk. He was already halfway across the street, walking in long, angry strides in the opposite direction.

"Sebastian, wait!" I didn't even consider looking both ways as I darted after him. The world spun for a moment before I regained my balance. "Please, slow down," I called out, only to crash directly into his back as he came to a sudden stop. Waves of angry heat poured from his body as he turned to face me.

"Having fun?" he asked in a clipped tone.

"I'm sorry," I said, trying my best to sound sober. It was quite hard to achieve after all the drinking we'd done. "I totally lost track of time. I wasn't planning to stay late, I promise."

"I told you tonight was important."

I didn't know what to say. I could barely remember the details of our conversation at DuLane. "I'm sorry. I didn't mean to forget."

He wore a bitter smile as he said, "I can't tell half the time if you're even listening to me. I don't ask for a lot. I let you pretend that what we're doing here isn't serious, when it obviously is. I take the scraps that you offer without complaint. I let you use me as a distraction when you don't want to think about whatever family shit you're dealing with." Sebastian stopped himself short, and his shoulders sagged inward as he let out a long, low sigh. "It was just one night, Grace. I wanted one night to have a real conversation."

My stomach turned sour at the defeat written across his features. "I'm so sorry. I've been having a hard time—"

"I don't want to hear excuses right now," he cut in. "It's late, and I have a really important game tomorrow. I just wanted to make sure you were safe."

No. No. No.

"Wait, Sebastian!"

"Go inside. You'll freeze out here without a coat."

And then he strode off into the night, disappearing around the block without another word.

CHAPTER 21

Grace

"Welcome back to the living."

Was I imagining things? I could have sworn that sounded like—

"Sam is here," called a familiar voice, likely one of my roommates.

I blinked through a world of pain until the scene came into focus. Sam was perched on my bed looking down at me, which could only mean—yep, I was on the floor, a pillow tucked under my head and a bucket placed several inches away. My roommates hovered in the doorway, dressed in comfy pajamas, each clutching a coffee mug between their hands. There was sunlight pouring in from the hallway beyond, so it was safe to assume it was morning.

"Did I miss something?" I croaked, wincing at the soreness in my throat.

"What you missed was lunch and dinner, and then you went out with your roommates and drank everything in sight. Including some random man's beer, which, by the way, is always a terrible idea."

Sam was livid, more so than I'd ever seen her before. I glanced at my roommates for help, but they looked equally frustrated,

Caroline watching the scene with pinched lips as Lydia shook her head. *What the hell happened last night?* The last thing I remembered was—*oh, no.* Sebastian.

"I don't remember much of that," I said, bringing a hand to my throbbing head, "but I did eat lunch. You're right about dinner, though."

"What were you thinking?" Sam exclaimed.

"They were the ones who suggested I go out!" I said, pointing at Lydia and Caroline like they were to blame for my own reckless actions.

"We also dragged you home after you refused to leave or stop drinking," Caroline muttered. There was a long silence in which all three of them seemed to be having a wordless conversation. A moment later, my roommates disappeared into the hallway.

I looked down at my hands, inspecting the partly bitten nail beds with great interest. Eventually, I plucked up the courage to speak. "Why are you here?" I asked softly.

Sam and I hadn't spoken for weeks. To say her appearance was a surprise would be an understatement.

"I was sick of you being too cowardly to answer my calls, so I drove up after work last night," she said with a nonchalant shrug. "Now your turn. What were you thinking, drinking on an empty stomach like that? Was your goal to contract mild alcohol poisoning? Because that's what you did."

There was fear interwoven with the anger in her voice, and a sudden wave of shame crashed over me. "I needed to forget for a little while. And then Sebastian showed up, and he was so angry, so I wanted to forget even more."

"It was dangerous! You could have been kidnapped or raped or—"

"I know, I'm sorry." The words came out in a sob, and suddenly, there was nothing to stop the rush of tears from streaming down my face. Sam knelt on the floor beside me, pulling me into her arms. Everything I'd been holding in for the past month rushed out with the force of a tidal wave.

"Please never ignore me like that again. You can be mad at me all you want, but don't shut me out," she said, and the words only caused me to weep harder, my body shaking with each gasping breath.

"I don't know how to deal with everything. They betrayed me, Sam. They lied to me for over a year, and they're supposed to be the people I trust the most." My chest jumped as a hiccup forced its way out of me. "When we spoke over the phone, it felt like you were taking their side. But it's not okay what they did."

"They shouldn't have lied to you, and you have every right to be upset about that," Sam assured me, rubbing circles into my back. I felt foolish for ignoring her, but I'd been so terrified that another person I loved was turning on me. "I only wanted to help you see things from Gabby's point of view."

"She wants me to forgive our mom, but what if I can't?"

Would Gabby hate me for the rest of our lives? Our family had already been torn apart once. This felt like history repeating itself, only this time, it wasn't just my mom abandoning me, it was my entire family.

"You don't have to forgive your mom, but Gabby needs to understand why you feel so hesitant about letting her back into your lives."

I wanted to shield Gabby from the truth, but Sam was right. If we were ever going to move on from this chapter in our lives, I needed to be honest. We sat in silence for a few minutes, Sam's hand running up and down my back in comforting sweeps as the last of my tears dried.

"So," she said eventually, and I could tell by the tone of her voice she was gearing up to tease me. "What happened with your boyfriend?"

"He's not my—"

"Boyfriend, I know. I wanted to see your face when I called him that."

I pinched her side. "Don't be such a bitch."

"Still keeping things casual?"

"I'm not sure they were ever casual," I confessed. "As much as I tried to convince myself they were." It felt better than I'd expected to admit it out loud. All this time, I'd been terrified to let Sebastian into my heart, but there was no denying that he was already embedded within the walls of my chest, his very essence coursing through my blood.

"Congratulations, you've made it to the first step of acceptance," Sam exclaimed, and it sounded like she was reading from a self-help book.

"Which is?" I asked.

"Acknowledgment."

"And what's the next step?"

She shrugged. "I'm not sure. It's something that stars with the letter *A*, but I haven't read one of those recovery pamphlets from work in a while, so I couldn't say."

"Apology it is," I muttered. "That's the only way I'm going to make things right with Sebastian."

>> <<

Sebastian

Grace
I'm so sorry.
Please answer your phone.
You were right about everything.
Seb, please.
You can't ignore me forever.
I'll be at your game, just like I promised.

>> <<

Penn State's starting center lined up across from me and stared into my eyes with a hardened look that promised blood. Max Henderson was a well-known agitator. I'd even had the pleasure of skating with him in my youth hockey days, and he wasn't any nicer before his balls dropped. Rather than support his teammates, he spent his time on the ice disrupting opposing players and causing maximum pain. The guy could teach a course in chirping. Personally, I preferred to let my scoring do the talking, but guys like Henderson got off to the sound of their own voice. Under normal circumstances, I'd have no issue handling someone like him. Loudmouthed, dirty-playing opponents didn't faze me. But I was hanging on by a thread after the last twelve hours—tired from a sleepless night, angry at Grace for standing me up, and disappointed in myself for pretending like I was fine to step onto this ice before having a real conversation with her. I should have answered her call this morning, or heard her out last night, but I'd been too angry to think straight. And right now, my head wasn't fully in this game.

Henderson cracked his neck as the referee approached. I willed myself to have a quiet mind and sound heart, but as the puck dropped, the image of a drunken Grace flickered to life in my head. The split-second distraction was enough to cost me the face-off. Henderson backhanded the puck to his right wing before I even moved, and the group instantly dispersed. I flew after the opponent, desperate to right my mistake and force a turnover. Thankfully, Bryce intercepted a lazy pass back to Henderson and flung the biscuit out to Bishop before things got out of hand. Bishop made a quick wrister to Kent, who passed the puck to me as I crossed through the neutral zone. Crisis averted. The second line came on before anything fun happened, and as soon as my ass hit the bench, Coach was in my ear. "You okay, son?"

I nodded my head in a bold-faced lie, scanning the arena for any sign of Grace. I wanted to believe she was out there, even after our fight, but I had my doubts. She'd already let me down last night; what was one more no-show?

Get yourself together.

Damn me for being too stubborn to pick up the phone this morning, and damn Grace for having such a chokehold over my sanity.

"Sebastian. Go!"

Dawson's piercing command had me flying off the bench and onto the rink in a matter of seconds. *Quiet mind, sound heart. Quiet mind, sound heart.* I repeated Bryce's pre-game mantra, hoping the words would steer me right. From that moment onward, time passed in a strange haze, some sections of play crawling by while others sped by in a blur. I felt like I was trapped in a fever dream. Every moment I was on the bench I spent searching the crowd for Grace, hoping to catch a brief glimpse of her face. When I was out on the ice, she would emerge from thin air, appearing like a goddamn mirage at the worst possible time. By the first intermission, I felt like I was losing my mind; there was no other reasonable explanation for what was happening to me.

"You all need to pick up the intensity."

Coach Dawson's voice echoed across the packed locker room. Around him, all twenty-five players sat in silence, some with their heads hung, other's with pained expressions painted across their faces. The first period had been a chaotic scramble resulting in a tied score. Penn State was playing to win, there was no doubt about that.

"Bryce and Bishop, keep an eye on number sixteen. He's been cherry-picking all game, and I don't want to see another goddamn breakaway. And please don't fall victim to Max Henderson's taunts. The next time he's in the sin bin—and there will be a next time—use that to our advantage. Assess and execute. Those are your orders."

Coach paused, and his eyes sweep over the room in a dramatic fashion, gaze catching on me for a prolonged moment. We both knew I wasn't all-in this game. To make matters worse, Landon was being assessed for a concussion, which meant we were down our best goalie. I needed to be present, but no matter how many times I tried to pull myself together, my thoughts kept drifting to *her*. Grace had never been a distraction on the ice, not until now.

"We are the better team, and we are more than capable of handling a pest like Henderson. Don't let his chaos distract you."

Even the sound of his name made me grimace. Since the first whistle, the only things that seemed to shock me out of my distracted stupor were the asshole's explosive hits and smart mouth. Each dig thrown my way felt like another broken thread in the rope holding together my control. It didn't help that the jackass was responsible for Landon's injury. The entire team had a bone to pick with him, and I was nearly at my breaking point.

"Let's get out there and show them what we can do!"

A chorus of chanted "Ravens" rose from the group as we filed out of the locker room and back into the noisy arena. I tried my hardest to concentrate on the task at hand: winning this game. But it wasn't enough to stop the nauseating sense of déjà vu that fell over me as I returned to the ice. I'd been here once before, with another girl on my mind at another consequential game. But tonight, the stakes were a great deal higher. The girl in question had a much stronger hold over my heart, and I was fighting for more than a title—I was fighting for my future career.

"I got your back, okay?"

Bryce's voice was a much-needed reminder that my teammates were relying on me. There could be no more distractions. *This is your future, Sebastian.* Henderson took his place across from me. For one blissful moment, the roar of the spectators softened to a low thrum. With the blade of my stick against the ice, I watched the referee lean down between us, the puck clutched in his hand. There was barely a flicker of movement before it dropped and my stick was cutting across the center circle. Carbon met rubber with a loud smack, and the puck shot perfectly into Kent's waiting stick. My sense of hearing returned a moment later when the booming crowd blinked back into existence.

Within the first few minutes of the second period, Penn State grew more desperate. Every moment we kept the puck away from them was another crack in Henderson's already flimsy restraint, especially after Bishop scored our second goal. He came crashing through our players like a wrecking ball any chance he got, and it didn't take long for their sloppiness to work to our advantage.

After a breakaway from Bishop and a beautiful assist from me, Kent slammed the puck between the pipes, securing us even bigger lead.

But the excitement of our goal wasn't enough to hold my focus. In the back of my mind, I was rereading those text messages. *I'll be at your game, just like I promised.* I spent every free second desperately eyeing the packed arena, searching for her among the masses, convinced the sight of her face would end this insanity.

"Evans! Get your ass out there!"

Yet again, it took Coach Dawson screaming my name to notice that I'd nearly missed the line shift. With ice once again under my skates, I tore across the rink and threw myself into the thick of things. The entire time, I felt like I was being pulled in different directions. I just needed to see Grace once. That's all it would take for me to get back into this game.

In a moment of recklessness, with the game moving at full speed around me, I scanned the stands. Relief flooded my system when I saw a familiar head of blond hair jumping up and down: Caroline, and beside her was Lydia. I followed the long line of hockey players squished together in the row, my eyes peeled for Grace. None of them were her. Each pass over the group drove a dagger of disappointment deeper into my gut.

She said she would be here—why isn't she?

The blade twisted.

My momentary lapse in concentration meant I had no warning to brace for the hit. A large force pummeled into my back, launching me forward and into the plexiglass with a loud whack. My teeth rattled as my bucket smacked against the barrier, and I felt my lip split against the bars of my cage. Hot iron flooded my mouth. Distantly, I heard the whistle blow, but nothing mattered outside of Henderson's arrogant smirk. The world shifted to red as I launched myself at the asshole and took him down, my fists swinging. Logic evaded me. There was only burning rage, no common sense left to temper the anger. Henderson's flailing arm clipped my chin and knocked my helmet free. I scrambled forward to land another hit, even as someone pulled me away, my fists punching nothing but air. It wasn't until Bryce's face filled my vision that the world around me slammed back into place.

Thump. Thump. Thump. All I could hear was my own pulse booming in my ear, and the referee shouting something unintelligible from behind me. A few more seconds passed before the full force of my actions walloped me over the head. For the first time in my entire hockey career, I was about to be disqualified for a major penalty—one that would assure my ass got plenty of bench time. A game disqualification meant that I was automatically suspended from our next match.

Even with that knowledge, I couldn't stop myself from searching through the thousands of blurry dots in the arena. But she wasn't there. I'd spent years searching the stands for my father's face, knowing he wouldn't be there, that he couldn't, but somehow, this felt even worse. In my utter desperation to feel her support, to know that she was out there like she promised, I'd thrown all my convictions to the wind. After all this time, Grace turned out to be everything I feared she would be: a colossal distraction.

>> <<

Grace

This could not be happening. I could not miss a single moment of Sebastian's game. This was my penance for standing him up last night—being accosted by a pound of melted cheese just moments into the second period. I heard the distinct swell of cheering that indicated something exciting had happened, but there was nothing I could do in my current state of undress. I desperately scrubbed the synthetically colored cheese from my DU-branded sweatshirt, hunched over the sink inside the women's restroom at DuLane. It would have been easy to blame the inebriated Penn State fan who'd collided with me in an explosion of nacho cheese and jalapeños, but I was a firm believer in karma. I deserved worse than a cheesy shirt after blowing Sebastian off to get drunk with my roommates.

I wrung out the moisture and held the material under the hand dryer, considering ditching it altogether and walking to my seat in nothing but a bra. How many topless guys had I been forced to watch on the big screen, their hairy, paint-covered chests displayed for the world? *Gross.* But I couldn't risk getting kicked out, not when I'd promised Sebastian I'd be here. Desperate not to miss any more action, I fished out my phone and pulled up Sam's contact. She had an extra jacket I could wear, even if it might be a little snug. Before I could press Call, the screen flashed with an incoming notification. A flutter of nerves filled my stomach. It was Gabby.

"Hello?"

My greeting was met with the unmistakable sound of crying. On the other end, Gabby was gasping for breath as sobs spilled out of her.

"It's Dad," she wailed, barely intelligible though the crying. "He—I think he's having a heart attack. The ambulance is coming now."

The fear in her voice sent me straight into big-sister mode. I responded as calmly as possible, shoving down my own feelings of panic.

"Where are you?"

"At home."

"Is he conscious?"

There was a short pause before she responded, "Yes, still conscious. He's having a hard time breathing, and he was dizzy before I made him sit down. But his chest hurts."

I could hear the muffled sound of my father on the other end of the line.

"Is he speaking with the dispatcher? Did they say when the paramedics would arrive?"

Gabby sniffled and said, "They should be here within the next few minutes. He's talking to them."

A small breath whooshed out of my lungs. "That's a good sign, Gabby. He's alert and speaking."

"I'm so scared." Her words were barely a whisper.

"I'm right here. I'll stay on the line until they get there, okay?"

Silent tears streamed down my face, but I couldn't let her sense my distress. Right now, I had to stay strong for my little sister.

"Okay, they're here."

There was an onslaught of muffled voices coming from the line. With shaking hands, I put the call on speaker and sent an SOS text to Sam. I could hear bits and pieces of the conversation, though it was hard to make out more than a few words through the phone. When things quieted down, I called Gabby's name. It took three times before she finally answered.

"They're taking him to St. Jude's. They said I could ride in the ambulance with them."

Thank goodness.

"I'm going to have Sam take me straight to the hospital. I'll be there in under two hours, okay?" Though I couldn't see her, I imagined Gabby was bobbing her head up and down in a nod. "Call me if anything changes."

The line went dead a moment later. I pulled the phone away from my ear just as Sam flew through the bathroom door. "I can't believe Gabby called—"

"Heart attack," I croaked. "My dad is having a heart attack. They're taking him to the hospital now. He's alert."

Sam's eyes grew wide and then she was asking me questions about his vital signs that I didn't know the answers to. At the same time, she took off her sweatshirt and pulled it over my head. I told her what I knew, starting with the fact that he was alert and talking to the first responders. Again, she inquired about his vital signs, but I just shook my head and asked if she would take me to the hospital.

"Can you let Caroline and Lydia know we're leaving?"

"Of course. I'll be right back."

I followed Sam out of the bathroom and watched her run toward the rink entrance. The concourse was silent, save for the echo of her shoes smacking across the floor. Wiping the tears from my face, I braced myself for the oncoming wave of shame. It had been weeks since I'd spoken with my father. My phone contained countless unanswered texts and missed calls from him. I couldn't deal with the truth about my mother, so instead of talking to my father like an adult, I'd ignored him. I packed away the hurt and shoved it down like I did with all the other feelings I couldn't face.

In the distance, a door slammed. Craning my neck, I peered down the empty concourse as a figure came into view. With each slow step he took in my direction, it became easier to make out the familiar shape of Sebastian. But as he grew closer, I noticed there was blood crusted on the corner of his mouth and a light bruise forming across his cheekbone. He looked absolutely worn down, like the life had been sucked right out of him. His brows were pulled together, green eyes unfocused as he walked with his hands hanging limply at his sides. I knew once our gazes connected that something was terribly wrong. I'd only just begun to call out his name when Sebastian's mouth curled into a snarl. He wasn't looking at me the way he normally did. Even months ago, when we were feuding over the training space, I'd never seen such brazen hate behind his eyes. A stranger stood before me.

"I should have listened to logic," he said with a shake of his head. "I should have trusted my gut when it told me you were nothing more than a pretty distraction."

I took a step closer, but Sebastian flinched away, as if he couldn't stand the thought of touching me. What the hell was going on?

"What happened? Were you hurt—"

"I can't do this anymore," he snapped.

Is this some sort of joke?

"That's not funny, Sebastian."

"I'm not being funny. I'm being honest. I know that's a hard concept for you to understand, but not everyone is afraid to speak the truth."

"You don't mean that," I said, trying to convince myself as well as him.

There were footsteps in the distance, someone coming up behind me. I searched his face, my eyes traveling over the slope of his nose and the familiar set of his lips for any sign of affection. I couldn't see anything past the fury burning in his eyes.

This was all just a terrible nightmare. It had to be.

"I'm so sorry about last night, and I'm sorry I made you feel used. Please, just hear me out. You have to hear me out."

His voice was low when he spoke next, but there was no mistaking his words. "You were a mistake, and whatever you thought we had, it's not real."

I reached out for him, but he only took another hasty step away.

"Don't touch me. Just leave me the fuck alone."

A gasp sounded from behind me. I didn't have the energy to chase after him as he turned to leave; all the fight in me was gone. *I'm not going to leave you, Grace.* His promise was etched into my memory. *I would never do that.* I guessed it had all been a lie.

"What the hell is going on?" Sam stepped into view, my roommates at her side. They all shared the same horrified expressions.

"I don't know, but I need to get going."

My voice hitched as another wave of tears threatened to break free. I had a feeling that if they did, I'd need another twenty minutes in the bathroom to collect myself. That was time I didn't have, not when my father was on his way to the hospital and my sister needed me.

"Take all the time you need," Sam said, reaching out to squeeze my hand. "When you're ready, we'll get you out of here."

I didn't need any time. All I wanted was to leave and never look back.

CHAPTER 22

Grace

It was late when we arrived at the hospital. Sam's father was idling in the parking lot, waiting to take her home. She pulled me into a hug, whispered that everything would be okay, and gave me the keys to her car. I watched her father's Ford pull out onto the main road and disappear into the darkness. St. Jude's stood before me like a haunted image from my dreams, the gray building cast in red light from the bold emergency sign. I couldn't move. The last time I'd stepped inside this hospital, I'd come against both of my parents' wishes, desperate to catch a glimpse of the woman who'd raised me.

Be brave, Grace. Do it for your sister.

There was a lone security guard waiting inside the front doors. He looked me over with a bored expression as I walked on shaky legs to the front desk. A middle-aged woman asked for my name without looking up from her computer. She continued to type away as I rattled off my name and reason for visiting.

"Room 224. Elevators are down the hall on the left," she said, handing me a sticker with my name printed across the top. I pressed it to my chest without checking to see if it was right side up.

The hospital was eerily quiet, save for the swish of scrubs from the lone nurse traversing the hallway. The sound of my breathing felt impossibly loud as I boarded the elevator for the second floor. They'd already moved my father from the emergency department into the critical care unit.

Room 224 was at the very end of the hallway, a corner unit cast in dim fluorescent light, the blinds drawn over a large window along the back wall. My dad was awake, the corners of his mouth twitching up into a half-hearted smile as I entered the room. I bit back a sob at the sight of him lying in bed. There was an IV bag pumping fluids into him and a pulse oximeter attached to the tip of his finger. A chorus of different beeps from the various machines permeated the air. In the armchair beside the bed, Gabby lay curled around her knees, sleeping. The sight of them together was all it took for the sense of betrayal hanging over my head to vanish. My shoulders relaxed. With light steps, I rounded the corner of his bed and reached out to grab the hand he'd extended for me.

"Don't wake her up," he said in a whisper, nodding to Gabs. "She was crying up until the moment she fell asleep, even though the doctor says I'm doing well."

I didn't know what to say. After weeks of ignoring his calls, I couldn't help but feel somewhat responsible.

"Is this all my fault?" I asked, unable to keep my darkest thoughts inside.

He looked at me incredulously. "How could this be your fault?"

"I've been ignoring your calls for weeks. That wasn't fair to you. You get so stressed when—"

"You're not to blame for this, Grace. It's ridiculous for you to even think that."

"Then what happened?"

"It was a minor heart attack. I'm okay, I promise."

"What caused it?"

He let out a long sigh. "They mentioned a few things about my diet and my drinking habits, but the most important thing is that I'm doing fine. I'm on meds to break up any clots, and if my vitals remain stable, I can probably leave in a day or two."

Relief coursed through me, but it didn't lessen the feelings of guilt. In some cases, heart attacks could be brought on by chronic stress. It wasn't that ridiculous to think that I was partly to blame for his anxiety.

"This is not your fault," he said as if he could hear the stream of thoughts inside my head. "Sometimes things just happen."

"I'm so sorry for ignoring you. I shouldn't have—"

"None of that matters now," he assured me. "I'm just glad you're here."

A quiet sob broke free from my lips. I covered my mouth to muffle the noise.

"I was so scared," I admitted, a perfect imitation of Gabby's confession to me over the phone. "And I'm scared for Gabby. I don't want Mom anywhere near her."

"I felt the same way in the beginning. I was terrified when she showed up on our doorstep asking to see Gabs. But I couldn't be the one to stand in the way of a daughter and her mother. And despite her past mistakes, everyone deserves a second chance. Don't you think?"

Every particle in my being screamed *hell no*. I didn't want to give Mom the chance to fuck up her other child. "Is she different?"

His head tilted to the side in consideration. "In some ways, yes. In others, no."

"How can you stand to be around her? Isn't it painful? I can't even think about her without feeling like my lungs are going to collapse."

"It is painful. It always will be. But it's worth it to see the excitement on Gabby's face when I mention her mother's coming to visit. My pain will always be worth her happiness, and yours as well."

>> <<

Gabby didn't say a word to me when we left the hospital in the early hours of the morning. I didn't want to push her after the stressful day we'd both endured. Silence filled our walk to the parking lot, and the car ride home, and the space in our front foyer where we stood and watched each other in a strange tension until Gabby disappeared into the privacy of her bedroom. That night, no five-star podcast or curated playlist was enough to stop me from reaching out for a warmth that wouldn't be there or dreaming about Sebastian. *You were a mistake.* I couldn't un-hear his words. Sebastian was just another person who regretted me, and it was my own damn fault. I'd been afraid to open up. Instead of listening to his pleas for me to be honest about how I was feeling, I'd used him to distract myself from the pain. And when it was finally time for me to return the favor, I'd chosen numbing myself on shitty tequila over showing up for him.

A feeling of bone-deep exhaustion followed me into the next day. When I glanced at myself in the bathroom mirror before heading downstairs, I was greeted with the sight of bloodshot eyes and swollen skin, half-moon smudges of purple decorating the flesh below my waterline. Thankfully, my dad was a coffee lover, and just the smell of roasting grounds was enough to ease some of the tiredness from my body. After a fifteen-minute check-in with my dad, I set to work preparing breakfast, determined to have something ready by the time Gabby woke up. I'd just poured the final pancake onto our countertop griddle when she walked into the kitchen rubbing sleep-bleary eyes.

"I spoke to Dad this morning," I said as she slipped onto a stool along the kitchen island. "He asked if we could bring him some lunch just after noon."

Gabby remained silent, though she reached for one of the plates I'd set out and used a fork to snag a pancake off the top of the leaning stack. I hadn't heard her voice since she'd called me in a panic the night before, and I was beginning to feel desperate for her to speak.

"Do you want any coffee?"

Dad didn't let her drink coffee on a regular basis, but I figured she could use the caffeine after the last twenty-four hours. Gabby glanced up from her barely eaten pancake, brow furrowed in a look of disbelief.

"Dad doesn't let me," she said, and I had to hold in my laughter at the unexpected response.

"He'd make an exception for today."

She scoffed. "Like you'd know. You haven't spoken with him in weeks."

I schooled my expression to keep the pain of her words from showing on my face. With a determination to win her over, I grabbed a mug from the shelf above the stove and poured a cup of coffee. I topped it off with a good amount of hazelnut creamer before setting it on the counter in front of her.

"Do you want me to call him and ask?"

Gabby just shook her head and pulled the mug closer, letting the steam waft up and warm her face. After removing the last pancake, I turned off the griddle and leaned against the counter directly across from her. Despite her earlier feistiness, she wouldn't meet my eyes.

"I know you think I'm a coward," I said, ripping off the bloodied bandage, "and I might be, but there's a lot you don't know about our mother. If you really want to understand why I'm so hesitant to forgive her, I'll tell you."

Gabby looked like she was holding her breath as she nodded for me to continue.

"You were too young to see how devastating it was when she left. Dad blamed himself every day for years, even after doing everything right to help her. And I had to step up and help take care of you." I winced at the confession, hoping that Gabby realized I'd never resented her for it. I'd do it all over again, and I told her that, but it shouldn't have been my job as her sister. I was still a kid, and she'd needed a mother. We both had.

I talked about how cruel the other kids had been once their parents found out, how no one had wanted to be friends with me after Mom's stint in the hospital. Gabby hung on to every word I spoke, and I could see in her eyes that this was what she'd needed all along—the truth.

"I felt so alone back then, even before she disappeared, and eventually all the sadness I felt at losing her turned to anger. Up until recently, I couldn't fathom why you even wanted to know her. And then I realized something. You'll never understand what it felt like waking up in the morning to learn that she was gone. You were a baby, barely three years old. The truth is, I'm terrified that she's going to break your heart like she did mine. But you're old enough to make your own decisions, and I can understand wanting to know our mother, even if part of me thinks it's a mistake."

For the first time in over a year, Gabby was looking at me like she used to. Like I was someone she wanted to be, someone she could trust with everything. I focused all my efforts on blinking away the pressure behind my eyes.

"I'm sorry for calling you a coward," she said, and then, after a moment of hesitation, she added, "What if I want you to know her too? At least, the person she is now."

I was already ready with my answer. The idea had come to me while I was lying in bed this morning, unable to sleep. "If you agree to start seeing a therapist, I'd be willing to give her a chance," I said, and disbelief flashed behind the blue of her eyes. Our mother's eyes.

"You'll meet with Mom?" she asked excitedly.

"What if I start by reading one of her letters? Baby steps, okay?"

"Yes," she said with a nod of agreement. "But I have my own conditions. You have to go to therapy too. We'll do it together."

I held out my hand, extending my pinky finger for her. It was a promise.

"What else? You said conditions."

"It's more of a question, really . . ." Gabby bit her lip, looking suddenly unsure of herself. "Did they really love each other back then—Mom and Dad? They're so different from each other now."

"They've always been like that, even when you were a baby. From what I remember, Mom was the opposite of Dad in a lot of ways: talkative, loud, even dramatic. She made mundane things like going to the grocery store seem like an adventure. Dad was her anchor, and she was his sail. They balanced each other that way."

Gabby smiled at me, and it felt like a beam of sunlight shining down on my face after months of nothing but overcast skies.

My dad had been right after all. Seeing a spark of happiness in Gabby was worth the ache in my heart that came with speaking about our mother.

>> <<

Sebastian

Saturday morning came with a world of pain, in more ways than one. Outside the obvious symptoms of my hangover, which included (but were not limited to) a torturous throbbing in my head and an unrelenting bout of nausea, there was the resounding realization of having fucked up spectacularly.

"Your parents are here."

Bryce wouldn't look me in the eye. In the twenty minutes since he'd woken me from the floor of my bathroom with a cup of cold water to the face, he hadn't said more than a few words to me. It was for the better considering that I could barely think straight, let alone speak. The same five words cycled through my mind on a loop: *I've made a terrible mistake.*

"Sebastian!"

That was definitely my mom. When I glanced up from my hands, Bryce was no longer standing in the threshold of my room. Slowly but surely, I dragged myself out of bed and made my way downstairs. They were waiting for me in the living room, my mother sitting cross-legged on the sagging leather couch and Bill pacing back and forth over the creaky floors.

"You scared me to death!" she exclaimed.

"How much did you drink last night?" Bill asked.

I've made a terrible mistake. I've made a terrible—

"Tell me what's going on, Sebastian." This time, when my mother spoke, her voice was soft. There was concern etched onto her face, concern that I didn't deserve.

"I'm sorry," I said, reaching out a hand to brace myself against the wall as a powerful wave of queasiness hit.

"You should sit down," Bill suggested.

Numbly, I did as I was told, slumping onto the cushion next to my mom.

"What happened?" she asked.

I didn't know where to begin. After leaving DuLane, everything turned a bit blurry. All I knew was that last night had ended with me at the bottom of a whiskey bottle, failing to drown out the look of horror in Grace's eyes as I told her we were over. *What the hell is wrong with me?*

"I ruined everything." There was no other way to put it. "It doesn't matter anymore. Not Grace, not my future in hockey. I blew it all up."

"What do you mean it doesn't matter? Is Grace the girl you've been neglecting to tell me about?"

"Like I said, it doesn't matter. I ruined things with her and with hockey."

"Don't be so dramatic," she said, but there was so much my mom didn't know, so much that I'd been terrified to share with her.

"You're not the first guy to lose his cool on that ice, and you won't be the last. Don't they let you do that stuff in the big leagues? I'm sure they see it as you getting in some practice," she continued.

She was right. Fights were bound to happen in hockey, but this was about more than a fight. Detroit had been radio silent these past few months. If they were still planning to sign me, I'd have heard from Duncan or another representative by now.

"They don't want me anymore," I admitted.

"Why would they send a package over to the house if they weren't going to sign you?"

My head shot up. "What do you mean?"

"I was going to tell you after the game. On Wednesday, we received a package from the office in Detroit. It's loaded with Red Wings gear: shirts, sweats, some branded compression shorts, and a couple of water bottles. I figured they wanted you to wear them around campus—show off your future team."

I shook my head in confusion. "That doesn't make sense. I haven't heard from Duncan, not even for my mid-season report. He hasn't answered a single one of my emails or phone calls."

The color drained from her face. I couldn't bear to the see the disappointment in her eyes, so I hung my head in shame.

"I'm so sorry, honey, I must have forgotten to tell you. We got some news in the mail over Thanksgiving break. Duncan is no longer with the Red Wings. I don't know much, but they ended on bad terms. They sent your report and some other information to the house because that's the address they have on file."

My heart stopped. "Are you serious?"

Disbelief. I was in utter disbelief. There was no other way to describe the tingling in my chest.

"I'm so sorry. I can't believe I forgot to tell you," she said, reaching over to clasp my hand in both of hers. "I was planning to send you home with everything after winter break, but you left in such a rush because you wanted to make it back to school before the storm hit."

"I've spent the last three months thinking they didn't want me anymore. Three months feeling like a fucking failure. Knowing that I let him down."

My ears rang loud enough to muffle the sound of my mother's voice. She must have said something to Bill because a moment later, he kissed the top of her head and left the room.

"You could never let your father down, Sebastian," she said, gripping my hand tighter. "Why would you think that?"

"Dad gave up everything to help raise me. I just wanted to make him proud. Do what he never got the chance to do because of me."

"Your father didn't give up anything. He got a job in town because he wanted to see you grow up. He didn't want to be away all the time. You were no sacrifice to him, and I know that he's proud of you." She shook her head, tears pooling in her eyes. "Your dad was so happy to share his passion with you, but that doesn't mean it has to be your future. He just wanted to spend as much time with you as possible, and hockey was something he knew he could teach you." She let out a small, sniffling laugh. "You were so good right from the start. I remember him rushing into the house every time you learned something new. To him, you hung the moon."

A lump formed in my throat. All I could do was squeeze her tight and soak in the words as she told me everything I'd ever wanted to hear.

"The Red Wings want you. But you don't have to accept a contract if you're only doing this to make your father proud. You've already done that. You do it every day." After a long moment, she added, "You haven't let anyone down, Sebastian, least of all your father."

Was that still true after last night? A half laugh, half sob escaped me. I'd never imagined I'd feel so miserable learning that my dream was going to come true. Everything I'd worked for was about to pay off. If what my mother said was true, I'd be playing for Detroit in a matter of months, living the life I'd set out to achieve when I was only twelve years old. But I could no longer see that perfect picture I'd painted of my future, the one where I was standing alone. It hadn't been that way since I'd met Grace, even if I hadn't realized it until now. I needed to fix this—to go to her and explain how fucking sorry I was for everything I'd said.

"I need to find Grace."

My mom must have sensed the urgency in my tone because she didn't question me as I raced from the living room in pursuit of my phone. But in my haste to reach my bedroom, I nearly collided with Bryce at the top of the stairs.

"She's not here, Sebastian," he said flatly, and I realized he must have been standing up here, listening to our conversation. "Grace left to go home last night."

"She left—because of me?"

He made a frustrated noise in the back of his throat. "Not everything is about you."

"Then why did she leave?"

"First, tell me what was going through your head last night."

Bryce's face was tense—all furrowed brow and flattened lips, a hard look in his eyes that made me want to take a few steps back. "I know I fucked up. I let down our teammates—"

He let out a bitter laugh, and the sound stunned me into silence. "I was referring to the best thing that's ever happened to you: Grace. You know, the girl you completely destroyed after your little tantrum on the rink."

Destroyed. The word brought forth an image of her standing in the concourse at DuLane. I could still see the devastation written across Grace's face as I tore into her deepest vulnerabilities. The things that I'd said—there was no coming back from that. Bryce was right, I'd destroyed Grace. How could she ever trust me again?

"What were you thinking?" he asked, and I shook my head, unable to find the words.

In only a few months, Grace had become the most important person in my life. That was why I'd been so torn up when I'd realized she wasn't there last night. For the first time since my father died, I was going to look into the crowd and see someone I cared for, someone I *loved*, someone who truly understood what hockey meant to me and appreciated every moment on the ice for how special it was.

"I built up this stupid moment in my head, and when it didn't come true—" I stopped short at the sound of my own words, realization dawning on me. Last night was no one's fault but my own, and there was no excuse for how I'd acted.

"I'm sorry," I said, knowing that it wasn't enough. "I've been such a self-centered asshole since the accident."

Bryce gave me a slow clap, his lips twisting into a sardonic smile. "I'm glad you finally figured out that the world doesn't revolve around you."

A crushing weight pressed down on my chest. The people in my life deserved more from me: Bryce, Grace, my teammates—Kate.

"When you're with Grace, you're like the old Sebastian, the one who was fun to be around and didn't blame everyone else for his problems."

He was right. I'd let my life be defined by hockey, and when that was taken from me, I'd lost myself. But Grace had helped me realize that I was someone outside of the rink. She was the best thing about me, and last night, in a moment of selfish rage, I'd thrown it all away.

"I'm going to make things right."

"It's not going to be easy, not after what you said to her. Not after—" He stopped himself short.

"Not after what?"

A telling silence hung in the air between us. I was missing something.

"Why isn't she here, Bryce?"

His lips pressed together in a slight grimace before he said, "Her dad had a heart attack. She was rushing off to the hospital to see him when you . . ."

When I accosted her. Shame wrapped itself around my body in a smothering embrace.

"Is he okay?"

Bryce gave a solemn nod, though it did little to ease my conscience. I'd ruined *everything* over a split-second feeling of betrayal that wasn't even real. I had to make things right, even if hell was more likely to freeze over than Grace forgiving me.

"She needs time at home to heal with her family. Give her that."

"And in the meantime?" I asked, feeling at a complete loss for how to move forward.

"Figure out what the hell you're going to do to make things right."

CHAPTER 23
Sebastian

Every instinct was screaming at me to pick up the phone and call Grace. It felt like the longer we went without speaking, the less likely she was to forgive me. But her dad was in the hospital, and Bryce was right. She needed time at home to heal with her family. That was what was most important. Not my own anguish or the sense of growing panic I felt at the thought of losing her.

I couldn't sit still or wait around, so after my parents left, I took a long shower to wash off the remnants of my hangover and immediately set off for DuLane. Once a place of refuge for me, the training center now carried with it the shame of my greatest mistakes. I walked the deserted corridors, drowning in sorrow at the lost sense of comfort I'd come to expect within these towering walls. When Coach Dawson's office finally came into view, my misery doubled.

The surly man was hunched over a mound of paperwork, his glasses perched at the very tip of his nose. They looked one sneeze away from sliding right off his face. The room was in its usual state—cluttered with half-open boxes of equipment and empty bottles of Diet Coke, the whiteboard behind his desk hidden beneath a drawing of a three-on-two jailbreak drill. I hovered in the doorway hesitantly, working up the courage to step forward.

"Are you waiting for me to invite you in?"

Straightening my shoulders, I took a deep breath and stepped inside. Coach motioned for me to take the chair in front of his desk. For a long time, he said nothing, so I sat across from him and watched him work. The first few minutes of silence were the most awkward. Several times my mouth dropped open, an apology poised at the tip of my tongue, but the words never came. Something told me that this discussion needed to be on his time, and I was right. Eventually, he set down his pencil and leaned back into his chair. When I saw the look in his eyes, my stomach sank.

"I've coached for over twenty years now, and in all that time, I've never had a more talented player on my ice. You've got something special, Sebastian, no one can deny that," he said, and I knew what three-letter word came next. "But if you can't see past your own two skates, you'll never make it in the pros. It's more than proving *yourself* on that ice. You've already done that. Now you have to prove that you're worthy of this team."

"Understood, sir," I said, my voice thick. "I'm sorry for letting everyone down."

"I hope so. Just to make sure, I'm going to give you the week off so you can think about how you might serve this team better when you return."

That was a nice way of saying he was suspending me for seven days, not just one game. "You should make Bryce the captain for the remainder of the year. He's earned it," I said.

Coach nodded in agreement. "That would be easy, wouldn't it? But that's not how life works. I want to see *you* earn the title you were given. This team depends on your leadership, and I won't let you back down now that things have gotten tough."

"I'm not the same guy I was when you made me captain, and I don't think I ever will be," I admitted.

"You don't need to be that guy; you just need to be better than the guy you were last night."

>> <<

If my weeklong suspension taught me anything, other than the obvious lesson of humility, it was that I needed more hobbies. It became painfully clear within the first twenty-four hours that I was aimless without hockey, and even more so without Grace. Every time I felt tempted to reach out to her, I remembered what Bryce had said when I'd told him I was going to make things right. *It's not going to be easy, not after what you said to her.* I'd thrown salt in her deepest wounds, and only moments after she'd learned that her father was in the hospital. If I wanted Grace to forgive me, I needed something big. Something that showed how enormously sorry I was and proved without a shadow of a doubt that I'd do anything to make it up to her. It would take time, and help, which meant in the meantime, I needed to find some way to keep myself distracted.

Given my need for self-reflection, the most obvious choice was to pick up a book. This turned out to be an immediate failure when, upon walking into Nelson Library, all it took was the familiar scent of musty books to remind me of how much time Grace and I had spent hiding between the dusty shelves, exchanging heated looks when we were supposed to be studying. My next attempt was even feebler, given how doubtful I was from the very beginning, but the opportunity fell into my lap when I overhead a girl in my econ class talking about an upcoming poetry slam at the student union. I barely made it through the first set without losing it. When the student organizer standing in the corner of the café noticed my muffled laughter, she gave me the stink eye and I took it as my cue to leave.

It wasn't until the fifth day of my suspension that I succeeded in finding something that stuck. In addition to the fact that it didn't require an innate set of skills, cooking could be done in solitude, within the comfort of my own home. I was terrible at first, often resorting to calling my mother in a panic when something didn't turn out or YouTube couldn't help me. It was hard to keep up with once I returned to the rink, but I dedicated my free evenings to trying new recipes. With each passing day, I grew more confident, and things felt a little less tense with Bryce and my other roommates once I started feeding them on a regular basis.

One night, after scouring a baking website that my mother had recommended, I came across a recipe that hurtled me into a memory from sophomore year. Kate and I were at the beginning stage of our relationship, tucked into a corner booth in the back of Coaler Café. It was late, we were up cramming for Monday exams, and the dim lighting was making it hard to keep our eyes open when Kate's stomach let out a low grumble loud enough to startle me out of a doze. "Eat something," I said, "or the owner is going to kick us out for a noise complaint." Eventually, Kate agreed, and after scouring the menu she decided to order a sweet from the bakery display at the bar. I'd never forget the look on her face at that first bite of pastry, like she was tasting a little bit of lemon bar heaven.

I got to work on the recipe immediately, realizing the sign for what it was: a push to find closure in my past relationship. How could I ever move forward with Grace when I hadn't owned up to the mistakes I'd made with Kate? At the very least, she deserved an apology for how I'd treated her. That afternoon, I made several batches of lemon bars until one came out looking exactly the recipe online. The kitchen smelled amazing, and I was tempted to steal one for myself.

The sun was playing hide-and-seek when I set off to find Kate. Beams of yellow light flashed in and out of existence as the scattering of clouds overhead shifted with the wind. March in Wisconsin was like a girl in a shoe store—it didn't know how to make up its mind. Today, the air was brisk, but the warmth of the sun was enough to chase off some of the cold. We'd finally reached that awkward transition between winter and spring. The grounds were covered in half-melted snowbanks and patches of soggy brown grass with puddles the size of small ponds cropping up along the sidewalks where the cement dipped.

Kate wasn't difficult to locate. We still shared each other's locations. I wasn't sure why—maybe she wanted to know where I was so she could avoid running into me—but I hadn't even thought to change my settings after we broke up. I took up a post outside of Kenworth Hall and waited. Twenty minutes later, students began pouring out of the building. When Kate emerged, my grip tightened around the container of lemon bars.

Seeing her for the first time in several months stirred up a lot of emotions within me, though none were as visceral as the guilt gnawing at my insides. She looked every bit the Kate I remembered, but there was something different in the way she held herself. Our eyes met, and without hesitation, she crossed the courtyard in my direction. As she grew closer, I felt myself tense in anticipation, my mind wandering back to the last time we spoke. The more I thought about it, the more I realized how wrong I'd been for letting things end that way. She might have pulled the plug, but it had been my own careless actions that had doomed our relationship.

"Hello, Kate."

"Such a formal greeting," she said tersely, coming to a stop in front of me and crossing her arms over her chest. "To what do I owe the immeasurable pleasure of seeing my ex?"

"I came to give you lemon bars." I held out the container of carefully baked pastries, watching as confusion swirled in her eyes. "And I came to say that you were right."

One eyebrow arched. "Feel free to elaborate."

"After the accident, I changed, and I blamed you for the injury, even though I knew it was wrong. I was so focused on myself that I couldn't see how much I was hurting you. I'm sorry."

"I was in love with you, and stupidly hopeful that things would get better. That's why I held on for so long. Why did you?" I couldn't help but notice the crack in her voice as she spoke, the way her expression softened at the mention of loving me.

"I didn't want to lose you, and I didn't want to break your heart, not after everything you'd sacrificed for me."

"You stayed with me out of guilt?"

I couldn't lie to her, not anymore. "Partly, yes, but I also kept hoping that things would get better."

Kate steadied herself at my words, her shoulders straightening as the confidence crept back into her body. I knew that nothing I said could make up for how I'd treated her, or the way things had ended, but I wanted her to know I regretted it.

"You're going to find someone who's willing to put you first. I'm truly sorry that couldn't be me."

"I think I already did," she said, the corner of her lip curving into a blissful smile.

Kate glanced over her shoulder, and that was when I realized someone was waiting for her across the courtyard. There was a woman leaning against the side of Kenworth Hall, one foot kicked back against the ivy-covered stones. She wore an oversized leather jacket and a bold red dress that I knew belonged to Kate. Our eyes met. Her expression was clear, even from more than fifty feet away. *Don't try anything stupid, pretty boy*, it screamed.

"You've definitely upgraded," I said, and an unexpected burst of laughter spilled from Kate, who took a step closer and reached for the lemon bars.

"I'd suggest the whole grand gesture thing," she said, and for a moment, I was utterly lost as to what she meant. Then it clicked.

"You still talk to Bryce, don't you?"

Her smile was answer enough. "You were the one I dumped, not him."

Kate gave me a nod goodbye before she headed back across the courtyard. She said something that made the girl in the red dress laugh, and I watched them walk hand-in-hand until they disappeared into the dining hall. The slightest bit of pressure eased from my chest.

"She's right, you know."

I whirled around, and there was Lydia, perched on a wooden bench no more than ten feet away from me. I'd seen her around campus here and there, but like all the other players on the women's team, she'd been dutifully keeping her distance. Slowly, I approached the bench and sat down beside her, my eyes falling over the sketchpad in her lap. She didn't look up. A rush of wind pulled at the edges of her paper, and a few strands of loose hair whipped around her head. I studied her hands as she worked—one made precise sweeping motions with a short piece of charcoal while the other rubbed at the paper to blur the lines of her drawing. The clouds shifted, a stream of sunshine breaking free and bathing the bench in warmth.

"Right about what?"

Lydia finally looked up at me. "A grand gesture. She'll forgive you either way, but if you make it special, I'll forgive you too."

The revelation came as a complete shock.

"You don't even realize it, do you?" She rolled her eyes in exasperation. "Grace thinks she's just as much to blame as you are. If you ask me, you're both stubborn idiots."

Grace blamed herself?

"I don't understand."

"Yeah, you and me both."

Lydia's fingers stilled over the sketch of a woman's face. There were blurred tears streaming down her sunken cheekbones. The emotion etched within the eyes could not be mistaken for anything other than misery.

"It doesn't matter if you're both to blame. What you said was inexcusable, especially after I told you to be careful with her, so you need to be the one to apologize first."

"I know I messed up. I regret everything I said to her that night." I waited for Lydia to ask me why I'd done it, but after a long pause, I realized she didn't care about the why. "I think I know how to make things right, but it might require your assistance."

"I thought you'd never ask."

>> <<

Grace

March was a month for missing, one that flew by and dragged on all at the same time. In the first two weeks, I missed more school and hockey than I had in my twenty-two years of life. I missed our conference championship game (we won), I missed Lydia's twenty-third birthday, I missed *him*. When I got back to school, the missing was a little different. I missed my sister, even though she was texting me every day, sending endless updates about the most mundane parts of her life. I missed my dad's quiet comfort, Sam's chaotic energy, and the bubble I'd lived in when I was home and away from it all. Away from *him*.

School was a much-needed distraction, one that kept my head above water when I returned to campus. Grad school acceptances began to fill my inbox, but even the prospect of my future wasn't enough to lift the gloom. Thankfully, there was an endless list of papers, tests, and projects for me to make up, which meant I didn't have time to feel sorry for myself. On the hockey front, the intensity of our training regimen ensured that my nights were dreamless and my days devoted to preparing for the potential of a national title. Fortunately, we no longer shared ice time with the men, a change the athletic director had implemented after our transition from the regular season into the NCAA tournament. Without the fear of having to be in close quarters with Sebastian, I thought that practice would become an easy escape. But it was impossible to find peace within the walls of DuLane, not when everything reminded me of him.

Regionals came. We won, and as all my teammates celebrated our climb to the semifinals, I *tried* to feel excited. But for the first time in my life, hockey was nothing more than an opportunity to numb myself for an hour or two. I did everything with full power and half a heart; I was a force on the ice for my teammates, but I didn't show up for myself, on or off the rink. Worst of all was the shame—knowing that the fearless girl from the beginning of the school year was buried alive under this version of myself that I was beginning to hate.

I held on to some semblance of my dignity until the big day. It felt strange to achieve something I'd always hoped for while simultaneously feeling miserable. I could hear my teammates screaming as the final buzzer rang, announcing our win over Northeastern for the national title. Frozen Four champions, that was what we were. I was caught in the rush of bodies swarming around Pearson. It was her incredible save that had clinched our win. All the while, I felt like I was watching things unfold from outside my body, wondering when I would start to feel things again. It wasn't until I'd downed an entire bottle of celebratory champagne that I did, and the resulting breakdown was even worse than when Sam had showed up at the apartment the night before Penn State. When the sobs finally subsided, I lowered my head into Caroline's lap. We were having floor time at the hotel, and Lydia was sitting on the other side of me.

"I hate that I miss him." I spoke the words quietly, half muffled by Caroline's pajama pants. "I hate that I let him ruin this for me."

"I know," she said, her fingers brushing through my hair in what could only be described as a motherly gesture. Lydia slowly removed the champagne bottle clutched in my hand, replacing it with a water bottle.

"Are you cutting me off?"

"You'll thank me in the morning when we board the bus for our long drive home."

She intertwined our fingers and squeezed.

"I'm sorry that there's nothing we can do to change things. But now that you've spilled all your darkest secrets, you're stuck with us for life. And that means we will always be around for a drunken cry," Caroline said.

"You should be out with the team celebrating."

Lydia just shook her head. "We're right where we need to be."

>> <<

Things got better after we returned to campus. I'd been holding on to so much hurt that breaking down after the championship game served to ease a bit of the pain. But I was still far from healed. As the school year stretched into April, I found myself feeling more and more desperate for closure. It was something my new therapist said I was owed. We talked a lot about Sebastian at our weekly sessions, almost as much as we talked about my mom. I hadn't yet worked up the courage to open her letters, but I thought about it every day. As I warmed up to the idea of letting her back into my life, I grew more terrified at the prospect of confronting Sebastian. I was scared to look him in the eyes and see that it was truly over.

On days when I didn't want to get out of bed, or even go to class, I had two pesky roommates who were determined to see me smile. Caroline started taking me to the local animal shelter to volunteer, and I'd become a frequent third wheel to Lydia and her girlfriend, Nina. But the strangest new development came in at six feet six inches tall. One day, Bryce appeared from between the bookshelves in Nelson Library and sat down opposite me. I wasn't sure how he'd known to find me there, or who'd told him to come, if anyone had, but I didn't question his motives. It was weird at first, hanging out just the two of us, but we didn't speak much, and it didn't have to be said that Sebastian was not to be discussed.

The end of April came with the news that the men's team were advancing to the final round of the Frozen Four. When the big day finally arrived, I felt a strange sense of bitter excitement. Sam was here for the weekend, and I had every suspicion her insistence on visiting was because of the championship game. I was being babysat by all of my friends.

"I don't know if I can be here," I admitted, taking in the projector mounted along the back wall. The game stream hadn't started yet, but the feed showed an image of the rink as two announcers chatted about their predictions for the match. Caroline had reserved a room at the student union so that the whole team could watch together.

"Sebastian isn't the only one on the team," Lydia reminded me. "Don't you want to see the other guys play?"

Guilt tightened my chest, but it didn't stop my stomach from turning at the thought of watching Sebastian and his perfect fucking form as he dominated the ice.

"Please just do this for me?" Lydia asked, reaching out to squeeze my arm. "It'll be therapeutic."

Beside me, Sam nodded and said through a mouthful of chips, "If it's not, I'll take you to that Bust-N-Stuff rage room when the game is over. You can picture his face as you smash up someone's old computer."

"Just please give it a chance," Caroline begged. "If you want to claw your eyes out after the first period, you can leave."

"Fine."

I sucked in a sharp breath as the men took the ice, the announcers rambling off each player's name. My jaw clenched when

Sebastian's photo flashed across the screen. As they gushed about his successful recovery, I focused on a spot along the wall above the projector and pinched my leg. *Breathe. Just. Freaking. Breathe.* Eventually, Sam reached over to halt my fingers, pulling my hand into hers to keep me from abusing the flesh along my thigh.

When the game finally started, I couldn't look away. One moment I was scrolling through Instagram, and the next I was watching with bated breath as Sebastian cut across the ice in a beautiful breakaway. From the very start of the game, it was clear that both teams were determined to win. Denver played with a bit more physicality. They were focused on overpowering their opponents with hard hits and sheer muscle. Meanwhile, our men played a carefully coordinated game of skill and speed, one that resulted in quick defense and smart offense.

The score was still zero by the first intermission, both teams having worked fiercely to protect their nets. Given Denver's triumph over Dallard in the conference championship, our men were out for retribution. Every one of them was playing like it was their last day on the ice. When Lydia caught my eye at the start of the second period, she gave me a knowing look that said, *I told you so, bitch.*

"Oh, shit, did you see that hit? Bryce is a monster," Sam said, showing her normal display of awe for the massive defender.

"I knew you didn't come for moral support. You came to eye-fuck the hockey men."

She grinned and said, "Just one of them, large as he may be."

As the clock wound down, a tense anticipation could be felt throughout the room.

"Fifteen to go, and they're tied up," Lydia said.

This game was going to be a battle until the very end. So far,

Denver had responded to each goal by Dallard with one of their own. It was a constant back-and-forth that would only end when the clock hit zero. Fortunately, with one Denver player banished to the sin bin, we had the advantage. I watched as Kent, Bishop, and Sebastian cycled the puck around the perimeter of the offensive zone until a gap opened. Kent's backhanded goal unfolded beautifully on screen, and the entire room erupted in cheers as the horn blew.

Then Sebastian lined up for the face-off, and it happened so quickly that I almost didn't notice. The referee dropped the puck, but Sebastian hesitated, the other center's blade making first contact. His stutter was barely noticeable, but it was enough to make me realize that he'd done it on purpose. I glanced around, checking to see if anyone else had noticed, but everyone seemed focused on the game.

Maybe I made the whole thing up in my head. But as the game continued, so did the same strange pattern of Sebastian purposely losing face-offs. There was no other explanation for the sudden dip in his performance. I was starting to feel like I was going insane when I caught my roommates exchanging conspiratorial looks.

"What the hell is going on?" Neither of them spoke. "One of you better start—"

"Here," Caroline said, handing me a sheet of paper attached to a clipboard.

I glanced down and was met with a table of numbers. They were stats—mine and Sebastian's. More specifically, goals, assists, and face-offs won. Caroline had been updating the numbers throughout the game, her pen marks littering the page. I shook my head in disbelief, my eyes darting back to the screen just in time to see the referee call offside on Denver. Sebastian lined up and lost another face-off, though this time it was more obvious than the last. He barely even moved when the puck was released, handing over the win to Denver's center. The clock continued to run, and my heart thrashed within the confines of my ribcage with every dwindling number. When the seconds finally ticked down to zero and Dallard began celebrating under a rain of confetti, Caroline spoke in a soft, sure voice.

"You won the bet, Grace."

I felt bewildered by the revelation, my mouth opening and closing as I tried to formulate a single coherent thought. "What's going on?"

"You won the bet. Remember, the one that you and—"

"I remember the bet." I cut her off, unconvinced by the look of innocent confusion on her face. "Why was he—"

I stopped myself short, worried that I might sound insane if I implied that Sebastian had lost those face-offs on purpose, especially during the most important game of his college career. Then there was Caroline and her stupid little clipboard, and Lydia's plea for me to be here—even Sam's insistence on visiting this weekend. What the hell was going on? Why did it feel like everyone was conspiring behind my back?

"Did you think the bet was off?" My head snapped in Lydia's direction. She was wearing the same questionable look of innocence as Caroline. Beside her, Sam just shook her head and shrugged.

"Was this planned?" I watched their faces carefully, trying to detect a slip in their half-assed attempt at seeming nonchalant.

"I've been keeping track of the stats all year," Caroline said cooly. "Just be happy, Grace. Think about how much this money will change the women's program. *You* did that."

>> <<

The thing was, I wasn't convinced I had.

I barely spoke another word the rest of the evening, which passed by in a blur despite my sobriety. Sleep evaded me, and after a few hours of listening to Sam's gentle snores, I retreated to the living room, made a cup of sleepy tea, and curled up on the couch. My mind was littered with images of Sebastian on the ice, purposely losing face-offs like he wasn't playing the most important game of his life. I hadn't thought about the bet in weeks, too distracted with my family and our fallout to even consider the trivial competition. I couldn't make sense of any of it.

Eventually, sleep came, though strange dreams visited me in the early hours of the morning until a knock at the door startled me awake. Bleary-eyed, I checked the time on my cell phone. It was four in the morning. Another knock came, and then another. Still half asleep, I stood up and slowly made my way to the door, muttering under my breath as I cracked it open. Clearly, in my haze of sleep and confusion, all survival skills had escaped me.

My muttering petered off as I discovered the most unexpected sight. Sebastian Evans, captain of the Dallard University men's hockey team, breaker of my heart, and two-time national champion, was here, staring back at me with immeasurable affection written across his handsome face. I let myself drink him in from top to bottom, like one last indulgence before a diet. His hair was messier than usual, the chocolate locks crumpled in some places and spiked up in others. Even with dark circles under his eyes and a wrinkled T-shirt with stains across the front, it was impossible to ignore how fast my blood pumped at the mere sight of him.

But Sebastian didn't seem like his usual confident self. He was shifting back and forth on his feet, one hand cupping the back of his neck and the other shoved into the front pocket of his jeans. How the hell was he here? The game hadn't ended until ten, which meant he must have driven all through the night to be here, standing on my doorstop at this ungodly hour of the morning. Sebastian held out a white envelope with my name written across the front. I stared at the letter in disbelief, my body frozen in place.

"Before you slam the door in my face, please read it."

I nearly melted right then and there at the sound of his voice. I hadn't realized until now how much I'd missed that low, whiskey-smooth rumble. Goosebumps erupted over my arms.

"Take the letter, Grace."

Like a creature of habit, I followed his command. My hands shook as I accepted the letter and turned it over. Slowly, I slid my finger under the seal and ripped it open. The page inside was unmistakably handwritten by Sebastian. I'd seen his terrible penmanship too many times to mistake it for anyone else's.

Dear Grace,

I know you're not a huge fan of letters, but I'm hoping this one changes your mind. I'm sorry it's taken me so long to find the proper words. Everyone told me I had to do this right, and if there's one thing I'm confident of, it's that you deserve the grand gesture. So here it is, written on this page for you to take or leave. Please bear with me as I bare my heart to you.

For as long as I can remember, my life has revolved around hockey and hockey alone. I've dedicated myself to mastering the sport because I believed it would bring me closer to my father. I wanted to honor his memory, and to ensure that my parents' sacrifices weren't made in vain. But after the accident, when the one thing I knew best was suddenly taken from me, I lost myself. I turned into this selfish and angry person, and I blamed everyone around me for my own mistakes. There was nothing and no one with the power to make me see past my own selfish desires. And then I met you.

From the very second I saw you on the ice, things changed. You were fearless, disciplined, and persistent as hell—all things that made me want you and loathe you all at the same time. So, I tried to keep you at a distance, far enough away that I wouldn't have to spend each day fighting the attraction I felt and struggling for control of myself. I faulted you for being a distraction, for bringing about the end of my relationship with Kate, and for making me lose sight of my dreams.

Then we were forced together because of my own stubborn antics, and it didn't take long for me to realize how wrong I'd been about everything. How could you be a distraction when you made me a better person, on and off the ice? And how could you bring about the end of a relationship that was already crumbling apart due to my own mistakes? The truth is you didn't make me lose sight of my dreams. You changed them, just like you changed me.

There are not enough words to express how sorry I am for the things I said, and for the way we started, but

I'm happy to spend every day for the rest of my life thinking of new ones if you'll let me.

If it wasn't obvious by now, this is me declaring my love for you.

P.S. Please don't lose the check.
Sebastian

My hands were shaking uncontrollably, the paper bouncing up and down between my fingers like it was attempting to escape my grasp. I blinked away silent tears as I read the letter for a second time, and then a third. Was it possible to move past all the awful things said and done between the two of us? I still thought about his confession outside of Remmy's, how I was responsible for making him feel so small and unheard in our relationship. And it was hard to forget the night he'd ended things, how intentional he'd been in exploiting my greatest fears. But I was sick of letting fear rule my heart. Even after everything that had happened, there was no denying my feelings for Sebastian.

I read the letter one final time, soaking in every last bit until I got to the end. *P.S. Please don't lose the check.*

"What does—"

I glanced up to find Sebastian holding out another piece of paper. This one was much smaller, and my eyes widened at the six-figure number written across the bottom.

"The women deserve every penny, not just half. The donor was in full agreement."

He was prepared for what came next, unlike the first time I'd thrown myself into his arms. Sebastian swept me off my feet in a graceful spin. When we kissed, it felt like I was breathing life back into myself. There was fire on his lips, burning me up from the inside out. And beneath all of the fervor and heat, there was a single promise made to each other, a vow of devotion that couldn't be put into words.

"If you guys are going to bang, please do it inside the apartment. I'm pretty sure they have cameras out there."

I laughed against Sebastian's mouth as Sam's voice carried into the hallway. Sebastian lowered me to the ground, slowly dragging me down the length of his body. I was reminded of how well we knew each and every inch of muscle and flesh between us.

"I'm sorry, Sebastian. I should have been honest with you, and it was wrong for me to—"

"I don't need you to apologize to me, Grace." His voice was thick, brows drawn together. "I'd like you to forgive me."

"I forgive you," I said with a shaky laugh. "Of course I forgive you." Then, after a moment of hesitation. "But I do have a request."

Sebastian shook his head in amused disbelief. "Other than the hundred thousand dollars?"

"She does drive a hard bargain," Sam called, the little eavesdropper.

"Will you read my mother's letters with me? I don't think I can do it alone, but I promised Gabby I would."

Sebastian's cheeks flushed, his gaze dropping to the floor as he reached into his back pocket and pulled out another envelope—no, envelopes, a little bundle of letters tied together with a blue ribbon.

"That reminds me," he said, fingers fiddling with the edges of the papers. "I wrote more than one letter to you over the last couple months. There's ten, one for each letter from your mom.

I know you said that revisiting the memories would be painful, so I wanted to make it a little easier. I thought maybe, if you ever decided to read the ones from your mom, you could read these after. Kind of like a palate cleanser. I tried to make them lighthearted. I had so much to say when we were apart, so every time I thought of you, I wrote it down. It's probably too much. I just..."

I was speechless. There were no words to adequately express the depth of gratitude I felt for Sebastian. No one had ever done something quite so thoughtful for me. With a lightness in my limbs, I reached out, fingers brushing over the mass of letters. It was as thick as a notebook—he must have thought of me *a lot*.

"I love you too, Sebastian."

He cupped my face in his hands, his thumb stroking the side of my cheekbone. There was such marvel behind his eyes, as if he couldn't believe that I was here or that this moment was real. I felt exactly the same way.

"I'd do anything for you."

I believed it.

EPILOGUE
THREE MONTHS LATER

Sebastian

Grace sat astride me, her head tilted back and her breasts bouncing with every roll of her hips. Tiny specks of dust drifted lazily in the beam of morning light that stretched across her torso, twirling around in loops like they'd be forever suspended in air. I loved taking her like this—in the early-morning haze when her eyes were still clouded with sleep.

The only sounds to be heard were our labored breaths and shifting sheets. My fingers marked a path along the side of her stomach and up to her breast, thumb brushing over the point of her nipple. Grace took her pleasure riding me, her palms splayed across my chest, nails etching marks into my flesh. *Magnificent.* I met each roll of her hips with a languid, measured thrust, pushing deep inside of her. Her breath hitched, a low whine spilling from her mouth. And then Grace bore down on me harder, her pace beginning to quicken.

"Good girl"—a low hiss—"you're almost there."

At the sound of my voice, she gripped me like a vise, and I nearly busted right then and there. That all too familiar tingle at the bottom of my spine warned me that I wouldn't be able to hold out for much longer, and based on the way Grace was moaning in ecstasy, she was just as close to falling over the edge.

"I need your eyes on me. I want you to look at me when you come apart."

Her eyes shot open to meet mine, pupils blown wide and glazed over in unmistakable bliss. Grace didn't slow, not even as her heaving breaths turned to gasps. She swirled her hips, rocking back and forth to find that perfect spot, cheeks flushed in exertion. Every passing second was another test of will. When it was finally all too much, my body at the precipice of pleasure, I reached down and pinched her clit. We flew over the cliffside together. Black spots dotted my vision as Grace collapsed against my chest. Her lips found mine as we rode out the shockwaves of our orgasms, writhing against one another.

We lost track of time tangled up together in bed, neither one of us willing to be the first to leave. Grace traced patterns across my bare skin and kissed the scar along my knee. In answer, I whispered dirty promises against the shell of her ear.

As the early afternoon approached, the rest of the house began to stir. Sounds of clinking dishes and slamming cabinets drifted up from the first floor. Eventually, a hollered, "Get your asses up!" forced us out of bed and into the shower, where we continued to tease each other until there was no time left to waste.

Grace and I emerged from my bedroom at the same moment Kent's door creaked open down the hall. We froze, watching silently as Caroline poked her head out, her eyes going wide as saucers when she realized we were there. Grace's shoulders shook in silent laughter at the sight of her roommate's face turning fire-engine red.

"I, uh—"

"Left your underwear in the shared bathroom last week," I said teasingly, remembering the smug look on Kent's face when he'd claimed them from a load of towels Bryce had washed.

Caroline covered her face with her hands and groaned. She and Kent had been fooling around for weeks. I wasn't sure what made her think we didn't know about it. Kent was terrible at keeping secrets, and both were majorly lacking in the stealth department.

"Liar, liar, pants on fire," Grace sang in a mocking tone, and Caroline chased her down the hall screaming something completely unintelligible.

The sun was high above our heads as the day's activities commenced. It was blisteringly hot, and not a single cloud could be seen across the wide expanse of blue sky. A single line of sweat slid down my back as we gathered on the front lawn.

"On this beautiful day, we all say goodbye to an old friend—one who saw us through the many trials and tribulations of college. Each and every one of you has made memories here—"

"Most of which we can't remember." Caroline snickered, and Kent shot her a warning glare for interrupting his speech.

"Each and every one of you has made memories here, memories we will cherish for this lifetime and into the next." He paused for dramatic effect. I didn't have to sneak a glance at Grace to know she was rolling her eyes. "And so, to honor our great hockey house, which stands tall and proud after decades of—"

"Get on with it already!" Landon shouted as he threw his red Solo cup across the yard. It landed less than a foot away from Kent, and cheers broke out amongst the group.

In under a week, the house would stand empty, awaiting a new ensemble of hockey players who would move in and continue the tradition of debasement. Today was our chance to give the house a proper sendoff via a day of lawn games and binge drinking. But Kent's farewell speech—one he gave standing atop an overturned bucket—was far too dramatic. The small crowd of people gathered around were restless, hot, and eager to begin drinking.

"Fine, you guys are no fun," Kent muttered, slapping away an empty beer can that was launched at his face. "Today, we are hosting the first and last Beer Olympics, a tournament of drinking games to be played in teams of two. Five worthy pairs will advance to the semifinals, but only two will compete for the championship title. In the last test of bravery, the final pair of partners will compete in the Great Shoe Race. The pair who completes the basement obstacle course first, without losing a shoe, will be our champions. If at any point your shoe comes off, you must restart from the beginning. Crocs will be provided as footwear, but the adventure straps have been removed to increase difficulty."

"What do we get if we win?" Lydia asked.

At this, Kent looked perplexed. His eyes darted to Caroline for support. She'd clearly taken the lead in planning today's activities. Kent didn't have the organizational skills necessary, and Caroline was too much of a perfectionist to let him wing it.

"You get bragging rights, of course," she said, shifting around to face the half circle of competitors. "And the chance to dole out some seriously nasty punishment. The champions get to select one person to shoot the boot, aka, the legendary Adidas."

A chorus of disgusted groans came from the crowd. "I'm not sure what that means," Grace whispered, her lips warm against the side of my jaw.

"It means the winner gets to choose someone who has to

chug a beer straight from the Adidas that's been stuck to the floor in the basement since before we started living here."

The corners of her lips curled down. "Is that safe?"

I sent her a playful wink. "I guess we'll find out."

As everyone huddled to speak with their partners, Caroline slipped into the house and reemerged with a massive white poster board containing a bracket. The official team names were a mashup of each partner's first name, and I laughed when I saw *Greb* written in bold red letters across the bottom of the board. A plethora of games were dispersed about the yard, including tables for beer pong and flip cup, one cornhole set, ladder toss (or, as Kent refereed to it, testicle toss), and a large spray-painted circle for beer darts.

"What are you best at?" Grace stood with her feet planted shoulder width apart, hands on her hips and jaw set in a firm line as she surveyed the lawn. She wasn't just my teammate because she was my girlfriend; she was my teammate because we matched each other in our competitive natures and determination to win.

And hotness.

"Just about everything," I said with confidence, quickly adding, "but I can be a little heavy-handed when it comes to flip cup."

She smirked. "You know I'm happy to pick up your slack."

The games kicked off shortly, but only after Kent's theatrical countdown and insistence that everyone shotgun a beer. Grace studied me with mirth as I wiped away a few drops of the PBR that had escaped in my attempt.

"What's that look for?" I asked, pulling her into my arms. She just shook her head. "Come on, tell me."

"I'm just excited to crush the competition with you."

"As if," came a voice from behind, and Sam stepped into

view, Bryce trailing behind her. *Bram*. She barely came past his elbow, but there was determination in her eyes that made up for the lack of height.

"She's small but mighty," Grace said, eyeing her best friend carefully. "Do not underestimate her."

"You better be just as much bite as you are bark," Bryce muttered, pulling her toward the cornhole set for their first game against Pandon (Pearson and Landon).

Grace held out her knuckles in a fist bump and said, "Game on, baby."

We took on Mishop (Bishop and Macy) in the first round, lining up across a folding table for beer pong. Things were neck and neck until the final three cups, when Grace and I both sank our shots. On balls back, Grace bounced one in for the win.

"Your team name is stupid," Bishop taunted in the wake of defeat.

"At least it doesn't sound like it should be a condiment," Grace shot back.

The sun beat down relentlessly as Grace and I approached the cornhole set. Kent was stretching in preparation for our matchup, and his overly zealous arm circles nearly took out Nina as she passed behind him. The cursed combination of his and Caroline's name (Kentoline) was subtle foreshadowing for their disastrous run as teammates, which resulted in more bickering than playing. Grace and I made it to twenty-one before they even got nine points on the board.

Gameplay grew sloppier with each passing hour, the pile of empties growing larger and larger. Funnily enough, there were a few individuals that only seemed to get better the drunker they got. Bryce sank four bags in a row during his match against Mishop, carrying team Bram to victory with little help from Sam, whose motor function was rapidly declining.

The semifinal round was a game of sudden death beer darts with a twist—the highest-ranked team (Greb, of course) received two cans of beer instead of one, increasing their odds of continuing to the final. Within the first thirty seconds, Bryce took a dart to the shin, which was an automatic disqualification for Lyna (Lydia and Nina).

"That's bullshit!" Lydia shouted as her girlfriend dragged her away from the circle, tears of laughter streaming down her face.

To Bryce's credit, he didn't complain. He simply reached down, pulled out the dart, and poured some vodka over the wound without so much as a grimace.

"That was insanely hot," Sam said, eyeing Bryce like he was a snack.

Grace and I were edged out of the final round by a collaborative effort. Bryce and Landon, despite being on different teams, were determined to see us eliminated. Even with our two-can advantage, we didn't stand a chance. Not when there were at least four players always targeting us. Though we'd never admit it, Grace and I were happy to escape participating in the shoe race. The only downside was the chance of being selected to shoot the boot.

The basement was large, but it was still a tight squeeze to fit everyone given the sprawling course built from old training equipment and random furniture. Along with an agility ladder and a scattering of cones, there were two tables, a smelly-looking armchair, and a couch that had once housed a nest of squirrels. In the end, Bram won due to a lack of clearly defined rules, because Kent had never clarified that each partner needed to complete the course on their own. Pandon made quick work of the obstacle course one by one, while Bryce just tossed Sam over his shoulder and carried her to the finish line in half the time. Despite an uproar from Landon, Caroline declared Bram as the official winning team of the first and only Beer Olympics.

I would have cheered along with the others if I hadn't caught the gleam of mischief in Bryce's eyes as he surveyed the group with the Adidas in hand, ready to distribute the punishment. Sam confirmed their intentions with a devious smile.

"This can only go to one person," Bryce announced, holding up the Adidas like a trophy, "as penance for their foolish behavior this school year. Though we have forgiven Sebastian, his idiocy cannot go unpunished."

Well, fuck, it looked like I was getting the foot beer. In all fairness, Bryce was right. I'd been a selfish prick this year, and if anyone deserved to drink a warm beer out of a mystery shoe, it was me.

"Come forward, Sebastian, and accept your unholy goblet!"

Before I'd taken more than a few steps, Grace was tugging me back. "Hold on, I need to borrow him for a minute before he does," she announced.

She led me toward the storage room off the bottom of the stairs. The place reeked of must and sweaty hockey bags, but Grace didn't seem to care. She closed the door behind us and pushed me against it.

"What are you doing?" I asked, peering down at her through the dim light.

"Isn't it obvious?" she said playfully, fisting the material of my shirt in her hands. "I wanted to kiss you one last time in case you die contracting athlete's foot of the mouth." Grace stood on her toes until her lips hovered inches from mine. "And if you don't die, there's a chance I won't kiss you for a week, so make it good, Evans. You'll need the memory to get through these next seven days."

I cupped her face in my hands, the tips of my fingers delving into the hair at the base of her neck. Grace let out a contented sigh as I leaned forward. She smelled of her cherry perfume laced with a hint of beer. It was a strange combination, but I would have bottled the scent if I could have. I'd bottle this day too, if it were possible, and every other day we spent together.

ACKNOWLEDGMENTS

Returning to a story that I wrote twelve years ago has been an unbelievably fulfilling and, at times, indescribably frustrating experience. Through the many highs and lows, I was reminded of why I fell in love with writing in the first place, and the importance of asking for help in times of doubt. Some things can't be done alone. Without the incredible people below, reimagining Grace and Sebastian's journey would not have been possible.

Thank you to my sister, Ali Novak, for introducing me to the world of storytelling and for helping me see that my words are worth sharing. Your guidance has been instrumental in bringing this novel to life. Every time I second-guessed myself, you were there to steer me right.

Thank you to my mother, for always reminding me that I'm capable of anything I set my mind to and for feeding me when I could do nothing but write for weeks at a time. To my brother and his friends, for helping brainstorm the best hockey group chat name in history.

Thank you to Maddie, whose relentless ambition inspired me to make my own dreams a reality. Your tenacity is truly contagious.

To my roommates, who witnessed my late-night writing sessions and subsequent crash-outs, your words of encouragement kept me going when I wanted to give up. Thank you to Vicki, for lending an extra set of eyes to my copy edits, and to my boss Peter, for reassuring me that this exhausting journey was well worth the double shifts.

Thank you to Deanna, my editor, for seeing something special in a story that I wrote when I was sixteen and for giving me the opportunity to make it into something more.

Finally, to my readers on Wattpad that have supported me over the years and the friends I've made along the way. Thank you for welcoming me into this beautiful community with open arms. I'm inspired by each and every one of you and grateful for every moment we've shared.

ABOUT THE AUTHOR

Flynn Novak grew up in Wisconsin and graduated from the University of Minnesota with a BA in global studies. Her love for writing can be attributed to her older sister and fellow author, who shared her first stories with Flynn when they were kids. In addition to writing, Flynn loves reading and collecting books—which are indeed different hobbies—traveling the world, pierogis, movie marathons, and dreaming up fantasy worlds before bed.

Want more from Flynn Novak?

THE BENEFITS of SEXTING

Danny Ashmore has a plan: get over the man who broke her heart, finish the spring semester strong, and flee the country to spend her final year of college abroad. She never anticipated sharing a class with her ex, and she definitely never expected to hear her seventeen-year-old sister utter the words "I'm pregnant." Now, Danny is forced to make a difficult decision: give up her dream of studying abroad to help raise the baby or, in her mother's words, abandon the family just like her deadbeat father.

When it seems like things can't get any more complicated, Danny receives a filthy text message from an unknown number and is thrown head first into Sawyer Armstrong's life. Dirty-mouthed and drop-dead gorgeous, Sawyer is the last thing Danny expects or needs. But as a mutually beneficial agreement leads to an unlikely friendship, she quickly realizes that he may be the key to turning her luck around, and the only person capable of helping her find the strength to stand up for herself.

Coming soon from W by Wattpad Books!